IMPOSSIBLY HANDSOME

"I fight my own battles," she said. "If you can't accept that—"

"What? You'll pour coffee over my head? Sic Mojo on me? Ban me from Bessie's Diner?"

"Don't tempt me." Her tone was cool. But her skin felt hot. And not strictly from anger.

It didn't help that he looked impossibly handsome and as rugged as the mountains.

Clean-shaven, with his dark hair tousled by the wind and the effects of his hat, he was all rough-and-tough cowboy, ready for a rodeo or a fistfight, or to wrestle a calf to the ground. His white T-shirt and snug-fitting jeans emphasized the hard bulge of muscles and sinew.

Lord help her, looking at him made her knees melt....

Praise for Jill Gregory

Books by Jill Gregory

Once an Outlaw
Rough Wrangler, Tender Kisses
Never Love a Cowboy
Just This Once
Always You
Daisies in the Wind
Forever After
Cherished
When the Heart Beckons

JILL GREGORY

THUNDER CREEK

A DELL BOOK

THUNDER CREEK
A Dell Book / August 2003

Published by
Bantam Dell
A Division of Random House, Inc.
New York, New York

ISBN 0-440-23732-7

Manufactured in the United States of America
Published simultaneously in Canada

OPM   10 9 8 7 6 5 4 3 2 1

To my family
With love

THUNDER CREEK

Prologue

SHE LAY STILL AND COLD IN A GRAVE DUG BY HER killer, a grave carved deep and hidden into lonely ground. No one had ever found her. No one had ever missed her. No one had ever mourned her—except for one.

Rain, snow, and storm had besieged the place where she rotted, and years had passed. And the dark secrets she took with her had long ago seeped like her very blood into the earth.

But the secrets were not dead. Secrets never die. They waited to emerge, like moldering worms squirming, crawling to the surface. Her secrets would be told.

Three men had used her. One killed her. And one wept for her.

Now he was dead too.

The wind on autumn days seemed to carry her voice. A voice that whispered above the rush of the creek, above the rattle of the crimson leaves. It whispered one word. Always the same word.

Murder . . .

Chapter 1

IT HAD RAINED THE DAY KATY TEMPLETON LEFT HER family ranch in Thunder Creek, Wyoming, for a new life far from all of her childhood memories, and it rained the day she came home. Pouring, gunmetal-gray rain that tumbled in violent sheets, soaking the towering Laramie Mountains and drenching the grazing lands all through the beautiful winding bluegrass country where she'd spent the first eighteen years of her life.

The first fourteen of those years had been happy, carefree, and sunny—the last four hell on earth. The girl who'd left was running away from the pain of loss and loneliness that had left her shaken and reeling inside, a pain that made her never want to look back—but the woman now returning was trying to find something she'd lost. She wasn't sure what it was or where she'd lost it, she only knew that when her mother called her in New York on Sunday morning and told her about her grandmother getting pneumonia and Bessie's Diner all boarded up and closed, about her parents' planned trip to Paris, their first vacation in fourteen years, which her father was all set to cancel, it had seemed like the only right thing to do was go home.

Home. What did that mean anymore? Katy wondered wryly as she wheeled her bag through the Natrona County airport in Casper. For the past few years, home had been too many places—and she didn't really belong to any of them. She wasn't sure she belonged here either, not anymore, but she was needed, at least for a while, and so she had come.

But the moment she saw her father striding toward her, his grim face looking grayer, sterner, and even more downcast than usual, a knot tightened in her stomach and she wondered if this was really what she needed after all. Dad hadn't been the same since the accident, since Matt died, and neither had she. Actually, nothing had. Certainly not Thunder Creek.

That's why she'd left.

But Gram needs you, and so does Mom, she told herself—and in a way, her father did too. He was going to take Mom to Paris if they both had to drag him by the boots kicking and screaming all the way.

The image of her plump little ash-blonde mother dragging Big John Templeton by his boots had her grinning even as she dropped her bag and threw her arms around her father.

"Hi, Daddy, you didn't have to come. I told you I could rent something."

"Reckon I can pick up my own daughter when she comes to town," he grunted. Their hug was brief—he broke it first, as always withdrawing from any physical or emotional contact beyond the bare minimum. His gray eyes, the color of the rain torrenting down, squinted at her beneath his hat, taking in her aqua silk sweater and chic black skirt, the delicate diamond drop at her throat, as if wondering where this strangely citified creature had come from.

"You look mighty fancy," he grunted.

"I hopped a plane straight from work."

"When are you going back?"

"When I'm good and ready." She spoke evenly, then softened her words with a smile that had beguiled bankers and CEOs in half a dozen states and a few European capitals.

Almost, Big John Templeton smiled back, but he managed to swallow the urge just in time. He gave another grunt and seized the handle of her wheeled bag in one calloused fist.

"Let's go, your mother's waiting to see you. But if you think your being here is going to make me go on that damned trip, you can just turn around and scoot back on that plane."

We'll see about that, Katy thought, but merely fell silently into step beside him, sensing this was not the time to argue. She'd inherited her father's iron will and felt herself every bit a match for him, but she'd also learned to pick her battles and when to fight them. And the moment she set foot in Natrona County was not the right moment to fight.

So instead she tried to let herself adjust to the rapid change of her surroundings, going from her twenty-fourth-floor corner office that looked out on a sea of glinting skyscrapers and roaring traffic, to this wide open landscape with rain sheeting down upon prairie, hill, and mountain, from jammed streets to open spaces so broad and deep they dazzled and gripped the heart, from the smells of sweat and garbage and perfume and hot dogs from the corner vendors to the smell of damp earth and greenery, of air so sweet and pure it could make you drunk faster than a shot of Johnnie Walker—and to the company of the grim, weathered man who drove the pickup with the same fierce concentration he reserved for picking out just the right quarter horse to purchase at auction and negotiating shipping rates for his cattle or oil.

Big John Templeton was a superb rancher and businessman, and a friend to most everyone in Thunder Creek, except a few fools he'd no more give the time of day to than he would sit in a cow pie. But in the husband department, Katy reflected with a sidelong look at his stony profile, he needed a good kick in the ass, and she was going to give it to him.

That was only one of the reasons she'd come home. The other was Gram and the diner.

"How's Gram?" she asked as they headed outside toward the pickup. It was still pouring but far be it from Big John Templeton to put up an umbrella. He had his hat after all, a big gray Stetson with a black band around it, and the water ran in rivulets from the wide brim. "Did the antibiotics kick in?"

"They're helping some. She's holding her own. But she's still too weak to get out of bed."

Katy had tugged her mini-umbrella from her tote bag and snapped it open, almost wincing as she thought of her robust grandmother, who always smelled like a black currant pie and who was used to scampering around the diner faster than any of the waitresses forty years her junior, now laid up in bed, struggling to breathe and to clear the pneumonia from her lungs.

"She's going to be all right, though, isn't she?" As they reached the truck and she swung the door open, she caught the tightening lines around her father's mouth as he loaded her bag and eased his six-foot frame in beside her.

"Hard to say. She's getting on."

"Daddy, she's only seventy-five. That's not so old." Dismay and apprehension made her voice shake, and Katy struggled for the cool control she'd mastered over the past ten years, the control Seth Warfield had expected in his wife, his partner in business and in bed.

"Her heart isn't what it used to be. Better brace yourself before we get home. You haven't seen her in a while."

He eased the truck forward even as she snapped on her seat belt, realizing with a little shock that what he said was true. How long had it been since her last visit home? Two years? Three?

She'd left Thunder Creek when she went off to college, intending never to come back, not to live anyway, and she'd stuck by it. Except for a few visits at Christmas or Thanksgiving, or for her mother's birthday, she'd been a stranger to the Triple T ranch where she'd grown up, keeping in touch with her parents and Gram by phone, and of late by e-mail, but rarely returning to the big stone ranch house set in the shade of Thunder Creek, or to the town where Bessie's Diner stood on a sun-dappled street near Krane's Drugstore and the real estate offices of Turnow and Barnes.

Coming back hurt too much. Home and the town were full of memories. Memories of Matt. And for a long while the pain of losing him had been like a whip on the back of a horse, making her want to run, run, and keep running.

Now the pain was a sorrow that lived in her heart. Deep and abiding, but it no longer drove her. Something else drove her. Another death, so different from the accident that had claimed her brother, yet so familiar in the agony it caused, in the biting, throbbing loss that swallowed and destroyed and pervaded everything else, coloring the world a mottled and sickening gray.

That death, and her divorce and the general falling apart of what had once appeared a perfect marriage, a perfect life, had driven her back home, where she was needed, and where, strangely enough, she needed to be.

At least for now.

It took them nearly two hours to reach the ranch, two hours of steady driving on rain-slicked roads that twisted through sagebrush scented hills and valleys. By the time they drove up the long gravel road that opened onto the two-story house Big John's father had built, and glimpsed the barns, stables, corrals, paddocks, and various other outbuildings all spread upon the valley floor in the shadow of the Laramie Mountains, Katy was exhausted.

She'd gone into work at seven-thirty this morning, trying to finish up as many projects as she could before her leave of absence began, and after the hurtling cab ride to the airport, her flight to Salt Lake City where she'd changed to a Skywest plane for Casper, and the long, mostly silent drive beside Big

John through the rain-gouged countryside, she felt drained and weak-limbed. But something happened as they pulled into the wide circular driveway before the house. Something happened just as Mojo came bounding out onto the porch barking frantically, and then her mother stepped outside, a dishrag flung over her shoulder, behind her the lights of the square windows glowing yellow against the thickening dusk.

The rain stopped, and for a moment a beam of sunlight shone in the gray-green sky. It was near dinnertime, and the sun would set soon, but for a moment its silvery glow lit the huge old house and the thick pines behind it. And it lit the beaming face of her mother and Katy felt something slide off her shoulders, something dark and heavy and old, and her heart lightened in a blink as she threw open the door of the truck and ran up the porch steps.

"Mom!" She flung her arms around the woman who gave a gasp of happy laughter and embraced her in a hug that smelled of sourdough bread and corn. "It's so good to see you."

And it was. She hadn't seen her mother, seen any family, since she'd lost the baby, since the divorce. An overwhelming flood of emotions surged through her, emotions she'd sought to keep stifled for longer than she could remember, and she suddenly had to fight back tears.

It felt so *good* to be home.

"The steaks'll be done in a twinkling, so if you want to change before supper, now's the time," her mother declared. "And I've got corn on the cob and your favorite honeyed butter for the sourdough rolls." Then her mother added in a whisper straight into her ear, a whisper no one else could hear, "So glad you're home, Katy."

And then the rain started again and they ducked inside, leaving the cold, wet night behind them. Big John Templeton sat and watched them from the cab of the truck, his throat tight as the two women, one tall, leggy, and lanky, a sophisticated beauty with hair the color of wild dark honey, and the other short and agreeably plump, wearing blue jeans, a big plaid shirt, and tennis shoes, disappeared into the glowing warmth of the house where once four of them had lived as a close and loving family.

He patted Mojo's silky black head and then retrieved Katy's wheeled bag, hefting it up the porch steps as the rain fell harder and night began its stealthy descent from the mountains.

"Gram?"

Stepping into the dimly lit room that had once been the "company" bedroom, and that her grandmother had moved into several years ago, Katy stared at the motionless woman in the bed. The first thing that struck her was that Bessie had lost weight—a great deal of weight. Tucked beneath a crisp white sheet and a pale blue cotton coverlet, her grandmother looked as pale and fragile as an antique wisp of lace. The iron-gray hair that ringed her square-jawed face looked dull and lifeless, and her normally ruddy skin had a pasty sheen to it that made Katy's heart clench with dismay.

"C-come in, girl, and don't look so scared." Gram's voice sounded thin and dry, not at all like her usual crisp staccato. Each word seemed to take an effort. "I . . . never did bite and I'm not about to start now." She broke off into a fit of coughing—hard, violent coughing that racked the body that had somehow, since Katy had last seen her, become spindly, the body of a tired old woman. Katy took a deep breath and hurried forward.

"Well, Gram, even if you did bite, you know you wouldn't scare me," she forced herself to say with a bright smile. Moving to the side of the bed, she clasped the sun-freckled hand that had first shown her how to whisk an egg, how to sprinkle just the right amount of pepper and garlic on a five-pound meat loaf. She held that hand as Gram coughed and groaned, and tried to catch her breath, then as the coughing subsided, the old woman with Big John Templeton's sharp gray eyes leaned her head weakly against the pillow.

"Never could scare you, Katy girl," she muttered, and the glint in those tired eyes held approval.

"Mom said you hardly ate anything tonight. I wanted to know if you'd like some banana cream pie."

"All I want is to sit up and look at you proper. Help me, please. This damned pneumonia's made me weak as a kitten."

Katy propped the pillows beneath her and lifted her by the shoulders until she was leaning against them.

"Stop... looking so worried. I'll be all right. It's just going to take some time. You didn't need to come all the way here. I'm sure you've got better things to do than keep company with a sick old lady like me."

"Actually, Mel Gibson was busy tonight, so I figured, why not go to the ranch and bother Gram?" Grinning, Katy seated herself on the side of the bed, pleased by the snort of laughter her words evoked. "Honestly, I think you're all falling apart without me. So I'd better pay a little more attention," she said lightly.

"Hmmm. Who's paying attention to you? You're thin as a shoelace."

"I'm fine, Gram."

"And there's something in your eyes. You're not happy, Katykins, don't try to fool me."

"I'm fine, Gram. Nothing stops a Templeton woman, you know that."

"Hmmmph." Gram turned slightly and started to reach out a shaking hand for the glass of ice water on the bedside table. Katy handed it to her and waited silently as she sipped from the long white straw, the glass trembling a little in her fingers. She handed the glass back to Katy, licked her dry lips, and studied the girl's face as she returned the glass to the table.

"It's that ex-husband of yours, isn't it? Ran off and had himself an affair, didn't he?" Indignation shook her voice. A series of coughs overtook her and it was a moment before she could speak. "Right after you lost that baby."

"Gram—"

"Regular skunk, he was. No sense moaning over him, he's not worth it. And he certainly wasn't worthy of *you.*"

"I'm not moaning over Seth, Gram." Katy swallowed. It was partly true. She'd never want him back, not after what he'd done, after everything that had happened, but... it still hurt. Hurt like hell. Her own failure in judgment hurt perhaps more than anything.

"The divorce has been more complicated than I'd like, what with dividing up the business and everything, but—"

"And he married that little bimbo he was carrying on with, didn't he?"

"Gram. Bimbo? Now, really." But there was a strain to the sound of her laughter.

Gram's eyes were still sharp, despite the pneumonia, despite the weakness pervading her body. They missed nothing, Katy realized as her grandmother's gaze seemed to x-ray her face... and maybe even her heart.

"And she's pregnant now, so your mother tells me."

"Mom talks too much." It took all her efforts to keep her tone light, her expression pleasant. The memories of Seth, of losing the baby they'd tried for so long to conceive, of his affair and the subsequent divorce, burned her still with sharp fire. The loss of her baby hurt the most, it stung, and burned, and tortured, causing more agony than anything she'd ever known, except the loss of Matt. Katy knew that losing the tiny life that had been growing within her was something she'd never get over, that there was an emptiness inside at the core of her soul that would never be filled. Her marriage to

Seth she'd dismissed as a failure and a stupid mistake, but losing the baby...

The pain still cut like glass and she knew it always would.

"Listen. Don't waste your energy worrying about me, old lady," she told her grandmother in a voice that shook only a little. "I came here because I'm worried about *you*."

Bessie Templeton stared at the granddaughter who had worked side by side with her in the kitchen and dining room of Bessie's Diner since she was old enough to ride a bicycle. Katy had changed before dinner into a loose white cotton sweater, jeans, and boots, but she still looked a far cry from the pigtailed, scraped-kneed monkey who had cooked and served and washed dishes at the diner every chance she got. She was a true beauty now, Bessie observed, her heart swelling with pride and with pure bursting love, and she was smart too—yet still down-to-earth, not snooty like the Winters girl who had gone off to Columbia and come back only once—for Christmas—with a fancy degree in medieval studies, looking down her nose at the folks back home. Katy was a good girl. And she deserved better than what she'd got from that fancy-schmancy husband of hers.

What she saw beneath the surface of her granddaughter's striking gray-blue eyes bothered Bessie. There was more than a hint of sadness, and a kind of wariness too, like a high-spirited filly who'd been broken in rough and knew the feel of the whip. But with time, Bessie told herself, that old intense sparkle just might come back.

Losing the baby, and her husband on top of that, may have shaken her to her core, but she still had her head up, her spine and shoulders straight. *She's too strong to get beaten down for long,* Bessie concluded, and slowly her lips relaxed into a thin smile.

"Worrying about me is a waste of time. I'll either lick this damned pneumonia or I won't." But as Katy began to protest, concern crossing her face, Bessie swept on, imperious as a queen.

"It's your mother you ought to concern yourself with. Your father wants to cancel that Paris trip of theirs. Says it's because of me. Ha."

"It isn't. That's silly. I'm here now and I'll look after you—and the ranch. He just needed an excuse," Katy said quietly.

"That's right. My boy or no, John's a fool. Giving up on life. Giving up on everything, everything but the ranch. Your mother's been looking forward to this trip more than anything. So—you going to let him get away with it?"

"What do you think?"

Katy met her grandmother's eyes and held her keen, searching glance. Her own blue-gray eyes were calm and intent.

"I think it's a good thing you came back." Gram sagged back against the pillows again. "I'm tired now. Think I'll sleep awhile."

"That's an excellent idea. I didn't mean to tire you out." Mom had warned her not to stay too long. For a moment she scanned Gram's face anxiously, fearing that it looked even more drawn than before. She turned and hurried toward the door, but even as her fingers touched the knob, her grandmother's voice stopped her.

"You heard about the diner?"

Katy turned back. "I heard it's closed."

"I guess that's the end of it." Bessie spoke bravely, but Katy didn't miss the slight quaver in her voice. "I opened that place more than forty years ago, when your grandfather died, and now it's ... the end."

"Like hell it is, Gram."

Bessie blinked at her from the pillows. "There's no one to run it, Katykins. That Daffodil Moline who works for me can barely carry a tray without dropping it, she can't—"

"I will." Katy's smile glowed brighter than the small lamp on the bedside table that reflected Gram's face. "That's one of the reasons I came home. I want to reopen Bessie's Diner. Keep it going until you're strong enough to come back. If you *want* to come back."

For a moment there was stunned silence. "You ... have a job. In New York. Your own restaurant ... a chain of them ..."

"Bessie's Diner comes first, Gram. It will always come first." Katy spoke softly. She felt an odd wrenching in her heart as she saw the hope and wonder, and at last, the feeble flicker of happiness in her grandmother's face. Whatever the diner meant to her, it meant ten times more to Bessie.

"I've taken a leave of absence. An indefinite leave of absence. It'll give me time to figure things out—and get the diner open again and humming with business. Don't you worry about a thing. Bessie's Diner will be waiting for you good as new as soon as you're ready to go back to it."

"I ... well ... bless you, Katy. I don't know what to say."

Her throat ached as she saw the shimmer of tears in Gram's eyes. She came back across the room and leaned down to kiss her grandmother's forehead, as the old woman clutched and then squeezed her hand. "Get some sleep," she whispered. "If Daddy thinks I can't be trusted not to get you all stirred up, we'll never get him out of here."

She was rewarded by a thin cackle of laughter as she slipped out the door.

Chapter 2

THERE WERE NO VOICES WAFTING FROM DOWNSTAIRS as Katy made her way to her own room, breathing in the clean cedar and lemon and cinnamon scent that belonged to this old ranch house. It smelled good. Familiar and natural, like a combination of the outdoors and a big, cinnamon-crusted pie. The house echoed with the soft sound of her boots on the varnished wood floor. She guessed her father would be in the den reading the *Wall Street Journal,* a shot of whiskey on the table beside his green leather easy chair. He probably had the TV on, a game show or sitcom, with the volume turned down low. Big John liked to accomplish more than one thing at a time. Her mother, with all of her ranch book work and housework done for the night, had been working crossword puzzles in the kitchen when Katy had come up to see Gram. She'd had a cup of coffee and a dish of strawberry ice cream on the table beside the laptop she used to check on words or places she didn't know. And the *Paris for Dummies* guidebook had been on the corner shelf with all of Mom's cookbooks. Its pages looked well used, the edges bent, and the cover no longer glossy.

If Mom wants to go to Paris, she's going, Katy thought, her lips compressing as she switched on the light and closed her door, then unzipped her bag and began unpacking.

Aside from her laptop, she hadn't brought more than a few of her belongings: some pants, shirts, a pair of jeans, and two sweaters, along with a sundress, and a pair each of sneakers and sandals. Most of her clothes and other belongings she'd had shipped. And even more had been left in her apartment on the Upper East Side. She was subletting it indefinitely to her secretary's niece, who'd just landed her first job in New York as an account manager at American Express. But Katy didn't want to think about New York or about her apartment, or about anything having to do with the Rattlesnake Cafe Company. There would be headaches enough tomorrow when Seth got wind that she'd flown the coop.

Katy had been practicing the words "Talk to my lawyer" all the way home on the plane.

Tomorrow she'd no doubt have to put them to good use. But tonight, just for tonight, she wanted to savor her first night back. And not think about anything except taking care of Gram, getting her parents off for their vacation, and re-opening Bessie's Diner.

She walked to the window and stared out at the dark night lit by a myriad of stars so bright they burned blue in the sky. The Laramies were only a charcoal shadow on the horizon, and the foothills that veered up from the lush grazing pastures of the Triple T ranch were phantom silhouettes in the night. But the sounds of insects and unseen animals in the brush were real and vibrant, and so was the fresh, cold wind sweeping down across the corrals, and up into her bedroom window, billowing the white lace curtains.

She thought of all the nights she'd sneaked out this window, latching onto the limbs of the willow tree, and shimmying down to the ground to go exploring with her best friends, Margie Birch and Smoke MacIntyre. Sometimes they rode their bikes to Eagle Point, sometimes they hiked to the creek and set up a tent, pretending they were a posse waiting to pounce on the rustlers or poachers that now and then plagued Thunder Creek and nearly every other ranching community. But most times they tried to either follow or find Matt and his best friend, Jackson Brent, on their far more daring adventures.

Matt and Jackson were four years older and far wilder in both imagination and nerve. They'd meet other boys for midnight poker games in the cemetery, smoke cigarettes, and go night swimming in the creek. Once they "borrowed" motorcycles from two members of the Hell's Angels who were passing through town and had parked their Harleys in the lot outside the Tumbleweed Bar and Grill. Matt and Jackson spent several boisterous hours racing each other up and down the dirt road that led up to Jackson's father's ramshackle old house.

Sheriff Harvey had paid Big John Templeton a visit after that. And Matt had been grounded for five days, and had to miss the freshman football tryouts at Thunder Creek High. It was the spring before he entered high school and he was already taller and broader than most other boys his age—except Jackson. For two years he'd talked of little except making the team, and suddenly he wasn't going to be allowed to try out. So naturally he'd argued and protested and begged Big John to let the grounding start the day *after* tryouts. But Big John had refused to back down, and, tight-lipped and determined to do the right thing, Dorsey Templeton had backed her husband.

But Matt Templeton, handsome, straight-A student, talented artist, and the boy voted most popular in his junior high class, was not for nothing known as a golden boy. The coach of the varsity team had heard about the middle school's star player, and he allowed Matt to try out after everyone else. He'd reserved a place for him on the team. And the rest had been history. Matt had been quarterback, Jackson (who'd never been punished for the motorcycle incident and had tried out on the regular date) had been the defensive tackle, and together all through high school they'd ruled on the football field—and just about everywhere else.

Just looking out at the night, Katy could almost see Matt and Jackson bounding out to Jackson's old pickup truck as they had so many times, laughing and hollering, in a hurry, always in a hurry either to get to the diner for hamburgers and shakes before Gram closed up for the night, or to pick up Allison Pritchard, Matt's girlfriend, and whichever girl of the moment had caught Jackson's eye. Or to go off and paint houses or barns or fences, whatever anyone wanted—Matt's idea of a way to earn extra money for college.

Their little painting business had kept them more than busy that last fall of their senior year. Gazing out the window, Katy found herself clenching the delicate curtains. *If only they'd washed cars instead,* she thought, her throat aching. *Or dug fence posts. Or worked at Slade's gas station. If only Jackson Brent had never asked Matt to take his place painting the Jenssens' barn that last night, all because he wanted to go to the drive-in with Holly Sue Granger. If only Matt had stayed home instead, and never fell off that ladder . . .*

A sweeping sadness shot through her. She still missed him. Probably everyone who'd ever known him still missed him, but not like his family did. Not as much, as deeply. Funny, she'd never minded being called Matt Templeton's kid sister. She'd been honored. There'd never been anyone like him—no one as smart, as funny and good-natured, as talented at pen-and-ink sketches or wildlife drawing. And certainly no one as full of ideas and plans for the Triple T ranch, for the future.

And there never would be again . . .

"Honey, mind if I come in?"

Her mother's voice outside the door dragged Katy at last from the window and the moving ghosts she'd seen below, and back to the present. She crossed the room with quick strides.

"Not a bit. Finish your crossword puzzle?"

"Every line." Her mother grinned smugly. "Did you know that a musical form often used for the final moment of a concerto is called a rondo?"

"Can't say that I did."

"You didn't know your old mother was so smart, did you?"

"I know you're smart, Mom. You've done all of the books for the ranch since you and Daddy got married and I don't think you've ever once not balanced the checkbook."

"Well, once, there was a problem, but it was the bank's mistake." Dorsey Templeton strolled inside and glanced around the room, which still looked exactly the same as it had the day Katy left for college. The Templetons weren't big on change. She seemed to realize for the first time that the shelves of stuffed animals, horse show trophies, and the poster of Tom Cruise in *Top Gun,* along with the faded yellow coverlet and throw pillows in Thunder Creek's high school colors of green and blue, didn't exactly suit the elegant young woman who was part-owner of one of the country's most successful restaurant chains. A young woman who had been written up in *Newsweek* as one of the top twenty-five businesswomen of the year.

"We really should fix up this room—especially if you're going to stay awhile," she mused. "I should have thought of that before. Maybe I can drive into Laramie next week and—"

"Next week? Mom, you're going to be in Paris next week."

Her mother shook her head. "Your father's made up his mind. He was never crazy about traveling out of state, always thinking something terrible would happen here when he was gone—"

"Because of Matt." Katy sighed. "The two of you being in

Butte at that horse show had nothing to do with Matt falling off the roof. And Daddy knows it."

"I'm not so sure he does." Dorsey shrugged. "Or maybe he's just superstitious. Over the years he's taken it into his head that if he leaves, disaster's going to strike this ranch, or someone, something he loves. Now with Bessie being sick, that seems to him like a message: *Don't go to Paris*. And with Cleo having problems, he probably thinks if he dares leave—"

"Oh, no, what's wrong with Cleo?"

Her mother sank down on the bed. "She's in foal, but there's complications. When we were trucking her in from the back thousand acres, there was an accident, and the trailer overturned. She had a lot of lacerations, and she's healing, but still . . . there's a danger of placental detachment. Especially since she lost two prior foals."

"I remember."

Katy sank down on her narrow single bed. Cleo was her favorite horse on the ranch, the horse she'd practically raised from the time she was a foal until she was two years old. A beautiful chestnut brown cutting horse, with four white feet and an unusually sweet disposition.

"Poor Cleo," she murmured. "When is she due?"

"Sometime in the next three to five weeks. There's no reason we shouldn't be back from Paris on time, unless she's early, or something goes wrong. But of course your father's taken it into his head that if he leaves, Cleo's going to lose her foal, or Bessie's going to have a relapse and need to go into the hospital, or the cattle will all come down with foot-and-mouth disease. Or that some other disaster will befall us."

She tapped her head. "It's all up here, but there's no reasoning with the man."

"Looks like I'll just have to convince him that I won't let anything happen to anyone or anything while he's gone."

"You can try." Dorsey sounded doubtful. "I already told him if we don't go, he can sleep in the den for the next month. You know what he said?"

Katy wasn't sure she wanted to. "Okay, I'll bite. What'd he say?"

"He just laughed. And told me there's no way I could go more than two nights without him sleeping beside me and he wasn't going to make me suffer like that. Said I'd just be punishing myself—and he wouldn't allow it. The conceited old bull." She burst out laughing, a mixture of amusement and ruefulness in her tone. "But he's right, damn it. Heaven help me, I do love that man, despite his hard head and that gloomy puss of his. If he can't bring himself to go, well, then we won't go. At least not right now. Maybe in the fall, after Bessie's better and Cleo's had her foal."

But Katy saw the wistfulness in her mother's eyes and vowed silently not to let Big John off the hook that easily. He might be stubborn and superstitious, and feel like everything would fall apart at the ranch if he set foot on a plane, for— heaven forbid—a pleasure trip, but he did love his wife with all of his being, and it was time he started acting like it.

Not that I'm exactly an expert on love and marriage, Katy acknowledged ruefully, as she emptied her sneakers and a pink satin lingerie bag from her suitcase and zipped it shut. She'd thought Seth loved her too. She'd thought their marriage would last forever. *Yeah, right.*

Well, she might have been young and stupid once, but not anymore. She was twenty-eight and she no longer believed in the tooth fairy, stars in your eyes, or happily ever after. At least not for herself. She'd decided on the day she filed for the divorce that from that moment on, when it came to her own life, she'd stick to what she knew best, what she was good at: running a restaurant her own way, cooking to her heart's content. She'd steer clear of men and all the trouble they caused, and keep her life simple and uncluttered.

Just the way she liked it.

As if reading her thoughts, her mother spoke in an overly casual tone. "So . . . your divorce. It's been three months now since everything was finalized. Are you all right?"

"I'm fine, Mom." Katy spoke lightly, but her mother's gaze missed nothing, and caught the tensing of Katy's shoulders, the way her mouth compressed. She also caught the hollow note in her daughter's voice. Inwardly, Dorsey cursed Seth Warfield, not for the first time.

"I know how rough the past year has been for you. I wanted to fly out, Katy, and be with you . . . when you lost the baby . . . and when you found out about . . . about the affair, but . . ." Dorsey shook her head sadly. "You said you didn't want me to come. You didn't seem to want any company."

"I needed to get through it myself, Mom." Katy spoke quietly. "Some things you just have to tough out." She took a deep breath. "And I did. I'm fine now."

"Just a little ragged around the edges, maybe?"

"A little." Katy met her mother's worried gaze and smiled. "But not much."

"Well, being home with family and old friends will put you to rights. Margie can't wait to see you. She and Lee just had their second little boy two weeks ago. The first one's two now and a holy terror, but cute as a button. Oh." Dorsey sucked in her breath. "Sorry."

Katy ignored the pain that had thrust like a dagger through her heart at the mention of her childhood friend's babies. She was happy for Margie, truly happy, but that didn't mean it didn't still hurt like hell to think about babies and bibs and booties and remember the precious little life she'd lost less than a year ago.

"It's fine, Mom. I'm glad for Margie." She closed the dresser drawer and came back to sink down on the bed, gazing at her mother, who held a stuffed monkey Matt had won for Katy at a county fair. "I'll pay her a visit tomorrow. I definitely want to meet the holy terror."

"Luke Dillard stopped your father in town yesterday and asked about you. He'd heard from Smoke that you were coming home."

"How is Luke?" *Still an asshole in stud's clothing?* she wondered, but didn't say it aloud. When she was a sophomore in high school and Luke was a senior, they'd served on the homecoming committee together, and he'd asked her to the dance. Afterward he'd seemed to feel he was entitled to more than just a good night kiss. A whole lot more. She'd had her hands full fighting him off in the woods off Bear Trail where he'd parked the car. And then, to make matters worse, Jackson Brent had come along...

The only person she'd be more loath to encounter than Luke Dillard was Jackson Brent. But at least she didn't have to worry about that. Jackson had moved away a few months after the homecoming incident—which had been just fine with Katy. Every time she'd seen her brother's best friend, pain sharp as shrapnel had sliced her heart. Just the sight of his handsome, hard-planed face had served as a bitter reminder that if he hadn't been itching to get Holly Sue Granger into the back of his pickup at the drive-in that night, Matt never would have *been* at the Jenssens' barn. He wouldn't have fallen off that ladder. He'd be alive today.

"Luke's divorced now," Dorsey chattered on. "Dixie moved to Denver—I hear she's remarried—but he never has. So far. And do you remember Wood Morgan, the oldest of the Morgan boys? He was a year ahead of Matt in school. He's been running the Circle M since old Odell died. He's thinking of turning a ten-thousand-acre parcel on the north side of the creek into a dude ranch..."

They chatted comfortably for a while, her mother filling her in on the doings and gossip of Thunder Creek until with a yawn she took herself off to bed.

It was after ten. Katy considered getting ready for bed too, but she rarely went to sleep before midnight. And even then, sleep was usually a long time coming. Tonight she wasn't sure if she'd get much sleep at all. Tomorrow she'd have to face the town of Thunder Creek, everyone who'd known her since she was a baby, everyone who'd known her as Matt Templeton's kid sister. She'd have to face the questions, the stares, the drawn-out reminiscences of how much she'd grown, changed, of how she ought to best get on with her life. In small towns, everyone had an opinion about everyone else and often felt entitled to voice it.

But she couldn't avoid it—she'd have to go take a look at Bessie's Diner and see what needed to be done before it could be reopened.

Yet that was tomorrow, and tomorrow was still hours away. She wasn't quite ready to face those long silent hours tossing and turning in her bed, nor was she ready to endure the dreams that sometimes woke her, leaving her staring bleakly at the ceiling, longing for morning to come.

She took one glance at her old bed with its school pillows in green and blue, and headed for the door.

The night was dark as sin. The rain had ended, but there were no stars, no moon to light the way, only scudding clouds and stillness. But Katy knew the way to the horse barn blindfolded, and she reached it without once stumbling or doubting. She opened the door and stepped inside, surprised to see a light on.

Perhaps Daddy had the same notion I did and came to check on Cleo.

"Daddy?"

There was a rustling sound, the faint scrape of boots on straw. Not her father. Her father would have answered her right away. Her heart leaped with a sudden jolt of fear.

"Who's there?" she demanded, and took a swift step

toward the pitchfork that hung on the barn wall only a few feet away.

But suddenly a man stepped out of the shadows near the first stall and grasped her arm before she could yank the pitchfork off its hook.

"Whoa, there. You won't be needing that."

The man who gripped her arm was definitely *not* Big John Templeton. He was even taller—a rangy six-foot-two of lean and coiled male muscle. His hair was dark as the night outside. His face was hard and handsome, and so familiar it made her flinch with remembered pain.

"Jackson Brent," Katy gasped. She shook off his hand, her eyes narrowing in the close dimness that smelled of horses and leather and hay. She gave him a push back, instinctively, to give herself space, as anger and pain surged through her. "You left town years ago. What the hell are you doing sneaking around our barn?"

Chapter 3

"SORRY. I DIDN'T MEAN TO SCARE YOU."

Jackson held up both hands, palms out, as if to show her he was harmless. His voice was low and steady, and every bit as deep as she remembered. That deep drawling voice, she recalled, had seemed to enchant all of the girls at Thunder Creek High School. Almost as much as his cool blue eyes and lazy, sexy smile. "Take it easy, Katy."

"Just answer me. What are you doing here?"

Those blue eyes, the color of gunsmoke, watched her impassively. "I came to look in on Cleo."

"And why would you do that? Cleo's no concern of yours. You're trespassing."

One eyebrow cocked. "You're jumping to conclusions." He spoke quietly. "Why don't you just simmer down and let me explain?"

Something in his tone touched the quivering anger beginning to unravel within her and she quickly coiled it into a tight, compressed ball once more. She wasn't fourteen anymore, she reminded herself, as she'd been when Matt died. She wasn't going to lose control the way she had after the funeral, crying and shouting, ordering Jackson from the house when he'd come, all silent and pale, to pay his respects. She blinked, pushing the image from her mind.

The last time she'd seen Jackson Brent hadn't been much better. It was equally humiliating, in a different way. That had been the night Luke Dillard had cornered her in his Chevy at the edge of the woods. Tried to corner her, she corrected herself grimly, and pushed that memory away too.

From one of the stalls came a soft whicker, and from another she heard the restless movement of hooves.

"Explain then," she told him, forcing herself to use a more level tone.

"I'm Cleo's vet." Jackson pretended not to notice the shock that widened her eyes. He eased his shoulders back against the stall and went on in that low, deep voice she couldn't help but remember. "She's had a tricky pregnancy and I stop in every chance I get to monitor her. In this case, I just finished sewing up the Andersons' dog. Old Clancy got hit by a car on Lost Wolf Road tonight. He was lucky, though—he's going to be fine. But since the Andersons' place is only a few miles down the road, I swung by to check on Cleo."

"*You're* a vet? Cleo's vet?" Incredulity ran through her. "But I thought you moved away."

"I did. I moved back. Six months ago. Want to make something of it?" He smiled as he said the words, as if trying to coax a returning smile out of her, but Katy couldn't smile. Not at this man. Just looking at him brought back swarms of memories. Memories of Jackson and Matt, of their adventures, their schemes, their girls—and now, too, she remembered all the slobbering strays that used to accompany them in the back of the pickup truck. "*Jackson and his strays,*" her mother always used to say, shaking her head. But she'd said it fondly. Her mother'd always had a soft spot for Jackson Brent.

"I guess you have a right to move back if that's what you want." She shrugged, and raked a hand through her hair, shoving it back. It felt warm in here. Too warm. Though

Jackson Brent, his wide shoulders encased in a hooded blue sweatshirt, didn't seem to have noticed.

"How is she?" she asked crisply.

"Who?" Jackson had been studying her while she took in everything he'd said. His gaze had swept over her sweater and jeans, her hair, the contours of her face, and now he sounded distracted. *No doubt shocked that Matt's kid sister is all grown up,* she thought in irritation. Married, divorced, everything.

Katy frowned as he continued to stare at her blankly. "How is who?" he asked again.

"Cleo." She brushed past him, walking down the line of stalls to the third one. Cleo stood there, gazing back at her, her solemn brown eyes bright and knowing. Even in the dim light, the mare's chestnut coat glistened. "Do you remember me, sweetheart?" she asked softly, reaching out to let the mare sniff and nuzzle her hand.

"This pretty lady's having a hard time of it, but she'll be all right."

"She will? You've dealt with something like this before?" The words came out more sharply than she intended, as if she was questioning his competence, but he merely nodded and went on in that easy way of his.

"Plenty of times. It's not all that uncommon. I mean, there's no guarantees—the accident was serious, and her history is troublesome, but I've been doing transabdominal exams every week and so far, so good. With the right care, and a little luck, she should come through the birth just fine. I intend to give her all the right care."

"And . . . the foal?"

"The same. I'll be on call whenever I'm needed and I can get here fast."

Katy stroked the mare's mane, wondering if she knew something was wrong, wondering if she was worried about the new life she carried inside her. The ache that was always there intensified inside her as she smoothed her hand through Cleo's mane. She herself had had no clue that anything was wrong—she'd had a normal first trimester, when the danger was supposedly the greatest, and then at the end of her fifth month, after she'd already felt life, felt the tiny kicks and quivers, there had come the cramps, the pain, the loss...

She drew in her breath. "You're going to be fine, girl," she whispered. "Just fine."

Jackson went into the stall and knelt in the straw to retrieve his stethoscope and electronic thermometer. He stuffed them into a small black satchel, moving with agility and efficiency, and purely male grace. His tall athlete's frame appeared hardier and tougher even than she remembered. A day's growth of heavy beard darkened his jaw, and the burly, laughing boy who'd whooped and hollered in the pickup truck with Matt could barely be detected in the brawny, cooleyed man who paused before leaving the stall to rest a big, gentle hand on the mare's neck. All that dangerous handsomeness remained, perhaps even intensified by the years. Jackson Brent exuded dark, sexy masculinity—the broad shoulders and sharp cheekbones, taut muscle and powerful sinewy strength—in contrast with the surprising gentleness in his speech and manner. That gentleness was startling in a man who looked as physically formidable as he did. He looked so solid, so strong, and so potently male that any woman within ten feet of him would have to look and look twice.

Katy had no doubt women still went wild over him just as the girls had in high school. But at least she knew she was immune. All she could think when she saw him was that it was too bad he hadn't grown up a little sooner, that he hadn't been responsible enough to follow through that October night fourteen years ago, the night he'd promised to paint Bob Jenssen's barn.

"Rest up, sweetheart," he told the mare. "I'll be back to make sure you follow doctor's orders." He strode from the stall, glancing at Katy. "You staying?"

She nodded, stepping aside so he could pass her without touching. "Do you have a cell phone or a pager or something? In case something happens while you're out on calls?"

She said it as if she doubted he would, and his eyes met hers with a touch of amusement. "I've got both. Your dad has the numbers. You want them too? I have a card here . . . somewhere . . ." He began digging through his jeans pocket, but Katy shook her head.

"Don't bother. I'll get it from him."

She realized how abrupt she sounded, bordering on rude, but she didn't know what to do about it. Jackson Brent stirred up the worst in her. The worst memories, of a time that was both precious and lost forever, of a grief that might not have been, of her own furious, uncontrolled behavior after the funeral. She just wanted him to leave.

"You still hold it against me, don't you?" He halted, his feet planted apart. His gaze was riveted on her. "Tell the truth, Katy. I can see it in your eyes."

"Don't be ridiculous—"

"It spooked you, seeing I was back. Even after all these years."

"I was surprised, that's all. The last I'd heard you'd moved away. I came out here tonight because I didn't think I could sleep and I wanted to be alone and—"

"And seeing me brought everything back to you. Matt, that night."

"Yes . . . no . . . I . . ."

"You still blame me." His jaw jutted out. "Fair enough. I still blame myself," he added coolly. "So we're even."

"I don't blame you, Jackson. Not anymore. It's just hard, that's all. I wasn't prepared to see you, not tonight. I'm not that same child who lost control at her brother's funeral," she assured him. "That was a long time ago." But her voice quavered for a moment, and she had to fight the threatening rush of emotion. With an effort, she continued in a cooler, steadier tone that almost precisely matched his. "I know in my head that none of it was your fault. It was an accident, pure and simple. I had no right to blame you, so I hope...I hope you'll forgive me. You have every right to be here, to live here, to take care of Cleo, but—"

"But the sight of me makes you sick."

She flushed and shook her head. "I didn't say that."

Jackson Brent met her gaze squarely, his eyes darkening with some emotion she couldn't quite read. "You didn't have to."

An uncomfortable silence fell between them, broken only by the sounds of the horses shifting, breathing in their stalls. Jackson studied her for one brief moment, then strode toward the door. As he pushed it open he glanced back at her, his face shuttered. "We're bound to run into each other now and again in town, but don't worry, Katy. I'll do my best to stay out of your way."

And with those words he was gone, vanished into the chill, dark Wyoming night with only the echo of his footsteps and the clean leathered scent of him to remind her he'd been there at all.

Katy sank down on a bench and let weariness flow through her. Weariness of body, weariness of spirit.

She hadn't counted on Jackson Brent being in Thunder Creek when she'd decided to come back, but she'd just have to get used to it. She'd come back here for her own sake, for Gram, for her family—and to sort out her pathetic excuse for a life, and she wasn't about to let Jackson Brent or anyone else chase her away.

So deal with it, she told herself as she leaned back against the hard wall of the barn, listening to the soft sounds of the horses snuffling, shifting in their stalls.

He said he'd stay out of your way.

And she sure as hell planned to make things as easy as possible on both of them and stay out of his.

Chapter 4

"KATY! KATY TEMPLETON, HOLD IT RIGHT THERE."
Smoke MacIntyrc dashed across First Street and grabbed
Katy in a bear hug just as she stepped out of Gram's Blazer
in front of the diner. He'd gained thirty pounds since high
school and his once-skinny frame was now softly padded in
the stomach, but not much else about Smoke had changed
since the days that he and Katy and Margie had been best
friends. Except that now he had a beard and a paunch, and
there were a few early silver strands mixed in with his thick
brown hair.

"Hot dog, it's good to see you. You're gorgeous, Katy. If I
weren't a happily married man I'd be falling over my feet in
love with you."

"You'rc not so bad yourself, Smoke." She grinned at him
and gave him a kiss on the cheek. "How's Ellen?"

"She keeps me on a short leash, that woman. Lucky for
her, I like it that way." His chuckle was the same, low and
hearty. "Did your folks tell you yet about the barbecue?"

"What barbecue?"

"Saturday is my parents' thirtieth wedding anniversary.
Ellen and I are throwing a big party for them at our place
next Saturday night. You come, and I'll consider letting you
in on my secret recipe for spicy barbecued steak." He winked

at her. "You'll be wanting to put it on the menu at Bessie's Diner. I figure you can call it Smoke's Special Spicy Steak."

Katy laughed. "I'll think about it."

"About putting it on the menu or coming to the barbecue?"

"Both." Katy punched him in the arm. "I wouldn't miss it, Smoke. Want me to bring something?"

"Just yourself, Big John, and Dorsey. Don't suppose Bessie will be up to it?"

Katy shook her head.

"So what's going on with this place?" Smoke turned and scanned the Closed sign on the front of the diner. "Do you think she'll be coming back here or you going to sell it or what?"

"I'm not selling Bessie's Diner. It stays in the family."

"I heard that Tammie Morgan was eyeing it for some new gift shop she wants to open. Wood's already talked to your dad about buying the space."

"No one's turning Bessie's Diner into a gift shop." *Least of all Tammie Morgan,* Katy thought. The idea of her old high school rival selling knickknacks and snow globes in her grandmother's diner made her want to spit—or kick somebody.

"What does she need with a gift shop? I heard she and Wood are turning some of their back acres into a dude ranch. I'd expect that big an operation would keep her occupied."

"Yeah, well, from what I hear, Tammie got it into her head that the tourists coming out to the place might want to do some shopping in town. Souvenirs, gifts. Stuff like that. She and Wood want to make Thunder Creek more 'tourist friendly.'"

"The tourists can be as friendly as they want inside Bessie's Diner. We'll be glad to serve them just like everyone else and make them feel right at home," Katy said firmly as she dug the keys to the diner from her purse.

"Sounds good to me. I'd hate to see this place close up. Remember when we came here, the night before graduation? You, me, Margie. Our last night, all together? Bessie brought us chocolate shakes and peach pie."

"And you told us you were going to get married to Ellen." Katy smiled, the memory floating back. "And Margie said she was coming back in four years as soon as she got her teaching degree."

"And you said you were never coming back." Smoke studied her, his brown eyes serious for the first time. "Margie started to cry. I did, too, but I pretended it was just something in my eye."

A rush of fondness surged through her as she looked into Smoke's face. "Well, I'm back now. Guess I didn't know everything back then."

"Hell, none of us did, Katy."

"Not nearly as much as we thought we knew," she murmured with a faint smile.

"You're famous now." Smoke shook his head. "We all read about you in *Newsweek*. Your mom ordered twenty issues from the bookstore in Casper. They called you one of the top twenty-five businesswomen in America."

"And to think you used to know me when I burned my first apple pie right in this very kitchen," she chuckled, turning toward the diner.

"Know you? Hell, I was the one who ate it and told you it was good. Me and Matt," he added, sobering just a little. "He even asked for seconds. Margie just pushed it around on her plate."

"And thought I wouldn't notice. But I did. I knew who my real friends were. Just for that, you get a free slice of pie next time you come in."

"All *right*." Smoke swept her into another bear hug then stepped back and watched as she fitted the key into the lock. "When are you planning to reopen this place?"

"Soon as our suppliers can get a shipment here. Probably by Tuesday."

"I'll be by for some of that pie. But don't forget about the barbecue Saturday night."

She watched him lope down the street toward Merck's Hardware and then turned the key in the lock and stepped into the diner. Just walking through that door, seeing the whitewashed wood tables and chairs, the four booths back to back on the right-hand side, the long counter with the ancient cash register she'd learned to use when she was ten, brought back a flood of memories, and she could almost smell Gram's biscuits and stew, and the huge platter of fried chicken with mashed potatoes and gravy that was nearly everyone's favorite. But today the diner was dim and quiet, the air warm and close. The ceiling fan was still, the windows closed, no pies cooled on the counter under the back window. Katy breathed in the silence for a moment, and glanced at the scrubbed blue linoleum floor, the white walls decorated with old photos of ranches going back four generations, and with soft watercolors of the Laramies and the Tetons.

Now I'm really home, she thought, her heart lifting as it hadn't in a long time. She switched on the lights, and sat down at the corner table, then reached into her purse for a pad of paper, a pen, her cell phone, and her planner.

And got to work.

Margie Birch hadn't changed a bit. Her name was Margie Davis now, but she was still petite and saucy, and her auburn hair, though shorter than it had been in high school, still curled neatly around her heart-shaped face. Her river-green eyes still tilted slightly upward at the ends, giving her a constantly quizzical expression.

She rushed out of the house, a baby at her shoulder, even

as Katy slammed the Blazer's door. At the sight of Katy walking toward her porch steps, she gave a muffled screech.

"It's you! I tried to reach you all day! Your mom gave me your cell phone number, but every time I called it was turned off. I left you three messages. How *are* you?"

And so saying, she flung herself at her friend, holding the baby at her shoulder and leaning her head against Katy's with a fervent excitement that was palpable in the warm May air.

"I'm fine and I can see I don't have to ask how you are. Who's this little cutie?"

"Cooper. Cooper Randall Davis." Margie shifted the infant into her arms so that Katy could see the tiny, puckered face and big dark blue eyes. "Is he the handsomest thing you ever saw or what?"

"The handsomest ever." Cooper Randall Davis was a heartbreaker all right. He had Margie's nose, Katy decided. But the rest of him was the spitting image of Lee. The lump in her throat tightened. She saw Margie peer at her and a shadow of dismay flickered across her face for a moment.

"Do you want to hold him, Katy?" she asked quietly.

Katy nodded.

"Here you go then." She placed the baby in Katy's arms and then touched her friend's shoulder. Katy felt pain quiver through her as she held the tiny warm bundle. Hollow, aching pain. But there was also a tenderness that swelled in her heart, a tenderness that felt good. Holding Margie's baby felt good. Cooper was warm and adorable and healthy. She wondered if her friend knew how lucky she was.

"Come on in and have some coffee, sweetie." Margie spoke softly. "But don't trip over Dougie's truck. The monster left it in the middle of the floor." Margie pushed the screen door wide. "Now tell me what's the point of having a cell phone if you keep it turned off?"

While Margie measured out coffee and water and set blue

earthenware mugs and cream and sugar on the table, Katy
studied the baby's expressive little face. And explained that
after she'd finished her own phone calls at the diner, she'd
been avoiding an incessant series of calls from Seth.

"Seth? You mean the bastard, don't you?"

"Margie—"

"Well, what does he want from you now?" Margie flipped
on the coffeemaker and scooped a red toy truck from the
linoleum floor, tossing it into a plastic toy bin in the corner
near the pantry.

"Business stuff." Katy shrugged. "He's furious that I took
a leave of absence so suddenly and without asking his permission. I sent him an inter-office memo yesterday morning,
telling him I was leaving, a mere hour before I took off." She
gave a tight smile, which relaxed into a genuine one as the
infant in her arms suddenly gave a loud gurgle.

"Well, good for you." Margie tucked a strand of auburn
hair behind her ear. "Can't he understand that your grandmother's sick and your family needs you here?"

"Seth only understands that the Rattlesnake Cafe in
Boston is falling apart. The manager there had been dipping
into the accounts for more than six months and no one knew.
And three cooks in a row have quit at our Phoenix location—
he wants me to fly down there and troubleshoot. I told him
no. And that I'm out of it." She gave her head a tiny shake. "I
think I want out of the business, Margie. He can deal with
my lawyer—let them figure it all out. As far as I'm concerned, I'm done with the Rattlesnake Cafe Company."

"But you started that company, honey. You opened the
first Rattlesnake Cafe in Chicago all by yourself. Before you
even met Seth Warfield."

It was true. She had. Two years out of college, she'd
opened her first restaurant, a tiny, hip, upscale version of
Bessie's Diner in a space not much bigger than a closet, and

the young and trendy and the older and wealthy had flocked to it.

"Down-home cooking with just the right twist of upscale imagination," the *Tribune* reviewer had raved. Lines had formed outside the door every night for one of the twelve tables, and weekends were packed. By the time her lease was up she was ready to move to a bigger location, but even with thirty tables and a heftier rent, crowds and money poured in.

Katy had been ecstatic. Of course, she'd worked seven days a week, doing much of the cooking herself, hiring and training her staff, handling all the books and all the ordering, even picking out the tiny twig vases where a single larkspur was placed in the center of each table. She'd been exhausted, exuberant, and triumphant—the successful owner of her very own business.

And then she'd met Seth Warfield.

Seth had an MBA from Harvard and had made his first million in real estate development within three years of entering the business world. He'd made his next million in a coffee shop franchise that had gone national in record time, and had been looking for another business to invest in and expand. Having heard all the buzz, he'd brought a willowy blonde to dinner at the Rattlesnake Cafe and ordered Thunder Creek Rib Steak with Cactus Butter and Down-Home Herbed Potatoes. By the time he was served cappuccino and rhubarb-ginger pie, he'd fallen in love with the food, the restaurant—and the owner.

Looking back, Katy knew exactly why she'd fallen so hard and so fast for Seth. He was tall, brash, and high-powered, with tawny hair and eyes the color of whiskey. He was exciting and energetic, like a speedboat, sleek and swift and sure, with sporty lines and a sophisticated flair, and he left all waters churning wildly in his wake.

Their courtship was a whirlwind of champagne and crème brûlée, of theater tickets and parties, weekend trips to

Martha's Vineyard and Hilton Head and nights of languid, intoxicating sex.

Seth had convinced her to hire a staff to run the cafe so she wouldn't be tied to it seven days a week; he'd come up with an investment and expansion plan where she could open a chain of Rattlesnake Cafes—not too many, just five or six, in select cosmopolitan cities—and reap more profits than she'd ever dreamed. He asked her to enter the expansion venture with him, as equal partners, using his business know-how and her restaurant savvy to morph her little cafe into a major player across the continental United States. And he'd asked her to marry him.

She'd said yes to both.

And everything had been wonderful for the first few years, until Katy began to feel the rat race of business and money and stress eating them both alive, and began yearning to slow down a little, yearning for them both to be able to start enjoying their success and each other—and to crown everything golden that had happened to them since they met with the best treasure of all—a baby.

A baby? She'd never forget the startled look on Seth's face when she'd broached the subject over breakfast one Saturday morning in their condo overlooking Lake Michigan.

"What's going on—is your internal clock ticking or something?" he'd asked warily, but then he'd cut the discussion short when the phone rang, and slipped out for a jog while Katy fielded the call from a friend. He'd eventually ceased dodging the subject, and had even begun to seem receptive, especially when his older brother Richard and his wife became pregnant. Seth had always competed with Richard, and looking back, Katy could see how that had influenced his change of heart.

Three months later, she was pregnant, overjoyed, and devouring every baby book she could get her hands on.

But she'd never had the chance to use even one morsel of

information she'd absorbed...or even to hold her baby in her arms.

She'd lost her baby near the end of her second trimester.

It had left her devastated.

But not Seth. Seth had little tolerance for any kind of failure, and little inclination to dwell on what might have been. What was done, was done. He'd put the loss of the baby behind him and moved on more quickly than she would have dreamed possible.

"I just want out. A fresh start," she told Margie. "And that means cutting loose from the Rattlesnake Cafe Company. Being tied to Seth Warfield through business the rest of my days is not my idea of getting on with my life."

"I see what you mean. So...what do you want to do? Your mom said you're reopening Bessie's Diner. Are you moving back here for good?" Margie asked eagerly.

"That's something I haven't figured out yet. Along with everything else about my life," she added with a rueful smile. "Right now, I'm just taking it day by day. It feels good to slow down, though, you know?"

"Not really," Margie laughed, as a horn sounded from outside, the telephone rang, and a red-haired toddler in denim overalls barreled into the kitchen with an orange Nerf football clutched in one jam-smeared fist. "I don't get to slow down too often, not around here. Whoa, mister, hold it right there," Margie ordered and picked up the cordless phone even as she grabbed a rag and knelt down to swipe at the jam and Kool-Aid stains surrounding her son's mouth.

Cooper started to fuss in Katy's arms and she stood up, carefully easing the baby up to her shoulder and rubbing his back. She glanced out the window just in time to see Jackson Brent getting out of a black Ford truck. As she watched, he slammed the door of the truck, and headed up the front walk.

Chapter 5

"HE'S HERE RIGHT NOW, LEE, WHAT DO YOU WANT ME to tell him? Okay, bye, darlin'." Margie released her son, set down the phone, and hurried to the kitchen door.

"Jackson, come on in. Lee's delayed in town—he'll be here in about twenty minutes. Want some coffee while you wait?"

"Sure, Margie. Sorry about the horn, I forgot that the baby might be sleeping—" He broke off when he saw Katy standing there, holding Cooper at her shoulder. "Didn't mean to interrupt," he said curtly.

"Katy and I were just catching up—or trying to. Dougie, what *is* it?" she asked as the little boy tugged on her hand, making little whiny noises.

"I have to go bafwoom."

"Well, if you have to go, you have to go. Come on. I'll help you, let's just put your brother in his crib—"

Snatching Cooper from Katy, Margie scooted out of the room with Dougie at her heels, calling over her shoulder, "Katy, help yourself to the coffee and pour a cup for Jackson, will you?"

When she disappeared there was an awkward silence in the ranch house's kitchen.

"Would you like some coffee?" Katy asked stiffly.

"Nope. Think I'll just wait in the truck." He spun around and started back toward the door, but Katy's voice halted him.

"Wait. You don't have to sit for twenty minutes in your truck just to avoid me," she said in annoyance. She picked up her purse from the kitchen chair and slung the leather strap over her shoulder. "I'll leave."

But as she took a step toward the door, he moved unexpectedly to block her, his tall, rangy frame seeming to fill the small kitchen. "You haven't finished your visit. Margie said you were just catching up."

"Well, I'll come back and catch up another day." She started to edge past him, but he snagged her arm.

"If anyone's leaving, it's me." His voice was cool. "I'll just take some coffee out to the truck with me. That way you won't have to feel bad about kicking me out of the house."

"Kicking you out of the..." Katy bit back her temper. "You're the one who *offered* to leave."

"Because," he said evenly, "any fool can see you'd rather sit and have coffee with a skunk than with me."

You're damned right about that. But she wasn't about to let Jackson Brent or anyone else see that he could get to her.

"On the contrary. It makes no difference to me whatsoever. We'll both stay and have coffee. Will that make you happy?"

"If you knew me better," he said, and she thought she detected an edge of mockery in his tone, "you'd know it takes more than that to make me happy."

"Oh, really?" She tilted her head up so that she met his gaze challengingly. "What does it take? If it's anything more than cream and sugar, I'm afraid you'll have to look elsewhere."

"Actually, at the moment, all it would take is a beer. It's hot as blazes out there and I'm dying for something cold. Think Margie would mind?"

"Help yourself," Margie answered him, rushing back into the kitchen, minus two children. "What'd I miss?"

"Nothing important," Katy said quickly. "Where's that gorgeous baby?"

"Sleeping, thank heavens. At least for the next half hour, I hope. If he ever takes a normal two-hour nap, I'll probably faint."

"Mommy, come pway with me. Read me a stowy!" Dougie bounced back into the room, his voice high and demanding.

"I can't right now, Dougie. In a little while. Say hi to Katy and Jackson first," Margie instructed her son as she took a beer from the fridge and handed it to Jackson.

"Hi."

"Howdy, pardner." Hunkering down, Jackson offered the toddler his big hand. Dougie smiled delightedly and grasped his knuckles with his own small fingers, pumping up and down.

"Will *you* wead me a stowy?" he asked the dark-haired man.

"He can't now, sweetie. He's going with Daddy to look at some sick calves." She threw Jackson a grim look. "Lee's praying it isn't a virus. But there's three of 'em down as of this morning."

"We'll find out soon enough."

"But I want someone to wead me a stowy!"

Katy leaned toward the little boy, smiling. "I will." She held out her hand. "Come on, show me the storybook you like best."

She was rewarded with a huge grin. "I want the hoss stowy," Dougie announced.

Katy glanced up at Margie, as Jackson watched, taking a long swig of his beer.

"He means *Tony and the Magic Pony*," she said. "It's on the couch in the living room. I read it to him ten times a day."

"*Tony and the Magic Pony* it is." Katy grinned and let herself be dragged from the kitchen.

Jackson's gaze followed her as she and Dougie disappeared through the short hallway that led to the living room.

"Sorry about that." Margie sighed. "For a minute there I forgot . . . about you and Matt and Katy."

"Yeah. It's okay."

"Must've been a little awkward."

"It was fine."

"I'm sure after all these years, she doesn't still hold you responsible for what happened to Matt."

"You're sure? I'm not." He took another swig of beer. "The sight of me still seems to shake her up. Even with all that city gloss on her." His eyes darkened for a moment with memory. "Guess I can't blame her."

"It's just that she's not used to seeing you. She's been away for the past ten years, and you were away, too. Every time she sees you it probably still reminds her of Matt, of what happened. Give it time."

"She staying in Thunder Creek awhile?"

"Maybe. She's keeping the diner going while Bessie's sick. But I'm not sure how long she'll be here and neither is she. With the divorce and all, she's still sorting things out."

He nodded. He'd heard snatches of talk about Katy Templeton's divorce. Something about a high-powered husband and career. She'd had a miscarriage, Jackson seemed to remember. He wondered how much of that accounted for the lost look he'd glimpsed for just a moment in her eyes last night in the barn, for the sadness he'd seen even today deep within those smoky blue-gray depths. He knew what it felt like to have your world shaken up, changed irrevocably, to have to take stock and figure out what you wanted, where you were going. He'd done that himself more than once.

And he'd ended up back here where he'd started. In Thunder Creek. He wondered if Matt's little sister would too.

Either way, it didn't matter to him. She'd get used to seeing him around and wouldn't stiffen up like a cornered filly every time she saw him. Or maybe it wasn't all because of him. Something might have spooked her along the way, something even more than losing Matt.

But it's none of your business, he told himself. *The best thing you can do for Matt's kid sister is stay out of her way.*

He could hear her voice, soft and lilting, as she read to Dougie in the living room. She had a nice voice, soothing, smooth, feminine. Actually, he thought, remembering the way her white T-shirt had outlined her breasts and the way her jeans had encased those long, slim legs, she had a nice everything. And if she were any other woman he'd have been calculating how many dates it would take to get her into bed.

"Thanks for the beer, Margie. I'll wait outside for Lee. That way she can come back in here after finishing the story. You two can get on with your visit." He set the beer bottle on the countertop and swung out the door before Margie could protest, and at that very moment, Lee pulled into the drive.

Which was just as well, Margie thought, considering the way Jackson Brent and Katy reacted to one another. She watched Lee and the vet drive off toward the north pasture as she whipped out a fry pan and the chicken pieces she'd been marinating since this morning. By the time Katy returned to the kitchen Margie had them sizzling in olive oil, and was peeling red-skin potatoes at the sink.

"It's okay. The coast is clear. He's gone."

"Jackson Brent doesn't bother me, Margie."

"Ahuh. I saw the look on your face when you were trapped in here with him. And the tension—you could have cut it with a spatula."

"I'm not fond of the man, that's all. End of story."

"He really is a good man, Katy. And he's a great vet. It's only been about six months since Doc Howard retired, but Jackson moved back to town and just took charge. He's done a great job. Lee thinks the world of him. And he's built a brand-new clinic on the site of his old house; remember the Brent place, down Lonetree Road, where he and his father lived?"

"Not really." She'd never been to Jackson Brent's home, though Matt surely must have gone there some time or other. As she recalled, they'd usually hung out at the Triple T— or the diner. But she did have a vague memory of seeing Jackson's father around town. Clayton Brent had been a gaunt scarecrow of a man with unkempt salt-and-pepper hair and bleary eyes. And a sour temper.

Now that she thought about it, she began to recall something else. Talk in town, talk about Jackson. About how his mother had run off and abandoned him and his father. Talk about Clayton Brent, drinking too much, letting his small-beans horse ranch go to hell.

"He's completely remodeled the place. The facilities are all modern, up to date, and he trucks in all the latest diagnostic equipment from Casper." Placing the peeled potatoes on a wooden cutting board, Margie began slicing them into wedges. "Half the women in town are crazy in love with him," she added.

"Great. They can have him." Katy picked up her coffee mug and carried it to the table.

"You'll see for yourself at the barbecue. Oh." Margie half turned from the sink. "Did Smoke tell you about the barbecue yet?"

"This morning."

"It'll be a great chance for you to see everyone again. There's a lot of people buzzing about you coming back. Including . . ."

She broke off with a mischievous grin.

"Who?" Katy asked suspiciously.

Margie returned to slicing the last of the potatoes. "Roy Hewett, for one."

"Roy! What's he doing these days?" Katy had gone steady with Roy her senior year of high school.

"He runs the real estate office. And he's divorced from Patty Watkins. And then there's Luke Dillard. I'm surprised he hasn't dropped in on you yet, you've been here a whole twenty-four hours. He's single again too. And Lee saw him at the Tumbleweed the other night and told me Luke kept asking questions about you."

"Lovely."

"What's wrong with Luke?"

Katy had never told anyone about the night Luke Dillard had gotten way more than friendly after the homecoming dance. She hadn't told Margie, or Smoke, or her parents. Looking back, she knew she'd been embarrassed by what had happened and had felt it was partly her fault. She'd worn a lot of lipstick and eye makeup that night, had slathered herself with perfume, and had been liberally flirtatious with her date. It wasn't until years later that she realized nothing she had worn or done could excuse the way Luke had treated her. She hadn't known the term *date rape* back then, but it was the only way to describe what he'd tried to do to her... what he probably *would* have done... if Jackson Brent hadn't come along.

She drew a deep breath just thinking about the way Jackson had dragged Luke off her, and punched him in the face. She'd yelled at him to stop, but he'd hit Luke in the stomach too, and then knocked him to the ground.

Her stomach clenched as she remembered how she'd started to cry, something she never did, something she hadn't done since Matt's funeral. Both times Jackson Brent had been there to see her lose control. That was the most galling thing of all. He hadn't said a word to her, had just put her in his rusted old truck, climbed behind the steering wheel, and driven her home. And the whole time she'd railed at him, told him she didn't need him to protect her, she could take care of herself, that he wasn't her big brother, and could never take Matt's place, and she didn't want him ever interfering in her life again.

Interfering. That's what she'd called it.

He'd saved her, saved her from Luke's groping hands and long, ropy body. And she'd never even thanked him. Maybe she'd have been able to fight Luke off herself, to make him stop—and maybe not. She'd never know. She only knew that it was humiliating to have the boy she'd kicked out of her house after her brother's funeral come to her rescue, to owe Jackson Brent even the smallest word of thanks.

"Luke's as good-looking as ever, and he's made a great success of the Dillard ranch since his dad and brother died in that plane crash and he took it over," Margie rambled on. She dumped the cut-up potatoes into a pot of cold water and snapped the burner switch to high. "Last year he bought out the Quinns and added their cattle and another ten thousand acres to his place. And he was dating Corinne Thomas, this waitress at the Tumbleweed, for a while, but she broke it off a few months back—so then he moved on to this school-teacher over in Bigrock—but she left town soon as school let out for the summer."

"That's what I'll have to do if you keep touting the virtues of all the single men in town." Katy eyed her friend over the rim of her coffee cup. "The last thing I'm looking for at the moment is a man in my life. I'm trying to get one *out* of my life."

Margie came to the table and slid into the chair beside Katy's. "I know. Sorry. God, after all you've been through, you don't need me pushing you to date someone before you're ready. Not that anyone could ever push you into doing anything you didn't want to do, Katy," she added. "But . . . forget it. You need time. It's only . . ."

"Only what?"

"I've missed you. And I just keep hoping you'll decide to

stick around in Thunder Creek. And you know, if you met a man here, one of our homegrown cowboys, there'd be a lot better chance of that happening, right?"

"Margie, you dork, I don't need a man to keep me in Thunder Creek. I have friends, family... Bessie's Diner. And—the funny thing is—it's still home."

She turned her head, gazing out the window a moment at the wide, turquoise sky where the sun blazed like molten gold, at the scraggly hills rising to the west, and at the cool green valley to the north, studded with cattle as it meandered into the distance.

The beauty of it all stole her breath away.

"I missed this. All of it," Katy said softly. "I'd almost forgotten how beautiful it is here. How peaceful."

She turned from the window to meet Margie's glance levelly, suddenly intensely aware of the delicious aroma of sizzling chicken, of Dougie's childish voice singing the *Sesame Street* song to himself in the living room, of Margie's understanding gaze fixed on her in the homey little kitchen.

"I need this right now. I need everything that's here in Thunder Creek. As for the future," she shrugged, "who knows? But for right now, this is where I want to be."

"Well, that's the best news I've heard. Exactly what I like to hear." Standing up, Margie hugged her. "Why don't you stay for supper? I have enough mashed potatoes to feed the National Guard and there's plenty of chicken."

"I'd love to, but not tonight. I'd better head home and get to work butting heads with my dad." She grimaced. "He and Mom are supposed to leave for Paris next week and he's aiming to cancel. I'm aiming to get him on that plane, even if I have to load up a shotgun to do it."

"Shotgun vacation, huh?" Margie grinned. "You wouldn't have to hold a gun to my head to get *me* to go somewhere." Dougie began shouting in the other room and from a distance, they heard Cooper begin to wail in his crib. "*Anywhere*," Margie said fervently.

Katy stayed another half hour, keeping Dougie occupied with colorful foam building blocks while Margie nursed the baby, then setting the table while Margie threw together a salad. When she finally turned the Blazer out of the drive and onto the rocky track that wound down through the valley, she couldn't help thinking that her own baby would have been ten months old now, if she'd lived. *She'd have been crawling by now,* Katy realized, a lump in her throat. *And on the verge of learning how to walk. And I'd have been planning her first birthday party, picking out party hats and paper streamers and balloons, deciding what kind of cake to bake . . .*

She felt the familiar pain welling up in her chest, the sting of tears in her eyes, and quickly blinked them back. *No more wallowing,* she told herself.

Wallowing.

That had been Seth's word.

You stay home and wallow in your suffering if that's what you want, Katy. I won't. And if you won't go to the Allerton party with me, I'll go myself.

Pain shot through her, and she forced away the memories the same way she'd forced away the tears, by sheer will.

Think about something else, she told herself, taking a deep breath. *Think about anything else.*

Gram and the diner. As the Blazer jolted over a particularly rough stretch of road, she focused her thoughts on all that still needed to be done if she wanted to reopen the diner by Tuesday. The questions she needed to ask Gram about her suppliers and about possibly printing up some fresh new menus swirled through her mind, and she reminded herself that she still had to call Daffodil Moline after dinner tonight and set up a work schedule for next week. At the top of her to-do list was the need to hire another worker, preferably a part-time cook/waitress who could give her a hand in the kitchen if she had to run home to help Gram while her parents were in Paris...

Concentrating fiercely on everything she had to set into motion within the next few days, Katy never saw the Explorer SUV barreling around the corner as she neared the fork in the road. She didn't see it until it was almost upon her. She heard a roar, and high-pitched laughter, then suddenly saw the flash of metal and green paint, a teenaged boy behind the wheel and a blonde girl next to him—and she screamed even as she jerked the steering wheel hard to the right.

There was a screech of tires and the SUV rolled onto the track and kept going, narrowly missing her as the Blazer careened into a ditch and nearly flipped over. At the last moment, Katy managed to keep it upright, but the jolt as she struck the ditch jerked her forward like a rag doll and rattled her teeth until lights sparked in her head.

She could do nothing but gasp for a moment, dizzy and shaken, her hands trembling on the steering wheel. Her heart pounded like thunder.

Slowly, then, she flexed her muscles, and was relieved that nothing hurt, other than a slight ache in her neck and shoulders. But her entire body tensed as a white Ford Ranger suddenly sped around the corner from the opposite direction, coming toward her. But fortunately it stayed well on its own side of the road, and then to her surprise, the driver braked abruptly just past her, backed up until he was alongside her, and opened his window.

"Hey, lady, are you— *Katy*!"

Roy Hewett stared at her in shock. Before Katy could even speak, he had his door open and was striding toward her.

"What the hell happened?" Roy still had the same mop of dark hair and sexy, puppy-dog brown eyes she remembered from high school, but his face was more weathered, his body whipcord lean. "You okay?"

"I'm . . . fine, Roy. Just a little shaken up."

"You're white as a sheet. Can you move?"

"Yes. Ye . . . es, I think so."

"Hell, Katy, seems to me when you left Thunder Creek, you knew how to drive. Guess you didn't get much practice in New York." The crooked grin she remembered curled his lips and Katy gave a shaky laugh. Roy had always had a way of making her laugh.

"Give me a break, Roy. There was an SUV . . . teenagers. They were coming so fast, I couldn't even really see who it was—"

"I could. And I did." Roy's lips thinned. "It was Corey Dillard driving—Luke's nephew. His brother's son. Daffodil Moline—she works for your grandmother as a waitress— was practically in his lap when they flew past me a minute ago."

"Luke's nephew? Great." She sighed. "He came out of nowhere. I forgot about that side road and I never saw them."

"The kid was going way too fast. He's wild as a wolf. Probably drinking, too." Roy shook his head. "His mother sent him back here to live with Luke for a while after he got into some trouble when they moved to Sioux Falls. Luke's doing a helluva lousy job straightening him out, if you ask me. Think you can get out of the car, make sure everything's all right?"

"I'm fine, Roy, honest. I really need to get home."

"Why don't you let me get you out of that ditch?"

Katy scanned the angle of the car against the rocks and brush, catching her lower lip between her teeth. His offer was tempting. But she wasn't about to start leaning on anyone at this point in her life. Especially her old boyfriend.

"I can manage, Roy. Don't worry about me."

"You sure?"

"Absolutely. I have to prove that living in New York hasn't softened me up too much for Thunder Creek, don't I?"

Roy laughed. "You don't have to prove anything to me. Tell you what, I'll stick around and make sure you get out of there okay. You just might need a little push."

As it turned out, she didn't need a push, but it took her ten minutes of sweat and swearing to wrestle the Blazer back onto the track. By the time Roy jumped back into his Ranger and took off with a wave, Katy felt like she'd been riding wild broncs for an hour.

She headed home, hoping she had time for a quick shower before dinner and her next battle of the day: a knock-down-drag-out fight with Big John himself.

Chapter 6

"YOU'RE GANGING UP ON ME, HUH? WELL, IT WON'T do you any good." Big John Templeton glared around the kitchen table from his wife to his daughter, his expression grim. Scowling, he set down his coffee mug and pushed back his chair. "That trip to Paris is going to have to wait. I've made up my mind."

"So have I. Sit down, Daddy. We're not finished yet."

Katy's tone was every bit as firm as his. Dorsey threw her daughter a quick worried glance and sighed.

"It's not worth fighting about," she said as she stood and began clearing away the dinner plates. "If you really can't bring yourself to go now, John, then I guess we'll wait—"

"No." Katy too pushed back her chair and stood. Her father hadn't taken his seat again, but he hadn't walked out of the room either. She still had his attention, and her mother's too, though Dorsey had carried the plates over to the sink and was rinsing them. But she was listening to every word.

"If you call the airlines and cancel the trip, you'll never get to Paris. Or anywhere else. Mom, you'll wait forever." She came around the table to face her father, her blue-gray eyes meeting his dark gray ones with equal determination.

"Daddy, things are never going to be perfect. Either on the ranch or in your life. It's never going to be a perfect time to go to Paris. As a matter of fact, this is about as good as it's going to get. Because I'm here right now. I can take care of Gram. And the ranch. There's nothing holding you back—except yourself."

"What do you know about the ranch? You've been gone for ten years. You don't know what's going on with the cattle, the crops, the oil operation—"

"I'm a quick study. And Riley will fill me in. He's been your foreman for seven years now, right? And Rod and Punchy are good hands. They'll be here, and they can come to me with any questions or problems, and I'll call you in Paris if there's something we can't handle."

"You forgetting about Cleo?" His brows drew together. "She could go into labor—"

"Jackson Brent will take care of Cleo. And based on her prior gestation date, you know as well as I do that there's a good chance she won't have this foal until you're back. Either way, Daddy, you know I'll watch out for her night and day. I want her to have a healthy foal as much as anyone."

A slight throb in his daughter's voice made Big John wince inwardly. He knew how Katy loved that mare. There'd been a bond between the two of them from the first time Katy saw her—that's why he'd bought the horse for her in the first place. He wondered if Cleo's troubles reminded Katy of her own doomed pregnancy. He wondered if it hurt her to think about Cleo losing her foal, just as she'd lost her own baby. The thought of his first grandchild never having made it into the world was enough to make him want to bawl and roar and hit something—he could only imagine how it affected his daughter. But if Cleo's endangered pregnancy brought back painful memories for Katy, she gave no sign of it, other than that tiny, almost undetectable quaver in her voice.

It never occurred to him to ask her. Big John didn't believe in bringing up painful subjects. Better just to stick to business, to concentrate on getting everything right you possibly could, because sooner or later, something would go wrong and there'd be hell to pay, and you'd best minimize the damage.

And who knew what damage would happen along while he was off fooling around on a damned "vacation" in Paris, of all places.

"You're forgetting about Bessie," he growled. And glared at his wife and daughter. "She's too weak to be left alone."

"She won't be alone, John, not if Katy's here." Dorsey spoke up quietly. She turned from the sink and regarded her husband with a steady gaze that still held a small flicker of hope.

At least Katy had John *voicing* his worries. She could never get him to say much about anything. John Templeton was a doer, not a talker. And what he did was work. Since Matt died, he'd cut nearly every pleasure and pastime from his life, busying himself with the ranch, the cattle, the oil, the land. The only pastime he retained was his bi-monthly poker game, and his only pleasure was a purely physical one—sex. The sex between them was still as vigorous and intense as it had been on their honeymoon. So was Big John. But in bed he could allow himself to be gentle, allow himself to show the feelings he kept inside, the ones he never talked about. Need, hunger, want, fear, sadness, joy. All of that he expressed when they were in bed together. He spoke to her, not in words, but in each stroke of her cheek with a callused thumb, each deep, needy, and possessive kiss, one after the one, trailing over her body.

And he spoke with his eyes, those hard, sorrowful eyes, which only the sheen of passion seemed able to soften. Dorsey knew how to read him in bed. She could always reach him there. But outside of their bedroom with its blue-and-violet flowered quilt and soft blue curtains, Big John Templeton was a lone, stoic man, who spoke in the shortest possible sentences about only a limited range of topics—a man who refused to partake of the joy or adventure or beauty of life, who had given up on all that when he'd buried his son.

"Katy's going to have her hands full running the diner. She won't be around to help Bessie bathe and get dressed, to bring all her meals up to her and make sure she doesn't start to run another fever or fall down, or any one of a hundred things that could happen."

"Well, I spent a good hour with Bessie before supper, when I brought her tray up," Dorsey said, wiping her hands on a dishrag, and walking toward the table again. "She seems to be feeling a little bit stronger each day, like Doc Evans said she would. She even talked about going off to Las Vegas on that trip with Ada in a few weeks, just like they'd planned. And Katy had a word with Riley on her way in tonight," she continued, undaunted by the flash of ire in her husband's eyes. "He told her Pat would be more than happy to stay here with Bessie while Katy's working at the diner. They could use some extra money, it seems, with their son in college now and wanting to go to law school."

"You've both got it all figured out, don't you?" John Templeton felt cornered, and when he felt cornered, like a bear, he lashed out.

"Fine, then. I won't fight both of you, damn it." His mouth tightened and the lines at the corners of his eyes seemed to deepen, further creasing the furrows in his already weathered face. "If that's how you want it, we'll go on the damned trip. But if anything happens while we're gone, Dorsey, it's on your head, yours and Katy's. And don't say I didn't warn you."

He wheeled around and stalked from the room, his heavy footsteps rattling the plates and knickknacks in the china cabinet. A moment later, they heard the front door slam.

Wearily, Dorsey turned toward her daughter. "It's no use. The trip was supposed to be fun, for both of us." She shrugged, and started gathering up the rest of the plates, as well as what remained of the roast chicken and stuffing on the big china platter. "It's not going to be much fun for either one of us if he's in a temper the whole time."

"No kidding." Katy gritted her teeth. "I'm going to talk to him some more." But her mother shook her head as she was about to march out after Big John.

"Not yet, Katy. Wait. Let him cool off some."

"But we need to make him see—"

"No one can make that man see anything he doesn't want to see. He knows, deep inside, that this trip would be good for him, good for both of us. He just has to come to terms with it."

Dorsey returned to the sink and began rinsing the rest of the plates. For a moment, Katy just stood and watched her.

She knew her mother was right. From her own experience, she understood all about coming to terms with things. It had taken her a long time to come to terms with Matt's death after he fell off that roof. And it had taken months for her to even come close to coming to terms with the miscarriage. And no one could have rushed her. Not Seth, not some shrink, no one. She'd had to deal with it herself in her own time, her own way. And she still was. Maybe she always would.

But it had been fourteen years since Matt fell off the roof of the Jenssens' barn. Enough was enough. Her father needed to stop grieving and start living before what remained of his own life passed him by entirely.

Still, she suddenly realized, that was something Big John needed to figure out for himself.

We're just giving him a little push, she told herself as she carried the leftover green bean casserole to the kitchen counter. *If we're lucky, maybe it will nudge him in the right direction.*

By the time the table was cleared, the dishes loaded into the dishwasher, and the pots scrubbed, dried, and put away, she felt drained. It had been a long day, and her shoulders still ached from the near collision with Corey Dillard's Explorer. She swept the floor while Dorsey scrubbed the sink, then went upstairs intending to speak to Gram about the new menu items for the diner. But Bessie was asleep, and Katy quietly retreated from her room, closing the door without waking her.

She paused in the hall, staring for a moment at the opposite door, the door to Matt's old room. It was always kept closed, unless her mother was in there, dusting or sweeping. Katy hadn't opened it once since she'd been home, and before that, for several years.

She studied it for several seconds, then on impulse, she grasped the doorknob and turned it. She braced herself as if for a blow as she pushed it open and gazed into the room.

Memories rushed back at her so strongly that for a moment she was dizzy. The room still smelled faintly, vaguely of Matt, of Brut aftershave and Wrigley's gum, of sage and the outdoors. Or perhaps it was just her imagination, just her senses playing tricks on her as she gazed at all the familiar objects she'd seen in this room so many times before, all kept spotless and dusted and arranged tidily on shelves or hooks, as if waiting for Matt to come back and pick up where he left off. Matt's football jersey and his sketches and his cleated shoes. The blue ribbons from horse shows crowded together with books and photographs on the shelf over the bed. Matt's blue and green checkered bedspread, the ends just touching the floor.

There were half a dozen wood-framed photos lined up on the desk shelves as well, and his favorite drawings were tacked to the walls in random arrangement. And on his desk was the twelve-by-fourteen inch sketchbook filled with doodles and minisketches and full-fledged drawings.

Matt had loved drawing almost as much as he'd loved football and riding. Since he'd received his first box of crayons and drawn his three-year-old version of a rearing horse on the living room wall, he was forever sketching something or other, and in a few swift strokes could capture the majesty of the mountains, or the wistful expression of a child gazing longingly at an ice cream cone. He was good— good enough to study art if he'd chosen to, but he'd always kept the drawing as a hobby and had planned on attending the University of Wyoming for his degree in business, so he could use what he learned when he returned to work for the Triple T.

The ranch had been his first love, something he and Big John shared, the way they shared a love of riding and fishing, but capturing images on paper, often only in pen and ink or charcoal, had been a special pleasure.

His backpack, still bulging with school books, was slung over the back of his desk chair. Katy doubted it had ever been opened since the day Matt died.

But the funny thing was, she thought, as she sank down on the bedspread and gazed around, letting herself feel and remember, Matt wasn't here anymore. Only his belongings were here. It was good to see them, because it brought back memories, wonderful memories, but they didn't bring Matt to her, not anymore. His spirit didn't inhabit them.

Because now his spirit was in her heart.

Stunned, she sat a moment on the bed, taking this in, searching her memories, letting them drift warmly through her mind, and finding for the first time more pleasure than pain.

She remembered Matt teaching her how to ride, how to swim, how to throw a ball straight and hard. And also, when she was seven, how to walk a split-rail fence. She'd fallen off the first few times, but he'd caught her before she could tumble into the hard gritty dust. And she remembered how he'd caught her another time, this time sneaking out of the house one night when she was eleven, wearing Passion Pink lipstick and blue Maybelline eyeshadow. He'd never tattled to their mom, but had told her two years later that he'd followed her to the creek that night, and made sure she met up with her friends all right, and that she was only drinking Coke and eating potato chips and not getting mixed up with drugs or beer or cigarettes—or boys.

She'd never known he was there, but he always had been. He'd always watched out for her.

She wondered if Matt had lived, if he'd have warned her that Seth Warfield was not the right man for her, if with his keen vision and remarkable perception about people and life, Matt would have been able to see what she had not: that she never should have married Seth in the first place, that when push came to shove, she hadn't been able to count on him. Not the way a woman should be able to count on a man.

But most likely, she reflected wryly, that was something she'd inevitably have had to discover for herself.

She spent the next half hour poring over sketches and photographs. Her weariness was forgotten as the vivid details of her brother's life and loves and friendships flowed back to her.

She suddenly didn't want to keep all these pictures of Matt and their family, and his friends and girlfriend, Allison, locked here in this room—she wanted them framed, out on the mantel in the living room, or perhaps in her father's den, where they would be part of the family. Matt was still a part of this family even though he was gone, and he didn't have to be shut away anymore in this "shrine." He could join them, be part of them, and so live on, she thought, and with this realization she felt something like peace settle over her heart.

It's also time, she decided, *to go through some of this other stuff.* She surveyed the crowded desk and shelves, the backpack still bulging. Impulsively, she unhooked it from the chair, plopped it in the center of the bed, and unzipped it.

Textbooks and notebook paper and old gum wrappers

filled every inch of the deep canvas pocket. She lifted out the textbooks first—the *Contemporary World History* text was only slightly thicker than *Introduction to Calculus*. There were pens, pencils, a squashed, empty Milk Duds carton, a Hershey bar wrapper, and a spiral-bound lined pad of paper with doodles on the upper half of the first page.

On the bottom half a few words were scribbled, each on their own line.

Call Allison.

Study for Calc quiz.

Tell Sheriff Harvey & Dad.

And at the bottom was more doodling, except...she peered closer. It looked more like a sketch, a rough sketch done in plain blue ink, but it was clear enough. A girl, a young woman, really, with very long, very wavy hair lying facedown in what looked like tall grass. From the angle of her arms, the glimpse of lifeless eyes, the way her face was half buried in the grass, she looked...

Dead.

Katy felt a jolt like that of ice scraping down her spine.

Her fingers tightened on the pad. She read the list over again, studied the drawing again.

Tell Sheriff Harvey & Dad. A chill trickled along her spine once more.

What on earth would Matt have to tell Sheriff Harvey? And who was that girl?

She wanted to drop the pad on the bed, but she couldn't. For some reason, her fingers continued to clutch it, as if held by an unseen hand.

A coolness, like a ghostly breath, just touched the back of her neck and was gone.

Katy stared at the page again.

It doesn't mean anything, she told herself. But she found her eyes drawn again to that strange rough sketch of the girl in the grass. Beside her was a tree stump, and in the distant background, a hill.

Matt, what is this? she whispered, trying to shake off the uneasy feeling in the pit of her stomach.

Was it something he'd created out of his imagination... or something he'd seen?

She flipped that top page over, and saw that the next page was blank. And the next.

This list, this drawing, must have been made the day he died—or only a day or two before. She closed her eyes, searching back in her mind, and was pretty sure that on the day he died, Matt had indeed been studying for a calculus quiz. She vaguely remembered him grumbling about it when telling her how he had to go paint the Jenssen barn, because Jackson suddenly had a hot date with Holly Sue Granger that night. How he'd have to study when he got back and he hoped painting the barn wouldn't take too long. How Allison was mad at him because he'd promised to go over to her house and help with homecoming decorations, and now, instead, he had to work as well as study.

Call Allison.

She began riffling through the rest of the backpack but came up with nothing more unusual than a flashlight, an old musty T-shirt that had been rolled into a ball at the bottom, and a pocket English/Spanish dictionary.

Katy stuffed everything except the pad of paper back inside and zipped it closed. She hesitated, eyeing the pad of paper, then something made her tear off the top page and carry it from Matt's room to her own.

The drawing disturbed her. She couldn't shake the feeling that the girl it depicted was not sleeping, not just lying in the grass. She was dead.

Never, to her knowledge, had her brother drawn a dead person or animal before. So why, on the day he died...

She drew a deep breath and decided she was letting her

imagination run away with her. She slipped the drawing into her desk drawer and slammed it shut. Then she crossed the room and curled up in the window seat.

Outside, the Laramies seemed to loom closer, like great monstrous shrouds. Despite the half-moon, the sky looked unusually dark. Even the shadows of the trees seemed more ominous and dense, more full of secrets than they ever had before. *You're being ridiculous,* she told herself, and pushed open the window, taking slow gulps of the clear, pine-scented air.

Why should a fourteen-year-old drawing make goose bumps prick the back of her neck?

From somewhere in the distance she heard the screech of an owl, hunting its prey. A coyote howled in the hills. And the wind picked up, sweeping across the valley with a flutter of leaves and brush, and a sound like an eagle's rushing wings.

She sat there a long time, in the window seat of her girl-hood. And sitting there, gazing at the darkness and at the crystal glow of the half-moon, she knew what she was going to do.

She'd go see Sheriff Harvey tomorrow and find out if Matt had spoken with him the day he died. And if so, what about.

No doubt it was something simple, she told herself. *Something ordinary, and completely irrelevant to a drawing of a dead girl—and to the somber tone of the sketch that was most likely the very last sketch of my brother's life.*

Chapter 7

"ANOTHER BEER, JACKSON?"

Corinne Thomas paused at Jackson Brent's table and waited, her head tilted to one side as he seemed to pull himself out of a daze. She doubted he was drunk—Jackson never had more than a few drinks on any given night, and there was only one empty Budweiser bottle at his elbow. But he seemed to be lost in thought, caught up in whatever problem was hog-tying him, and he hardly seemed to hear her until he noticed her standing beside him, and sat up with a start.

"It's okay, honey," she chuckled. "I only want to know if you'd like another beer."

"Sure, Corinne, why not?" His smile, she noticed, was halfhearted and still distracted.

"Something wrong? You're doing a powerful lot of thinking here. And not much dancing tonight," she added.

Three or four couples were swaying together on the darkened dance floor in the Tumbleweed Bar and Grill. At the bar, Luke Dillard swiveled on his stool, ignoring his burger and his beer as he watched Corinne through narrowed eyes, studying the way her shaggy blonde hair glistened in the dim light, the way she balanced the drink tray on her hip, the way she was standing so close to Jackson Brent.

"Well, Corinne, maybe I just haven't had the right invitation." Jackson shot her a grin, looking much more like his old self. He leaned back in his chair. "You want to dance?"

"Why, sweet thing, I thought you'd never ask."

He laughed and stood up, taking the tray from her and setting it down on the table. As he led her over to the dance floor and wrapped a friendly arm around her waist, he tried to figure out what the hell was wrong with him.

He'd been restless tonight after finishing his rounds, making his phone calls, caring for his own horses and the two dogs and ginger cat that had adopted him a few months back, shortly after he returned to Thunder Creek. Too restless to stay home, too restless to relax.

The cabin he'd built, a half mile up from the small ranch house where his father had drunk himself into oblivion every night after his mother had abandoned them, had for some reason pressed in upon him tonight, and so he'd taken Jiggers for a ride in the hills. He'd even considered spending the night camping out under the moon, usually one of his favorite diversions, but even that notion hadn't appealed to him.

So he'd come here, hoping for a drink and a dance, some music and some company, thinking maybe that would help, and that perhaps he'd run into Kelly Jones, buy her a drink.

Or take her to bed, he amended silently as he made idle chatter with Corinne on the dance floor while Patsy Cline's *Crazy* crooned from the jukebox.

Kelly worked at the bank, and was fairly buttoned-down by day, but at night she liked playing pool and hanging out at the Tumbleweed. Theirs was a casual relationship, which sometimes included drinks and dinner, sometimes popcorn and a movie—and frequently, long nights of highly satisfying sex. She was stunning with short, red hair, a milky complexion, and wide green eyes the color of the grass that grew deep in a lush Wyoming meadow. She was fun, easy to talk to, and best of all, after having gone through two divorces, she was totally uninterested in any kind of serious relationship.

Which suited him just fine. Jackson ran from serious relationships the way Spaniards in Pamplona ran from the bulls. Ties, commitments, and certainly marriage were not in the cards for him, not now, not ever.

Getting too close to people always ended badly—he'd learned that a long time ago.

Which is why he scouted out the women in his life carefully—and steered away from any who seemed needy, or in search of a husband. He didn't want to hurt anyone and he didn't want to end up hurt—sure as hell not hurt like he and his father had been when his mother ran out on them twenty years earlier. Mary Alice Brent had taken off for parts unknown, and never looked back.

And his father had buried his misery in a bottle.

Jackson had promised himself every night, as he listened to his father's drunken sobbing and his pleas for Mary Alice's return, that he'd never end up like that. He'd gone to sleep listening to his father's cries and curses, and he'd awakened to the stench of spilled liquor and vomit, and stale sweat. He'd vowed to himself that he'd never let anyone— man or woman—mean that much to him, enough to turn him into a sniveling, hopeless drunk.

Then, in seventh grade, Matt Templeton had become his best friend, and he'd let himself get involved in a friendship that had brought joy and fun and purpose to his life, in a family—Matt's family—that had welcomed him like an adopted son, and invited him to dinner and on fishing trips, and cattle roundups, a family whose door was always open to him, and that had given him a sense of belonging he hadn't even known he missed until he found it.

And then Matt had died, and something in himself had died too. Matt's sister had blamed him for the accident and he'd discovered that the very sight of him was like a punch in the gut to her, so he'd stayed away, from her and from Matt's family.

And he'd rediscovered that it was no good getting too close to people—no good caring too much about anyone, letting them *make* you care, because in the end, there was no guarantee they'd stick around. No guarantee any of it would last.

And you'd just end up lonelier than before.

The song ended and the jukebox in the Tumbleweed went silent. The sound of pool cues clicking against balls, of glasses clinking and low talk and laughter floated around the murky, smoke-filled room as Corinne rested her arms on his shoulders, still standing close and gazing at him with worried eyes.

"What's wrong, Jackson? You're not yourself tonight. You got woman trouble? Is it Kelly Jones?"

"Nope," he answered, realizing it was only half the truth. Because it wasn't Kelly Jones who bothered him—he'd only been wanting to see her tonight in the hopes that she'd take his mind off the real source of his irritation.

And that was Katy Templeton.

Katy Templeton. She pretty much loathed him. He shouldn't care, he knew that. But for some reason, her looking down her snooty nose at him even after all these years rubbed him the wrong way. It didn't help that she was gorgeous. Matt's little sister was no longer all elbows and knees, like she'd been at fourteen. She looked good, she smelled good, she walked good. And she was bad for him in every way.

Nursing any kind of attraction to her wasn't practical and it wasn't smart. And over the years he'd been supporting himself, scraping together enough money for college and veterinary school, working three jobs at a time, and keeping expenses to a minimum, Jackson Brent had taught himself to be both of those things.

"Could be I'm just upset," he told Corinne, leading her back to his table, "because I heard you and Roy Hewett have been getting cozy. Could be I'm jealous."

"Like hell." Corinne snorted and threw back her head and laughed. "You're a good friend, Jackson, but you couldn't care less if I slept with a grizzly bear. Now, *that* one's another matter," she added as she picked up her tray again. Jackson saw she had glanced over her shoulder at Luke Dillard.

"Just because we went out a few times, Luke thinks he owns me. Well, I guess he's finding out different," she muttered.

Jackson threw Dillard a long glance. "If that jackass gives you any trouble, you let me know," he told Corinne, still steadily holding the other man's hostile gaze. He refused to withdraw his stare, and Dillard glanced away first, swiveling around on his bar stool to grab his beer.

"Thanks, honey, but I can handle Luke myself." Corinne gave her head a toss and moved on, murmuring over her shoulder, "I'll bring you that fresh Bud in a jiffy."

She'd no sooner hurried off to take drink orders from another table than Luke Dillard swung off his stool and bore down on Jackson's table.

"Nearly shot one of your dogs this morning, Brent. That red mutt of yours came round, started chasing some of my calves. I thought he was a coyote and damn near shot his tail off. You'd better keep your strays off my land. No telling what can happen."

Jackson stiffened. His "red mutt" was Ajax, an Irish setter/golden retriever mix he'd found abandoned and starving along the highway a few months back. Jackson had taken him in and fed him, bathed him, brushed him, and quickly found that there was no better-natured, more loyal dog than

Ajax. He stared up at the hard-eyed, sandy-haired man loom-ing beside his table and spoke quietly.

"That better not be a threat, Dillard."

Luke Dillard shrugged, and gave Jackson the innocent look he'd used on teachers all through high school whenever someone had bombarded their turned backs with spitballs. "Just a friendly warning," he said. But his bland smile didn't hide the ice in his tobacco-colored eyes.

"And here's one for you." Jackson leaned back in his chair and regarded the other man steadily. "Anything happens to any of my dogs, any of my animals, and I'll beat the crap out of you."

All the false amiability drained from Dillard's face. "Think you can, Brent?" he scoffed, his mouth curling deri-sively.

"You don't want to find out." Jackson continued to speak quietly from his seat, not even bothering to unfurl his six-foot, two-inch frame.

He watched the other man's jaw clench, then turned his attention to Corinne as she returned and set his beer down.

"Thanks, Corinne."

"Everything okay here?" She glanced uneasily between the two men.

"Just dandy." Dillard caught her by the arm. "Hey, want to dance, beautiful?"

"Maybe later. I'm the only one serving now. Andi went home sick."

She eased her arm free and breezed off toward the bar, and for a moment Luke Dillard glared after her.

It was all Jackson could do right then and there not to pop him one. He was in no mood for Dillard's preening self-importance, or the possessive way he treated any woman who passed within ten feet of him. He'd seen the kind of ass-hole Dillard was years ago, when he'd been a high school

senior getting rough with Katy Templeton in the woods near
Bear Trail.

Dillard had grown up since then, had become a shrewd
businessman and rancher, and had added some acreage to his
parents' property. He now was considered one of Thunder
Creek's most prosperous ranchers. *But he's still a punk and
still a bully.*

And not exactly a lofty role model for his brother's kid.

"Heard your nephew nearly had a wreck today up near
Snake Road." Jackson tilted the bottle back, took a swig.
News traveled fast in a small town, and he'd bumped into
Roy Hewett at the drugstore. "The kid was speeding. Ran
someone off the road. You might want to have a word
with him."

"Yeah, who'd he run off the road? You?" Luke Dillard
looked amused.

"Katy Templeton. Sent her car into a ditch."

Dillard stuck his hands in the pockets of his jeans.
Jackson saw the quick interest light his eyes. "Yeah? That's
too bad. Katy okay?"

"No thanks to Corey."

"Maybe I'll have to stop by and see how she's doing."
Dillard smiled. "And don't you worry about my nephew.
He's just a boy, full of high spirits. He doesn't mean any
harm."

"Rein him in, Dillard. It's the kindest thing you can do for
him—before he gets himself into some real trouble."

"Look who's giving advice on raising kids. You ever
raised any yourself, Brent? Or maybe you just learned from
your own pop—but then old Clayton Brent wasn't exactly a
model husband and father, was he? Otherwise, maybe your
ma wouldn't have run off the way she did."

Jackson came out of the chair slow and easy, but his fist
shot out like lightning, slamming into Dillard's mouth with a
sickening crack.

Luke Dillard went down like a playing card flicked by a fingernail. Blood spouted from his lip. As Jackson took a deep breath, he fought the cold rage sweeping through him.

"You loco bastard," Dillard gasped, pushing himself up with his hands.

Jackson forced himself to relax his fists. Hell knew, he was itching for more, but this wasn't a damned school playground. And he wasn't a kid anymore. *So don't act like one,* he told himself.

But a part of him wanted Dillard to get up and give him a good dirty fight—he was in the mood to hit something, and why the hell not this bastard who'd nearly raped Matt's sister all those years ago? It would feel good to go one hard round with Dillard. That's about all it would take.

And it seemed—as the other man came heavily to his feet, seemingly unaware of the blood dripping from his lip, staining the front of his short-sleeved white shirt, while his eyes glinted with fury—that for one of the few times in Jackson's life, he was going to get exactly what he wanted.

"Where'd you learn to punch like that, Brent? From your old man?" Dillard gave a jeering laugh. "I heard that even before he turned into a drunk, he used to bat you around. Maybe he did the same to your ma—"

Jackson hit him again. Dillard staggered backward but managed to stay on his feet, and after one muttered oath through his bruised lips, he charged at Jackson like a maddened bull. Both men went down and then they were rolling around on the old sawdust floor as other customers edged nearer to watch, and Corinne and the bartender darted toward them, both shouting for them to stop.

Dillard landed a mean left hook to Jackson's jaw, but it was the only blow he got in. Jackson punched him again, and then again. As the other man fell back, striking his head against the floor, Jackson could have straddled him, could have held him down and beaten him bloody, but instead he got to his feet, and once more stood over him, breathing hard.

"Had enough?" he asked curtly.

Dillard's right eye was half closed. "Go to hell."

Jackson was about to grab him by the shirt front and heave him to his feet, then hit him one more time for good measure—until he saw Corinne's face.

"That's enough, Jackson," she ordered, but her eyes pleaded with him to stop. Slowly the anger dropped away and he stepped back, putting a few feet of distance between him and the man struggling up from the floor.

"Yeah, Corinne. I reckon it is." Jackson yanked some loose bills from his pocket, handed them to her and turned toward the door.

She followed him, grabbing his arm as he reached the exit. "Good Lord, for a man so gentle with animals, you've got a hell of a right hook." As she shook her head, a ghost of a smile touched her thin, peach-tinted lips. "He's not worth it, don't you know that? But I have to say, from what I heard, he had it coming."

"Forget it, Corinne. It's no big deal."

"I just hope he doesn't call the sheriff," she fretted, casting a glance over her shoulder at Dillard, who was refusing a bag of ice for his lip.

"Let him."

"What's gotten into you tonight? You're usually the calmest man I know. Something's eating you."

The hell of it was, she was right. But he'd never in a million years admit what—or rather *who*—had gotten under his skin. For an instant, Katy Templeton's lovely face and wary eyes filled his mind.

"Ever get an itch you can't scratch, Corinne? That's all it is. A damned itch. If you ignore it long enough, it eventually goes away."

"I guess," she murmured doubtfully, but then he was gone, striding out into the clear, cool night, as someone punched in a Lonestar tune on the jukebox and two couples drifted onto the dance floor, and Ray the bartender coaxed Luke Dillard back to the bar and bought him a beer.

Chapter 8

Seated at the front booth in Bessie's Diner, Katy studied the list of weekly specials she'd typed up on her laptop. Sweet Pea Soup, Steak and Cheese Wrap, and Coyote Chicken. The special dessert for the first week would be Devil's Canyon Chocolate Cake, in addition to the regular offerings of apple, blueberry, and ginger-rhubarb pie.

It looked perfect. And she was excited to be expanding the menu items at the diner. Of course she'd continue to serve all of the standards: Bessie's meat loaf and stew, turkey pot pies, and BLT sandwiches, the ribs and fries, hamburgers, and of course, the deluxe fried chicken platter. For breakfast there would be flapjacks and waffles and eggs with hash browns and sausage. But she was also going to start serving bagels and muffins and yogurt with granola.

Until she had time to design and print up new menus, she'd add the new items on separately printed weekly specials, and give people a chance to get used to them. And she'd need to start training her new short-order cook to help with the extended menu preparation.

Even as this thought flashed through her mind, the kitchen erupted with the sound of clattering pans, then a crash.

Katy suppressed a wince.

"Billy, are you all right?" Jumping up, she hurried past the counter and grill to the small, open kitchen that looked out on the diner. Billy Stone, the sixteen-year-old grandson of Bessie's dearest friend, Ada, was already kneeling on the floor in the midst of two large fry pans and a shattered glass bowl, wiping up broken eggshells, yolks, and glass that had spattered across the old linoleum.

"Sorry, Ms. Templeton." Billy gave her a sheepish grin. "I was carrying too much at once, I guess."

"You'll get used to it, Billy. Here." She handed him another roll of paper towels. "Watch out for the glass—we'll get that with a broom. Hold on."

Her cell phone rang as she lifted the broom and dustpan from the supply closet.

"No, Seth, this is *not* a good time to talk. I'm right in the middle of something."

"Katy, I don't give a damn what you're in the middle of." His voice pinged with crisp authority into her ear. "You have to get yourself on a plane and get out to Dallas. Today. And to Phoenix by Monday morning. The shit has hit the fan and unless you step in—"

"Have you spoken with my lawyer, Seth? I'm sure Maxwell has told you that I'm out of it. What don't you understand about those words? *Out of it*. That means no matter how many managers quit, or how many computer systems go down, or how many liquor shipments get delayed, it's not my problem anymore."

He wasn't listening to her. That was part of Seth's problem, she reflected, closing her eyes for a moment and trying to summon her patience, trying to banish the hard little rock of tension that always formed in her stomach now when she had to speak to him or think about him. He was a brilliant businessman, in top form with number crunching and projections, but he didn't listen enough to people—either those who worked for him or those in his life. It was always about *his* agenda, *his* timetable, *his* priorities.

That was why Katy had been in charge of human resources and management on a day-to-day basis.

But not anymore. *Now,* she thought, sweeping broken glass into the dustpan as Billy Stone fetched a mop and bucket and Seth went on and on about wait staff shortages, *all I have to worry about is getting the ceiling fan fixed, teaching Billy how to cook, and getting Daffodil Moline in here to arrange her work schedule.*

Daffodil had promised to report in at eleven, and it was already a quarter of twelve. *The first thing I'll have to teach that girl is how to tell time.*

And the Rattlesnake Cafe Company will just have to muddle along without me.

"Seth . . . *Seth.* What part of 'I can't help you' don't you understand? Call Stephie, see if she can help you. Yes, I know she was my secretary, but she's sharp and she's familiar with my management style and she'd probably jump at the chance to get her feet wet with the staff in Phoenix and Dallas. Seth, give her a try, I can't do it and I'm—"

She broke off as the door to the diner opened and a petite blonde bombshell bounced in. She was all of five foot three, squeezed into Gap denim shorts, a pink and orange striped tank top, and clunky little black sandals that showed off her precisely painted pink toenails. Her pale gold hair was caught up in a ponytail that bobbed back and forth as she propelled herself through the door. She tripped over the leg of one of the chairs, nearly fell against the table, choked on her gum, and then caught herself from falling just in time.

"Ooops, damn." She took a deep breath, stuck her fingers in her mouth and extracted her gum, then stuck it blithely beneath one of the tables. "Miss Templeton, I'm Daffodil Moline. Sorry I'm late but I lost the note I wrote for myself and I wasn't sure what time you said. Then while I was eating my breakfast—I always have oatmeal every day for breakfast, but not just plain oatmeal, you know, I like the old-fashioned kind with raisins and bananas and chocolate chips added to it—my mom taught me to make it that way when I was a little girl, and it's really good—but anyway while I was eating it I remembered that you said eleven and so I stopped eating right then and there and I ran right outside and jumped in the truck, and here I am!"

"Seth," Katy said firmly. "I have to go."

She ended the call with a push of the button and set the phone down on the counter. "So." She met the teenager's saucer-shaped blue eyes, surprised to see that they weren't vacuous, as one would expect from such an apparent ditz. "You're Daffodil Moline."

She went forward, past Billy who had gone silent and still, and held out her hand.

"I'm Katy. My grandmother's told me a lot about you."

"She has? Oooh, isn't she sweet? How's Bessie feeling?"

"Better, thanks. Do you know Billy Stone?"

"Yeah, I guess you could say I do. Seeing as he used to be my boyfriend. *Used to be* being the operative words." She gave her ponytail another toss.

Billy scowled. "Yeah, well, that was the dumbest mistake of my life."

"Mine, too," Daffodil flashed, her blue eyes narrowing on him, and all of the sugar fading from her voice. "Don't tell me you're hiring him too, Miss Templeton. I mean, Katy. I don't think there's room in this diner for the both of us."

"Really? I'm sorry to hear that."

"It just wouldn't be comfortable for me working with my ex, you know. And . . . and my new boyfriend wouldn't like it much. Corey's really jealous, you know, and he doesn't like me hanging around with other guys, even though I'd never look at anyone else, not when I've got Corey. And besides, the one thing you can say about me is once I'm done with a boy, I'm done, you know what I mean?"

"I believe I do." Katy gave her a warm, bright smile. "Well, then, thank you for coming in. Billy and I have a lot of work to do so just make sure the screen door latches on your way out, okay?"

"On my way out? Well, what about... my schedule? I need to know my hours—that's what I came for."

"Yes, but you just said..." Katy allowed a puzzled expression to cross her face. "I thought you were refusing to work with Billy. I've hired him, you see, as my assistant cook, in charge of the grill, and I certainly have no intention of firing him. He's an excellent worker and eager to learn and he's going to be invaluable to me. So if you can't work with him, I'm sorry, but I'll have to find someone who can."

From the corner of her eye, she saw Billy visibly relax. Daffodil merely stared at her, shock registering on her small, pert features.

"You mean... you'd pick him over me? But I have *experience*!"

"Billy can cook," Katy explained pleasantly. "And I need him, especially since I'm expanding our menu, plus I'll have to leave now and then to check on my grandmother. I can always find another waitress, but a cook—"

"No!" Daffodil bit her lip. "I... I need this job. I'm earning money for college and I... I need this job," she repeated. She threw Billy a wrathful glance, then added airily, "Fine, if he can handle working with me, I can certainly handle working with him."

"It's settled then." Katy suppressed a smile as Billy snorted and returned to his mopping. "Come sit down, Daffodil, and we'll figure out your schedule. I'm reopening Tuesday morning, if all of my deliveries arrive on Monday as planned. I'll need you *promptly* at 8 A.M. Not a minute later."

.   .   .

It wasn't until midafternoon that Katy had a chance to walk the two blocks through town to Sheriff Harvey's office. She had asked her father that morning if Matt had told him anything interesting or unusual on the day he died, and Big John had stared at her as if she'd lost her mind. When she pressed him, he'd reminded her in a low tone that he and Dorsey had been away in Butte the day Matt died, and though they'd spoken briefly on the phone that day about the horse show, he couldn't remember Matt saying anything out of the ordinary.

Then her father had demanded to know why she was asking such a thing fourteen years later, and Katy had decided not to tell him about the sketch. Not yet. It might not mean anything and why stir him up over nothing?

So she'd jumped up and left the table in a hurry just as she had when she was a teenager and Big John had questioned her about tests and homework. Now, as then, he'd scowled after her and then merely gone on chewing his toast.

But with her father out of town, maybe Matt had gone first to Sheriff Harvey ... if he indeed had something to tell, something of any significance.

Something about a dead girl ...

Katy shivered and forced her thoughts away from that grisly image.

The day was warm, crystal clear, the sky a shimmering blue pool so big and blue you could drown in it. There was a peacefulness in the pine-scented air that lulled her, a low-key kind of quiet that touched something long-ago forgotten. Despite the heat, one could glance over at the surrounding mountains and see cool silver waterfalls tumbling in the distance, and rocky plateaus where elk surveyed the valleys, and most refreshing of all was the sight of the glistening snow that frosted the tips of those looming peaks.

The beauty of wide open spaces and rugged mountaintops and valleys rich with bluegrass enveloped her, all bathed in silence, all soothing something in her soul. Thunder Creek was about as far from the crowded, blaring streets of New York as you could get.

And she had switched off her cell phone before leaving the diner to make sure that it stayed that way.

Sheriff Stan Harvey's office was in a one-story brick building at the end of town, down the street from Merck's Hardware. She walked through the paneled lobby, cooled by several fans, and past a secretary's unmanned desk to find him in his office. He was handing a sheaf of papers to a little bird of a woman with glasses perched on her nose.

"Katy Templeton! Heard you were back! It's about time." Stan Harvey's eyes lit and he pushed his big frame out of his chair as the secretary gave her a nod and slipped through the door. "And Big John tells me you're reopening Bessie's Diner. Good girl!"

The sheriff lumbered around the desk, a broad smile creasing his bullfrog face. He was an enormous, deep-chested man, still in good physical shape for a man nearing fifty, and he wore his bulk well, moving with surprising speed and agility for all his heft.

His thick, wiry hair was as brown as ever, still worn in a crew cut, and his ruddy skin was clean shaven. Most of all, he had the alert spryness of a cop in him, and it showed in the sharp flash of his dark brown eyes, in the crispness of his speech. He'd been a cop in Butte before marrying his late wife, Ardelle, and settling in Thunder Creek, and in addition to his sheriff's duties he helped manage the oil interests Ardelle's father had left to her when he died, as well as the Last Trail Ranch, a five-thousand-acre spread that had been in her family for four generations.

"You're still going to serve fried chicken and mashed potatoes, aren't you? That's my favorite. As you can see." He patted his belly, and chuckled.

"Absolutely, Sheriff Harvey. I'm not taking anything off the menu. Just adding a few things."

"Oh, Lord. Fancy-schmancy things, like folks eat back east?" he asked in mock dismay.

Katy laughed. "Wait till Tuesday and you'll see. But if you don't like my brand-new steak-and-cheese wrap, it's on me."

"Well, you've got yourself a customer. I guess you must know what you're doing, don't you? Your dad showed me that article about you in *Newsweek,* with a picture and everything. He was mighty proud."

"Thanks." Her gaze fell on the photograph of Ardelle Harvey set in a silver frame on his desk. Sheriff Harvey had been devoted to his wife. She'd suffered for years from congenital heart disease, and had died last year on Christmas Eve. "I'm sorry about Mrs. Harvey. She was a lovely woman."

"Yes. She sure was. Despite her suffering, she always had a smile on her face." He sighed and she saw the shadow of sorrow in his eyes. "The truth is, I feel kinda lost without her. It's real hard, being in that house all alone. I haven't told your dad yet, or anyone else, but I'm thinking about selling the Last Trail and the oil interests. Thinking about retiring, just moving away. I wouldn't mind a little fishing cabin someplace up in the Tetons, nothing to do but fish and hunt and maybe start that book I want to write."

"I never knew you were a writer."

"Well, a man sees a lot in all these years of law enforcement, and I think I've got a few good stories in me. Might just get around to telling 'em—or trying, anyway."

Everyone in town knew Stan Harvey didn't need to work anymore. Ardelle had left her entire estate to him and it was considerable. Yet Katy couldn't imagine Thunder Creek without the staunch lawman who had been her father's friend and the town sheriff for as long as she could remember.

"Your poker partners will miss you something fierce," she told him. "You and Mr. MacIntyre and Doc Evans and my dad still play every other Monday night, don't you?"

"Yep, but don't tell the cops," he said in a stage whisper. "Gambling's illegal outside of Nevada."

And she laughed right along with him.

"But you didn't come here to talk about poker games, or Bessie's Diner, I'm guessing. Have a seat." Those sharp lawman's eyes settled on her, calm and probing as she slipped into the chair opposite his desk.

Harvey sank into his worn black leather chair and placed his palms on his desk.

"What can I do for you, honey?"

Now that she was actually here, about to ask him about a scribbled note and drawing from fourteen years ago, Katy felt a twinge of hesitation. In the light of day, outside of Matt's room and all the mementos surrounding her when she'd gone through the photos and his backpack, it seemed ludicrous that a rough sketch at the bottom of a pad of paper would hold any significance. And that Matt's intention to "tell" Sheriff Harvey something could be connected to the drawing in any way.

Yet . . . she was here, and something about the sketch still haunted her. She couldn't explain why, but even now she could see it in her mind's eye, the girl with the long wavy hair, the way she'd been lying facedown in the grass. The chilling sensation that had come over her as she'd gazed at it.

She met the sheriff's eyes as he studied her, patiently waiting for her to speak.

"I've come about Matt, Sheriff Harvey. I was going through his room and some of his belongings last night and I found sort of a . . . a to-do list, which I think was written on the day he died. One of the things he'd written down was:

'Tell Sheriff Harvey and Dad.' I'm curious," she went on in a rush. "Did Matt come and see you about something before he died?"

Stan Harvey gazed at her in surprise. "No, not that I recall."

"You're sure?"

The sheriff's eyes sharpened. "I don't remember much more about that day except the accident, but I think I'd recall talking to Matt. If there's something upsetting you, something I should know, why don't you just go ahead and tell me what it is, Katy? Maybe I can help."

Katy heard low voices outside the office door. A man and a woman. The secretary, she realized, inviting someone to have a seat.

Sheriff Harvey is busy. It shouldn't be long.

"Well," she said quickly, feeling foolish to be taking up his time with something as flimsy as an odd sketch and a scribbled note. "There was a sketch. On the to-do list." She bit her lip. "It was sort of... unusual, for Matt. It looked like a drawing of a... a dead girl."

His eyebrows shot up and Stan Harvey stared at her with that penetrating gaze. "You recognize her?"

"No... no... I'm not even sure she was dead. It was just a little sketch. At the bottom of the page. It wasn't in his usual style, but then that doesn't mean she was real, or that she was dead—"

"You want me to take a look at it?" he interrupted.

Katy bit her lip. "No. I was just... trying to see if Matt had reported anything. I'm positive I would remember if a girl had died in Thunder Creek the same time Matt did."

"I sure as hell would. But if it'll set your mind at rest, maybe I should take a look—"

"No, that's all right." Katy stood up and slipped the strap of her purse over her shoulder, suddenly in a hurry to get out of there before the sheriff insisted on seeing the sketch. The last thing her parents needed was for her to start dredging up talk about Matt's accident after all these years, all stemming from her own wild speculations about a sketch. "I've taken up enough of your time. I just wanted to make sure . . ."

"If you want, bring it in." He came around the desk. "I'm not exactly swamped these days, as you can see, and I'm never too busy for you or Dorsey or Big John, that's for sure. The fact is, we're lucky enough to have a good peaceable little town here—that makes my job easy. Right now the only thing I really have to worry about . . ." He offered her a twinkling smile, ". . . is folks getting caught up in a stampede when you reopen the doors to Bessie's Diner."

"I'll call you if the crowd gets out of hand," she assured him as he walked her to the door.

"Hell, Katy, I'll be the first one in line," the sheriff promised.

A man pushed himself out of a waiting room chair as she stepped out of the office. He wore dark aviator sunglasses and had a swollen lip. His features were sharp as rock, his sandy hair cut short. He smelled of an expensive cologne, something with woodsy notes and spice and tobacco.

"This must be my lucky day," Luke Dillard said. "I've been wondering when I'd run into you."

He looked much the same as he had in high school, smoothly handsome, full of himself, confident to the point of cockiness. He had filled out some in manhood—yet his body was still lean and firm, his face deeply tanned. And he looked prosperous—his black shirt and khakis looked crisp and starched, his boots shone.

But all Katy could really see when she looked at him was the boy who had tried to rip her homecoming dress off in the dark woods near Bear Trail.

"Well, now you can stop wondering, can't you?" she said evenly, and kept walking.

Behind her Sheriff Harvey greeted Luke with respect, and

asked what he could do for him, and as she reached the door she thought she heard Luke say something about Jackson Brent. She didn't slow her steps, didn't hesitate, just twisted the knob and bolted out into sunlight and heat.

Quickly, she began walking up the street, back to the diner, working very hard to sort through her thoughts. Luke Dillard didn't matter—she wasn't worried about him. But she still found herself thinking about the sketch.

Face it. You're never going to know why Matt drew that girl in the grass, she told herself. *And maybe it doesn't matter.*

But it bothered her—gnawed at her in a way she couldn't explain.

Maybe, after things had settled down a little, after the barbecue, and the diner reopening, and Mom and Dad getting safely off to Paris, maybe there was one more person she should ask about that sketch. One person who'd been closer to Matt than anyone else, even Katy, even Jackson Brent.

Allison Pritchard, Matt's girlfriend.

If anyone knew the details of Matt's life that particular autumn day, Katy reflected, blinking a little in the afternoon sun, it would be Allison.

And if there was any chance Allison could settle this one niggling question that was plaguing her, why not simply ask her?

Chapter 9

TWO NIGHTS LATER, ALL DRESSED FOR THE BARBECUE, Katy peeked into her grandmother's room.

"Need anything before we go, Gram?"

"You bet I do. I need you to come closer so I can get a look at that dress," her grandmother ordered.

Grinning, Katy obeyed, and Riley's wife, Pat, who was staying with Gram while the family went out, tsked with pleasure from her chair.

"Don't you look pretty." Her eyes moved approvingly over the silky blue sundress that emphasized Katy's slim figure and fell in soft filmy folds just below the knee. Katy had twisted her hair into a pretty braid that fell in a single sleek strand down her back, and the only jewelry she wore were small shell-shaped silver dangle earrings and her delicate diamond drop necklace. Even her strappy Prada sandals looked as elegant and sexy as high-heeled pumps.

"Which cowboy you after?" Bessie demanded.

"Roy Rogers."

"He's dead. Come on, now, which one?"

"Gene Autry."

"He's dead too," Pat offered helpfully, smothering a laugh.

But Gram was eyeing her with Templeton determination.

"Come on now, pick a live one, honey, and fess up. No girl gets herself dolled up that pretty unless she's got a man in her sights."

"You've got me, Gram." Katy sighed. "I heard a rumor that Butch Cassidy's going to show up. He's been haunting Smoke and Ellen's ranch for years."

"Go on with you." Bessie gave a snort of laughter. "Whoever he is, he doesn't stand a chance."

"*He* doesn't exist, Gram." She hurried over to the bed and dropped a kiss on her grandmother's cheek. In the past few days, Gram had begun to recover some of her color, and her cough had eased, much to the family's relief. "I've sworn off men for the rest of my life," Katy announced. "They're too much trouble."

"Ain't that the truth," Pat chuckled. "Your granddaughter's a smart girl, Bessie."

"Hmmpph. A smart girl wearing mighty sexy perfume." Gram watched her fixedly as Katy rolled her eyes and crossed to the door.

"Don't worry about us, honey, we'll be fine," Pat assured her, drawing a deck of cards from her purse. "We're going to play a little blackjack and get your grandmother primed for that Las Vegas trip of hers—in case she ends up being able to go. So have yourself a good time."

A good time? I wish, Katy thought, her stomach clenching. Somehow, she doubted a good time was in the cards for her tonight.

She'd been to her share of parties large and small in cities all across the United States, and more than a few abroad, but the idea of facing nearly everyone she knew and had ever known in Thunder Creek, all in the same place at the same time, was enough to make her want to head for the hills. It was the whispering and gossiping that gave her pause—in a town this size, everyone would know about her divorce, losing her baby, her totally screwed-up life in the big city. And what they didn't know, they'd ask.

But, she told herself, as she grabbed her purse and went downstairs to find her parents, better to get it all over with at once than in dribs and drabs when the same people started coming into the diner.

During the drive to Ellen and Smoke's ranch her parents surprised her with the news that they'd be leaving for Paris the next week as planned. Katy was thrilled. Somehow, she and her mother must have gotten through to her father, because Big John had changed his mind, and was now resigned to the trip. During the entire drive, he listened in stoic silence without a single complaint as her mother chattered about the hotel she'd booked, and the restaurants she wanted to try, and the top ten sites she wanted to see. But his mouth was grim, Katy noticed, and it was obvious he was as excited to be going to Paris as he would be going to a funeral home to pick out his own casket.

As they neared Smoke and Ellen's ranch deep in the foothills, her thoughts turned to the goal she'd set for herself tonight. Instead of worrying about answering questions about her ex-husband and ex-life, she was going to ask a few questions herself—and find someone who knew what had happened to Allison Pritchard. Her mother had told her that Allison married a boy she met in college and never came back to Thunder Creek, and that her parents and brother had moved away as well. So far, no one—not Dorsey, not Bessie, not Margie—knew the name of the man Allison had married or had kept in touch with her over the past years, so this would be a good opportunity to bring up Allison in conversation and find out if anyone had her married name or address—if anyone knew if she even still lived in the state.

There was quite a crowd milling around the chairs and tables set up outside by the time they arrived. Katy spotted her grandmother's old friend Ada Scott talking to Ralph and

Diane MacIntyre, Smoke's parents, near the barn, and on the big open patio area in the rear of the house, Smoke was grilling steaks and hamburgers, and Ellen had filled up every inch of the long tables with bowls of potato salad, baked beans, platters of corn on the cob, sourdough rolls in big baskets, and a chicken-and-rice casserole.

As her parents headed over toward the barn to greet the guests of honor, she worked her way through the throng until she found Ellen in the kitchen, putting the finishing touches on a pink frosted anniversary cake, while Margie was scurrying outdoors with a huge bowl of macaroni salad.

"Just in time," Margie exclaimed when she spotted Katy. "Would you mind bringing out the cookies and the brownies? Lee was supposed to be watching Dougie, but the little monster has somehow disappeared. Again. I swear, that kid's going to be the end of me." Blowing her hair out of her eyes, she rushed outside.

Ellen MacIntyre lifted the cake platter and threw Katy a welcoming smile. Her black hair was cut short, emphasizing her waiflike features. "I told Margie that Doug's probably in the barn chasing the kittens, but until she finds him, she's going to be a total wreck. If you don't mind, the brownies and the cookies go on the smaller table near the patio chairs. I've got Daffodil Moline watching my kids, but the baby just woke up. I'll be back in a sec."

She dashed outside and Katy lifted the big oval platter brimming with sugar cookies and chocolate frosted brownies. She whirled around toward the door, only to collide with Luke Dillard.

"Whoa, there, honey. You need to watch where you're going."

"I could say the same to you, Luke." She started past him, but he sidestepped, planting himself directly in her path.

"I just want to catch up with you, Katy. It's been a long time."

"Not long enough."

He stared at her. In his open-collared gray shirt and navy slacks, he looked handsome and polished and cool, even though the kitchen was warm and close. "Come on, Katy. Are you going to hold what happened all those years ago against me?"

"Figure it out for yourself."

"Look, I'm sorry. All right? I was a kid then, a dumb-ass kid. I got carried away. I've grown up since then, if you haven't noticed. So have you."

"Congratulations. Now, please get out of my way. I'm busy."

"How long are you going to keep running away from me?"

"I'm not running away, Luke." She met his eyes, her own clear and cool. Her voice was low, almost pleasant, except for the thread of steel under it. "I'm walking away—there's a difference. Watch."

She marched around him and this time he made no move to stop her. She felt his gaze on her though, burning into her backside, but she didn't slow, didn't look back. Pushing at the screen door with her hip, she went out into the heart of the party.

Smoke led her to the cooler where there were cans of beer and soft drinks, and she was soon surrounded by old friends and neighbors, some who'd known her grandmother for more than half a century and others, like Kelly Jones—who worked at the bank now, Margie told her—who'd only moved to Wyoming over the past few years. The swirl of laughter and calling voices, the aroma of grilled meat and the bright beauty of the early summer evening, soon wrapped her in a festive spirit and she found herself relaxing, sitting down to dinner beneath a shade tree with Margie and Lee and Dougie and Cooper, with Roy Hewett, along with his date, Corinne Thomas, and with Ada Scott and several of her mother's friends.

She was drinking coffee and nibbling on a cookie when she spotted Jackson Brent, his dark head bent as he listened attentively to something Kelly Jones was saying.

There was an intimacy about the way Kelly's hand rested on his upper arm, and how close she was standing to him, that suggested they were more than casual acquaintances. She felt a flicker of surprise. No one had told her that Jackson was involved with anyone. Not that it mattered, Katy reflected, taking another bite of the cookie.

Neither did it matter that Kelly and Jackson made a stunning couple. She with her pale skin and striking red-haired beauty and Jackson Brent, tall and lean and bronzed. He was as dark and dangerously handsome as any Old West gunfighter, while Kelly, in her cropped white pants and tight little red tank top, was the epitome of modern casual chic.

They look like they stepped right out of a magazine ad for perfume or breath mints, Katy thought. *Or for condoms . . .*

"Katy . . . Katy, honey, didn't you hear me?" Ada was tapping her on the shoulder, peering intently at her through faded brown eyes the color of the corral posts behind her.

"Sorry, Ada, I was daydreaming. What did you say?"

"I said, it's good of you to give Billy that job at the diner. He wants so bad to go to college, and I wish I could help him more, but a body can only do what a body can do. What I've got left won't buy enough to support a flea, so Billy's going to have to earn his own way all the way through. Unless when I go to Vegas with Bessie and bring my jelly jar of change, I hit a whopper of a jackpot." She gave a breathy little chuckle. "Wouldn't that be something? But I guess I can't count on it now, can I? Billy's going to have to work hard to pay for college, that's all there is to it."

"Well, I'm thrilled to have him—if he'd like, he can stay on through the school year. We can work out flexible part-time hours so his schedule won't interfere with his senior year workload. Once he's all trained, I'd hate to lose him until I have to—"

"So it's true." A woman's whiskey-soaked voice interrupted beside her. Katy paused and looked up into Tammie Morgan's angular face. "You're going to stay, you're going to keep Bessie's Diner open?"

"That's the plan."

She bit back a sigh as Tammie dragged over an aluminum chair and sank down right beside her, forcing everyone at the table to shift their chairs in order to make room for her.

"But why? For how long?" Tammie demanded, the black center of her amber cat eyes darkening.

She looked downright annoyed, Katy thought, as her old high school rival set her lips together in the exact same way she had after the drama teacher announced that Katy, only a freshman, had won the lead role in *Oklahoma* instead of Tammie, who was a junior and considered herself entitled.

"At least until my grandmother is well enough to make some decisions about it."

"And if she decides it's too much for her?" Tammie asked quickly, a bit too eagerly. "It's not easy to come back after a bout of pneumonia, you know—especially for a woman of her age. She might not want all that work, the long hours—"

"Then I'll stay on to run the diner, Tammie. Indefinitely."

"Indefinitely." Tammie said the word as if it were a toad rolling around on her tongue. She pushed back her long black hair and the three-carat emerald-cut diamond on her finger shimmered in the flames of the setting sun. Tammie Morgan looked every inch the wife of a millionaire rancher, with her braceleted arms, her V-necked cream silk blouse, and scalloped-hem denim skirt with its glittering wide silver belt studded in turquoise. She was tanned, slim, and hollow cheeked, thanks to liposuction and the Canyon Spa, and the platinum earrings cascading from her ears were studded with tiny diamonds and slivers of amethyst as they framed her long chin and deep plum lips, which were painted the exact same shade as her fingernails and sandal-clad toes.

"But surely you've got your fingers in bigger pies than Bessie's Diner." Tammie seized a cookie, broke off a corner of it, and popped it in her mouth. "What about all your wonderful restaurants? I'm sure you'd rather be in New York or Boston or Dallas, not stuck here in pokey old Thunder Creek."

"And what's wrong with Thunder Creek?" Ada demanded.

"Well, nothing. Wood and I *love* Thunder Creek, but we're settled here with our own home, a big ranch to run, and our kids and all."

If she'd wanted to draw blood with that one, she did. A quick jab of pain pummeled Katy's chest, but she kept her expression impassive as she'd learned to do at countless board meetings, when Seth had schooled her in the ways of corporate bludgeoning.

She didn't react, didn't flick an eyelash, even as the small cat smile tilted Tammie's collagen-ballooned lips. "Why, you're a city girl now, Katy. Footloose and fancy-free and all that. Lucky you. I can't imagine that you'd want to be cooped up here all winter for instance—"

"Sweet of you to worry about me, Tammie, but I'll be fine. I'm sure you have enough to do planning your new dude ranch. You don't need to bother your head about me."

"But that's just it. I'm thinking about you *and* the dude ranch." Tammie beamed, revealing a grin just a tad too toothy for real beauty, but she made up for it in wattage. "Wood and I think Bessie's Diner would be a great location for a little gift shop. You know how people love to shop and all. We're buying up several locations in town, and planning to build a quaint little shopping boulevard. We're going to have an old-fashioned ice cream shop, and a store featuring homemade quilts and antiques, and Bessie's Diner is just the right size and just the right place for this little gift shop I have in mind. You know, the kind of place with cowboy hats and fancy belt buckles, and snow globes of our dude ranch. We're prepared to take it off your hands for an excellent price."

Ada snorted, and leaned back in her chair, a disapproving frown settling over the sweet lines of her face. Katy smiled at her grandmother's friend as she stood up. "That's real kind of you, Tammie, but Bessie's Diner is not for sale. I'm sure you'll find another location that'll suit you better."

Even as the other woman opened her mouth to argue, Katy leaned over and touched Ada's hand. "How about letting me get you some more coffee? Or some tea?"

"No, thanks, honey, I think I'm going on over to talk to your ma. The air's getting a bit close out here," she said loudly and several people glanced over at the three of them. Then without even glancing at Tammie, she let Katy help her to her feet, patted her arm, and simply walked away.

Katy tried to flee too, but turning around she ran smack into Wood Morgan, Tammie's husband, who'd also been her high school sweetheart. They'd been a couple about as far back as Katy could remember.

"Wood, honey, there you are." Tammie's smile was brilliant. "You have to talk some sense into Katy here. Go on, talk to her. She thinks she wants to keep Bessie's Diner and try to run it herself and I was just telling her she'd be silly, just plain silly not to take us up on our offer."

Wood's razor-sharp, light brown eyes glinted from beneath thick brows that matched his mustache. They were the only distinctive features of his rather bland face. "Tammie's right," he told Katy bluntly. "You don't want to be burdened with a little business like a diner in a town like this. Look at you, you're a beautiful, sophisticated woman—you belong out in the world, Katy, traveling, dancing till dawn, not cooped up in a town that's barely a speck on the map."

"Well, thanks for the pep talk, Wood, and for your concern, but Bessie's Diner isn't for sale. It's staying in the family."

"Oh, now, but you haven't heard our offer yet. How about I stop by and go over some numbers with you and we can—"

"My answer is no." Katy held onto her temper, but just barely. She glanced from one to the other of them and felt a prick of disgust. She'd never succumbed to strong-arm tactics and she wasn't about to start now. Tammie and Wood were perfectly matched in ambition and love of wealth, and she wasn't about to judge them for that, but she wanted nothing to do with their latest expansion. Bessie's Diner was Gram's and hers, it was part of their history, with irreplaceable memories. She'd be damned before she let Tammie Morgan tear out the old booths and the grill and the tables and start peddling snow globes and keychains from within those much-loved blue-painted walls.

"I won't change my mind—no matter how good your offer is, Wood. Find another place. Now if you'll excuse me..."

She walked away without giving either of them a chance to argue, and ran straight into Roy Hewett.

"Just the girl I was looking for. Want to dance, Katy?"

She hadn't even realized that Smoke had turned up the volume on his boom box and Shania Twain's voice was lilting through the night. Several couples were already dancing on the grass beneath the first stars popping out into the dusky lavender sky.

Katy smiled at Roy. "I'd love to. But...your date..."

"Corinne had to leave early. New girl at the Tumbleweed has a habit of calling in sick, and she has to keep covering for her."

"She seems very nice," Katy said as Roy's arm encircled her waist and they began to sway in time to the music.

"Yep, Corinne's great. But...we're just dating, we're not together. My options are wide open."

Including you. He didn't say it but she could sense it in the way he was looking at her, at the warm interest in his crinkled brown eyes.

"When you left Thunder Creek, I never thought you'd be back. Seeing you here again has brought back a lot of memories."

"For me, too, Roy." She didn't want to hurt his feelings by telling him flat out that she wasn't looking to rekindle any old flames or to start any new ones, that her return home was all about figuring out her life, not making it more complicated. And men definitely made life complicated. So she changed the subject, asking him about people they'd gone to high school with and then casually mentioning Allison Pritchard.

To her disappointment, Roy had no idea what had become of her. Neither had Ada, Katy reflected, trying not to feel discouraged. Then Smoke cut in, and after that she danced with Smoke's father, and with Randy Purcell, a burly wrangler on Lee and Margie's ranch.

They danced past Jackson Brent, holding tight to Kelly Jones, and she couldn't help but notice how seductively Kelly was whispering in his ear.

Some things never change, she noted in annoyance. Women were still falling all over Jackson Brent, just as Margie had said. Katy fought back her irritation, but it surfaced again when she saw him dancing later with Thunder Creek's quiet young third-grade schoolteacher with the big eyes and dark jet hair, and with Candy Merck, whose father owned the town hardware store.

Several dances later, she was out of breath and ready for a break when Margie ambled over to say good night with Cooper wrapped in a blanket in her arms. Then she spotted her mother on the patio apparently saying her good-byes, too.

"Ready to leave, Mom?"

Dorsey peered about distractedly. "Yes, as soon as I can find your—oh, there he is now. No doubt worrying about Cleo again." Katy turned and saw her father deep in conversation with Jackson and Ada over near the paddocks.

"That trailer accident really threw your father." Dorsey sighed, hooking her arm through Katy's as they began to walk toward Big John. "He's got his heart set on Cleo having a healthy foal. Good thing Jackson's taking care of her . . . no one else would be so patient with him. Any other vet would be pulling out his hair for all the time your father takes up with his questions and extra tests and monitors and things."

"Maybe we should wait until they're finished," Katy began, slowing her steps as Jackson glanced up and saw them coming, but her mother shook her head.

"Your father could go on talking about that mare all night. I want to go home and check on Bessie. And I need to start figuring out what to pack. If I don't start a list, Katy, I'll be sunk—there must still be a million things for me to do before I can get on that plane. But, honey," she murmured as they reached the little group, "you don't have to leave now. You stay and have fun."

"Don't be silly. I'm ready—"

"What? Ready to go home? So early?" Ada made a clucking sound with her tongue. "Katy, honey, *I'm* ready to go home, but you . . . for heaven's sake, girl, the night is young!"

"That's what I was trying to tell her," Dorsey said.

"In my day . . ." Ada began, then she gave a dry cackle. "Never mind, you don't want to hear about the olden days. But you're too young and pretty to leave a party just when the sun goes down. Why, I bet you haven't even danced with half the young men here who're dying to ask you. What about you, Jackson? Have you danced with our Katy yet?"

"No, ma'am." Jackson's tone was carefully polite. "I can't say I've had that pleasure."

"Well, there you go." Ada nodded in satisfaction.

"Honey, Ada's right." Dorsey glanced around at all the couples dancing under the stars. "Why don't you stay and enjoy yourself? I'm sure someone will bring you home later. I can just ask Smoke—"

"I'm sure Jackson wouldn't mind bringing her home, would you, Jackson?" Ada piped up.

For an instant Katy thought Jackson looked like he'd been asked to walk barefoot over splintered glass, but he recovered quickly. "Er, no. Of course not. If that's all right with Katy," he added coolly.

Now she knew how a rabbit felt when it was caught in a trap. There was a challenge—a subtle one—but still a challenge in those unreadable eyes of his. Something in her instinctively rose to meet it. She'd never run scared from anyone or anything and least of all would she run from Jackson Brent.

"Fine," she said, with a sweet, taut smile. "That's very... nice of you."

"If that's all settled," Big John interrupted impatiently, "let's get rolling. Ada, you're coming along with us, right?"

She was, and as Big John herded Dorsey and the older woman toward the truck, Katy found herself alone near the paddocks with Jackson. The faint strains of a country-and-western ballad floated through the night.

"I might as well claim that dance now," he said.

"You don't have to dance with me," she assured him. "That was pretty shameless of Ada to railroad you into it, but I prefer to find my own dance partners—"

"So do I." Jackson snagged her arm as she tried to step past him. "And right now, I pick you."

She looked up at him and as their eyes met, Katy felt a tremble within her like the first rolling pebble of a landslide.

Before she could say anything, he drew her closer. He

hooked an arm around her waist, and clasped her fingers in his free hand.

Without even realizing exactly how it happened she found herself drawn into the dance with him, their bodies touching, swaying to the slow dreamy melody that drifted like wood smoke through the night.

Chapter 10

IT WAS STRANGE, BUT SHE FELT EASY IN HIS ARMS. HE held her close, but not too close, and his powerful body seemed to vibrate with danger, yet she couldn't bring herself to pull away. The stars bloomed across the sky as they danced, the whisper of night creatures hummed behind the music, and Jackson Brent's breath ruffled her hair.

Neither of them spoke until the music ended.

Then Jackson eased back just a little, still clasping her waist, still holding her hand. "That wasn't so bad, was it?" he asked.

"Speak for yourself." Yet she made no move to pull away.

He smiled, and his fingers moved lightly over hers.

"How about another?"

Dancing with him was like playing with a loaded grenade. *You're trying to cut down all the complications in your life, not add to them,* she reminded herself as she gazed into that formidably handsome face and tried not to be sucked into the intensity of smoke-blue eyes that seemed to singe her soul.

"For two people who're trying to stay out of each other's way, we're not doing a very good job of it. I think we'd better go back," she replied crisply.

"Afraid?"

There was that challenge again. A faint but discernible gleam flickered in his eyes. Her chin shot up. "I hate to break it to you, but I'm not afraid of you or of anything. What are you talking about?"

"You. Me." Without thinking, Jackson brushed a strand of hair from her eyes. His blood heated as he watched the way the wind blew that slinky sundress around her soft, lithe little body. If they were any higher up in the mountains, she wouldn't be able to wear that gorgeous wisp of a dress this time of night. She'd freeze to death, or he'd have to find a way to keep her warm . . .

Suddenly realizing just how much he'd enjoy that task, he broke the train of thought. What the hell was he doing? This was insane. Katy Templeton wasn't looking for a fling, someone to warm her, in or out of bed. Hell, she was just coming out of a bad time in her life and he'd seen the pain in her eyes that first night in the barn. She was vulnerable beneath that cool facade of hers and she sure as hell wasn't up to his version of romantic roulette. So why was he dancing all alone with her out here, why was he even thinking about reasons to get her back into his arms?

He always kept things light with the women in his life, and he always picked women who liked things just as easy and uncommitted as he did—women who weren't looking for permanence or promises or love.

He wasn't sure what Katy Templeton was looking for, but he doubted it was a one-night stand. And he couldn't promise any woman more than that.

He needed to start thinking with his brain, not his body, and keep his damned distance.

"You and me?" She looked incredulous. "For your information, there *is* no you and me. Just two people who shared a dance thanks to a well-intentioned but interfering old woman."

"You're right." He spoke offhandedly. "Never mind." He

started to walk back toward the patio and the lights, apparently expecting her to fall into step with him, but she seized his arm.

"Not so fast, Jackson. Tell me what you meant."

"I thought you were in a hurry to head back."

"I am—but you started this. I'd like to finish it before things get complicated."

"Nothing to finish. We had our dance. I enjoyed it. Hope you can say the same. That's it."

Anger flicked through her. He was dodging her, she knew it, but she couldn't very well tackle him, pin him down, and force him to explain. Besides, Katy decided, the low burn of anger seeping through her, whatever he'd been on the verge of saying, she didn't want to know. *You. Me.*

She *definitely* didn't want to know.

It was just a line, she told herself with a small edge of disgust. *He probably has dozens of lines, and a lot of practice using them. And maybe Kelly Jones and Candy Merck get off on them. But I'm a little too smart to fall for smooth-talking bull from a country veterinarian.*

And it pleased her to think she'd made that perfectly clear.

"Great." She shrugged her indifference, and strode off ahead of him. But she could hear him following at an easy distance behind her.

"Just let me know when you're ready to leave," he remarked as she reached the glow of the lanterns on the patio. All through the yard and the porch, people were drinking, talking.

"I'm ready now, but it's no concern of yours."

"It is since I promised your mother I'd drive you home."

"I'm releasing you from your promise."

"Sorry. It doesn't work that way." He caught up to her, and smiled grimly. "A man's word is sacred. Guess I'm just stubborn about things like that. It's another one of my flaws, if you're keeping track."

"I'm hardly interested enough to do that."

"Fair enough. But I'm still taking you home. If you want to go now, that's fine, we go now. If you want to leave at three in the morning, that's fine, too. I'll be playing cards with Smoke and Ralph and the guys in the kitchen. Let me know when you're ready."

He sauntered off to join Smoke and his father and Roy Hewett, deep in conversation near the outdoor grill.

Katy could only stare after him. She was still inwardly fuming at his colossal arrogance when Ellen walked toward her, cradling a cup of coffee.

"There you are. Uh-oh." She glanced at Katy and followed her steaming gaze to Jackson Brent. "Is something wrong?"

"Nothing. The party's been wonderful. I'm just a little tired." Katy saw Tammie and Wood hovering near the cooler, looking her way, as if they were debating coming over to speak to her again. Just what she needed. She saw Luke Dillard talking with a dishwater blonde in jeans and a purple halter top, and caught her breath as his gaze shifted from the girl to settle on her. The appraising look he shot her made her stomach clench.

But it was enough to decide her.

"I think I'm going to call it a night, Ellen. Jackson Brent's offered to drive me home. I'll help you clean up a little first, and then—"

"Oh, don't bother about cleaning up." Ellen waved a hand. "I've got it covered. But . . . Katy, if you feel funny about going home with Jackson . . . for any reason . . ." Her voice trailed off.

Katy knew it was because Ellen, like everyone else in Thunder Creek, remembered the nasty scene after Matt's funeral, between Matt Templeton's sister and his best friend.

"I know it must be hard for you, with him being back here too, just when you've come home," Ellen said quietly. "I'm sure, if you'd rather, Smoke would be glad to take you home."

Katy glanced toward the grill, where Sheriff Harvey had just joined the group, and Smoke was handing out cigars.

She couldn't do it. She couldn't pull Smoke away from his own barbecue just because she was annoyed with Jackson Brent—and with her own reaction to dancing with him.

"There's no need to bother Smoke," she told Ellen, trying to keep the resignation out of her voice. "I don't have a problem with Jackson Brent. None at all."

A half hour later she was sitting in Jackson's truck, bumping down a road almost as narrow and rough as the one where she'd encountered Corey Dillard and his SUV.

The thought of Corey reminded her of something she'd nearly forgotten. It seemed as good a way as any to finally break the taut silence blaring between her and Jackson, so she informed him that she'd seen Luke Dillard in Sheriff Harvey's office and heard him mention Jackson's name as she headed out the door.

"Not that it's any of my business. But he didn't sound like a big fan of yours."

"No big surprise there. Never has been. And the feeling's mutual. Actually, I know all about him going to Harvey's office. He filed a complaint against me."

"Why would he do that?"

"Because he's a son-of-a-bitch." Jackson took the car easily around a rocky curve, then glanced sideways at her. "He claims my dog Ajax crossed onto his land and chased his cattle. He's demanding Ajax be kept on a lead—or else he threatened to shoot him."

"Shoot him!"

"Stan Harvey apparently calmed him down some, and

talked him out of filing a formal complaint. But Harvey did pay me a visit and now Ajax is on that lead. He's not too thrilled about it either, poor guy."

Jackson had known all along that going to the sheriff with a complaint against Ajax was just Dillard's way of getting back at him for wiping the floor with him in the Tumbleweed. Luke couldn't exactly whine to Harvey that he'd gotten his ass kicked—that would make him look like even more of a wimp. So he'd had to resort to complaining about a dog instead.

"Can't say that I blame Ajax much for hating that lead," he went on, as the truck bumped over a rut in the road, and a fox slithered in the brush at the edge of the track, caught for a fleeting moment in the headlights. "Once an animal's tasted freedom, he doesn't much like being tied down."

Katy considered this for a moment, wondering if Jackson Brent was talking about more than his dog. Was he warning her, perhaps, of his own philosophy? Did he think she was a naive little girl about to fall in love with the big bad freedom-loving, bed-roaming wolf? That would be the day.

"Did someone try to tie you down once, Jackson?" she asked coolly.

"No one ever got that close." Adroitly, he changed the subject. "What were you doing at Sheriff Harvey's office in the first place? Did you go about Corey running you off the road?"

Katy stared at him. "How did you know about that?"

"I have my sources."

"And they are?"

He shrugged. "Roy Hewett mentioned it."

"Oh." Katy had forgotten how swiftly news travels in a small town. "No," she said slowly, "I didn't go about that. I went about . . . something else."

In the pause that followed, she heard rustling in the brush

beyond the open windows of the truck, and the sudden, lonesome wail of a coyote from the hills.

"Something else." Jackson glanced at her. "Jaywalking ticket? Double parking outside Merck's Hardware?"

Katy was too distracted to even grant him a smile. She was considering how to answer, and suddenly realized that Jackson was the one person she hadn't yet asked about Allison. And not only that—after Allison, he was probably the person closest to Matt at the time of his death.

What if he knew something about the drawing, about the girl in the grass?

He was a whole lot more accessible right now than Allison Pritchard.

"I went to see Sheriff Harvey to ask him about something I found in Matt's room the other day. It was a sketch Matt drew, but it was different from any of his sketches I'd ever seen. And ... I think he may have drawn it on the day he died."

For a moment silence ticked between them. *The day he died*. That day held so many memories for each of them. That day had rocked and forever changed both of their lives.

"Do you want to tell me about it?" he asked.

"It was a sketch of a girl." Katy spoke into the darkness between them. "He drew it at the bottom of some kind of to-do list. The list mentioned something about telling our dad and Sheriff Harvey. I thought that possibly the sketch and his wanting to talk to the sheriff might be related. But Sheriff Harvey didn't know anything about it. Matt never got to him before he died. And he never said anything to Big John either."

"What was it about the sketch that made you think it involved the sheriff?"

"I told you it was a sketch of a girl. She looked ... real. Very real. You know how Matt always drew things he'd seen, not things he made up in his imagination? Well, it made me wonder if he'd seen the girl in the sketch . . . and who she was. Because it was creepy."

"That doesn't sound like Matt's work." He frowned. "Matt saw beauty and whimsy in the world."

"I know. That's why the sketch bothered me so much. That's why I'd like to find out who the girl might be. I didn't recognize her, but I wondered if she was someone real, someone Matt had seen—like that," she murmured, thinking of the girl's closed eyes, her arms awkwardly akimbo in the grass. "I thought maybe Allison would know, that Matt might have shown her the sketch or told her about it, that she might know who the girl was—but I haven't been able to find out where she lives now, or even her married name. Do you know it?"

"As a matter of fact, I do. Allison and I have kept in touch over the years."

"Can you tell me her married name? Do they still live in Wyoming?"

"They live in Medicine Bow. Her husband's name is Leggett. Rusty Leggett. They've got two kids, both boys. But I don't think she's all that happy—I get the impression she never got over Matt."

"Oh . . . How sad." Katy shook her head as she thought of the laughing, pony-tailed young girl who'd been in love with her brother. "Matt was unforgettable. But still . . ."

Still . . . Life went on. As she and her family knew. It changed, but it went on. A little emptier than before, so you had to fill it up in other ways.

"There's something you're not telling me about the sketch," Jackson said as he turned onto the gravel drive that led to the Triple T ranch house. "You haven't explained about the creepy part."

The creepy part. What could she say? The woman in the sketch looks like she's dead? The sight of her lying in that grass makes my skin crawl?

"Maybe you should see it for yourself. Actually I'd like your opinion." She hated saying those words to Jackson Brent, but in this case they were true. Despite how she felt about him, he'd been close enough to Matt to possibly be able to shed some light on that sketch. As he braked in front of the ranch, where only the porchlight and the light in the hallway glowed, she suddenly wondered if he'd recognize the girl. If he could answer all her questions with a simple explanation. "I could show it to you now, if you have the time."

"Fine with me. You've definitely piqued my curiosity." *In more ways than one.* Jackson opened the door of the truck and came around to help Katy down, hoping she couldn't see his uneasiness.

All this talk about the past, the sketch. The last thing he wanted was to see any harm come from digging up events that had taken place fourteen years earlier.

There were things about that time he hadn't understood, things Allison had mentioned way back when. But after Matt died, none of it had seemed important anymore, and he'd put the entire matter out of his head.

Now, for some reason, Katy was asking questions, and it made him wonder. He wanted to see this sketch, see if it could have anything to do with the way Matt had been behaving. But even after all these years, Jackson was damned sure Matt wouldn't want his little sister stepping in and uncovering his deep, dark secret, whatever it had been.

Unfortunately Katy didn't strike him as a woman to back off once she set her mind to something.

As he lifted her down, making sure her thin-heeled sandals found a grip in the gravel drive before letting go of her, he saw with chagrin the determined look upon her face.

She hurried toward the house, her braid swinging along with her hips. "I'll get the sketch—it's in my room," she flung back at him as Mojo began to bark and she pushed open the door. As the dog joyously greeted each of them, she led the way toward the living room.

"I'll only be a moment. Make yourself at home."

Then she left him with Mojo without a backward glance and hurried up the stairs.

Chapter 11

JACKSON WAS SEATED ON HER MOTHER'S FLOWERED chintz sofa when she returned downstairs with the sketch. Since he hadn't turned on the lights, the only illumination came from the hall. In the dimness of the living room, his broad shoulders looked enormous. His long legs were stretched out before him as Katy paused in the doorway, taking in the sharp planes of his face, and the dark mood of reflection in his eyes as he sat half in shadow.

The house was quiet as only a sleeping house can be, and the familiar cedar and lemon and cinnamon scent floated ever so lightly in the breeze that stirred the curtains. She came toward Jackson and switched on the table lamp beside the sofa, startled to find Mojo curled up on the rug at his feet.

"Tell me what you think of this." Handing the sketch to him, she dropped down onto the tufted Queen Anne chair across from him, watching his face as he scanned the to-do list. When his gaze shifted lower, to the drawing at the bottom, she saw his eyes narrow.

"What the hell is this?" he muttered half under his breath.

"Do you think . . . it seemed to me . . . she looks . . ."

"Dead." There was shock in his voice.

"Yes." Katy's stomach dropped. "That's what I thought too."

Jackson was still staring at the sketch. "It's not only her

position in the grass, and the angle of her head and arms. It's something in the sketch itself. Matt captured it... he captured..."

"Tragedy," Katy supplied, her tone low. "I couldn't put my finger on it, but it's disturbing, isn't it? And terrible. It's how he must have felt when he looked at it... at her."

"I'd guess this is something... someone... Matt saw. Not something he made up out of his imagination."

"You don't recognize her, do you?" Without thinking about it, Katy shifted over to sit beside him on the sofa, stepping around Mojo so that she could study the sketch alongside him.

"No. Not exactly." Jackson tried to quell the seed of fear inside him, the flow of memories of Matt that last week, the things that hadn't made sense. There was no need for Katy to know about any of that. But she was staring at him as if she sensed there was something he was holding back and he continued quickly. "There's something familiar about her. That curly hair..." His brows drew together in concentration, but after a moment he shook his head. "I think I've seen her somewhere, but I can't place her."

That, at least, was the truth. But Katy wasn't about to let it go.

"I'm wondering if Allison could. It's possible Matt told her about this girl, or about the sketch. She might have the answers." She tore her gaze from the sketch and met his eyes. "I don't know why, but I need to find out. I need to know why Matt drew a dead girl right before he died."

"How do you know when he made the sketch?"

She explained about the calculus quiz, referred to on the to-do list, pointing out that Matt had been planning to study for it the night he died.

"You've given this a lot of thought, haven't you?"

"I have to get to the bottom of it. And since you don't know who this girl is, Allison sounds like my best bet."

He handed the sketch back to her. "Probably. But . . . look, are you sure you want to start poking into all this now? Fourteen years have gone by. There's probably some simple explanation and all you're going to do is—"

"Find out who this girl is and why Matt drew this sketch," she said evenly. "That's what I'm going to do. I'm not asking for your help. All I'd like from you is Allison's phone number. If you don't want to give it to me, I'll get it myself."

"I never said I didn't want to give it to you." Irritation flared inside him. "Why don't I take the sketch to Allison? You have enough to do here between caring for your grandmother and opening the diner. I'll let you know what she says—"

"No way." Katy stood up, holding tightly to the sketch. "I'm visiting Allison myself."

"All right." Jackson rose to his feet, forcing her to look up to meet his eyes. "Mind if I tag along?"

"That won't be necessary."

"You got me involved by showing me the sketch. Now I'm curious about this girl too. What about next weekend?"

"You don't have to do this."

"I don't do much of anything I don't want to do, Katy. If you knew me better, you'd know that."

There was a pause while she considered this. Finally she nodded. "Suit yourself." She continued briskly, "I should have the kinks worked out of the diner reopening by then, and I'll schedule both Daffodil and Billy to work. If Gram's well enough, she's going to leave Saturday morning for Las Vegas with Ada, and if not, I'll see if Pat can stay with her. Either way, I should be free."

"I'll call you when I get ahold of Allison." As Jackson stepped past Mojo, the dog stirred on the rug, then closed his eyes and returned to gentle snoring. "In the meantime, don't worry about it. I'm sure there's a good explanation for that drawing."

Yes, Katy thought, setting the sketch on the coffee table, *but what could it be?* She had to admit she felt a vast sense of relief that Jackson didn't think she was crazy, didn't think she should just forget about the sketch. And that he knew how to get in touch with Allison. But she couldn't shake the sense of dread that came over her each time she thought about the drawing.

She followed him to the door and out onto the porch in silence. The Wyoming night glistened with stars, and the chirps of a thousand crickets sang in the pine-laced air. In the distance, the Laramies were faint hulking shadows above the vast stretch of pine forests and rolling, open land cloaked by darkness.

For the first time, Katy shivered in her sundress as a gust of cold wind blew through the valley.

"How are you liking it—being back?" Jackson asked suddenly, pausing at the edge of the porch. He turned back to study her.

"It feels good—at least for now. Like home." She gave a shrug and a short laugh. "Of course if I stay, I'm going to have to find a place of my own to live. Somehow, my old high school bedroom just doesn't fit the bill anymore."

He smiled. "I'd think not. Let me guess—same old pillows in school colors, horse show trophies and stuffed animals on the shelves—"

"How do you know all that? Don't tell me mom gives tours of her restaurateur daughter's room—five cents a go." She groaned.

"Actually, I haven't been upstairs in this house since Matt died, but I remember what it looked like, everything—including that you used to keep your door open to listen for when he and I came in and you'd tear into his bedroom and beg us to listen to some new song you liked on the radio, or to drive you to Margie's house or to Smoke's. And Matt always did exactly what you wanted."

She tilted her head to one side. "Are you saying I was a pest?"

"I'm saying Matt would have done anything for you."

Suddenly her throat tightened. Because she knew it was true. But as she looked at Jackson, another thought occurred to her. "That doesn't mean you have to, Jackson," she said coolly.

He leaned back against the porch rail and regarded her in amusement. "Do you really think I'm going with you to Medicine Bow because Matt would have wanted me to?"

"Aren't you?"

Something flickered deep in his eyes. He pushed away from the porch rail and stepped toward her with a purposefulness that made her heart jump. "Listen. Maybe looking after you because Matt wasn't here was the reason I decked Luke Dillard all those years ago in the woods—or maybe not. I know I'd have done the same thing if he'd been tearing off the dress of any other girl—but because it was you, Matt's sister, I wanted to beat the shit out of him, not just knock him on his ass. And I would have, I'd have taught him a really good lesson, if you hadn't looked so scared. I only stopped because I wanted to get you out of there."

Katy shivered, as memories rushed back of the terror and the awful humiliation of that night. "I suppose I *was* scared," she admitted. It was a ridiculous understatement. "And I was embarrassed, too—actually, I was mortified, because I'd let myself get into that situation."

"It wasn't your fault. You must know that by now."

"Yes. But back then I thought . . . it doesn't matter. What does matter . . ." Katy took a deep breath and then forced out the words she probably should have said a long time ago. "I never thanked you for that night. I . . . I resented having to be rescued, especially by you . . . and . . . it was stupid. Just like screaming at you after the funeral was stupid—"

"You don't have to apologize. It was a long time ago."

"I owe you an apology." She bit her lip. Her father had taught her—and Matt—that Templetons never shirk from paying their dues. Or owning up to their mistakes. She shouldn't have waited so long. She didn't want any unfinished business left between her and Jackson Brent. After tonight, she wouldn't owe him a thing. Not one damn thing.

"I appreciate what you did for me back then." Her voice was stiff, unnatural, but it didn't matter. It was done. She took a deep breath and hurried on. "So you'll let me know what Allison says?" She hugged her arms around herself as a gust of wind swept across the porch.

He took one look at her, shivering, her eyes soft and troubled in the moonlight, and turned on his heel. "You bet. Get inside before you freeze to death. I'll let you know."

Then he was gone, springing off the porch, striding toward his truck before she'd even drawn a breath.

"Good night to you, too," she murmured drily to cool empty air as the truck door slammed and he brought the engine roaring to life.

As she watched the truck rumble off, she heard only the crunch of the tires on the gravel, the rush of the wind, the screech of a hawk in the distance diving at some unseen prey.

And the uneven beating of her own heart as she clenched the porch rail and tried to clear her head of visions of a dead girl and Jackson Brent's piercing eyes and the memory of an eighteen-year-old boy they'd both lost a long time ago.

Chapter 12

"WHERE'S THAT STEAK WRAP AND BURGER?" DAFFO-dil Moline scurried around the corner, her ponytail bobbing and sweat dampening the blonde wisps of hair framing her forehead. "Table four's been waiting since—oh, finally! It's about time. Billy, give those to me, right now!"

She snatched the heaping plates Billy shoved at her chest and spun around.

"Hey, you're welcome," he growled after her, then turned to toss five more burgers and a chicken breast on the grill.

But Daffodil was already charging back into the front of the diner. She skidded to a stop in front of Corey and his Uncle Luke.

"Omigosh, sorry this took so long."

"That's okay, honey," Luke drawled. His gaze was not on the blonde teenaged girl with flushed cheeks before him, but on Katy, making change for Doc Evans and his wife at the cash register.

"Sit down and eat with us, Daff." Corey grabbed her arm and tried to yank her down upon the booth beside him, but she shook her head and just popped a fry into her mouth in-stead.

"Are you kidding? Katy'll kill me. We've got another half

hour till the lunch crowd thins. And Sheriff Harvey is waiting for his BLT."

She dashed off, back toward the kitchen, even as Katy left
the cash register and began cruising the tables.

She looks good, Luke thought, his gaze sweeping over the
sweet picture she made in a cool raspberry sundress and
cream-colored sandals, her hair caught in a barrette at her
nape. Casual, cool, and sophisticated, but not too sophisticated. Down to earth. And sexy as hell, he thought, his groin
tightening as she poured coffee at one table, then paused to
chat at another with Agnes Bean, who owned the hair salon
across the street from the drugstore.

A bell tinkled and Ada walked in. Katy's smile brightened—she whisked the dirty dishes from Agnes's table into
the kitchen and returned an instant later to lead Ada to the
only vacant table in the crowded diner: a small two-seater
with a vase of blue wildflowers atop it.

She's stopped at every damned table but this one, Luke
reflected, sipping his coffee. Resentment sparked in him.
Damn the pretty little bitch for holding a grudge.

"Can't a man get any coffee around here?" he asked
loudly, and heads flew up, turning his way.

Including Katy's.

She grabbed a coffeepot from the sideboard and came
toward him.

"Service is kinda slow, Katy. You'll have to work on that."

"It's our first day." She spoke coolly, but kept her tone
carefully polite. "We didn't expect to be packed like this.
Things will settle down."

*And if you choose not to come back again to see for your-
self, nothing could suit me better,* she thought, but kept the
comment to herself, knowing that Luke was only trying to
bait her.

"The burger's good." Corey shot her a grin, talking with

his mouth full. "And you've got yourself a hot little wait-ress," he added with a smirk.

Katy inclined her head. "See you leave her a good tip," she said evenly, and started off, but Luke grabbed her arm.

"How about coming with me to the Tumbleweed tonight to celebrate your opening?"

Katy shook her head. "I'm busy."

She tried to pull away, but Luke's grip tightened. "Doing what?"

"Filing my nails." Katy glared at him. Her arm hurt where he was holding it and she tried to break free once again, but his fingers dug in. It was all she could do not to wince. But she refused to give him the satisfaction. "Let me go, Luke. *Now*. If you want a scene, I'll give you one," she said softly, and moved the coffeepot so that the spout was just above his head. Slowly, she tilted it forward, the dark hot liquid tipping toward the spout.

Luke blinked uneasily, then let her go. She gave him a tight-lipped little smile and moved off without another word.

"You've sure got a way with women, don't you, Uncle Luke?" Corey cracked.

"Watch your mouth, kid." Luke eased back in his chair, but he was seething. He shot his nephew a warning glance.

"Well, what's up with her? She looked at you like she'd really pour that hot coffee over your head."

"Yeah, well, Katy Templeton's gotten a little full of her-self over the years. She used to like me well enough."

"Is that how you remember it? I don't."

A new voice spoke right beside him. With a start, Luke stared up into Jackson Brent's hard face.

"Where'd you come from?"

"The question is, where are you going, Dillard? You lay one hand on Katy Templeton ever again and I'll see you in hell."

"You don't tell me what I can and can't do, Brent. Who the hell do you think you are—" Luke was halfway out of his chair and Jackson's fists were clenched when Sheriff Harvey materialized beside the table.

"Simmer down, boys. What's this all about?"

Jackson didn't take his eyes off Luke's face. "Ask him."

"Goddamnit, Brent, don't you have anything better to do than poke your nose into other folks' business?" Breathing hard, Luke stood up, but when he would have shoved Jackson aside, the sheriff clapped a heavy hand on his shoulder.

"That's enough, both of you. I know there's been some bad blood between you two, but it's gotten worse—and I won't have trouble in my town. And Katy Templeton doesn't need trouble in her diner. Do I have to run you both in for disturbing the peace?"

Jackson at last shifted his gaze from Dillard's anger-flushed face. He swore silently as he realized everyone in the diner was staring at them—including an open-mouthed Daffodil Moline, not to mention Katy, her face taut with anger as she stood beside the cash register.

"That won't be necessary, Stan. I'm done here." He shrugged. "Think I'll just order me a yellow-bellied chicken sandwich," he added in a deliberate drawl, and for a good ten seconds, his eyes bored into Dillard's. Then he nodded to the sheriff and sauntered over to the rear booth that two ranch hands from the Morgan ranch had just vacated.

Daffodil Moline scurried forward to wipe down the table for him.

From where she stood, Katy struggled with the hollow anger welling in the pit of her stomach. Damn Luke Dillard—and Jackson Brent too. The diner's opening had been hectic and demanding, but she'd loved every minute of it—until this.

She'd already handled Luke Dillard just fine by herself, and now Jackson had shown up at the worst possible moment and made the situation worse. He'd turned it into a public spectacle. Not that it would be bad for business, she reflected with a sigh—there was nothing a small town loved more than cause for gossip—but she was already at the center of enough gossip and speculation. She didn't need more.

And she didn't want it boiling like burned stew inside her diner.

She glanced around at the customers, hoping no one else realized what this argument had been about. People were already returning their attention to their sandwiches and coffee, and Luke and Corey had slapped money on the table and were headed out the door.

Sheriff Harvey ambled over to the cash register.

"Know what those two were locking horns about?" he asked as he handed over a ten-dollar bill to cover his meal.

"Since when do two cowboys need a reason to lock horns?" Katy responded with a forced smile. "Maybe one of them didn't care for the taste of my coffee."

The sheriff accepted the change she handed him and grinned. "I thought your coffee was great. So was my BLT, Katy. Looks like Bessie's Diner is back in business, good as ever."

"We mean to please." She rang up Agnes Bean's bill, and handed over her change while she watched Stan Harvey stroll out the door, then she stalked over to Jackson Brent's table just as Daffodil was about to take his order.

"Ada's ready to order dessert," she told the girl quietly. "Bring her a slice of ginger-rhubarb pie, will you? On the house. I'll take care of this one." Daffodil took one look at Katy's set face, at those blue-gray eyes fixed unrelentingly on Jackson Brent, and scooted toward the pie shelf without a word.

"Don't suppose you'd care to join me for lunch." Jackson

shot her an engaging smile. When Katy only glared at him, he gave a shrug of those big shoulders. "Didn't think so. Maybe you could just tell me what to order. Everything on the menu looks so good, and—"

"Shut up, Jackson. Just shut up."

His gaze locked onto her face. "Go on, then. Let me have it."

"If I let you have it the way I'd like to, this whole town would be talking about it for a month."

"Going to dump coffee over *my* head next?" he asked. "I liked it when you held it over Luke. But I'd prefer it in a cup."

"I'd prefer it if you'd let me handle my problems by myself," she hissed, her eyes flashing. "Starting with Luke Dillard."

She slipped into the booth opposite him and leaned forward, keeping her voice low with an effort. Anger pulsed through her and it took all of her willpower to keep from shrieking her fury. "I don't need you to handle him or anything else and I don't want you doing it. I thought I'd made that clear."

"Did he hurt you?"

The quietly spoken words jolted her and for a moment she couldn't speak. She glanced down at her arm, where the red imprints left by Luke's fingers still marred her fair skin. She saw Jackson looking at them too.

"No, no, hardly at all," she murmured, then took a deep breath. His concern, his protectiveness stirred something inside her, something primitive and female, something she'd done her best to stifle since she'd first learned of Seth's affair. Since the devastating blow of that betrayal, she'd vowed not to rely again on a man, any man, not for anything, and now Jackson Brent was here with his gorgeous blue eyes full of concern, and she resented the way her heart and her body responded to his male protectiveness.

"Nothing worth fighting about," she said, and suddenly threw back her shoulders. "And if it was, it would be *my* fight. I can take care of myself. Nobody asked you to interfere."

"Fine, I get it. You can stick up for yourself. I only wanted to make sure he—"

"No!" She spoke so sharply everyone looked over at her again. Katy bit her lip. "I fight my own battles. If you can't accept that—"

"What? You'll pour coffee over my head? Sic Mojo on me? Ban me from Bessie's Diner?"

"Don't tempt me." Her tone was cool. But her skin felt hot. And not strictly from anger. It didn't help that he looked impossibly handsome and as rugged as the mountains. And totally without remorse for having stepped in on her behalf. Clean-shaven, with his dark hair tousled by the wind and the effects of his hat, he was all rough-and-tough cowboy, ready for a rodeo or a fistfight, or to wrestle a calf to the ground. His white T-shirt and snug-fitting jeans and boots emphasized the hard bulge of muscles and sinew. Lord help her, looking at him made her knees melt. Something like what she'd felt for Seth when she'd first met him, only deeper. Rawer. More primal.

She didn't know if it had anything to do with how angry he'd just made her, and she didn't want to stick around and find out. She had a restaurant to run, damn it.

People were lining up at the cash register.

"I have work to do." She pushed herself out of the booth but his voice stopped her in her tracks as she started toward the register.

"I spoke to Allison last night."

She whirled back. "And?"

"You're busy now." He nodded at the customers lined up, clutching five- and ten-dollar bills, waiting to pay and get on with their business. His eyes were unreadable, but she realized that behind their cool impassivity he knew full well he had her hooked. "I'm planning to drop by tonight to look in on Cleo and I thought I'd fill you in then. That all right with you?"

"Do I have a choice?"

He grinned at her, his gun-smoke-blue eyes warming, lighting, and Katy quelled the urge to throw her notepad at him. With a toss of her head she left him without another word, part of her seething to know if Allison had agreed to a visit, and part of her remembering that she'd never taken his order.

As Daffodil dashed by with two slices of chocolate cake, Katy told her to see what table five wanted to order.

Table five. That's all Jackson Brent was to her, a customer in the restaurant. Cleo's vet. And a link to Allison...

But part of her was looking forward to his visit tonight, and not only to seeing what he had to say about Allison. Part of her wanted to see him. *To match wits with him, lock horns with him,* she told herself. To show him that she was ready to take on all comers, even an impossible cowboy vet whose smile could melt rocks and whose rugged male energy made her blood pound.

She wasn't ready for another man in her life, but a sparring partner, someone to fight? Someone who needed to learn how to back off, how tough she could be? She could handle that.

Easily. Willingly.

If he thought she was some helpless lamb who would crumble because scum like Luke Dillard tried to hassle her, then he didn't know her at all. What she'd gone through, what she'd become.

She wasn't in high school anymore and she wasn't a grieving kid. She'd dealt with a lot worse than an egotistical asshole like Luke. If it was a contest of wits and wills Jackson Brent wanted, she could give him that much.

But only that much, she told herself, as she made change for Ada and slipped a ten-dollar bill into the drawer. *That much, and nothing more.*

Chapter 13

"Sounds to me like you need another waitress," Gram observed over the rim of her coffee mug as Katy pushed her chair back from the kitchen table and carried an armload of her mother's blue Fiesta dishes over to the sink. "Never used to be that all-fired busy at lunchtime. Or at dinner. Just a nice steady flow." She gave a satisfied cackle. "Must be folks have missed the place."

"And they miss you too, Gram. Everyone who came through the door asked about you. I told them not to worry, you're as hardheaded and mulish as ever."

"Hmmm. And don't you forget it. But they'll forget all about me once they get used to this good cooking of yours." Bessie glanced down at her plate with only a few crumbs remaining of chocolate-pecan pie, Katy's next weekly dessert special. Tonight was the first time she'd come downstairs to dinner since the pneumonia set in, and she'd eaten nearly all of her chicken chili and herbed French bread. Katy had pleaded with her to let her bring up a tray, but with the Templeton stubbornness that was harder than a walnut to crack, she'd insisted that she was ready to take meals at the table once more.

"If I don't start coming down those stairs for at least one

meal a day, my legs will shrivel up and crack off. Got to use 'em or lose 'em, don't you know that?"

"Yes, but there's no need to rush it," Katy had tried to argue.

"Rush, hush. I'm stronger every day. Bad enough the way your mother fusses over me, don't *you* start too."

Katy had relented, and now, as she loaded the dishwasher, and Gram trailed into the living room to rest on Dorsey's favorite floral-upholstered wing chair, she was relieved to acknowledge that Gram *was* stronger. Her color was better, she'd had no fever in nearly five days, and the coughing had all but disappeared.

By the time Big John and Dorsey returned in ten days, she hoped Gram would be well on her way to a full recovery.

And then Big John would see that traveling away from the ranch for a few days or a few weeks didn't send disaster an open invitation to descend upon his home and family.

Yesterday, when she'd driven her parents to the airport, she'd sensed the tension crouching on her father's chest like a vulture. Big John had been silent, and her mother had not even bothered trying to reassure him. She'd chattered nonstop to Katy, as if to compensate for his gloom, and later, no doubt, had squeezed his hand on the plane and tried to interest him in one of her travel books.

Katy could only hope that by now, Big John was so immersed in the sights of Paris that the Triple T, Gram and Cleo, and everything else in Thunder Creek were only a blip in the far corners of his mind.

But she doubted it.

Still, she felt a sense of relief that her parents had actually departed for their trip, that the diner had opened to bustling business and without any major catastrophes (except an argument beween Billy and Daffodil over the splitting of tips), and that Gram was improving.

The only things that had marred her day were the encounter

with Luke Dillard, and Jackson pushing his way into some-thing that was none of his business—and later, at the start of the dinner rush, the arrival of Wood and Tammie Morgan. Those were two customers she definitely could have done without.

They'd ordered steak wraps, seasoned fries, and apple pie, and then complained—loudly—that the fries were cold, the meat undercooked, the flatware dirty. And the pies tasteless.

Katy had been tempted to dump a whole pie smothered in whipped cream right in Tammie's lap.

She knew damn well that everything set before the Morgans had been just fine. She also knew that they'd only complained to try to rattle her, and to see if folks in Thunder Creek could be convinced that Bessie's Diner was slipping.

They were cheap tricks designed to make her rethink her decision about selling the diner. But it would take more than a few phony complaints to make her willing to sell to Wood and Tammie. *Nothing short of World War III will do it,* she thought with a grin as she scrubbed the sink and folded the dishrag over the faucet.

The sound of a truck roaring up the drive and Mojo's wild barking sent her spinning around, hurrying to the living room window.

Jackson Brent braked ten feet from the porch and stepped down from his truck, the setting sun illuminating the hard planes of his face, the easy way he moved across the yard, his broad chest, and those wide, iron shoulders.

A lick of fire skittered through her blood and she fought against it. She'd let Jackson be a friend of sorts, she'd be civil to him, but nothing more—and only if he behaved himself.

You threw your heart away on Seth and now that you've got it back, what's left of it, you're going to hang on to it and not waste it on a tall, handsome, quiet-talking cowboy who likes sexy redheads and open rangeland with no fences to hold him in . . .

"Who's there, Katy?" Gram asked from the chair, her eyes sharp and interested. Too much confinement indoors at the ranch had led her to welcome company with the eagerness of a flower opening its petals to the sunshine.

"It's Jackson Brent. He mentioned he'd be coming by to check on Cleo." She moved from the window, more than aware of her old khaki shorts and red T-shirt, her doing-the-laundry getup. Her hair was caught haphazardly in a loose casual ponytail.

This was hardly a glamorous look for greeting the heart-throb vet of Thunder Creek and she was aware that she'd deliberately dressed down just short of sweats for the encounter. Whether or not she was subtly discouraging any advances from Jackson Brent she couldn't say—she did know that after careful consideration she had decided she was too physically attracted to him for her own good and this was way too soon for her to even think about any kind of involvement with another man, physical or otherwise. She found herself bracing inwardly as Jackson bounded up the porch steps and rapped twice on the door.

"Well, let him in. What are you waiting for? The sight of a handsome man is better for whatever ails a woman than all the penicillin and chicken soup in the world."

Like hell it is. Katy straightened her spine and opened the door.

The sight of him, dark and strapping, brought back disconcerting memories of how it had felt to be held in his arms when they danced out by the MacIntyres' corral. With an effort, she pushed them away.

"Hope this isn't a bad time." Jackson stepped in without waiting to be asked and Katy felt a pulse of heat thread through her as he brushed past.

"Bessie." His eyes lit with warmth as they fixed on her grandmother, curled on the flowered chair. "They said you were real sick but you look prettier than a garden of poppies.

When are you going to quit lying around like a slug and come back to the diner where you belong?"

"Don't you like my granddaughter's cooking?" Bessie bestowed a saucy grin on him as he strode over and claimed a seat on the sofa, right next to her chair. "I taught her everything she knows. And then some."

"It shows. She's almost as fantastic a cook as you. But she looked like she could use some help today. Pretty wild crowd in there. My guess is she'll need someone to run the cash register full time. Maybe in a month or so you'll want to help her out, at least with the lunch crowd."

"A month or so? More like a week or so," Gram snorted. "After Ada and I get back from Vegas. I can't take too much more of this lying around."

"Must you encourage her?" Katy shook her head. "As it is she insisted on coming downstairs for dinner. All I need is for her to wear herself out and have a relapse." Her stern gaze fixed itself on her grandmother's sharply mischievous face. "Big John would never set foot off the Triple T again and you know it."

"Pshaw. Don't know how I raised such a worrier anyway." Gram waved a dismissive hand, then glanced back and forth between Katy and Jackson, her expression growing intent. "So . . . what brings you up to the house? Not that I'm not glad to see you, Jackson, but Katy said you were coming by to check on Cleo."

"Maybe I came by to see you."

"Is that right?"

She looked pleased, but still suspicious.

"I need a word with Katy, as well. Mind if I steal your granddaughter away for a few minutes, Bessie?"

Gram's smile widened and her eyes became almost shrewd. "If she wants to be stolen, don't let me stop you." She chuckled, and noting the tinge of pink color staining Katy's cheeks, she continued blithely, "Ada stopped by yesterday and told me how she set the two of you up in a dance the other night."

Katy spoke lightly. "She twisted his arm is more like it."

"That's not how I remember it." Jackson smiled at Bessie. "There wasn't *too* much pain involved."

"Speak for yourself," Katy retorted, before she even realized what she was saying. Then she flushed at her own rudeness.

Bessie peered back and forth between them once more, and a thoughtfulness suddenly stole over her face. She began pushing herself up from her chair.

"Well, now, glad to see you two getting along so well. But this old body is a mite tuckered out. Think I'll bundle myself off to bed."

Jackson stood up, and reaching out an arm, helped ease her to her feet. "How about letting me help you up the stairs?"

"Well, I surely wouldn't mind a strong arm nearby. I never was one to refuse the strong arm of a good man," Gram said. Tiny and spry, she lifted her head and stared up at him, a slow, approving smile spreading across her face. "You were always a good boy, Jackson. And a good friend to Matt. And now, of course," she said in a heartier tone, "you're also the handsomest man in town. If my grandson had lived, he'd have given you a run for your money in that department, but..." Her voice trailed off. "We can't change what is," she added with finality.

Katy followed Gram and Jackson up the stairs, a knot of worry beginning to clench in her stomach. Her grandmother suddenly looked all worn out, as if the exertion of the evening had abruptly caught up to her, and when Katy saw her knees trembling as she lowered herself onto the side of the bed, she insisted on staying to help Gram ready herself for sleep and to be certain she took her antibiotics.

When she returned downstairs to where Jackson waited,

she had her cell phone hooked to one of the loops in her khaki shorts.

"I told Gram to call me if she needs anything while we're out in Cleo's paddock," she explained, then lowered her voice. "Let's go outside to talk. I don't want her overhearing anything about Allison. There's no need to . . . to dredge anything up for her . . . or to set her to wondering about the sketch."

"Right."

In silence they left the house, Mojo trailing at their heels. After stopping at his truck for the electronic thermometer and stethoscope, they walked through thick rustling grass to the paddock behind the barn where Cleo grazed with two other horses as the first pearly beams of moonlight spilled across the fence posts.

When Katy pushed open the gate, she felt a wave of gratification as Cleo whickered at her and ambled over to nuzzle her neck.

"Hi, there, sweet girl. You feeling okay?"

For answer, Cleo tossed her mane and despite the tension of being with Jackson Brent in the moonlight, much like the night they'd danced, Katy laughed. She stroked Cleo's muzzle.

"You're going to have a healthy foal this time," she whispered, her voice catching. "A little beauty just like you. Doc Brent's going to make sure of it."

"You heard the lady, Cleo babe. Let's check you out."

As he took the mare's temperature, and checked her pulse and respiration, Jackson couldn't help but be aware of how good Katy was with her. She might look like a delicate New York sophisticate, even in khakis and T-shirt, but she was pure Wyoming ranch girl in the sure, gentle way she handled the mare.

When he was done, she gazed at him questioningly, a touch of worry in her eyes.

"Is she all right?"

"So far, so good."

Relief filled her face and she leaned her head a moment against the horse's muzzle, her eyes closed. Perhaps, Jackson thought, his gut twisting, she was remembering her own shattered pregnancy.

"She's strong, isn't she?" Opening her eyes, she searched his face. "She survived that accident, and she's hanging in here, despite all those lacerations, despite the trauma, everything."

"Yep, she's a true Templeton, I guess you could say."

"I didn't have any trauma," she said slowly. "It just... happened."

Her voice was so low he had to duck his head closer to make out her words. "You heard—I suppose everyone has—that I lost my baby?"

"I heard."

Her lips twisted. Small towns. She wasn't surprised. Swallowing, she continued, not even sure why she was telling him this, only knowing that the words were pouring out of her. "There was no warning. Nothing I could do. The umbilical cord... it twisted around the baby's neck. By the time I got to the hospital it was too late."

She drew in a deep, painful breath. Above, the stars glittered cool and distant as pearls, while the vast mountains hunched across the land.

"Sometimes it's just that way." Jackson spoke quietly. "No one knows why."

She nodded and turned quickly away, but not before he saw the tears gathered in her eyes.

"I'm sorry, Katy. Sorry about your baby."

If he'd touched her at that moment, she would have run. Broken away and run. She couldn't have borne it. But he didn't. As if sensing the pain that isolated and paralyzed her, he stayed where he was, silent and still, while she struggled against the tears, using pride as a weapon to beat back waves of agonizing loss that would overwhelm her, even now, if she let them.

After a few moments, she gave Cleo one last pat and turned back. Jackson opened the paddock gate for her and as they passed through she asked him about Allison.

"She was happy to hear from me. I sensed she's a little lonely, as if she misses Thunder Creek."

"Did you tell her about the sketch?"

"I didn't describe it. I only said that you'd found a sketch of Matt's and wanted to show it to her. She was glad to hear you were back in Thunder Creek. She wants to meet with you."

Her heartbeat quickened. "When?"

"Saturday afternoon. Her boys have a Cub Scout camping trip and her husband's the pack leader, so she'll be alone. Why don't I pick you up around ten that morning?"

Katy paused at the porch steps and faced him. "You really don't have to go along with me, you know."

"Yeah. I know."

"You must have something better to do with your Saturday."

"Well, I could always have a date with this little heifer up on Lonesome Ridge. And I heard the Pfisters have a new dog that needs neutering. Pretty exciting stuff, I have to admit."

"And what about Ms. Jones? Maybe she'd want to go on a picnic or to a movie or... to spend the afternoon with you—"

"So. That's what this is all about. You're asking me about my love life?"

His grin was slow and amused and Katy could have kicked herself.

"Don't flatter yourself," she retorted. "I merely want to make sure that just because I showed you the sketch, you don't feel that you have to hold my hand while I check into it."

"No chance of that. I'm not much of a hand-holder." Jackson gave her a long look, and seemed as if he was about to say something more. Instead he wheeled toward his truck and spoke over his shoulder. "See you Saturday then. Ten o'clock."

She watched him fire up the engine and switch on the radio and Clint Black's "Walkin' Away" poured out into the darkness. Without so much as a wave in her direction, he roared off into the night.

Katy stood alone on the porch for a while, gazing at the mountains, trying not to think about Jackson Brent and his quick retreats, or about the unsettling effect he had on her, focusing instead on what Allison might say when she saw the sketch. Only a few more days and she'd have some answers, and maybe this nagging fear in the back of her heart would disappear as suddenly as it had come.

She'd returned home hoping to find a sense of peace and a way to put the past behind her. But she couldn't do either of those things—not yet. Not until she knew why Matt had drawn that sketch—and the identity of the girl lying so still and so strangely, like a dead doll in the tall weedy grass.

Chapter 14

THE DAYS FLEW BY FASTER THAN KATY COULD HAVE imagined. Between working at the diner, caring for Gram, and fielding phone calls from her lawyer, her former secretary, and Seth, having to do with Rattlesnake Cafe business, she scarcely had time to even think about her upcoming meeting with Allison, much less to glance anymore at Matt's sketch.

But to her surprise, she found herself thinking far too much about Jackson Brent. She caught herself wavering back and forth between the absurd fantasy of having a casual fling with him, and the notion of cutting off all contact and driving up to Medicine Bow on Saturday by herself.

Grow up, a voice inside of her chided.

She was twenty-eight, for heaven's sake, and far too old and experienced to be dithering over a man, especially a man with a history as bitter as the one she shared with Jackson Brent.

Yet part of her toyed with the idea of succumbing to the attraction she felt toward him. He was sexy as hell, after all, and had the most gorgeous eyes, not to mention a phenomenal body. Why not leave her heart out of it and simply indulge? Casual affairs worked for him, and for zillions of other people, she reminded herself.

But they weren't her style.

Maybe it's time to start a new style, Katy argued with herself Saturday morning as she yanked a cream-colored sleeveless sweater over her head, then zipped up slim khaki capris.

Why not give in to the attraction and stop trying to fight it? Then you can get him out of your system. Frowning, she shoved her feet into low-heeled Prada sandals.

Butterflies tumbled through her stomach. He'd be here soon. *You're not even sure you* like *the man,* she thought. *Most of the time he rubs you the wrong way.* But all that rubbing had produced some kind of powerful electricity, she admitted. Sparks, hot ones.

Pull the plug, she told herself angrily. *And stop thinking like a teenager smearing on lipstick for a first date.* Picking up her purse, she hurried to her desk and dug the sketch out of the drawer. The sight of it finally distracted her from thoughts of Jackson, and she felt once again the prickle of ice along her spine she'd known the first time she looked at it. For several long moments she gazed at the curly haired girl's eerily prone figure, then she slipped the drawing into her purse.

Maybe today the mystery would be solved. Maybe today Allison would shed light on the identity of the woman in the sketch, and the reason Matt had drawn it. Maybe today it would all make sense, perfectly normal sense, and the sketch could be forgotten.

"Any word from your folks?" Jackson asked a half hour later as his truck wound its way along Highway 487, past hills blackened with dots of countless cattle. Above them the sun blazed like a golden coin in a sky so big and brilliant a blue it numbed the eyes.

There had been precious little conversation between them until now, except when he'd asked if Gram and Ada had gotten off to the airport all right. Since then, Katy had been trying to figure out a way to break the drawn-out silence, but he'd beaten her to it.

"Not since the phone call the night they arrived." She was relieved her voice sounded so normal. "But I know exactly what's going on: Big John's counting the days until he can get home, and Mom's soaking in everything she can."

"They'll be gone another week, right?"

"Yes, one more week." Katy tried to imagine her parents traipsing around the Left Bank, the Champs-Élysées, and the Louvre. She could just see her mother trying to chat unabashedly with everyone she met, reading her guidebook incessantly, taking roll after roll of photographs. Big John would be scowling, his hands in his pockets, his heart longing for the meadows and mountains of home.

"Now all I have to do is keep everything status quo at the ranch until they get back, and Mom might stand a chance of another trip with him sometime in the next millennium," she murmured.

"Anything I can do to help, just ask."

"You're helping today. Helping me settle this sketch business once and for all." She bit her lip and spoke briskly. "If I haven't thanked you before, let me just say it now. I appreciate everything you've done—calling Allison, setting this up. It will all probably come to nothing, I'm sure. And that's what I hope, but still . . ."

"You need to know."

"Yes. I need to know."

"That's understandable." Jackson glanced over at her, then back at the road. "But sometimes looking back into the past can do more harm than good."

"What does that mean?" Katy stared at his profile. "Do you know something I don't?"

"Not exactly."

"You said you didn't know who the girl in the sketch was or what she had to do with Matt—"

"I don't. I don't know anything about her—or about the sketch." He hesitated. "All I'm saying is that when you put the past under a microscope you sometimes find things you'd rather not see."

"Are you talking about Matt's past?"

"Anyone's. But maybe Matt's too."

A thread of panic jolted through her. "I'm not an idiot, Jackson. What do you know about my brother that I don't? Spit it out."

He stared straight ahead at the road, not glancing at her, not wanting to see the tension in her face. "He was my best friend, Katy. I loved him. And I lost him too. That's what I know."

"And what else?" she asked sharply.

She was a damned persistent woman. Jackson weighed his options. Okay, she'd asked for it.

"I only know that Matt was acting a little funny the last week before he died. He was upset about something, but he wouldn't talk to me about it. I think he may have told Allison," he continued quickly, "but that's only a guess."

"Funny—how do you mean funny?"

"It's hard to explain. Upset. Down."

That wasn't like Matt. Why hadn't she noticed? *Because he didn't want you to.* Her thoughts raced. "You never talked to Allison about it?"

"Once or twice, but I didn't have a chance to really get into it with her. And then, after the accident, I didn't want to press her about anything having to do with him. She always cried whenever anyone mentioned his name, so . . . I just let it go." He shrugged. "Who knows, maybe he didn't tell her what was wrong, or maybe it was something stupid. I think they may have had a fight, though. That could have been all it was."

He glanced sideways then and saw the tension in her face, the worry knitting her brows. "That doesn't mean any of it is related to the sketch," he added. "Or to the girl. I'm not try-ing to say that. I'm just warning you—"

"I know what you're doing. But there's no need to warn me about Matt." Her hands were clasped tightly in her lap, the knuckles white, as the hilly land outside the window flew past. "My brother never did anything he'd be ashamed of. I'm not worried about learning something awful about him. I just want to find out why he drew this sketch."

"So do I."

"Then why don't you drive a little faster?" The words burst from her. She knew she sounded like a total bitch, but she couldn't help it. Jackson's little "warning" had shaken her for some reason. Her stomach felt like it had just come through a blender. What was he implying? *And,* she thought, staring at him as if she could somehow penetrate his brain, *what is he holding back?*

To her irritation, he ignored her remark and didn't push down on the accelerator, didn't even glance at her. They sped on toward Medicine Bow, the speedometer continuing to hover at sixty when she suddenly wanted to be going eighty. She needed to talk to Allison.

Forcing herself to lean back against the seat, Katy stared out the window, not even noticing as the land flattened, and the road stretched before them. Neither of them spoke again until they'd rattled past the Shirley Basin, home of some of the richest uranium deposits in the world, and reached the gi-ant wooden sign welcoming them to Medicine Bow.

The cow town that had been immortalized by Owen Wister in *The Virginian* was now home to The Virginian Hotel, oil fields, and two gigantic wind tunnels built by the Interior Department to provide electricity for twelve hundred homes, one of which belonged to Allison and Rusty Leggett.

Allison's house stood six miles west of town at the end of a lonely dirt road. It was small, smaller than the Triple T ranch house by at least half, and it needed paint. The truck jolted over deep ruts in the road leading up to the barn and sheds, and at last reached the front yard and the house with its oblique, dark green curtains and matchbox-sized front porch.

The woman who opened the door smiled when she saw them. She pushed open the screen door, her brown eyes misting and then widening as her gaze shifted from Jackson to Katy.

"Wow, look at you. Just *look* at you, Katy Templeton!" Allison's glance swept over Katy's slender figure, the chic swing of honey hair, the cream-colored sweater and crisp khaki pants, and stared in awe at the diamond drop necklace at her throat.

"I can't believe it's you."

"It's been a long time, Allison."

Emotions welled in Katy as she stared at her brother's former girlfriend, framed in the doorway of the house. How many times had she seen Allison and Matt holding hands while they did homework at the kitchen table, chasing each other around the barn, kissing on the porch as if they'd personally invented the giddy feverishness of first love? How many sketches of the young girl who owned his heart had her brother plastered over the walls of his room, his locker at school, even the dashboard of his truck?

But this Allison was no longer the dark-haired, doe-eyed teenager who had practically lived in the Templeton house from the time Matt became her boyfriend. Allison Leggett was little more than thirty, but thin streaks of gray showed in her once glossy dark hair, and there were tiny crow's-feet at the corners of her eyes. Those eyes, once young and glowing, now looked tired—and defeated, Katy thought. But as Allison leaned past Jackson and embraced her, she caught the scent of the same Charlie cologne Allison had always worn, the scent that had clung to Matt for hours after he'd been with Allison for any length of time.

It brought back memories, good memories, Katy thought, hugging Allison in return. Maybe that was why Allison still wore it.

"Come in, I've made coffee. Are you hungry? I could whip up some sandwiches..."

"No, no, we don't want to put you to any trouble." Katy followed her into the house as the screen door thudded softly shut behind Jackson. "But coffee would be great."

"Just sit anywhere," Allison called over her shoulder, disappearing into the kitchen.

Moments later she returned with a tray holding three mugs filled with steaming coffee, cream and sugar bowls, some packets of Sweet'N Low, and a plate of oatmeal cookies.

The house—Allison's domain, Katy suspected—was as neat and cozy inside as it was run-down on the outside. The low-ceilinged living room was furnished with a green and tan upholstered sofa that had green throw pillows at each end, a maple coffee table and matching TV stand, and a stone fireplace whose mantel held an assortment of framed family photos, among them Allison with a short, stocky man in a flannel shirt and jeans. He had his arm around her, and standing in front of them were two boys with dark hair, cowlicks, and grinning faces.

"My boys." Allison jerked her head toward the photos as she spotted Katy studying them. "My husband, Rusty. And Boyd, he's my older one, and the spitting image of his father. The other's Neddy, my baby, who's going into fifth grade next year. He decided last week he wants to be a sports announcer." She sighed. "Last month it was a hip-hop star."

"What a beautiful family." Katy approached the mantel and studied the photograph. The boys looked scrubbed, wholesome, full of energy. She sensed that Allison didn't realize how lucky she was. "Your husband looks like a nice man."

"Rusty? Oh, he is. He's a fine man. He sort of lets things

go around here." She made a face. "No matter how much I nag, he just doesn't pay much attention to fixing things, and painting and such, never has time—you know what I mean—but he's devoted to the boys—and to me." She took a deep breath and stared at her hands. "He's good to us, real good, but he's no ..."

She caught herself, bit her lip, and then clamped both lips together. Katy knew somehow that she'd been about to say, "He's no Matt."

"Matt would be happy to know you have a good life. With someone who loves you." She spoke quietly as she returned to the sofa, and the other woman's eyes flew to her face.

"I guess he would. But..." Suddenly, Allison was blinking back tears. There was bitterness in her eyes. "But it isn't fair. You know, Katy? It just isn't fair. To this day, I wonder, I wonder a lot ... *why*. Why he had to die. And what my life would be like ..." She drew a deep breath. "If he'd lived."

She leaned forward suddenly and grabbed a coffee cup, as if to cover the moment with a normal gesture, but her hands were shaking and the coffee nearly sloshed over the edge.

It was Jackson who shifted on the sofa and spoke to her in a soothing, matter-of-fact tone. "Ally, we all wonder that. It's fine to wonder. But what you don't want to do is let it get in the way of the life you have now. The one you built. Because you can't go back—none of us can."

"Yeah. Tell me about it." There was acid in the words, even though she tried to smile as she spoke them.

Katy wondered if Rusty Leggett knew that his wife had never gotten over the teenaged love of her life. Then she wondered how he couldn't know. Pain stabbed her, for both of them, as Allison peered over her coffee cup with those sad, stoic eyes. *What a tragic way to live,* she thought, and then she thought of Seth. Would she ever get over *him* ... over his betrayal? Over what she'd lost with him? Would she ever be able to give herself heart and soul to another man, or would she end up like Allison, always remembering the past, wishing for it, deep inside her heart, unable to move on?

That's not what I want, she thought fiercely. *Matt didn't leave Allison deliberately. Seth did. He cheated. He lied. He abandoned me when I needed him most and turned to someone else.*

Her throat tightened and, for a moment, she closed her eyes. She opened them again quickly, reminding herself why she'd come here, and she quickly picked up her purse from the floor and opened it.

"I think Jackson told you that I wanted to ask you something today. There's actually something I want to show you. A sketch, a sketch Matt drew the day he died."

"A sketch of me? Matt made so many. I used to get aggravated with him, because he took that sketchpad everywhere we went. And even when he didn't have it, he'd draw something later on, and bring it to school, and hang it in his locker, and his friends would always tease me—"

"Hey, you wouldn't be talking about me, would you?" Jackson drawled with a ghost of a grin. "I was pretty relentless back then, wasn't I?"

"Well, I used to tease you right back, and so did Matt. You wanted Holly Sue Granger in the worst way in those days. You used to eye her like the wolf looking at Little Red Riding Hood. But she was no Little Red Riding Hood, as we all knew. Matt always said he wished you'd just ask her out already, and get her out of your system, since you'd already had nearly every other girl in our grade—" She broke off suddenly, clasping her hands taut in her lap. "And you did, finally. That night. The night Matt died."

Jackson's face had turned to stone.

Flushing, Allison glanced back and forth between him and Katy, obviously remembering Katy's outburst after the funeral. "I'm glad to see you've both gotten past ... everything," she stammered. "You ... you have ... haven't you?"

"Yes. Of course." But Katy avoided Jackson's eyes. Maybe she had forgiven him for the most part, but that didn't mean she had to let him into her life. Now her fantasy seemed more idiotic than ever. She wasn't about to become best buds or casual lovers or anything else with Jackson Brent. Especially now that she knew he'd been holding back information from her, information he might have shared when she first showed him the sketch.

"Here's the drawing, down at the bottom." She handed the paper to Allison. "It's not of you, Allison, but I hope you can tell me who this girl is. Do you recognize her?"

Allison gave a sharp intake of breath. "She looks dead!"

"We thought the same thing." Katy's chest felt tight. "But we can't figure out who she is. Is she real, someone Matt saw or knew, or did he make her up?"

Allison had gone pale as she continued to study the sketch. "He didn't make this up," she whispered. "Matt never made up the people or things in his sketches. And besides," she said almost to herself, "she looks familiar. I can't quite place her..."

Exactly what Jackson had said. He leaned forward.

"Did Matt ever show you this sketch, Ally? Could that be why she looks familiar?"

"No, no, he never showed me this. I'd have remembered this. It's so different from anything he ever drew. Matt drew kittens on fence posts, horses poised at the peak of a ridge at sunset, old people sitting on their front porch, holding hands ... he drew warm things, happy things ... not ... this."

"So who is she?" Katy murmured. "Try to remember, Allison, if you can."

"I can't ... can't place her name. But there's something about her hair, that long, wavy hair..." Suddenly her head snapped up.

"I know who she is." Her voice shook.

"Who?" Katy asked quickly.

"Her name was Christine, no—*Crystal*. Crystal something. I don't remember, but she used to work at the Tumbleweed Bar and Grill."

"That's it. You're right." Jackson turned toward Katy, his face grim in the sunlight that slid between the vertical crack in the heavy green curtains. "I knew I'd seen her before. Matt and I sneaked into the Tumbleweed one night—I think it was our junior year. We huddled at a back table, hoping no one would notice a couple of high school kids. She was a waitress there and she brought us each a beer before Elam caught us and tossed us out on our underage butts. After that I may have seen her in town once or twice."

He moved closer to Allison and stared down at the sketch in her hands. "I knew she rang a bell."

"Was she waitressing there up until the time Matt died?" Katy wanted to know. It was Allison who answered.

"I think so. At least, I know she worked there a few months before." Allison set the sketch down on the coffee table as if she couldn't bear to touch it any longer. "My brother came home from college over the summer and he used to go to the Tumbleweed a few nights a week," she said shakily. "I guess he had a crush on her because he used to mention her now and then. And once we ran into her in town and he turned bright red and stammered and I just knew he was madly in love with her. But he never went out with her. I asked him about her once and he said she worked at the Tumbleweed and he'd danced with her once or twice, but she wouldn't go out with him. She said she was already taken."

Suddenly, she broke off and her gaze shot back to the sketch. A muscle worked in her cheek, and without warning she snatched up the sketch again and as Katy watched in shock, she ripped it in two.

"Allison!"

Katy grabbed it from her before Allison could rip it again. "What are you doing? We need this. We need to find out—"

"No, no, you don't, Katy. Throw it away, forget about it."

"I can't. I need to know—"

"No!" Allison turned frantic eyes upon her. Her lips were trembling. "Let it go. Leave it be. My God, Matt was your brother—why can't you let him rest in peace?"

"What does this have to do with letting Matt rest in peace? Maybe he saw something, knew something about what happened to her—"

"For God's sake, Katy, why can't you just let it go?" Allison shrieked. She made a grab for the sketch, but Katy moved faster, stepping back and thrusting the torn papers behind her back.

Allison stared at her a moment, her eyes wild, then suddenly sank back on the sofa and covered her face with her hands. Sobs wracked her shoulders. "Jackson," she rasped, as tears soaked through her fingers, "you tell her. Tell her to just forget about it, about that damned sketch, just let the past go—"

"Take it easy, Ally." Jackson was almost as stunned by her reaction as Katy was. He stared hard at the sobbing woman and then looked over at Katy, tightly clutching the two halves of the sketch.

"Let's just calm down here," he began quietly, but Katy suddenly thrust the pieces of the sketch at him and sank down beside Allison. She spoke in a low, surprisingly steady tone.

"Allison, can I get you something? A glass of water?"

"No, nothing. I just want you to leave. I don't want to talk about that stupid sketch anymore."

"We have to talk about it. Why did you rip it up? I need to know."

"No, you don't. You don't need to know anything about . . . back then. About that girl."

"I need to know whatever you know. Tell me."

Allison lifted a wet face. Brown mascara ran with the

tears down her cheeks. "He was a wonderful boy, Katy," she whispered. "A wonderful boyfriend. I loved him with all my heart. Until that last week...everything was perfect. It's not fair now to dredge up something Matt never wanted anyone to know—even me..."

"What are you saying?" Katy felt the apprehension rising in her. "What didn't Matt want anyone to know?"

Allison stared at her, and swiped at the tears on her face, smearing mascara into her skin. "I don't really have any idea," she said softly, so softly Katy had to strain to hear her. "It was secret. All I know is that Matt was really quiet that last week—and irritable. He wasn't himself at all and when I asked him what was wrong—" She hesitated. "He told me he'd done something. Something terrible." Her shoulders slumped forward as if in defeat. "He wouldn't tell me anything more. He said he loved me, but..."

"But what?" Katy demanded, her stomach roiling.

"But he was...mixed up...about everything. Mostly himself. He said if I knew what he'd done, I'd hate him. Not that I ever could—" she added shakily. "But he just kept saying he had to think."

"That's it?" Katy spoke more sharply than she'd intended. "If that's all he said, why did you tear up that picture?"

"I don't know. I just remembered how my brother said Crystal was 'taken' and now you told me Matt drew this sketch—I never even knew he met her—but obviously, he did..." Her gaze traveled once more to the sketch in Katy's hands. She swallowed. "And what if... what if he was *cheating* on me, seeing her behind my back? Maybe when she said she was taken, it was Matt—" She leaned against the sofa, hugging her arms around herself. "Oh, God, Katy, I don't want to know, I just want to remember things the way they were. The way they were *supposed* to be."

The way they were supposed to be. *And what way was that,* Katy thought dazedly. The past she'd always seen so clearly, the past she'd thought of as carved in stone, had turned into a disturbing, fuzzy blur. Her brother, the most honest, outspoken, loyal person she'd ever met, had harbored a secret. And sketched a dead girl.

It looks *like a dead girl,* she reminded herself, as sweat trickled down her spine. *You don't know anything for certain yet... except that her name was Crystal...*

"Let's not jump to all kinds of conclusions." Jackson echoed her thoughts, but Allison's eyes darted nervously between her two visitors.

"I think we should forget the whole thing. I've got a bad feeling about this." She dug into the pocket of her dark denim jeans, but her fingers came up empty. "God, I'd kill for a cigarette right now. Rusty and the boys made me quit two months ago, but right now..."

Her voice trailed off. Katy shared that bad feeling she had, but she refrained from saying so. What they needed was information, a lot more information, and a chance to think things through.

"We should try to sort this out one step at a time," she began, but Allison jerked to her feet, fixing Katy with a glance that could have set wet timber on fire.

"I don't *want* to sort it out. It's over and done. The past died with Matt—that's what everyone is always telling me. And if Matt had wanted me to know, he'd have explained it all to me—why he was acting so weird, what he meant about that pact..."

"Pact? What pact?" Katy demanded.

Allison froze, her cheeks flushing.

"You didn't mention any pact," Jackson said.

"Well, I guess I forgot." She went on stiffly, reluctantly. "He mentioned something about some stupid pact he said he made. He wouldn't tell me with who, or what it was about, he just said he never should have agreed to it. I didn't have a clue what he was talking about."

"Is there anything else you're forgetting to tell us? Like who the pact was with?" Katy asked, her thoughts racing.

"No. Nothing. I told you I didn't know, except..." Allison bit her lip. "I saw him duck into the alley behind the Tumbleweed one day and I...I followed him. I never told him but I saw him talking to someone. Arguing, really."

"Who was he arguing with?"

Allison met Katy's eyes, her own filled with misgiving. "Wood Morgan."

Wood Morgan?

That was the last name Katy expected to hear. "Matt and Wood never hung out together in high school."

"I know that. That's why it seemed so strange. They weren't friends, particularly, never had been, so I didn't understand why they were in that alley..." Allison shook her head. "But I never told Matt I saw them, never asked him about it."

You wanted to bury your head in the sand, Katy thought. *You wanted to pretend that everything was fine. But it wasn't.*

She couldn't really condemn Allison though—not when she herself hadn't even had the wit to notice anything was wrong.

"Did Wood have something to do with the pact, or with what was bothering Matt—or did he know Crystal?"

Allison shook her head. "I told you, I don't know." Her tone was stony, and the gaze she fixed upon Katy held both anger and a kind of pathetic pleading. "But I think you're making a big mistake bringing all this up."

"I know you do. I'm sorry." Rising, Katy slipped her purse strap onto her shoulder, hoping neither Allison nor Jackson could see how her insides were twisted into knots.

"We've bothered you enough," she said quietly, and glanced at Jackson. "We ought to head back."

When Jackson rose and handed her back the two pieces of

the sketch, she folded them without looking at them and tucked them into her purse. Allison trailed them to the door.

"It was good seeing you," she said woodenly, but there was no joy or sincerity in her face or in her words. Resentment clung to her like weeds.

Katy nodded, then impulsively hugged the other woman's thin shoulders. "Thanks, Allison. I'm sorry we upset you—I know this was hard."

She made no answer. Jackson gathered her into his arms, and her gray-tinged hair fell forward as she rested her head for a moment against his chest.

"We'll be in touch, Ally."

"That's . . . fine. You're always welcome, both of you." She moistened her lips. "But I don't want to talk about this again."

Back in the truck, Jackson paused, key in hand, and turned to Katy.

"Are you all right?"

"I will be." Meeting his gaze, her eyes shone with anger in the hot afternoon sunlight. "As soon as I find out what the hell happened fourteen years ago—and why my brother's so-called best friend claims to know nothing about it."

Chapter 15

THERE WERE ONLY A HANDFUL OF TRUCKS AND CARS in the parking lot behind the Tumbleweed Bar and Grill when Jackson pulled in and parked across from the entrance. It was early yet—barely seven o'clock—and the place didn't really start filling up until closer to nine, which suited Katy just fine. She wasn't here for a social evening of drinking and dancing, she was here to ask questions.

And to get answers.

"It shouldn't be too difficult finding someone who knew Crystal." Jackson switched off the engine and turned to look at her. "Elam's been bartending here for at least fifteen years. And we can always ask Ted Paxton, the owner, if he's here tonight. Sometimes he doesn't come in until eleven or twelve though."

"I'll wait as long as it—" Katy broke off, staring across the parking lot.

"Well, now, how's this for serendipity?" she muttered.

Jackson followed her glance and saw Tammie and Wood Morgan just stepping out of their spanking-new Land Rover. As he watched, they began strolling toward the bar.

"I'm not exactly in the mood to be hit with their top ten reasons why I should sell them Bessie's Diner, but I wouldn't mind asking Wood a few questions." Katy pushed open her door. "If I can get him away from Tammie for a few minutes, that is."

"Maybe I can help you out there." Jackson swung out of the truck and slammed the door as Wood and Tammie disappeared inside the Tumbleweed. He knew that if Wood Morgan had any connection whatsoever to Crystal, he sure as hell wouldn't tell anyone about it in front of Tammie. Those two were already dating back when Matt had his accident, and Tammie had been born with a jealous streak as big as Texas. One word about another woman in front of his wife would make Wood Morgan clam up faster than you could slap a tick.

"Come on," Jackson said. "I'll buy you a beer and we'll see what we can come up with."

Maybe the beer would wash down the bad taste in her mouth, Katy thought. Not all of it was due to the food at the Blue Fin Diner in Eagleton where they'd stopped for dinner. True, the burgers had been greasy, the fries burned, and the service indifferent. *No comparison,* Katy had reflected with a small twinge of satisfaction, *to what customers find at Bessie's Diner.* But she'd had a sour, sick feeling in the pit of her stomach long before they'd reached the Blue Fin and she knew it was due to what she'd learned from Allison, and to wondering frantically what in the world had been wrong with Matt the week before he died.

Jackson had claimed to know nothing more than what he'd told her in the car on the way here, and she just about believed him. But that got her no closer to the truth. What had Matt been hiding from his family, from his best friend, and from everyone else in town—except Allison? And even Allison didn't know any details—or so she said.

A pact. Something terrible.

The sketch.

And Wood Morgan . . .

The interior of the Tumbleweed was dark and smelled of

whiskey, Old Spice, and Marlboros. Corinne waved them to a table not far from the dance floor. Elam wasn't working behind the bar—it was the other bartender, Ray, Jackson pointed out, and Corinne told them Elam called in with a flat tire, saying he'd be there by eight.

Jackson ordered their beers. But Corinne had no sooner hurried off to get them when Tammie slithered from her chair near the pool table, whispered something to Wood, and then came sauntering over, her open Budweiser bottle dangling from her manicured hand.

"Incoming," Jackson murmured. "This might be easier than we thought."

But Tammie's next words almost made Katy forget all about her plan to get Wood alone.

"Well, now, what have we here? Don't tell me you two are an item?" She arched a brow and grinned at each of them in turn, her chunky, dangling silver earrings catching the light of the single candle flickering in the center of the table. "No wonder you're too busy to work these days," she chided, wagging a finger at Katy. "Now if you'd sell us the diner, you wouldn't have to worry about lack of help, slow service, running out of pies—"

"What are you talking about?"

"You don't know?" Tammie opened her eyes very wide, then shook her head. "Sorry to be the bearer of bad news, but more than a few customers were mighty unhappy today at Bessie's Diner. It seems your little waitress played hooky with her boyfriend instead of coming into work. Poor Billy—he ran himself ragged trying to keep things going all by himself. But he was in way over his head, you know what I mean? Me and Wood, we stopped in for a piece of pie this afternoon with this architect who's drawing up the plans for our dude ranch, and there was no pie to be had—not a single piece. And the coffee was cold. And a few people just plain walked out before their food came, they were so fed up."

Katy's stomach clenched. *I'm going to kill Daffodil Moline,* she thought, but aloud she said, "Next time you and Wood come in, the coffee and pie is on me. That goes for the other customers who were inconvenienced today, too."

"Well, aren't you sweet? But, Katy, you shouldn't have to work so hard and worry your head. Now I don't know what kind of screws your ex is putting to you in the divorce settlement, but I do know that if you sell the diner to me and Wood, you'll have enough money to open a restaurant anywhere in the world, and hire enough people to run it properly."

Red-hot anger pulsed through Katy, but somehow she managed to speak in a calm, tight tone. "No one puts the screws to me, Tammie. No one. Now are you finished?"

Tammie was many things—pushy, self-centered, full of herself, and single-minded—but she was no fool. She saw the glint of danger in Katy Templeton's eyes, saw the tautness in the other woman's slim neck, the steam practically puffing out of her ears, and she figured she'd pushed as hard as was safe right now.

"Sure I'm finished. For the moment." Her smile was the gracious one she reserved for the important businesspeople Wood brought home, the ones they wanted something from. "You think about what I said, sugar. As soon as you're ready to let us take that creaky old place off your hands, you just give me and Wood a call."

Katy itched to throw the beer in her face, but before she could do or say anything, Jackson stood up. "I think you've made your point, Tammie. Time to quit while you're ahead."

"Am I ahead?" She slanted her eyes at him and chuckled, a deep and throaty sound like she was gargling whiskey.

"All right, come on." His grin was easy as he caught her hand. "Let's dance. I think both you ladies need a minute to cool off."

Her heels tapped against the pine plank floor as she allowed him to lead her onto the dance floor, the beer bottle still dangling in her free hand. Katy was already whipping out her cell phone even as Jackson's arm hooked loosely around Tammie's waist.

She punched in Daffodil's number but heard only an answering machine. "Daffodil, it's Katy." She spoke rapidly. "You call me the minute you get this message. I don't care what time it is. *Call me.*"

She dropped the phone back in her purse and shoved back her chair. Two seconds later she was dropping down beside Wood, who had turned to watch his wife dancing with Jackson. The Eagles crooned from the jukebox. *Take it eeeeasy.*

She smiled grimly at him.

"Tell me something, Wood."

"What's that, Katy?" His smile was at once warm and speculative. He never saw it coming.

"Tell me all about you and Matt—and that girl, Crystal."

Was it her imagination, or did Wood's color fade beneath his tan?

"Wh...at the hell are you talking about?"

She leaned back in her chair, as if she had all the time in the world. "I'm talking about the pact, Wood. You remember the pact."

"I don't know what you're talking about." He cleared his throat, shook his head. "How much have you had to drink there, Katy? You're not making any sense." He smiled then, with something of his characteristic self-assurance, but it was a forced smile. Oh, he was good, but not good enough. Seth had taught her a number of corporate skills, not the least of which was how to spot a lie, and she could spot one with the best of them.

"We can talk about this when Tammie gets back to the

table or we can talk about it right now," she said softly, pleasantly. "I want to know everything you can tell me about Crystal, and why you and Matt made that pact—"

"I suggest you go home and sleep this off, Katy." His tone had changed. The shock was gone. Wood Morgan had regained his composure and suddenly there was a stone-hard glint in those shrewd businessman's eyes. "You're not making any sense at all. And there's nothing to talk about. I don't know any Crystal, and I never made any pact."

"I don't believe you."

"That's your problem."

"Wood, I just want some answers." From the corner of her eye she saw Jackson sweet talking Tammie into another dance. There wasn't much time . . .

"If you have nothing to hide—"

"Damned straight I don't."

"Fine. But you were seen meeting in an alley with Matt right before he died and I know he made some kind of pact with *someone*—"

"Whoa, there. Who are you? Nancy Drew? Or Columbo?" There was scorn in his eyes and he laughed harshly. "Whichever, you're on the wrong track, honey. I don't know where this is coming from, but I suggest you back off. Way off."

"I will—right after you tell me what I want to know. I won't say anything to Tammie, if that's what you're worried about. I just want some information—"

"Information about what, sugar?"

Tammie and Jackson stood beside the table. Before Katy could say anything, Wood rose to his feet, and reached for his wife's arm. "Katy wants some figures on what the diner would be worth to us if she decides to sell."

"Well, now, that's real good news. And it's about time." Tammie's grin could have lit up the rafters of the cavernous bar.

"I'll crunch her some numbers later," Wood said casually,

and dropped a kiss on his wife's neck. "Meantime, let's you and me dance. Seeing you on that dance floor with Jackson made me more jealous than a tomcat."

He led her away without another glance at Katy, but she kept her gaze on him as he and Tammie began swaying together in the shadows, kissing and nuzzling each other as if they were still a couple of teenagers.

"He's lying," she told Jackson in a low tone. "He denied knowing Crystal, and having any knowledge of a pact with Matt, but he was clearly shaken when I mentioned it. And he completely changed the subject when Tammie showed up. He's covering up big-time."

"Maybe I should take the next round of talks." Jackson led the way back to their own table. "If he sees neither one of us is going to drop it, he may decide to cut his losses and talk. Or," he added, a slight frown between his brows, "he might just strike out like a cornered bear. Did he threaten you?"

"No, not exactly." At his long look, she shrugged. "He told me to back off, that's all."

"I don't like the sound of that. Be careful, Katy. Wood Morgan didn't get where he is today by playing Mr. Nice Guy."

"Do you think I care? This is driving me crazy. I have to know what was going on with Matt before he died. I have to know why he drew that sketch of Crystal, and how he knew her and—"

"And what happened to her." Jackson finished her thought.

"Yes." She spoke grimly. "I need to know what happened to her."

"We'll find out." Jackson tasted his beer. "There'll be plenty of other chances to talk to Wood. In the meantime, there's Elam. He'll be in soon. What about what Tammie said? Did you check in with Billy or Daffodil?"

"I left Daffodil a message." Katy dragged a hand through

her hair in frustration. "I never should have taken the whole
day off."

"Don't let Tammie get to you."

"Much as I hate to admit it, she's right about one thing: I
don't have enough help. I should have hired another waitress—I meant to do it," she added bitterly. "But I kept letting
myself get distracted by other things. Seth always told me in
business you can't afford to take your eye off the ball for
even a minute or . . . why are you staring at me like that?"

"It's the first time you've ever mentioned him. Your ex."

"It is?" Katy realized he was right and she grimaced. She
reached for her beer and took a long sip, forcing herself not
to gulp. "I guess you're right."

Get ahold of yourself, she thought. *Are you so shaken because things got messed up at the diner or because you found
out that the girl in Matt's sketch really existed? That Matt
had a secret, a pact, that he was mixed up in something that
he didn't want anyone to know about . . .*

And, a small voice persisted, *because he might have
known something about Crystal's death . . . if she is dead . . .*

"Seth . . . isn't exactly one of my favorite people these
days. I don't like to talk about him much," she said tightly.
"Or think about him."

"Does that mean you're not over him?"

The question came so quickly, so directly, that she could
only blink at first. "Over him?"

"Yeah." There was an edge to his voice. His blue eyes
looked like granite in the smoky bar. "As in, you're not in
love with him anymore and you couldn't care less if he fell
down an elevator shaft. That kind of over him."

Katy wasn't sure if the beer was going to her head or if
she was just tired out from the emotions of the past days, but
she heard herself speaking the truth abut Seth, without any
bravado or false levity for the first time since he'd asked her

for a divorce and informed her he was going to marry someone else.

"I'm working on it." She shrugged. "If you must know,
it's one of the reasons I came home to Thunder Creek. To put
my life back together, to give me some distance from Seth,
from everything. To figure things out."

She reached for the beer bottle again, but suddenly
Jackson's gaze moved past her, and his hand shot out, clamp-
ing over hers.

"Don't look now, but Elam just walked in."

She glanced around, saw the amiable-looking, brown-
bearded man in jeans striding toward the bar, and slid swiftly
out of her chair.

"What are you waiting for? Come on."

"Crystal? You mean Crystal Kirk? Sure I remember her."

Katy's heart jumped in her chest. *Crystal Kirk*. Somehow
knowing the girl's last name made her all the more real. She
kept her gaze glued to Elam Lowell's face, focusing on his
nearly lashless pale blue eyes that were sunk deep into sun-
burnished skin. The bartender was burly, with stringy brown
hair, a voice like gravel, and quick, deft hands that lined up
glasses and beer bottles all the while he talked.

"How long ago did she work here? What happened to
her?" she asked.

"Let's see now. You're talkin' way back, maybe fourteen,
fifteen years ago, I'd say. Hell, I remember. She left right
around the time me and Sally got our divorce. I remember
thinking too bad she was quitting and heading out of town,
now that I was gonna be single again." He chuckled. "She
was mighty pretty, was Crystal."

"Any particular reason why she left?" Jackson asked.

Sloshing whiskey into glasses on a tray, Elam shrugged.
"She said it was time to move on. She was a friendly girl and

all, but Crystal kept pretty much to herself. Started out dating one or two of the customers, then all of a sudden she just up and quit going out with anyone at all. Oh, she was still real flirty, real fun, but me and the girls always thought there was someone secret she was seeing. Hell, we didn't care. She always came to work on time, always worked real hard. And she got along with everyone."

Katy leaned forward. "Do you know where she went when she quit?"

Elam squinted, and for the first time, stopped pouring whiskey and setting out glasses. His brows knit in concentration. "I think she was headed home to see her family."

"Where was home?" Katy persisted.

The bartender shot her a keen glance as Corinne rushed up and grabbed the tray from his hands. "Why're you so curious about Crystal?" he asked.

"It's a long story, Elam," Jackson said. "But it's important. We need to find her."

"All right, then. Let's see. Seems to me..." He scratched his jaw as Corinne dashed off with the tray, then suddenly nodded. "Tucson." He snapped his fingers. "Damned if that's not it. She hailed from Tucson. Ted paid her that night at the end of her shift, she said good-bye to everyone, and said she was leaving the next morning, taking the bus to Tucson."

Corinne scooted up to the bar again. "Two Scotch rocks for Sheriff Harvey and Bob McCoy," she called breathlessly, then scooped four beer bottles onto a tray with a mug of pretzel thins and hurried off. The bar had begun to fill up.

"That's all I know. Haven't heard hide nor hair from her since."

It was Jackson who asked the next question as the bartender dumped ice cubes into glasses and reached for the Jack Daniel's.

"You said she dated a few of the customers at first. Remember who?"

"Well, no, can't say as I do. Wait a minute... There was Fred Byers; he was one of the young hands at the Hanging X ranch. And Luke Dillard. Both of 'em were sweet on Crystal right off the bat."

"Luke Dillard dated her?" Katy gripped the bar. "For how long?"

"Not long at all, as I recall. Maybe once or twice. It didn't seem to go anywhere. He was just a kid back then, still in high school, and I didn't let him in here too much, but we always used to see him hanging around outside, waiting for Crystal to come on duty or to get off. Seemed odd to me, you know, her being twenty-one already and all, but I found out later that Crystal had lied about her age when she first came to work. She showed me and Ted a phony ID when she was hired. Turns out she was only eighteen herself."

Eighteen. The same age as Matt. Katy felt a lump in her throat. "What about Wood Morgan? Did he date her too?"

"Wood? Nah. Don't remember him being one of those sniffin' around her."

"How about Matt Templeton?" It was Jackson who asked the question, the one question Katy most wanted to ask, with the answer she dreaded hearing. She held her breath as the bartender gave Jackson a long look, then shook his head.

"Nope, never saw her and the Templeton boy together, if that's what you mean." He noticed Corinne waiting to give him more drink orders, and half turned toward her. "Look, anything else, folks? I got to catch up here, you know."

"One more question," Katy said quickly. "You said Crystal left around the time you were divorced. When was that exactly?"

"Signed the papers October 15, '88. Saddest day of my life. Crystal up and left a few days before or after, I can't remember which."

Katy swallowed hard, her thoughts spinning. Matt had fallen off the roof of the Jenssens' barn on October 19, 1988.

Was it the same day that Crystal Kirk had quit her job and left town? Was it just a coincidence that he'd died right around the time Crystal left Thunder Creek?

And did she really leave? a voice inside of her asked. Maybe she never got on that bus. Maybe something happened to her, something terrible, unthinkable, something Matt sketched right before he died...

Jackson took her by the arm. "Thanks, Elam. If you think of anything else, will you give me a call?"

Even as the bartender responded, "Sure thing, buddy," Jackson was leading her back to the table.

"Katy, are you all right?"

Her face was pale as Irish lace, her lips dry. But she nodded.

"Something happened to her, Jackson. Don't ask me how I know, but I do—something terrible happened to Crystal Kirk."

"It's beginning to look that way."

"She's dead. And Matt saw her. Didn't he?" The words seemed to stick to the roof of her mouth. "You think so too, don't you?"

His expression was guarded. "I think it's possible."

Katy's heart thudded. "We have to get in touch with her family. We have to find out if she ever made it home, if they ever saw her again. Then we'll know for cert—"

She broke off as Jackson's cell phone rang.

"Jackson Brent," he spoke curtly, his eyes fixed on Katy as she sat with fists tightly clenched, her eyes dark and enormous in the shadowy bar. Then his knuckles tightened around the phone.

"*What?* Hold on, I'll be right there." He dropped the phone back into its holster clipped to his belt and grabbed her arm. "Come on."

"Where are we going? Is there an emergency? Oh, God, is it Gram? Cleo?"

Jackson was already tossing money onto the table, propelling her toward the door. "That was Hatcher, my foreman. Someone cut through my dog Ajax's lead, and he ran off. One of the hands just found him crawling home through the south pasture—bleeding to death. He's been shot."

Elam waited a good ten minutes after they left, then strolled unhurriedly into the john. It was empty save for the smoke and the grime on the tile floor, a roll of toilet paper on the edge of the sink, and an empty beer bottle beside the trash can.

He pulled out his cell phone and rapidly pressed a series of buttons.

"We got trouble," he said when Wood Morgan answered his cell phone from his table inside the bar. "Yeah, that's right. The Templeton girl. And Jackson Brent. You need to figure out what you want me to do."

Chapter 16

KATY PACED BACK AND FORTH IN THE WAITING ROOM of Jackson's veterinary clinic, her mind racing. Even so, she couldn't help noticing the curious combination of drab and cheerful that characterized the clinic's decor. She'd never been to his family's ranch home before, never seen what the Brent place looked like before he converted it into a clinic, but she got hints from some of the furnishings—like the depressing, weathered old sofa with the lumpy, faded green cushions, and the scarred pine rocking chair with a tattered pillow propped at its back. The new all-white linoleum floors and freshly painted warm beige walls contrasted sharply with the gloomy holdovers scattered through the waiting room, where only the large rectangular blue-and-yellow striped rug looked new.

The former Brent home was quiet—too quiet. Jackson had driven here as if the devil pursued him, his jaw clenched, his face gray beneath his tan, his lips pressed tightly together. When they entered the house, Hatcher had called out, "In here!"

Jackson had disappeared into what once must have been a kitchen and dinette—but now was a sleek, blue-tiled examining and operating room. Katy had only a flashing glimpse of spotless floors and sea-blue walls, but she caught sight of a reddish-brown dog wrapped in a bloody blanket and she heard the pitiful yelps and cries of the animal just before the door slammed shut behind Jackson.

Her skin crawled at the thought that someone would be so cruel as to shoot a dog. And then she thought with a chill of Crystal Kirk and the cruelty of whoever had killed the girl— *if* someone had killed the girl.

And what about Matt? If Crystal was indeed dead, how did Matt know about it, why had he sketched her?

An icy sick feeling swamped her. She sank shakily down upon the lumpy sofa and took deep breaths, trying to sort through everything she'd learned today. She had a bad feeling that Crystal Kirk hadn't ever made it home, a bad feeling that Matt had indeed seen her lying dead somewhere right before he died.

And as she sat in the Brent family's former home, waiting to hear if Jackson's dog would survive, she wondered if there was a connection between what Matt had seen and sketched, and the accident that had taken his life. Had it really been an accident? Had Crystal's death been an accident? Or had someone killed her?

Matt, what was wrong? What secret was so terrible that you kept it from all of us?

She felt sick. Sick and clammy and frantic all at once. She had to know. For Matt's sake and for Crystal's, she had to find the truth. The word *murder* popped into her head more than once, and each time she pushed it out. Matt had nothing to do with any murder, she told herself, but there was a knot in her stomach that grew tighter by the moment.

When the door to the examining and operating rooms swung open, she tensed, dragging herself out of the desolate swirl of her thoughts and focusing her gaze on Jackson. He looked exhausted, but his eyes were the storm blue that preceded thunder.

He was followed by Hatcher, a slight man with a long

bony neck and small, shrewd gray eyes. But she barely noticed the foreman—her gaze was locked on Jackson's taut
face as she pushed herself to her feet.

"Ajax—is he—"

"It looks like he's going to make it."

All the pent-up adrenaline and fear for the animal had
drained out of him, and now he looked unutterably weary,
and oddly vulnerable. For one brief flashing moment she saw
a ghost, a ghost of a little boy haunted by loneliness and uncertainty, locked in the soul of a man starved for comfort.
She moved toward him then, not thinking, acting on pure
instinct, and embraced him quickly, then just as quickly,
stepped back, wondering at her own actions.

"I'm glad he's going to be okay," she said, to cover the
moment. "I'm glad you saved him."

"For now, maybe." His eyes were seeing something in the
distance, something she couldn't see. "But this isn't over."

The vulnerable boy and the weary man had disappeared.
The lonely soul was nowhere to be seen and instead she
gazed into the icy blue eyes of a man whose anger was only
just held in check, a man who seemed steeled against all
other emotion.

"Jackson—"

But he stepped away from her and swung toward Hatcher.
"Did you see anything? Anyone?"

"No, boss. Just came back here after checking on some
strays, and found the lead cut."

"Cut? You're sure it was cut? Ajax didn't break it?"

"It was cut." Hatcher's face was grim. "Then Ed called me
from his cell—said he'd just found the dog crawling through
the grass. I told him to bring him here and then I called you."

Jackson's jaw was tight as he strode toward the door.

"Wait, where are you going?" Katy ran forward and
blocked his path. He stopped short, staring at her, or rather
through her, almost as if he didn't even see her.

"Hatcher will take you home, Katy. I have to go. This was Dillard's doing."

"You don't know that—"

"He threatened to shoot Ajax days ago if he chased his cattle again. Now he's deliberately cut the dog's lead, set him free just so he'd have an excuse to go after him."

"In that case, let Sheriff Harvey handle this."

He stepped around her, his mouth set. "I take care of my own."

"No, wait." She grabbed his arm and held on. He could have shaken her off with one gesture, but he didn't. He just looked at her, quietly, intractably.

From behind him came the foreman's scratchy drawl. "Boss, maybe you should listen to her."

"Go home, Hatcher."

"But—"

"*Go home.*"

The foreman sighed. "Miz Templeton, can I give you a ride?"

"Thanks, but I'm not going anywhere." Katy's chin notched up and she tightened her grip on Jackson's arm. She knew he could shake her off and stalk past her anytime he wanted, but she wasn't going to make this easy for him. "I'll hang on to your ankles all the way to Dillard's ranch if you make me," she said flatly.

Hatcher smothered a chuckle as he stomped toward the door, but Jackson's expression didn't change. He didn't even seem to be looking at her, but looking instead deep into some personal hell of anger she couldn't even fathom. When the door slammed behind the other man, Jackson clamped one hand over hers and removed her slender fingers from his arm.

"I'll drop you off on my way. You'll want to check on things at the ranch."

"Cleo's fine. I called and checked in with Riley while you

were in there. And Gram's plane landed safely in Vegas. Tell me about Ajax."

"He was shot in the back leg. He lost a lot of blood, but it was a clean wound and we got him in time."

"The poor baby—will you take me in to see him?"

"He's resting now. Still coming out from under the anesthesia."

"Shouldn't we stay here so you can check on him?"

"Listen, Katy." His tone was taut. "I'm damned if I'll stand by and let that bloodthirsty bastard get away with no more than a rap on the knuckles for shooting my dog. If there's one thing I hate in this world it's a bully. And men who shoot dogs and hurt women and beat kids are bullies. Drunk or sober, in anger or just for fun, it's no excuse. Trust me, I know. I saw it enough in my own father, before I got big enough to take him on. He shot our family cat one night in one of his damned drunken rages. Right before my eyes."

"Oh, God, Jackson—"

"I might not be able to stop all of them, but I sure as hell can stop Luke Dillard."

"Listen, it's not that I don't understand how you feel. I do. But you don't know what you're doing right now. You're in shock, you're angry and upset. That's why you shouldn't confront Dillard tonight—who knows what could happen? What it might lead to . . . what would happen to *you* . . ."

"Don't worry about it." He strode past her, out of the clinic, letting the door slam behind him.

She stared after him, biting her lip. *Don't worry about it.* It wasn't that easy.

She ran for the door.

Outside the night was abloom with stars. A full moon gleamed like a polished pearl and the air burst with the clean scent of pine and the song of a thousand crickets. She caught Jackson as he yanked open the driver's door of his truck, and snatched the keys from his hand.

"What the hell!" Anger blazed in his face. He snagged back the keys. "Damn it, Katy, this doesn't concern you."

"Maybe not, but right now you're too angry to know what you're doing."

"I know exactly what I'm doing." But as he turned back to get into the truck, she suddenly pushed ahead of him, blocking his access to the seat.

"Then I'm going with you. You went with me to Allison's— I'll go with you to Luke's."

He stared at her incredulously. Not only was it absurd that she thought she could stop him, it was even more absurd that she would care enough to try.

"What's going on, Katy?" An odd note entered his voice. "There's something more than what you've told me."

"Don't be ridiculous. I meant what I said, you're too angry to think straight and going after Luke Dillard tonight is madness—"

"So what's it to you?" His gaze suddenly locked on hers, intent and focused for the first time since he'd finished tending to Ajax. "Could it be you actually care if I get myself killed?" he asked in a low tone.

"Don't flatter yourself." She smiled faintly and shrugged, hoping she appeared suitably flippant, but her heart was beginning to hammer at the intent way he was studying her. "But we *are* looking into this Crystal Kirk business together and . . . and two heads are better than one." She waved a hand airily. "Still, I'm sure I can manage perfectly well on my own if you really are determined to get yourself killed—"

"Uh-huh. No doubt." Thoughtfully, he dropped the keys in one pocket. Then he placed his hands on her shoulders and drew her toward him. "So let me get this straight," he said softly. "You're officially denying that there's something more here, something going on between us—between you and me?"

Uh-oh. An odd electricity swooshed through her. *You and me.* Exactly what he'd said at the barbecue.

"I . . . I . . . just don't want to see you end up in jail or . . . shot. Luke could shoot you as easily as he shot Ajax—"

"So?"

"So . . . fine. Go ahead. If you want to behave like a lunatic, don't let me—"

He kissed her. He simply lowered his head and kissed her.

The unexpectedness of it was a shock, yet Katy felt herself sliding into the kiss instead of trying to push him away. It was a dark kiss, dark and hot and ferocious, and it sent a shudder through her blood. The night with its moon and its mountains faded into a black blur as he kissed her some more, long and thoroughly, and somehow more deeply than she'd ever been kissed before.

Katy moaned and clung to him. With a sound like a growl, he pushed her up against the side of the truck and held her there with his body, while his hands threaded through her hair. Her pleasure ratcheted up, escalating with each touch of his hands, with each burning brand of his mouth on hers.

"Jackson," she gasped at last, when he finally dragged his mouth from hers. Then more softly, like a cry, a plea. "*Jackson.*"

He answered her with a kiss filled with gentleness, yet at its center was a scalding need. His hands found her breasts and she closed her eyes at the soft pleasure that spilled through her.

"I want you, Katy." His mouth scraped against her ear. "You have no idea how much I want you."

"I want you, too." To her horror, the words just slipped out as her mouth found his again, as her hands slid down that superbly muscled back.

This shouldn't be happening, she thought in shock. *None of this should be happening.* Not between the two of them.

But it was.

Stroking her hands through his hair, she breathed in the soul and the strength of him as they touched and tasted each other beneath the burning white moon.

"If you wanted to distract me, you're doing a hell of a good job." His voice was ragged. As ragged as she felt.

"Whatever works," she managed to gasp, clinging to his neck, touching her tongue to his lips, tracing them, shuddering inside.

"You're so beautiful—so damned beautiful." His fingers closed around her breast, then slipped inside the lace of her bra to find her nipple. As she moaned and arched her neck, helpless to protest and demur, helpless to think coherently, or do anything other than nestle closer against him in the darkness, they were both startled suddenly by the long blaring horn of a car. Jackson tensed and glanced at the road, where headlights glowed for an instant before disappearing around a curve.

"Oh, my God. Did they see us?" Katy had whipped back, away from him. She felt ridiculously like a teenager caught making out in the backseat of a car. Jackson shook his head.

"Probably not. Most likely they honked at a squirrel or a fox. But who knows?" he added, grinning. "What do you say we find some privacy? Come on."

Then he was pulling her, dragging her along with him behind the truck, behind the clinic. She had no idea where they were going as they ran through the darkness, past sheds and a barn, as the wind whistled around them and the stars glittered, hanging so low, so bright, so close it seemed they could have reached up and snagged one, or two, or a dozen to hold within their palms.

They went through a meadow, bathed in moonlight, then through a winding stretch of woods, and finally up a gently sloping rise. Then, on the other side, another fifty yards ahead, she saw it. A cabin, small and snug, in the shadow of Cougar Mountain. A single rectangle of light glowed at a window, outlining the simple log structure set within the trees.

"What's this?" she gasped breathlessly, running alongside him.

"Where I live."

"Not back there? In your old house? I thought you'd have a room in there somewhere—"

"No. Not there. Not for years. Here."

He pulled her toward the cabin, pushed open the door, and holding tight to her hand, led her inside.

At first she could see nothing but pitch darkness, then a flick of a switch brought golden light and as the door thudded shut behind them, Katy blinked at a long tan leather sofa, and deep nubby black chairs with matching ottomans. She caught a glimpse of a rough-hewn black granite fireplace, and of white-and-tan striped curtains at the windows, blocking out the night. There were crowded bookshelves and a writing desk tucked into the corner, and a handsome bronze sculpture of a horse running free atop a small table beside the sofa. A bright woven rug caught her eye—it covered nearly all of the burnished wood floor—and there was an entertainment center on the far wall, wih a TV, DVD, and CD player tucked into its deep mahogany shelves. Beyond the living room she spotted a kitchen and a hallway.

The cabin was masculine and comfortable and peaceful, and somehow it suited Jackson like an old, beloved pair of boots, she decided. No sooner had they burst through the door than he began tugging Katy toward the sofa, at the same time that an orange tiger cat stretched and pattered forward to rub against his leg. Then a yellow lab pup romped out of the kitchen, yapping happily.

"Forget it, guys." Jackson barely glanced at the animals;

his slow smile was for Katy alone. "I know for a fact Louisa Hatcher came by to feed you both. Now it's my turn."

"You're not going to introduce me?"

"Cammi the Cat and Regis the Dog," he said, putting his hands on her shoulders. He backed her toward the sofa, his eyes gleaming. "Now where were we?"

"We were acting crazy." The blare of the horn had broken the spell, and Katy had had time to think while they'd made their way to the cabin. She was still dizzy and breathless with the power of Jackson's kisses, with the heady sensuality his touch had sparked in her. She still wanted to feel his hands all over her, but she was sane enough now to know she should put on the brakes. "I think we need to—"

"Pick up where we left off," he finished for her with a grin so lazy and so sexy, her heart flipped over. Then he eased her down on the sofa, eased himself over her, and his mouth touched hers again with infinite gentleness.

She wanted to argue, to be sensible and realistic and cautious, but she was lost. Lost in his kisses, in his arms. He stroked her face, then her throat, then her breasts. Soft, sure touches, so gentle and yet so strong. Butterflies danced in her stomach and an ache throbbed deep within her. Her hands scraped through the thick silk of his hair, then slid down to caress his lean jaw as his body shifted subtly, covering hers. Clever hands took hold of her sweater and tugged it over her head, tossing it aside. His gaze lit as it came to rest on her breasts, swelling above the peach lace of her bra. As he touched them, and his gaze burned, a rush of pleasure raced through her, electric and sweet.

It had been a long time since she'd been with a man. Then it had been with Seth. The last time they'd made love she'd been trying to forget, to forget the heartache of her lost baby, trying to capture hope and magic in Seth's firm, ropy arms and agile body. But it hadn't happened. Whatever magic they'd known hadn't been strong enough, or maybe *she* hadn't been strong enough.

Tonight was different, so different. A deep roaring need surged through her, and the intensity of Jackson's gaze both soothed and seduced her. Why did she feel so alive with him, so vibrant and aroused? Was it only that she was recovering finally from the past, from the dead dreams of her marriage and her pregnancy, or was it more...

All she knew was that his touch felt so good she wanted to stay here beneath him, close to him. She wanted these deep, longing kisses to go on, she wanted to feel him deep inside her. She wanted to heal the loneliness she'd glimpsed in him, the loneliness that echoed her own. She wanted to make him grin that damnably sexy grin...

Slow down, you fool. You're acting like an idiot. Panic rippled through her, icy and sharp. *It's too soon. You can't trust him. This is a physical attraction, nothing more, and that's not what you want, not what you do. Do you want to be just another notch on Jackson Brent's gunbelt?*

"Jackson...stop. Please. We have to stop." She wrenched her mouth from his, ceased her stroking of his broad back, and let her hands drop down to her sides.

He groaned. Or maybe cursed. "What's wrong?" He eased back, shifted. One hand, one warm, strong hand, with its callused, gentle fingers, lingered at the delicate fastening on her bra.

"Katy—"

"We can't...*I* can't...I'm sorry, let me up."

He groaned again, shifted again, easing back and letting her wriggle out from beneath him, leaving him alone on the sofa.

"You're a cruel woman, Katy Templeton."

"I'm sorry."

Breathing hard, he watched her pull the sweater over her head, and tug it down to cover those beautiful breasts.

"Are you all right?" His blood was hot, but cooling down now, rapidly, painfully, as he saw that her eyes were filled with uncertainty. "I didn't hurt you, did I?"

"No. No, you were ... you didn't hurt me. It's just that I can't do this."

"Why not?" He went to her, stopped right in front of her. God knew, he wanted to touch her again. But if he did, it would be hell to stop. "What are you afraid of?" he asked quietly.

"It's too soon. I told you before. I'm not ready."

"You sure felt ready. You felt right. Perfect. Seemed like you thought so too."

His muscles ached with the wanting of her, and the irony of the situation smacked him in the chest. He never brought the women he dated here. Even though Lee and Smoke and the guys kidded him that the cabin was a perfect bachelor pad, when he slept with a woman it was always at her place. Surrounded by her things, by plants and candles and silk sheets and the like, by dressers holding perfume bottles and powders and creams.

He never shared this place with anyone. Kelly had never been here, neither had Angela or Val or any of the others.

They touched his life, but they didn't belong to it. *In it.* Not in any way that mattered.

This cabin was his sanctuary, his refuge from the outside world, from everyone—even the women who touched his life.

So why had it felt right bringing Katy here? Maybe because she lightened it, brightened it, sweetened it with the way she moved, with the glow that clung to her. Even her hair gleamed in the ordinary lamplight like radiant bronze.

"I think you must be trying to kill me," he said with a rueful smile. "Don't you know, this kind of a letdown can really hurt a guy?"

"I'm sorry," she said again. "So, you hate me now, right?"

The apologetic smile she offered him heated his blood all over again and it was all he could do not to wrap his arms around her once more.

Hell, that bastard husband had really done a number on her. Hurt her bad. For a moment it was a toss-up which man he'd like to beat the crap out of more: Luke Dillard or Katy's ex-husband.

"Hate's a far cry from what I feel," he said. He raked a hand through his hair. "How about some coffee before I take you home?"

Relief flooded her face, rewarding him for what the words *take you home* cost him.

"Coffee would be great."

Not as great as sex, he thought. He started toward the kitchen then turned back. "You think you've won, don't you? You think you've distracted me from pulverizing Dillard."

"Haven't I?"

It was good to see the saucy grin return to her face.

He nodded. "For now."

"Good. I'll settle, for the time being."

"Yeah. I know what you mean. So will I." He continued to gaze at her, his eyes warm and deliberate in the lamplight, making her heart suddenly skip a beat.

"Only I'm not talking about Dillard," Jackson said. "I'm talking about us—you and me. I guess you could call it a delay of game—I'm giving you some time. As much as you need." Slowly, he came back toward her and took her hand. He enclosed it gently but solidly within his.

"But don't think for a minute that what started between us tonight is over. And don't even try to pretend that you want it to be."

Chapter 17

THEY SAT IN THE BRIGHTLY LIT KITCHEN AT A SQUARE pine table, with Cammi and Regis drowsing under a boot bench near the door, and with the heady aroma of fresh coffee filling the room. Beyond the window, moonlight bathed the mountains and the dark, rolling land, and the vastness of the night seemed to stretch forever. But here it was cozy and quiet and comfortably intimate and Katy sipped her coffee as Jackson Brent told her how he'd adopted Regis from a shelter in Butte, how Cammi had been a stray who just showed up one day and tried to move into the barn, and how he'd found Ajax abandoned and wounded on the side of the road.

"He's had some bad breaks in his life." He drained the last of his coffee and set the mug on the table with a small thump.

"Yes, but your finding him was his lucky day. He's going to be all right, Jackson."

"He'd better be."

The worry that knit his brows touched her more than she cared to admit. "Why don't we go back and check on him now? It'll make you feel better."

"In a few minutes. He's probably still out. Another half hour," he glanced at his watch, "and he'll be waking up. Right now, I want to know about you. The call came in about

Ajax and we never got to talk about what Elam said about Crystal."

"I've been working on taking it all in." She lifted her coffee cup, cradling her palms around its warmth. "I've got a horrible feeling that something terrible happened to Crystal Kirk. And that Matt knew about it before he died. I don't know how he knew, or what the pact was all about, but I'm going to find out. If that sounds like I'm jumping to conclusions, then I'm sorry, but..."

"I don't think you're jumping to conclusions. I think Matt did see something. Just what he showed in that sketch: Crystal was dead. But we can't prove it. Not yet."

Crystal was dead. Hearing him say the words aloud made it seem even more real, and more horrible. A shudder chased down her spine.

"And what about Matt?" he continued, very quietly.

A silence fell in the room. But Katy heard her own heartbeat drumming in her ears. "What about him?" she asked, unable to keep a note of defiance from her tone.

Jackson's gaze was steady and his tone even. "He told Allison he'd done something terrible. Don't you want to know what that was?"

"Of course I want to know. Matt was upset and depressed for the entire week before he died, and I want to know why. I want to know in case it ties in to this whole thing." She set down her coffee cup with a thump and glared at him across the table. "But if you're implying that the 'something terrible' was Matt killing Crystal, and then drawing a sketch of her body," she placed both hands on the table, her eyes flashing, "then you didn't really know my brother at all."

"Calm down," Jackson told her. "I didn't say he had anything to do with her death. And I didn't mention anything about murder. I know Matt would never have hurt anyone, least of all that girl."

"You're damned right about that." She swallowed, her throat

suddenly too tight and achy for her to continue. No, Matt would never have hurt Crystal, never... but still, there had been something going on in her brother's life that no one had known about. There had been a side of Matt she'd been unaware of and it disturbed her more than she could say. She'd openly idolized him all her life, even in the years after he died, and now, to find out that the boy she'd thought was perfect—grounded, wise, and as solid in his own sense of self as anyone she'd ever met—had actually done something "terrible," that there'd been an awful secret in his life before he died, cast a shadow over her heart. And made her wonder about the "accident" that had sent Matt falling to his death from the Jenssens' roof.

"Crystal may have died in some kind of mishap," Jackson mused, staring into the black depths of his coffee as if trying to peer back in time.

"Yes, but then why wouldn't Matt have come forward? Why didn't he tell Big John and Mom, and explain what happened to Sheriff Harvey?"

"Maybe he meant to. He did write Sheriff Harvey's name and your dad's on his to-do list. It seems to me he *meant* to go to them, but he never had the chance. He fell off the roof before he could tell anyone."

"Fell... or was pushed," Katy said slowly.

Jackson's expression was grim. "It does seem like a helluva coincidence that *she* would have died accidentally and then so did *he*. Especially considering his state of mind that last week."

"So maybe it wasn't an accident. Either one of them. Maybe Crystal was killed... and Matt was, too," Katy whispered. Horror rose in her as she spoke the words aloud, and she gripped the edge of the table. "Oh, God, Jackson, what if someone killed him because he knew what happened to Crystal?"

"Then we'll find out who that someone was and he'll pay."

Jackson paused, noting the sudden pallor in her face, and then went on, choosing his words carefully. "There's another possibility to consider, Katy. You won't like it."

She already knew what it was. She met his gaze directly, her heart lurching. "My brother did *not* jump off that roof intentionally. He didn't kill himself because of Crystal, or because of whatever secret he was keeping. Matt wouldn't do that."

"I don't think he would either. But—"

"No buts." Katy jumped up from the table, clenching her hands at her sides. "I don't care how upset he was, how depressed, or what kind of secret he was hiding, he wouldn't have done *that*. I won't let anyone say he did."

He stood too and came around the table, but when he reached for her, she stepped back.

"Do you know what this will do to my mother . . . and Big John? And Gram? All of this. When they hear . . ." She shook her head, and swallowed hard. "Even the mention of suicide would kill them. And who knows what Matt's secret was? What the pact involved? Oh, God, I wish I hadn't ever found the sketch. I should have left it alone. Whatever we find out is going to tear them apart and it's my fault—"

"Cut it out, Katy. None of this is your fault. The truth always comes out sooner or later, about everything, and if anyone was murdered, that needs to come out too, no matter who gets hurt. Your family can survive it."

"I hope to God you're right," she said through clenched teeth.

"I'm more concerned about you." He stepped closer, his jaw tight. "Can you handle whatever you might learn about Matt? Can you deal with it if you find out he wasn't really perfect after all?"

"I never thought he was perfect," she began with a spurt of anger, but then she broke off. Maybe she had thought that. Maybe she'd idolized Matt more than he deserved, more than any human deserved. *Or could live up to,* she thought in despair.

"Don't worry about me." She took a deep breath. "I can handle . . . whatever I need to handle."

He hoped to God it was the truth. Doubt flickered in his eyes as he noted the taut muscles in her throat, the weariness in her shoulders.

She noticed his careful appraisal and spoke quickly. "I'm not going to pieces, Jackson. It's too late for tears, for hysterics. Fourteen years have gone by. It hurts me, yes." Her voice trembled. "It's like a knife in my heart, slicing it into thin, agonizing strips, but I can't give in to it. Not yet. Because if someone killed my brother . . ." She sucked in her breath. Saying the words hurt so much she thought her chest would explode. But she had to get used to them. "If someone killed my brother, I'll find him . . . or her . . . whoever," she finished. "And whoever it was will pay."

"You can damn well bet on that." He didn't move so much as a muscle but there was a tension throbbing through him that communicated itself even to the sleeping animals. Regis lifted his head, looked at the man standing beside the table, and whined. The tiger cat eyed him alertly.

"We're going to get to the bottom of this and find out the truth. If after all these years it turns out that Matt's accident was no accident . . ." He drew in a breath. "God, Katy."

"I know."

The implications of it made her want to pound her fist through a wall, to howl and scream and weep. But she couldn't do any of those things. She could only try to be calm and smart, to dig deep, as deep as it took to uncover the truth. She owed Matt that. And she'd do it, no matter the cost.

"What about Sheriff Harvey? Do you want to bring him in on this?"

"Not yet." She shook her head, remembering her visit to the sheriff's office. What more did she know now than she'd known then? That Crystal Kirk, a waitress at the Tumble-weed Bar and Grill, had disappeared. That she'd supposedly left town around the same time as Matt's accident. That he'd sketched her shortly before he died, perhaps the very same day. And that she looked dead in the sketch.

None of that was proof of anything. She needed more, just a little more before she went to the sheriff. Enough to give him a compelling reason to open an investigation into events that had taken place fourteen years ago. If she went to him too soon, and then kept going back, with bits and pieces here and there, he might start dismissing her as some kind of nutcase.

But there was another reason she didn't want to go to the sheriff yet, a reason she wouldn't admit to Jackson, only to herself. Her family. She wanted to spare her parents and Gram for as long as possible from having to reexamine that time in their lives. From knowing about Matt's secret, and the mysterious pact, and hearing that he'd done something terrible. What if it was all a mistake, a horrible misunder-standing? All she had was Allison's words—and the sketch.

No, she decided, thinking of her parents blithely enjoying Paris, of Gram counting her winnings in Las Vegas. There would be time to go to the sheriff, time to shatter her family's peace of mind. And time to open an official investigation that could well lead to everyone in Thunder Creek finding out all the painful things she was discovering herself.

"Let's wait until we come up with some more," she told Jackson. She paced toward the window, then came back to face him, resolution in her eyes. "I think we should try to find Crystal's family."

"I can start searching on the Internet. My laptop's in the bedroom."

"It's all right, I'll do it at home. It's time I headed back." Staying here alone with him for much longer didn't seem like a good idea. She gathered up their empty mugs and carried them to the sink.

Watching her, Jackson fought the blunt sensation of loss he felt merely because she was going home. He still wanted her. He wanted to drag his hands through that soft, honey-colored hair of hers and kiss her until they were both gasping for breath. And he wanted to have sex with her right there on the rug, to taste every soft inch of her before the night was through.

What had happened between them tonight had only fired up his curiosity and his desire. And he had a pretty good feeling she felt the same. But she was scared, and wary. It would be better for both of them if they could keep this at bay, at least until they'd finished working together on what had happened fourteen years ago.

Jackson acknowledged to himself that if he let himself get too into Katy Templeton now, it would be a definite distraction. And considering the importance of what they were trying to figure out, neither one of them could afford to be distracted. But she was too damned sexy, too damned beautiful. She'd tasted like sweet wild honey. And he wanted more.

"I'd still like to peek in on Ajax before we go," she said as she set the cups in the sink.

"You've got it."

Jackson came up behind her, and rested his hands upon her shoulders.

An enticing warmth flowed through Katy as he turned her gently to face him.

"You're a damned remarkable woman."

She shook her head. "I'm not as calm as I seem. I'm simply . . . putting one foot in front of the other. Just as I've been doing ever since my d—" She bit her lip. "Never mind."

"Your divorce?"

For some reason, she didn't flinch at the word. Maybe it was the quiet way he said it.

"Yes. It's gotten me through."

"I never met the guy, but I can tell you, he's an idiot."

That made her laugh, a small laugh, but it was genuine enough, rich, low, and musical. "Seth wouldn't agree with you. He'd say he was smart... smart to get out when he did. I was dragging him down."

"You? Impossible."

"You don't know the whole story, Jackson." She forced herself to move away from him, away from the comforting strength of those hands on her shoulders. She edged closer to the boot bench where Cammi and Regis had curled closer together.

"Tell me."

"Usually when a couple decides to have a baby, it brings them closer together." Her mouth twisted. "That isn't what happened with us."

"Why not?"

"Seth didn't really want a baby. Not like I did." God, it hurt to say those words, even though she'd faced up to the facts a long time ago. She sighed. "He kept putting me off every time I brought up the subject—and then some of our friends started getting pregnant. So one day out of the blue he decided it was the thing to do. I think that part of it was an attempt to humor me, and part of it was... going with the flow, I guess you'd say. I don't know, he joked once that it would be cool to have a son, a little heir to the Warfield dynasty." Her mouth trembled. "The irony was, after our baby died, we found out she was a girl. He would have had to settle for an heiress," she added with a faint tinge of bitterness she couldn't suppress. She swallowed, trying to keep the pain from her voice, trying to speak with equanimity about something that cut too deep to ever fully heal.

"It broke me," she whispered. "Losing her. It tore me up more than anything ever had before... except maybe losing Matt. It was a month before I could go back to work. I just cried all the time. My doctor put me on antidepressants, and I started functioning somewhat better. I still felt sad, so awfully sad, but I went back to work—I tried to pick up my life. But I started hating all the traveling I had to do to different restaurant sites. And hating all the parties and meetings and schmoozing with the investors and with Seth's other business partners. I just wanted to spend more time at home, I wanted peace and quiet. Seth, on the other hand," she added, taking a deep breath, "picked up right where he'd left off, and he couldn't understand why I couldn't shake off the blues."

"Not only an idiot, a *dense* idiot," Jackson said.

"He told me I wasn't myself, that he missed the upbeat vivacious go-getter who'd managed a chain of five restaurants and made it look easy. But in the months after losing my baby," she said softly, "nothing was easy for me—not life, not business, not . . . my marriage."

"I'm sorry."

Her gaze met his, pain shimmering too brightly in her eyes. "I went into counseling, grief counseling. I wanted him to come too, I thought it would help us both, and help our marriage, but he said he was too busy. He was busy all right. With a babe on the side. A twenty-two-year-old assistant manager at our Boston restaurant."

She turned away again, and Jackson swore silently as she paced restlessly to the window. She hugged her arms around herself and stared out at the night.

"After I filed for divorce, Seth and his bimbo found out she was pregnant. Kind of funny, don't you think? He married her. Their baby is due in the fall."

"You're better off without him."

"You're telling me." She whirled to face him. Her face looked strained and weary, but her eyes were dry. "Sorry to burden you with my past," she said tightly. "But that's it. Now you know the whole story, and you know why I'm not ready to get involved with anyone, in any way. I might never be ready—"

"That's pretty extreme, don't you think?"

"No. I'm being honest." She forced herself to say the words. "I may never be ready to let another man into my life, not even casually, and certainly not someone who might—"

She broke off, biting her lip, and Jackson jumped into the breach, quick as a panther. "Someone who might what? Touch your heart? Make you care? Make you feel vulnerable again?"

"What are you, a psychotherapist?"

He grinned and went to her, framing her face with his hands. "You might say I know the syndrome. Maybe I even invented it. You and I have more in common than you think."

"God help me."

He laughed, and she couldn't help smiling back at him. She felt it surge again—that warm, dangerous pull between the two of them and a shudder ran through her.

She fought the pull.

"I won't let myself be vulnerable again. Not like that. It's only fair to warn you—"

"Okay, I'm warning you too." Jackson's tone was frank. "I'm not in the market for a lifetime partner. Otherwise known as a wife. Love, commitment, vulnerability, those aren't on my agenda either. So now we've both been warned. That said . . ."

He leaned toward her and she might have flinched away, but she didn't. She couldn't. His eyes burned into hers, and despite everything, she wanted him to kiss her again, wanted to feel that rush of emotion and awakening. She'd felt dead inside for too long. And Jackson Brent, who didn't want a wife, didn't want to fall in love, made her feel alive.

It was a hot kiss, the kiss of a man who'd kissed many women, and it was edged with life and danger and need. It sent arousal licking through her. Her body trembled. And when he raised his head, her eyes were closed, her lips moist and still parted.

"You . . . shouldn't have done that," she chided, but it came out as a sigh. "It's not fair."

"Tell me about it."

A small laugh broke from her. But when he bent to kiss her again, she pushed him away. "Jackson, I think I've lived dangerously enough for one night. I have to go."

He released her, even though his body burned for more. Much more. Digging out his keys he followed her out of the kitchen and through the living room to the cabin door.

"I'll take a rain check then," he said as he opened the door.

"I think that can be arranged."

Her heart lifted when he smiled at her. But she knew she was in trouble. Big trouble. She was passing Go without a cent in her pocket. And this was a tricky game, one she'd never really learned how to play.

You are so *out of your league,* she told herself. But she felt a rush of warmth as he slipped his hand around hers. Together they walked outside into the smooth dark of night.

Chapter 18

He dreamed of her that night.

Not the way he'd last seen her—lifeless and still, her eyes open, her red mouth slack, bruises on her throat. No, he dreamed of her the way she'd looked when she'd invited him into her bed for the very first time. Smiling, seducing, her laughter girlish, soft as summer flowers. The sight of her heavy breasts and sleek long legs had filled him with a lust raw as blood, and with a keening pleasure. He'd tangled his hands in her hair, that coarse bushy red hair that smelled of raspberry shampoo and cigarettes, and toppled upon her before she'd even unhooked her bra.

Her panties had ripped in his hands as he tore them off and she'd laughed as he plunged inside her.

No one like you ever paid attention to me before, she'd told him afterward, and she'd been as pleased and excited as he at what had started between them.

He awoke with the scent of her in his nostrils, of her sweat and her cigarettes and her thick, sweet hair. He almost felt her in the shadows, drifting closer through the dark.

He felt clammy all over and his own sweat drenched him like cool blood as he stared wild-eyed around the pitch-black room.

I never wanted to kill you, he whispered. *I never wanted to kill anyone. Jesus, leave me alone.*

He hadn't dreamed about her in a long time. He'd thought the dreams were over.

Until tonight.

Something was bringing it all back. No, not something. *Someone.*

Katy Templeton.

She was asking questions. A lot of questions. *But maybe she'll drop it,* he thought, lying rigid in the dark, staring in cold silent desperation at the ceiling. *Maybe she'll just let it go.*

Queasiness rippled through his gut. Katy Templeton would have to be watched. She'd have to be taken care of . . . if need be.

He prayed it wouldn't come to that. He'd give her a chance. A warning. It was only right. And if it went well, everything would be fine. This could all blow over and amount to no more than a hill of beans.

Yet, he knew deep down that he couldn't afford to deny the truth. Katy Templeton could ruin him. She could ruin everything—his life, his reputation. He'd have to do a damned good job persuading her to leave the past behind.

And to shut the hell up.

If she wanted to live . . .

Chapter 19

"I THINK YOU'D BETTER TELL ME WHAT HAPPENED IN here yesterday."

It was 7 A.M. and Katy had just whipped the first batch of blueberry muffins from the oven to cool, and placed two cherry pies on the center shelf when Billy let himself in through the unlatched kitchen door.

"You heard? Already?" Dismayed, his gaze darted to her face.

"Oh, yes, I heard." Drawing four cartons of eggs from the refrigerator, she set them on the counter. "But I want to hear your version of events. Particularly about Daffodil."

There was a pause, then Billy gave a shrug. "She had to go home, that's all. Stomachache. She was all doubled over—it looked real bad." He rushed on before Katy could interrupt with any questions. "So I handled everything myself. It wasn't too bad, not really. A few folks were mad because things got slowed down, and some of the food got cold, but I didn't charge them. I'll . . . I'll make it up out of my pay," he added quickly as Katy studied him intently, her expression carefully neutral.

"Daffodil got sick? That's not what I heard."

"What do you mean?" Billy started filling the creamers,

setting out coffee cups and plates for the early morning customers, who'd be arriving in less than an hour.

"I heard she took off with Corey Dillard."

Billy spilled some of the cream over the side of the creamer and swore as he grabbed a rag and wiped it up. "Who was the big mouth who told you that?" he muttered, refusing to look at her.

"That doesn't matter. I just want to know if it's true."

"Well, sorta. I mean, yes, okay, she did go off with that creep, but . . . you're not going to fire her, are you?"

The boy's gaze fixed upon her earnestly. "She needs this job, Katy. I know Daffodil acts like a ditz, but she's smart, and she wants to go to college. And her mom won't help her."

"Why not?"

"She's too busy trying to get Daffodil's sister into the movies, or TV or something." He scowled. "Rose is gorgeous, and she wants to be an actress. Mrs. Moline always wanted to be an actress too. She spends every penny supporting Rose in L.A. while she goes on auditions and stuff. Mrs. M always used to tell Daff that she'd be able to get a bunch of scholarships and wouldn't need help like Rose did. But Daff kinda screwed up her life and now . . ." He shook his head, his eyes dark with disgust. "It's a long story—just take my word for it. She needs this job."

"Billy, she ran off and left you all alone here while I was gone," Katy exclaimed, staring at him incredulously. "I'd have expected you to be the first one yelling that she deserves to be fired."

"Well . . . uh . . . I didn't say I'm not mad at her, but maybe if you just talk to her, you know, give her hell and all, she won't do it again."

He fumbled the cream again, knocked over one of the cups, and caught it just before it rolled off the counter onto the floor.

"Come here, Billy." Katy took his arm, pulled him over to

one of the booths, and pushed him toward the seat. "Have you had breakfast yet?"

"No, ma'am."

"Stay there. Don't move."

Three minutes later she set a glass of orange juice and one of the blueberry muffins hot from the oven down in front of him, as well as a hastily prepared omelette.

"Eat that. And you can talk with your mouth full because I want to know exactly what happened in here and why you're sticking up for Daffodil."

By the time he'd polished off the eggs and orange juice and left only a handful of crumbs on the plate where the muffin had sat, she'd pried the story from him.

The diner had been busier than usual, Daffodil and Billy were snapping at each other, rushing around trying to keep things on track, and Daffodil had accidentally dropped a plate of burgers and fries on the floor just as she was serving it to Randy Purcell. He'd yelled at her for her clumsiness and stalked out without waiting for another plate of food, and she'd burst into tears. The next thing Billy knew, Corey Dillard had shown up, told Daffodil that she deserved the day off, and hustled her out of the diner and into his Explorer, saying something about a drive in the mountains.

"For what it's worth, she tried to argue with him," Billy muttered, "but he just laughed and said he knew what was best for her, and why would she want to be stuck indoors working on a nice summer day like that when they could be together? Then he kinda dragged her toward the door." Scowling, Billy dropped his fork onto his plate.

"That's when I ran up front and told him to take his filthy hands off her. He started toward me, and I wished like anything he'd have tried to hit me, but Daffodil jumped in the way and then she started pulling on his arm, saying, 'Come on, Corey, let's go. Let's get out of here.'" Billy grimaced. "She told me to go to hell."

Katy studied him a moment. "Then what happened?"

"The fries were burning, so I ran back to the grill, and the next thing I knew, the door slammed shut and Daffodil and Corey were gone. I tried to keep up with all the orders, but I guess I wasn't fast enough. I didn't do such a good job, did I?"

"You did the best you could, Billy. Why didn't you call me?"

"I kept hoping Daffodil would come back. I . . . I guess I didn't want her getting in trouble."

That much was obvious. Katy spoke bluntly. "I thought you and Daffodil couldn't stand each other."

"We can't. At least, she can't stand me." He slumped back against the seat. "But I'm damned if I know what she sees in that jerk Dillard."

She didn't answer him. From what she'd seen, Corey Dillard was bad-boy smooth, and what most girls would call a hottie. He dressed well, he wore his hair in the latest style, he had what her mother had always referred to as bedroom eyes. Not to mention a know-it-all attitude. *Just like his uncle,* she reflected. Back when she was in high school, she'd thought Luke Dillard was hot stuff too—until she found out better one night in the woods.

A shudder slid down her spine, and she hoped Daffodil wasn't getting in too deep with Corey. Because if he was anything like his uncle . . .

"It's very noble of you to try to protect her," she told Billy, and his ears turned pink. Obviously the boy still cared about Daffodil—maybe more than he'd ever admit. No wonder he didn't want her getting fired. Not only did she need the job, Billy needed to have her around. Katy was willing to bet that the only chance he had to talk to her was when they were both working at the diner.

"But if anything like this ever happens again," Katy continued, "I need to know the truth. Immediately. Got that?"

When Billy nodded, Katy glanced at her watch. "Time to open for business. Let's get moving."

As Billy scooted for the kitchen and fired up the grill, she unlocked the door and flipped the Closed sign in the window to Open. But as she returned to the kitchen she temporarily forgot about the troubles in the diner and her thoughts turned to what had happened—or rather what had *almost* happened—between her and Jackson last night.

In the cold light of day, she couldn't believe she'd come so close to plunging into a red-hot involvement with a no-strings-attached man. It was so un-Katy. And it was the last thing she'd intended to do when she'd moved back to Thunder Creek. But even now, tingles danced through her as she thought of Jackson's deep, demanding kisses, of the smooth hot texture of his skin beneath her fingers, and the electrifying heat of his hard-muscled body pressed against hers.

But after all that had happened, he hadn't even kissed her good night when he dropped her off at home. *That's a good thing,* she told herself. Maybe he was letting her get some distance. Giving her what she wanted. Space. And time.

Or maybe he was having second thoughts himself.

Disappointment quivered through her. *Stop it,* she told herself. *Don't let whatever you're starting to feel for Jackson Brent get in the way of what you need to focus on now.*

And that was getting to the truth about what happened to Crystal Kirk. And to Matt.

Katy's spine tightened. Nothing could get in the way of that.

Last night, unable to sleep after Jackson brought her home, she'd started her on-line search for Crystal Kirk's family. Through the on-line White Pages, she'd located dozens of Kirks in Tucson, and their phone numbers, and tonight after work she'd start calling them, seeing if she could track down Crystal's family.

As a stream of people began finding their way into

Bessie's Diner, hungry for eggs and sausage and muffins and coffee, and to share the news of the day with their friends and neighbors, she was forced to shift her attention to the most immediate problem confronting her.

She needed a waitress, and she needed one now.

Daffodil Moline had not shown up for work, nor had she returned Katy's phone calls.

Gritting her teeth, Katy grabbed menus, setups, and coffee cups. Then she pasted a smile on her face and went to work.

The Moline house was in need of paint, a new roof, and a window-washing. Not much bigger than Bessie's Diner, it huddled, small and squat at the end of a dirt road five miles outside of town as if it were hiding from the rest of the world.

Pulling up into a weed-choked yard, Katy noted the beat-up Jeep Daffodil drove parked behind the house, but saw no other cars. The house's curtains were closed and there wasn't a sound in the still, hot air.

Maybe she's not here, Katy thought as she pressed the bell. She waited a minute, then pressed it again.

She was about to turn and walk away when she heard a muffled voice from the other side of the door.

"I'm sick, Ms. Templeton. You'd better go away, you don't want to catch it. I'll... I'll try to make it into work tomorrow."

"Open the door, Daffodil. I need to talk to you. And I'm not going anywhere until I do."

For a moment she was afraid the girl was planning to ignore her, but then she heard the bolt click and the door creaked open.

Katy stared at the bedraggled figure before her.

Daffodil wore a baggy sweatshirt and cutoff blue jean

shorts. Her feet were bare, and her normally lustrous golden hair hung in limp, uncombed tangles around her face.

And her face . . .

The pert, pretty features and milky-blue eyes didn't look quite so Kewpie doll cute today. Daffodil's eyes were red-rimmed and swollen from crying, her lashes still damp with tears, and there was a faint bruise on her cheek, which she'd obviously tried to mask with a thick layer of makeup.

It hadn't worked. The faint bluish bruise was still apparent on her soft, curved cheek, its outline dark and alien against the golden tan of her skin.

"Daffodil, what happened to you?" Katy asked quickly.

Flushing, the girl touched a hand to her cheek. "Nothing," she said defensively. "I . . . I told you, I'm sick. I—"

"You don't look sick. You look like someone used you for a punching bag."

"No, I fell. I fell out of bed in my sleep and . . . I have to go now, I think I might throw up. I'll come to work tomorrow."

She tried to close the door, but Katy stuck her foot against it and reaching out at the same time, placed a gentle hand on the girl's arm.

"Daffodil, let me in. Whatever's wrong, I want to help you."

"I don't need any help."

"Is your mother at home?"

Alarm flared in the girl's eyes. "No. She's in L. A. with my sister. She's coming back tonight maybe . . . or tomorrow. But please—don't tell her I'm in trouble at work, Ms. Templeton—she'd be really upset."

"Calm down, Daffodil. I'm not planning to tell her what happened at the diner. I just want to talk to you. Please, won't you let me come in?"

The girl's lips quivered. She looked like she didn't know whether to try to slam the door, or to just run away. Instead she stepped back, her shoulders slumping. "Whatever. I . . . I don't care," she said with a carelessness that sounded forced.

Following her into the dim hall, Katy couldn't help noticing the dingy pale yellow walls and tattered brown couch in the living room, the clothes and shoes strewn everywhere, the stains on the worn yellow linoleum floor. Somehow she'd never pictured Daffodil, who always looked fresh and pretty in stylish teen clothes, living in a home as badly in need of some spit and polish and a good spring cleaning as this one.

"Whatever Billy told you, it's not true." Daffodil sank down on the lumpy sofa and pulled her knees up, hugging her arms around them. "He hates me because I broke up with him. He just wants to get me in trouble. I'm sorry I had to leave early yesterday, but I'll make it up to you if you let me keep my job. I'll turn over all my tips to you for the next week and—"

"I don't want your tips, Daffodil," Katy said evenly. "I want to know why you left. And by the way, Billy didn't try to get you in trouble. As a matter of fact, he lied for you—he told me you were sick and had to go home, when the truth is, you left with Corey Dillard to spend the day with him. True or false?"

Daffodil was gaping at her. "Billy . . . didn't tell you . . . about me and Corey?"

"No. Not at first. He covered for you. Or at least, he tried to." Katy slipped into a chair whose upholstery was faded, with a ripped seam at the corner. "I don't think he hates you as much as you think he does. It sounded to me like he was trying to protect you."

"Billy wouldn't do that. He thinks I'm trash. Just because I got tired of having him for my boyfriend and wanted to go out with Corey." She raked a hand through her tangled hair, pressed her hands to her face, and began to cry. "Great decision that was, huh?" she muttered, half to herself.

Katy went to her, sank down on the sofa, and put a hand on the girl's trembling arm. "Katy, what happened yesterday? Did Corey hurt you? Did he give you that bruise?"

"No! I fell, I told you," Gulping in deep breaths, Daffodil managed to choke down her sobs. She pressed the palms of her hands to her eyes. "I need to go upstairs and take a shower," she said. "I don't want my mom to see me like this when she gets home."

"Maybe she should see you. Maybe you need to talk to her about what happened yesterday."

"What do you mean...about yesterday?" Daffodil's eyes widened, and her face went pale. "Oh...you mean, about leaving work."

"There's that. And there's also that bruise you're sporting. And the fact that you've obviously been crying all day."

"I just don't like being sick, okay?"

"If Corey hit you, Daffodil, you need to tell your mother," Katy said firmly. "Or me. Or someone. And you need to stay away from him."

"He didn't hit me! I never told you that. I never told you one word about yesterday!" Daffodil cried. She pushed herself to her feet, her eyes wide and frantic. "I think you'd better go—I'm going to be sick. I have to get to the bathroom."

She ran down the hall, the floor creaking beneath her bare feet. Katy hesitated. She wasn't getting anywhere with Daffodil. The girl clearly wasn't ready to talk—at least to her. Frustrated, she started for the front door, but turned toward the bathroom at the feeble sound of Daffodil's voice.

"Ms. Templeton?"

"Yes?"

From the bathroom doorway, Daffodil stared at her, blonde hair straggling across her face, eyes bleary, looking like an overgrown little girl who was lost and scared and alone.

"I still have my job, right?"

"Yes. Yes, you do, Daffodil. But you need to show up for work on time tomorrow and every day after that."

"I will. Don't worry, I will. I wish to God I'd never left yesterday." The girl grasped the wall and leaned her head against it. "I wish I'd stayed at the diner," she repeated, and gulped down another sob. "You don't have to worry, I won't ever leave work like that again."

"I'm counting on that." Still, Katy hesitated. It didn't feel right leaving her. Daffodil looked so fragile, so distraught, but it was clear she wanted Katy to go.

"See you tomorrow then," Katy said quietly.

No answer.

But just as she closed the door behind her, she heard the heartrending sound of more sobs. She stood in the fading sunlight, feeling helpless and torn.

If Corey hit her yesterday, Daffodil needs help, Katy thought, her fingers digging into her palms. *I might just have to speak to Mrs. Moline myself about what's going on.* She strongly doubted Daffodil would tell her mother on her own.

But the girl needed someone to talk to, that was clear.

For her own sake, no matter how difficult it was, Daffodil needed to tell the truth about whatever had happened yesterday when she and Corey Dillard left the diner.

Chapter 20

SIPPING COFFEE AT THE KITCHEN TABLE, KATY listened to the quiet that enveloped the ranch house. How calm and peaceful the valley felt as purple twilight glided toward night. The dinner dishes were all washed and put away, the leftover salad and grilled chicken she'd brought home from the diner were stored in the fridge, and the windows were open wide to catch the fresh mountain air.

She was alone—save for Mojo—alone in the ranch house for the second night since she'd returned to Thunder Creek. It would only be a few more days before her parents returned, and then Gram, and with Bessie feeling better, and the Paris trip out of the way, it would be time to start thinking about finding her own place to live.

If, that is, she planned to stay in Thunder Creek.

She closed her eyes and tried to imagine going back to New York, tried to imagine leaving the diner, her family, the pine-draped mountains and sagebrush behind. And at the back of her mind she saw Jackson Brent.

Why in the world should it seem difficult to imagine leaving Jackson Brent?

Something squeezed tight around her heart. She opened her eyes and sighed. She'd come here to figure out her life and she hadn't done that yet. In fact it was more confusing than ever. She wasn't ready yet to make any decisions, to move back or go forward. First she had to find the truth about the past, the truth about Crystal and about Matt.

Then . . . well, she would see about the diner, and everything else. And that included Jackson Brent.

Her gaze dropped to her cell phone, on the table next to her coffee cup and a pad of paper. Jackson hadn't called her today. She'd thought she'd hear from him—she'd wanted to know if he'd gone to Sheriff Harvey, and how Ajax was doing. But he hadn't called—the only personal phone call she'd received had been from Margie, inviting her to dinner tomorrow.

One time she'd actually picked up her phone to call him, but the diner had suddenly filled up with customers and she'd had to disconnect. It had been hectic nonstop after that.

I could call now, she thought, but then bit her lip. So could he. *Maybe he doesn't want to talk to you. Maybe he's thought better of what happened last night, of the idiotic way you ran hot and cold, unable to make up your own mind about what you wanted. Maybe you should just forget about him . . . and about everything else.*

Everything else. All she had felt and wanted when he'd kissed her. All that had swept through her when she'd come within a heartbeat of having sex with him.

Sure, she could forget that. Just like she could forget her name, the color of her eyes. The color of Jackson's eyes. The heat of his mouth claiming hers.

Mojo's whining at the front door dragged her thoughts away from Jackson and back to the task ahead of her. She let the dog out into the fragrant purple night, and returned to the kitchen table, focusing her thoughts on Crystal Kirk. She'd printed out the information she'd gleaned from the Internet White Pages—forty-two names, everyone in the Tucson area with phone listings under the name of *Kirk*.

She'd taped together the two pieces of the sketch, and now

Matt's drawing of the girl with the thick curly hair lay on the table alongside the list.

She stared at it a moment, picked up her cell phone, and began punching buttons.

It took twenty-seven calls before she finally hit pay dirt.

"Crystal Kirk?" The man's voice was rough, coarse as sandpaper. "She don't live here no more. What do you want with her?"

Katy was so stunned to have finally reached someone who knew Crystal that she nearly dropped the phone. "Is this Edward Kirk?" she asked quickly, checking the name on her list that matched the number she'd just called. "Are you Crystal's father?"

"Yeah. Used to be." He grunted. "But if you want to find her, you'll have to look someplace else. The little bitch has been gone for years."

"Gone?"

"You heard me." Total indifference. Crystal's family wasn't exactly the Brady Bunch. She heard a woman's voice in the background, then suddenly, the man muttered for her to hold on.

The next thing she knew a woman's thready voice came on the phone. "You know where Crystal is?" she asked, a throb of hope echoing through the thinness of her tone.

"No, I'm sorry, I don't. I was hoping you could tell me how to find her."

"Oh." The single word held a deep well of disappointment. And then there was silence.

"Mrs. Kirk, my name is Katy Templeton. I live in Thunder Creek, Wyoming. Crystal used to work here in town and... and then she left. I'm trying to get in touch with her. When was the last time you spoke to her?"

"Not for a long time," the thready voice said dully. "She ran away when she was sixteen, and I only heard from her one time after that. She said she was coming home, but she never did."

"When was that?" Katy held her breath.

"Fourteen years ago. Some weeks before Halloween." The woman sighed. "She was real upset. Crying. Crying like I hadn't heard her cry since she was a little girl. She said she needed to come home, she ... she wanted to see me."

Katy's pulse quickened. "Do you know why? Why she was crying?"

"Oh, it was some man. What else? It was always a man with Crystal. She didn't tell me his name, though. I could barely make out what she was saying, but she was in a bad way. I was worried, and I told her I'd send her bus fare if she needed it. She said she didn't, but she promised to come. Then ... I guess she changed her mind."

Katy was staring down at the drawing. Her fingers tightened around the phone. "You never heard from her again, Mrs. Kirk? After that phone call? You're sure?"

"I think I'd know." Weariness, more than anger, flowed through that thin voice. "I kept waiting, but she never came. Never even called again." Suddenly the voice quickened. "I was worried, you know. I even called the police after a few weeks when she didn't show up. But they weren't too interested. She was a runaway and all. They said most of 'em never do come home."

Her tone sharpened. "Why do you want to know? Have you seen my daughter? How long ago did she work there?"

"No, no, I haven't seen her," Katy said swiftly. "She worked here a long time ago ... right around the time she called you. I wanted to find her ... to ask her about something that happened here—around the time she left."

"Did Crystal do something? Something wrong?"

"No, Mrs. Kirk, it's nothing like that. It's just that people here thought she was heading home too. She said she was going back to Tucson and I wondered—"

"Like I said, she must've changed her mind." But the woman sounded nervous. "Or else...something happened to her."

"Do you have any reason to think something might have happened to her?"

"No...not exactly. It's just that she was so upset. She sounded kind of...broken. I really thought she was coming back."

The man's voice bellowed in the background. "Forget about her, will ya? When the hell are you going to forget about that little tramp?"

"I have to hang up now." The woman spoke rapidly. Katy's heart ached at the flat hopelessness of her voice. "But if you hear from Crystal...or if you find out where she is—"

"Of course—I'll call you, Mrs. Kirk. I'd like to give you my number, too, in case you—"

But there was a click and the line went dead.

She set down the cell phone and took a deep breath.

Crystal Kirk had never made it home. She'd told the bartender she was leaving, and she'd called her mother. But she hadn't made it. Maybe she'd never even made it out of town.

"Oh, dear God." Horror prickled the back of Katy's neck as she stared at the sketch. Crystal *was* dead. Matt had known it, seen it. He'd had a secret...he'd made a pact. With Wood Morgan?

Why?

"Matt. Oh, God. *Matt,*" Katy whispered as pain wrenched through her. She'd come to grips with Matt's accident, but this was different. Anything linking him to Crystal Kirk's possible murder made everything different.

You don't know for certain, a sane quiet voice whispered inside her head, but something in her, something deep and raw, knew. Something in her had known the moment she'd found the sketch.

She pushed back the chair, stood up on knees that shook.

She was cold. So cold. She needed to put on a sweater. She needed a glass of wine. She needed to find answers.

And at the same time, she felt dread at what they might be.

From outside came a shrill insistent barking. Mojo.

There was something odd about it. The sound seemed to be coming from the barn. From inside the barn. It was muffled, frantic, and unrelenting. She started toward the door, wondering how Mojo had ended up in the barn when the door was closed.

Unless someone had let him in there. Maybe Jackson was looking in on Cleo.

Suddenly the lights went out. Darkness clamped down over the house like a bomb and at the same moment Katy heard the rush of boots through the hall. Someone running, coming fast. Running toward the kitchen . . .

"Who's there?" she called, then instinct kicked in and she bolted toward the back door. But she tripped over a chair leg in the darkness, and the next thing she knew she was grabbed from behind. An arm coiled around her throat, a hand crushed her mouth, and she smelled wool and sweat and felt the thrum of excitement in a body much bigger than hers.

She struggled frantically, panic tearing through her, but the man held her easily, and his grip was cruel. She heard a car engine outside, a door slam, but then everything else was blocked out by a grating whisper in her ear, by the scratch of rough wool that felt like a ski mask brushing against her cheek.

"Stop," the man holding her whispered. "Stop asking questions."

Katy stamped down hard on his foot. She heard his grunt of pain, but even as she tried desperately to break away, his grip tightened, brutally pressing on her throat. She felt her senses swimming and she gulped for air.

"You've been warned. *Stop*."

Frantically, but with decreasing strength, she tore at his arm, but she couldn't budge it. She couldn't even gasp. That's when something hit her over the head. Pain exploded for one brief, blinding moment and then she went down into a tunnel of darkness that was endless and stifling and from which there was no return.

And as she plunged and fell and was swallowed up she heard another voice, far away. It sounded like Jackson's voice.

And it called her name.

Chapter 21

KATY. KATY, WAKE UP.

She was swimming, swimming through a murky black river, trying to reach the surface.

Katy!

She burst through, pain splintering through her head.

"Are you all right? Can you hear me? Katy!"

The voice was rough, insistent. She remembered now. Jackson ... calling her.

She forced her eyes open, blinking at the brightness set off by a penlight in his hand, blinking at his sharp, handsome face leaning close to hers, full of worry.

"There was a man," she whispered, clutching at his arm. "Did he ... get away?"

"There was no one here when I got in. He must have gone out through the living room—I came in the back door. Hold on a minute." Jackson lifted her into his arms and settled her on a chair. "I'll be right back, Katy. Don't try to move."

Move? She could barely breathe. Dizziness washed over her and she clung to the sides of the chair to keep from falling as he dodged through the darkness toward the living room.

She took slow, deep breaths, determined not to slip back

into a faint again. She couldn't faint, she had to think. Think about that voice. That horrible whisper.

Who was it? She couldn't recognize the whisper. *Try. Try to place it.*

She tensed up at the sound of footsteps running once more through the house, but it was only Jackson this time, returning to the kitchen, shaking his head. Mojo raced in at his heels, darted up to Katy, and pushed his wet nose against her arm, making whining noises.

"No sign of him—or of a car," Jackson said. "I found Mojo locked in the barn. Whoever was here made sure he was out of the way." He stopped beside her, and lifted her again, carrying her into the living room as if she weighed no more than a dandelion puff.

Her eyes were adjusting gradually to the darkness that had clamped down upon the ranch house. Moonlight, along with the penlight clipped to Jackson's belt, bathed the living room in a faint glow as he lowered her upon the sofa.

"Look at me, Katy. Let me check you out."

"Check me out?" She was feeling a bit stronger now, and boosted herself up on the sofa pillows. "I'm not a horse or a dog, Doc Brent," she said weakly.

"Yeah, I noticed."

He aimed the penlight at her eyes, studied the pupils, and checked her pulse.

Then he reached for the silk throw at the foot of the sofa and tossed it over her. "Let me get you some water."

"Better make it wine," she murmured.

He shook his head. "Later."

When he brought her the water, and eased her up farther to sip it, Katy closed her hand over his as he held the glass.

"If you hadn't come when you did, he would have killed me."

Jackson's mouth was a thin, hard line. "You need to tell

me everything that happened. What you saw, what you heard. Did he say anything to you?"

"He told me to stop. Stop asking questions. And he said I'd been warned. He...he had his arm around my throat, he kept squeezing harder. But I never saw him, Jackson. It was pitch black and he grabbed me from behind—I think he was wearing a ski mask."

She was trembling as the memories flooded back and Jackson eased down on the sofa and curved an arm around her.

"Just take it easy now. Do you want to go to the hospital?"

She shook her head.

"Where does it hurt?"

"My head...but it's not too bad," she said quickly. "He... hit me with something."

"I'm calling Sheriff Harvey."

"Jackson, no." Her eyes were wide. Her hand clutched his. "There's no need—"

"Damn it, Katy, someone tried to kill you tonight—in your own house. We can't ignore this. It's time we filled Stan Harvey in about what's going on—everything that's going on," he added grimly.

"Not yet."

"We've hit a nerve. And someone's hitting back. *Hard.* This isn't something to fool around with."

"I know, but...I can't imagine who it could be," she whispered dazedly. "I mean, I pushed Wood Morgan pretty hard last night with all those questions. But I can't believe he'd ever do something like this..." She moistened her lips. "Would he?"

"Who the hell knows." Jackson scowled. "All I know is we have to catch this guy before he comes after you again. After what happened tonight, this is police business, Katy."

"I'm not prepared to drag Sheriff Harvey in just yet—"

"What are you waiting for?" he demanded roughly. "Until

he kills you? Look." Jackson's hands framed her face. "This guy's running scared. Real scared. And that makes him dangerous. You won't be safe until we've caught him, and if we have to call in the National Guard and the Marines and every forest ranger in the state, then that's what's going to happen."

"I just don't want..." She bit her lip. "I don't want this to start snowballing, not yet. I'm not ready for everyone in town to start gossiping, speculating about Matt and Crystal—or for my parents to come home and find some big scandal has erupted, with people whispering that Matt was involved in who-knows-what. I want to learn more first, so we can prove that Matt didn't do anything wrong, that he somehow got caught up in something—"

"We'll prove it, Katy. We'll get at the truth. But in the meantime, we need to bring Harvey in now. Amateur hour is over. We need every resource we can get."

At her mulish look, he continued flatly. "It may not come out so quickly, you know. Sheriff Harvey can be discreet. Hell, he's one of your father's best friends. He sure as hell isn't going to start blabbing details of a potential murder investigation all over town."

"I suppose." She sighed. Deep down she knew he was right, but she didn't have to like it.

"All right. You win." She leaned back, away from him, and thrust a hand through her hair, forcing herself to accept the inevitable. "We have to tell Harvey, I can see that." She thought of the can of worms she'd opened—dirty, nasty worms that were now wriggling out uncontrollably from the past. Not for the first time, she wished she'd never looked through Matt's bag, never found the sketch.

"Let's get it over with," she said in a low tone. She straightened her shoulders and met Jackson's searching glance head-on. "Go ahead—call him."

.   .   .

Stan Harvey dusted the doorknobs and all of the electrical switches on the circuit breaker for fingerprints, but Katy knew he wouldn't find any. The man who'd entered the house and shut off the electricity and tried to strangle her in her mother's kitchen had worn gloves. But the sheriff dusted anyway, covering all the bases, he said, just in case the intruder had removed a glove at some point and left a stray print. He studied the ground outside for footprints, but found nothing clear, nothing usable. And he took meticulous notes on a legal-sized pad as Katy spent the next hour relating the entire story to him, everything she could remember about finding the sketch, its unsettling nature, and how she and Jackson had begun trying to learn the identity of the curly-haired girl Matt had drawn.

With his burly body seated on the wing chair in the living room, and his long legs stretched out before him, the sheriff wrote down in longhand everything Katy told him, including what she'd learned only tonight when she'd called the Kirks—that Crystal had never made it home.

"So this is what you really were poking into when you came to my office that day." He peered gravely at her. "Why didn't you level with me then?"

"I'm sorry, Sheriff Harvey. I should have told you everything right away. I just wasn't sure if there was really something wrong about that sketch, or if I was letting my imagination run away with me."

"I think it's about time you showed me this sketch."

"It's in the kitchen, on the table. I'll get it."

"Let me." Jackson was already on his feet, headed toward the kitchen. A moment later he returned, his face grim.

"It's not there."

"It has to be." She swung her legs off the sofa, startling Mojo, who lay only a few feet from her, and hurried into the kitchen, followed by both Jackson and the sheriff. She stared in disbelief at the table: the list of Tucson phone numbers was still there beside her cell phone, and so was her coffee cup, but there was no sign of the sketch. In dismay she scanned the floor, the countertops. The sketch was gone.

"He took it. Damn it, it was right there! He took the sketch!"

Somehow this angered her almost more than anything else. The sketch was her last link with Matt, the last drawing her brother had ever made, and the only existing proof that he'd seen Crystal Kirk's dead body.

"We have to find him, Sheriff Harvey. The man who took the sketch tried to kill me, and I'd bet my life he killed Crystal Kirk. And maybe Matt as well."

Stan Harvey's expression grew even more grim. "Come on back and sit down a minute, honey," he said somberly. "You, too, Jackson. Let's go about this in a sensible way."

Back in the living room, the sheriff patted Mojo's head a moment before pursing his lips and giving Katy a long look.

"Think carefully now. Who knew that you were asking questions about this Crystal Kirk, and about what happened all those years ago? Also, did anyone else see that sketch?"

"Only Jackson and Allison saw it," Katy replied promptly. "Allison is the one who recognized Crystal. And she told us that Matt was keeping some kind of secret before he died."

"And you think it had to do with this pact you mentioned." The sheriff's eyes watched her face, carefully, speculatively. "But you don't know for sure if that had anything to do with Crystal, right? Or who he made the pact with?"

"We only know that right around the time Crystal disappeared, Allison saw Matt talking with Wood Morgan in an alley," Jackson said.

"No law against that," the sheriff grunted, but he scratched a notation on his pad.

Katy leaned forward. "We went to the Tumbleweed last night and questioned both Elam and Wood. Elam's the one who told us Crystal's last name and where she was from—

and the approximate time period she supposedly left Thunder Creek. That gave us enough information to start calling people named Kirk in Tucson to see if she made it home."

The sheriff's pen moved rapidly across the page. "And Wood?"

"He denied knowing anything about Crystal or a pact. But he was shook up when I mentioned her name," Katy added. "And he definitely didn't want Tammie getting any whiff of our conversation."

"This is all mighty interesting—especially in light of someone breaking in here tonight—but to tell you the truth, it doesn't amount to a hill of beans. Katy, honey, what I need is some hard evidence." Harvey clicked his pen and his eyes swiveled back to her face. "You talk to anyone else about this?"

"No. Only Allison and Elam and Wood, until I called the Kirks tonight—" Suddenly she broke off. "I just remembered something."

Both men gazed at her expectantly.

"That day I came to your office, Sheriff Harvey, to ask you about Matt—when I was leaving, Luke Dillard was there. He was in the outer office, waiting to see you, and he could have heard me talking to you about Matt. I think I even told you that day that the girl in the sketch looked like she was dead. Luke may have overheard the entire conversation."

"Well, okay. Guess that's possible." But Stan Harvey looked skeptical even as he made another notation on his pad.

"There's something else, Stan." Jackson's eyes had narrowed. "When we questioned Elam, he mentioned Luke's name as one of the men Crystal dated when she first worked at the Tumbleweed."

"That's right," Katy gasped. A chill shot through her.

Sheriff Harvey pursed his lips.

"You sure about that?"

"We both heard him," Jackson said.

"Well, all right, I'll keep that in mind. But I've got to tell you, Jackson, I know there's some bad blood between you and Dillard. First he wanted to file a complaint against your dog, then today you said he shot the dog—"

"He did." Frowning, Jackson turned to Katy. "I didn't get a chance to call you earlier—that's why I was coming by tonight, to fill you in. I took your advice and went to see Stan earlier today about Ajax. It seems that Dillard has some sort of alibi for yesterday."

"A damned good alibi," the sheriff corrected him. "Two witnesses. They both swear he was in Carsonville all of yesterday afternoon and right through dinner."

"I don't care if you have a hundred witnesses, I'd bet my boots, my saddle, and my eyeteeth Dillard shot my dog," Jackson retorted.

"So you're telling me Luke shot Ajax." The sheriff turned to Katy. "And he dated this Crystal Kirk. And then he broke in here tonight and attacked you—all because he overheard you asking me some questions?" He shook his head. "I don't suppose there's anything else you two want to pin on him while we're at it?"

Katy flushed. "I know it sounds like we're ... throwing around accusations, Sheriff, but it isn't like that. We're just telling you what happened."

"You're telling me what you think happened. It's my job to find the evidence, my job to get to the bottom of this, and then, don't you worry, I'll be the one doing the accusing."

He sighed and made a few more notes before they all returned to the living room.

"When are your folks coming home, honey?"

"Tuesday."

"And Bessie?"

"Wednesday morning."

"You going to be all right out here until then?"

"Ye... es. Of course." She tried to keep her voice steady, but it wavered ever so slightly. She was grateful the sheriff couldn't see the knot in her stomach the size of Kentucky.

Sympathy flickered in his eyes and he reached out to gently squeeze her arm. "Here's what I'm going to do. I'm going to investigate the hell out of this thing in the next day or so. I vaguely remember this Crystal gal working back at the Tumbleweed all those years ago, but I'll talk to Elam and to Ted Paxton, and whoever else they think might have been tight with her, and find out all I can. Then I'll get in touch with her family in Tucson and see if they can give me any more information. If your theory is true, and something happened to her, I'm going to try like hell to get a lead on it."

"Whoever got to Crystal is still in Thunder Creek," Jackson said flatly. "He's nearby—probably someone we know. And tonight he tried to kill Katy, or at the very least, to scare her into dropping the whole thing."

"Could be, but you're going to have to slow down a bit, Jackson." The sheriff clicked his pen, and tucked it into his jacket pocket. "I want to get to the bottom of this as much as you do, but you're jumping to a whole bunch of conclusions here. I'm not saying you're wrong, I'm just saying that when it comes to the law, we need facts, not theories. You let me handle this, all right? First off, it sounds like whoever came in here and grabbed you, Katy, *was* only trying to scare you. Based on what he said, it was a warning."

"Well, he wasted his breath." She met the sheriff's gaze squarely. "He obviously doesn't know me very well. I'm not backing off."

"Sorry to break it to you, honey, but you *are* going to back off." Stan Harvey's brows drew together and he eyed her like she was a recalcitrant schoolgirl about to shoplift a lipstick from a drugstore shelf. "You're going to let me handle this investigation from here on out. And I don't want either of you saying a word about this to anyone. Not a word about that sketch, or about Crystal Kirk—or about what happened here tonight. I don't want you two becoming targets, and I don't want folks being forewarned about this investigation. Let me do my job. Keep quiet, act like nothing happened, and don't stir things up more than you already have. And just maybe I'll have a chance of getting at the truth about this thing."

"I want to keep what happened tonight quiet, too," she agreed quickly, feeling a wave of relief. "There's no way I'm going to lay all this on my parents or Gram one minute before they get home."

"Knowing your dad, honey, that's a good idea."

"God, yes, Big John would be on the next plane. And Mom . . ." She swallowed and shook her head. "They definitely don't need that kind of news while they're an ocean away."

"No argument here."

"There's something else, Sheriff Harvey." Katy flicked a glance at Jackson before turning back to the sheriff. She picked her words carefully. "Make no mistake, I *want* you to ask questions, I *want* you to discover the truth, but . . . the more discreet you can be about this, the better. At least for the next few days," she went on hurriedly, as he raised his brows. "I'd hate for Mom and Big John—and Gram—to come home to the whole town buzzing with questions and gossip about Matt." She licked her lips. "At least, not until we know what happened. Not until I've had a chance to think how to tell them . . . whatever it might be I have to tell them," she finished in a low tone.

He was silent a moment. "I understand, Katy. I'll try to be careful. Discreet, as you say. You do the same and lay low. Give me a chance to see what I can find out over the next day or two. By the time Big John and Dorsey get back, let's hope to God I have an idea on who was behind this. And on what might have happened to Crystal—and to Matt," he added quietly.

"Thank you." Katy glanced at Jackson, who nodded his agreement. "We'll hold off for the time being," she said. "We won't get in your way. But . . . you have to find whoever did this, Sheriff Harvey."

"I damn well intend to, honey. Don't you worry about that."

She walked him to the door. As he turned to pat her shoulder reassuringly, her gaze on his was level, calm, and determined. *Just like her dad's,* Harvey thought with a jolt of surprise. And admiration. *There's a look about her like Big John when he's holding a royal flush.*

"If you don't find him, Sheriff Harvey," Katy said, her voice low, but remarkably even for a woman who'd been attacked in her own home only an hour earlier, "I will." She drew a breath. "You can consider that a promise."

Chapter 22

A HALF HOUR LATER WHEN JACKSON RETURNED FROM the barn and from yet another check of the grounds, he stopped in the kitchen and retrieved a bottle of Riesling and two glasses.

"You ready for that wine now?" he asked Katy. She was lying across the sofa with her head on a pillow. Her eyes were open, staring at the ceiling.

She sat up and made room for him beside her. "More than ready. Coffee wouldn't do much for my nerves right now. I need to stay calm so I can think straight." She accepted the glass he handed her and regarded him over the rim.

"You certainly seem to know your way around our kitchen."

"Your mother's had me over to dinner a few times since I moved back."

"Interesting. And yet, when I came back, she never even thought to mention to me that you were here, much less that you were Cleo's vet."

"She probably knew that the mere mention of my name would make you rear up like a wild mustang filly. She must've wanted to wait for the right time and break it to you gently."

Katy took a sip of the wine, realizing he was probably

right. "I can't imagine how I'm going to break the news *we've* discovered to them gently. Or to Gram. Jackson, I hope they can handle this."

"You're handling it. They will, too."

"Why would anyone have wanted to kill Crystal?"

"It could have been anything, Katy. We don't know much about Crystal's life here except that she dated a few guys, and then claimed she was 'seeing someone.' Maybe it had something to do with whoever she was seeing... and, I assume, sleeping with, or maybe it was something from her past catching up to her. We don't know if the motive was jealousy or drugs or..." He raked a hand through his hair in frustration. "There's too many blanks to even start filling them in."

"*Yet*," Katy muttered. "We need more information." She took another sip of wine, then her eyes narrowed. "It still strikes me as a more-than-interesting coincidence that Luke Dillard was in the sheriff's office that day, and could conceivably have heard me asking Sheriff Harvey questions about Matt—and that he also just happened to have been one of the men hanging around Crystal back then."

"I'm not a big believer in coincidence. And there isn't much I'd put past Dillard."

"Me either—but even so, it's not enough. Not yet."

"There's one thing I *do* know." Jackson's gaze sharpened on her. "You're in danger."

She tried to quell the shudder that crept down her spine. "All those years in the city," she mused, "and I never once got mugged, never once even had to pull the cap off the pepper spray in my purse. Yet here, in Thunder Creek..." She broke off and shook her head. "I'll be fine. I'm planning to load up Big John's revolver and sleep with it under my pillow."

"That's not a bad idea. But I've got a better one."

He regarded her over the rim of his wineglass. "How

about bunking with me for the next few nights? Until your family gets home."

Katy stared into his eyes, surprised by the sudden rush of heat that surged through her. The idea of staying alone in the Triple T ranch house, revolver or no, held zero appeal. And the idea of staying with Jackson tantalized her with its possibilities. She'd be much safer with Jackson, there in that serene, cozy cabin. Safer from the outward danger, that is.

But there was another kind of danger she'd face if she kept getting into situations where she was alone with him, and kept letting herself lean on him. Her sense of caution, as well as her sense of duty, held her back.

"I don't feel right letting this . . . this monster, whoever he is, chase me away from the Triple T. Especially since Big John left me in charge. And what about Cleo? What if she delivers early?"

"Riley can keep a close eye on her and on the house. I'll check her each night before heading home, and you can tell Riley to monitor her each night until Big John gets back." His voice roughened. "I sure as hell don't want you heading out to the barn in the middle of the night by yourself to check on her."

"I'd have the gun," Katy pointed out.

"Would you have had time to use it tonight when he came at you from behind?"

She swallowed. "You have a point," she muttered.

"Big John wouldn't want you staying here alone under these circumstances."

"He wouldn't want me staying with you either," she retorted, and his eyes lit with laughter.

"Going to let that stop you?"

"And just what do you think is going to happen . . . between us . . . if I do take you up on your offer?"

"Whatever you want to happen, Katy. And nothing more. Scouts' honor."

She eyed him suspiciously. "Matt was a Boy Scout. I don't remember you being part of the troop."

"I wasn't." Jackson grinned, that slow irresistible grin that always seemed to turn her heart upside down. "Don't you trust me?" he asked. He set both their wineglasses aside and drew her closer, his arms sliding around her waist.

I don't trust myself, she thought. Then he kissed her, his mouth warm and seeking, and she knew exactly why she didn't trust herself. Jackson's kisses tasted too good, his mouth was too clever. His hands ... oh, God, his hands. They did things to her, dark and wonderful things, that stirred every sexual nerve in her body. She snaked her arms around his neck and nestled closer, opening her lips to him, inviting him in.

His hands slid down her hips to her buttocks and pressed her against him. Pleasure tingled through her and she slid her fingers down his back, even as his kisses became softer, deeper.

She clung to him, feeling so alive, so safe and warm and wanted that she didn't even want to think about pulling away or getting up. She didn't want to stay alone here tonight at the Triple T, not when she could be with him. She nibbled the edge of his mouth, enjoying the rock-hard tautness of his body against hers, enjoying the way he drew back and looked at her with those warm, contemplative eyes.

"I'll have to pack a few things," she murmured.

"Uh-huh. You do that." He grinned. He couldn't resist picturing a sexy teddy, lace panties, and bras.

Katy read his mind, and laughed. Men were so predictable. "Easy, cowboy. Don't get ahead of yourself. For all you know, I'm talking about long johns and toothpaste."

"You can bring the toothpaste," Jackson told her, his eyes glinting into hers. His arms were tight around her. "But those long johns, they'll have to go."

"You have something against long johns?"

Jackson brushed a stray lock of honey hair from her face, and grazed another soft kiss across her lips. "I just don't think you'll need them to stay warm."

From deep in the shadows, he watched them. Watched Jackson toss a small bag into the back of the truck, then hand Katy in and slam the door. Watched them drive away in a whir of gravel and dust, and caught a glimpse of Katy Templeton's pale face in a quick shimmer of moonlight.

So, it was like that between them, was it? Sweat glistened on his cheeks. Fear punched through his stomach. They were thick as thieves. And there were two of them, two working against him as one.

Shit.

He closed his eyes, remembering, remembering how narrow and fragile her throat had felt beneath his arm. How quick it would have been to end it all. How quick it *could* be—next time. He'd come so close to doing it tonight—he'd held her life almost literally in his hands. But he'd chosen to give her a way out, a chance to live.

Now it was up to her.

"That was the only warning you'll get," he whispered, staring at the retreating headlights as they glowed briefly at the top of a ridge. "I can't let you find out. No one can find out."

The lights of the truck were nothing now but a pinprick, a pinprick that burned into his eyes.

"Whatever happens," he muttered, as sweat pooled beneath his armpits, and desperation gnawed through his guts, "you can't ever say you weren't warned."

Chapter 23

"HOPE YOU DON'T MIND MY MENAGERIE," JACKSON said. "I'd rather not leave Ajax another night at the clinic. He and Regis and Cammi can hang out together while we get some sleep."

They had stopped at the clinic to pick up the injured dog on the way to the cabin, and Ajax had welcomed them with high-pitched, happy barks.

"I don't mind at all. He's so sweet, and so frisky—even being shot hasn't seemed to have gotten him down...too much." Katy couldn't help smiling as she glanced back at the scrappy dog seated on a blanket in the back, wriggling with happiness to be going home.

"I should have brought Mojo along."

"Tomorrow, if you want." Jackson smiled. "The more the merrier."

Katy peered out at the inky darkness of the night. The wine had soothed her nerves somewhat, and meeting Ajax had distracted her, but as they neared Jackson's cabin, isolated from the main road and set beneath the mountain, the full implications of the night's events sent a chill through her once more.

The suspicion that Matt's death might not have been an accident began to take firm hold in her mind. It no longer seemed like such a leap to contemplate that someone had deliberately pushed him off the Jenssens' roof, or moved the ladder, or done something to make certain Matt Templeton didn't break "the pact." If so, then Crystal's killer, and Matt's, was still here in Thunder Creek—and still trying to keep the truth from coming out.

And still willing to commit murder to ensure it didn't.

She was afraid. Her head no longer hurt, but the memory of helplessness and terror was imbedded in her. Was that how Crystal had felt, and Matt, in the seconds before they died? What pain, what fear had they known in those final moments? Rage and sorrow gripped her, making her clench her hands in her lap as velvet darkness rolled by outside her window, and Ajax whimpered softly on the blanket in the back, and the scent of sage and pine drifted in through the open windows.

She'd give Sheriff Harvey a few days, and she wouldn't say anything to anyone for the time being, but that didn't mean she wasn't going to keep trying to get some answers herself.

"I thought of something while I was packing," she told Jackson as he pulled up in front of the cabin. "Where did Crystal live when she worked here? If she rented a room somewhere, whoever she rented from might know who she was seeing, who her friends were—"

"Or her enemies." Jackson nodded. "That could be a good lead for Harvey to follow up on. Tomorrow I'll stop by the Tumbleweed and talk to Elam again. Maybe he'll remember."

"Call me as soon as you find out."

"I will. But Katy, you need to keep a low profile. Let Harvey do the digging. Whoever's out there already knows you're on his trail. If he wants to be worried about someone finding him out right now, let him start worrying about Stan Harvey."

"If I was the one who had died, or been killed—who was in trouble back then and no one ever knew it, Matt would never back off. He'd get the answers come hell or high water. And you know it, Jackson."

He cut the engine and turned to look at her.

"That's different."

"Why? Because I'm a woman?"

"Yeah, because you're a woman. And because if anything ever happened to you . . ." He stopped himself before he finished the sentence. Then he focused his attention on the relatively simple task of opening the door of the truck. "Come on," he said abruptly. "Let's go inside."

She brewed Maxwell House decaf in his kitchen while he settled Ajax in a large plaid dog bed in a small office at the rear of the cabin. Cammi and Regis rallied around the injured dog and inspected every inch of him, including the bandage that covered his wound. Then, Jackson told her when he returned to the kitchen, they promptly settled down on either side of him in the dog bed, trying to bring him what comfort they could.

But once in the kitchen, the only thing compelling Jackson's attention was the woman pouring hot coffee into two of his mugs. He watched her add a dollop of milk to hers, and stir it absentmindedly. He liked the way she moved around his kitchen, with smooth, graceful efficiency, as if she belonged there.

To look at her, you'd never know what she'd gone through tonight, he thought. Only the unusual pallor of her skin and the faint lavender shadows beneath her eyes gave any indication of the ordeal she'd experienced.

A knot tightened in his chest. If he ever got his hands on whoever had done this to her . . . Suddenly, the vehemence of his feelings took him aback and he reminded himself not to get overly involved. That wouldn't be a good thing for either one of them.

She brushed a lock of that gorgeous honey-colored hair out of her eyes and turned her head to smile at him then. That one smile made him go hard, made him want to touch her. It was like a punch in the gut.

It was amazing how having her here changed the entire feel of the place. It always felt welcoming to him, and comfortable as old sneakers. But now it felt warmer, softer—more intimate somehow. And even more like a refuge from the troubles of the world. Almost like a real home.

As she carried the mugs toward the table, she noticed the answering machine flashing. "You have some messages."

He took his coffee cup from her and then hit the button. A message from Roy Hewett, asking him if he'd have time to check out a horse Roy was considering buying from a breeder in Laramie, and a second message, this one from Margie, inviting him to dinner the next night. Then, just as Katy was digesting the fact that her best friend had invited both her and Jackson to dinner on the same night, another woman's voice came on.

"Hi, Jack, it's me. It's been weeks, sweetie. I thought we might get together this weekend. You left your socks at my place and I thought you might want them back. I even washed them for you. So call me." The voice became softer, more intimate and distinctly sexy. "Soon."

Jackson almost choked on his coffee. Katy's shoulders stiffened and her cheeks went pale as frost.

"That was Kelly Jones," he began, but she interrupted him.

"You don't owe me any explanations."

"Maybe not, but—"

"Your love life is your own business." She shrugged, hoping she looked a lot more nonchalant than she felt. "Now, if you don't mind, I think I'm going to turn in. If you'll get me some sheets and a blanket, I'll make up the sofa."

"Hold on a minute." He came around the table as she

pushed back her chair, and caught her to him. "She doesn't mean anything to me."

"Maybe you ought to be telling her that."

"She knows it. It was always clear between us, right from the start. Neither one of us wanted to be tied down or involved in an exclusive relationship."

"How nice for you."

"Yeah. It was nice. It was easy and it was fun and there were never any strings attached. Just the way I liked it."

Liked? Katy was intensely aware of his nearness, of the clean soap and leather scent of him, of his arms locked around her. *So he said liked. Not like. Don't make too much of it.*

"That's between you and Kelly, I guess. Don't drag me into it."

"Drag you in—" He gave a rueful bark of laughter and cupped her chin, forcing her to meet his eyes. "I hate to break it to you, but you're in it, like it or not, sweetheart. And you got there all by yourself. Don't you know that? Damn it, am I the only one feeling all these sparks between us?"

"Maybe there's some sparks but we certainly don't owe each other anything. I've already explained that I'm not ready to get involved with anyone, and the whole world knows *you* like to play the field—"

"Shut up, Katy," he said very softly, and touched a gentle finger to her mouth. "You're being an idiot. Only an idiot couldn't see what's going on between us."

She tilted her head back to meet his eyes. "And that would be?"

Shit. She didn't make things easy, did she? "I told you. I care about you." And then his hands slid down her arms, pulling her closer, nestling her against him. "And I want you so bad I can taste it. And unless I'm losing all ability to judge," he muttered, nibbling at the corner of her ear, "I think you want me too."

Delicious heated sensations flickered through her. Oh yes, she wanted him all right. She knew she should run like hell from him, but instead she lifted a hand to his face, and her fingers tingled at the wonderful roughness of his stubbled jaw.

"You're not," she whispered.

"Not what?"

"Losing your ability to judge."

He grinned and his hands slid lower even as he pressed a kiss to the corner of her mouth. "I can't tell you how encouraging that is."

"Since when does Jackson Brent need encouraging?" she murmured and he suddenly chuckled.

"Good point. Guess I should stick to taking what I want. Sure you can handle it?"

"I'm a big girl." Then she gasped, a delicious shiver enveloping her as those roving hands slipped inside her shirt. "I'm not... going to break." But she ended the words on a moan.

"Yeah? Well, I just might."

There was no mistaking the raw hunger in his eyes. "If I don't kiss you again in the next two seconds, I'm going to—"

"You're going to what?" She writhed up against him, and entwined her arms around his neck. *Playing with fire,* she thought. She, Katy Templeton, was actually playing with fire. The woman who had vowed not to get involved in any more relationships, not for years, if ever, was daring thunder to knock her off her feet, daring lightning to strike her down. She could feel his heart thudding, hard and hot against the tips of her breasts. She tilted her head back, challenging him with her eyes. Her smile was a beguiling invitation that made him groan.

"You're going to what, Jackson?" she whispered again, her lips an inch from his, her fingertips sliding slowly through his hair.

"Explode," he grated against her mouth and caught her to him so hard she gasped.

His kiss was powerful, awakening a hotbed of need deep in her core. If she'd had any doubts about this, about what they both wanted, they dissolved as his hand cupped her nape, and his tongue teased its way inside her mouth. Katy moaned, her fingers burying themselves in his hair. As her tongue twisted wildly, willfully against his, the kisses became wilder, fiercer.

"I take it back, we're not going to explode—we're going to implode," he rasped against her lips, and the blood pounded in her ears. Jackson's hands roamed over her body, igniting little fires everywhere he touched. And he touched everywhere.

First he unbuttoned her shirt and tossed it aside, then unhooked her bra in one second flat and threw it over his shoulder.

"Gorgeous," he murmured, his eyes feasting on her breasts.

Her heart was racing. "Two can play that game, Doc Brent," she whispered thickly as she stepped closer again and dragged his head down to her. Locked in another starving kiss, she tore at the buttons of his shirt, yanking it from his broad shoulders and away from those muscle-corded arms. Oh, God, his chest was beautiful—toned and muscled, bronzed by the sun, and threaded with wiry dark hair. Katy immediately began to explore it, brushing her lips and her fingertips across his chest, his nipples, reveling at his indrawn breath, his electric sensitivity to her touch.

He groaned, and reached for her with new urgency, as his body nearly shook with wanting her. He unzipped her jeans and slid them down her hips. The moment she stepped out of them, his hands found her breasts and began to stroke them, rubbing her already erect nipples, tormenting them, first with his fingers, then slowly, with his tongue, until she was dizzy and aching with pleasure. She wasn't the only one.

When his hands touched her pink satin thong she could feel the jolt as his whole body jerked with tension.

"Oh, baby, what are you doing to me?" he grated against her lips, and then her panties were gone too, and he was stroking her bare skin, her thighs, and the moist, soft nest between her legs.

She was so soft, so responsive, that Jackson could barely wait to get inside her. Her beautiful eyes shone with desire as he touched her, kissed her.

He scarcely remembered carrying her to the sofa, or lowering her down on the leather. Then they were lying, tangled, on the smooth cushions, and she was naked beneath him, her skin golden in the lamplight, and her hair soft in his hands. She reached for him, her face flushed and eager, and her fingers tore at the zipper on his jeans, stroked his arms, raked down his back.

"Katy Templeton, she-cat." His teeth and tongue encircled her nipple.

Katy gave a gasp of intense and exquisite pleasure. When his mouth began to suckle her breast, sensations burst through her, blocking everything else from her mind—everything except this man, this moment. *This madness,* she thought wildly. There was only Jackson, with his silky dark hair, his clever hands and mouth, his muscle-corded body so finely attuned to hers.

She moaned raggedly, incoherently as his mouth drove her wild, and then she had his jeans and briefs off, and they were both naked, both wild with the wanting. When she stroked the hard thickness of his shaft, the tension in his body seemed to vibrate through her, right down to her toes, and her breathing quickened with anticipation and desire.

She was more than ready when he shifted, easing over her and parting her thighs. She opened herself to him completely, clinging to his back and losing herself in the tender kisses he rained on her. She felt alive again, alive and whole and female, and she felt beautiful. When he slid inside her, she held her breath, and twined her legs around him. His eyes gleamed into hers, and she lost herself in their depths, then lost herself in the feel of him inside her, filling her. Her body arched toward his.

He felt her craving through every muscle of his body as he kissed her mouth, her eyelids, her throat.

"You're so lovely, Katy. So lovely." He spoke against her lips, his voice hoarse. "Ready to ride?"

"Ready or not, here I come," she whispered on a breathless, desperate laugh and then the laughter died from both of them as he pushed even deeper inside her, filling her, stretching her, making her gasp, and obliterating every rational thought and emotion from her mind. She arched up, and clenched her legs around him, holding him to her, inside her, and rocking madly with him as they began to soar.

The last thing she remembered was crying out his name.

Then there was nothing else, nothing but the two of them, only Jackson and Katy and this intense, brilliant pleasure. Only the thrusting, the heat, and the fire.

The ride took them both, whirling them away from the cabin, away from the earth, faster and faster in a dark tunnel of speed and fervor and power, of sweat and need and pure blinding passion. They rocked together, bodies fusing, burning. The rhythms of their blood and of their hearts matched, beating one to one. They tore together on a dizzying, rushing journey until at last they reached a peak—the highest peak— and sailed over. Far and high they sailed, and then at last, inevitably, shattered, splintering into a thousand pieces. They drifted down at last—to earth, to the cabin, to find themselves spent and broken and shivering in each other's arms.

They breathed again and were still.

.   .   .

Pale opal sunrise shimmered over the cabin and the peak of Cougar Mountain as Katy awoke in Jackson's arms. They were in his bed, though she only vaguely remembered how they got there. Forest green sheets were twisted around their bodies. Their naked legs were entwined, and her head rested upon his chest. As he shifted slightly in his sleep, she squirmed just enough so she could tilt her head to look at him.

He was gorgeous. His hair tumbled over his brow, his lean face was peaceful and yet so very strong, even in sleep. And he'd made her feel cherished, beautiful, every moment they'd made love last night, until they'd collapsed finally in each other's arms. She didn't think he'd released her once all through the hours they slept, and a kind of rare peace stole over her now that made every bone in her body melt into him. She reached up and very gently kissed that rough stubble on his chin.

"Morning." He spoke with his eyes still closed.

"Morning yourself. I didn't mean to wake you."

"Good thing you did. I have to get you home before I head in to the clinic. My appointments today start at nine."

"Oh."

Disappointment pricked her like a needle, deflating all the happiness of the moment before. He sounded so matter-of-fact, so ... businesslike. As if he couldn't wait for her to leave so he could get on with his day.

Well, why not? she asked herself, her heart dropping into the pit of her stomach. *Did you expect valentines and marriage proposals? Haven't you learned anything at all?*

She jerked out of his embrace, started to sit up and swing her legs toward the side of the bed, but a muscular arm swatted her back down as easily as if she were a butterfly, and in one smooth move, he had her pinned beneath him.

"Where do you think you're going?"

"To get dressed. You said—"

"I said I had to be at the office by nine. And you have to be at the diner, right?"

"Right. So if you'll just let me up, I won't bother you anymore—"

"Bother me? Is that what you call all those things we did last night—*bothering* me?"

"Jackson!" She couldn't help laughing, and he grinned at how beautiful she looked in the pale sunlight streaming in through the cracks of the shutters.

"You can bother me like that anytime you want," he chuckled. "In fact the way I figure it," he shifted his body lower, his hands starting to roam over her again, gently stroking the warm silk of her skin and the curve of her breasts, "we have time to bother each other like that at least two more times before we have to set foot outside this bed."

"Two more..." Katy moaned slightly as his hand slipped along the curve of her thigh and glided inside her. She was already moist, ready, welcoming.

"So, you don't want me to get dressed?" she breathed, her arms slipping around him, pulling him closer against her, fitting herself to him.

"I'd sooner throw all your clothes in the fireplace," he murmured against her lips, and when she laughed, a husky silken laugh that reminded him of roses rustling in a breeze, he caught her mouth in a kiss so tender that she shivered and wrapped her legs around him.

"Maybe I'll throw yours in first," she whispered with a small challenging nip at his lower lip, and then she was drowning in fire, the hot, sweet fire of his kisses. His body moved over hers, rough and rhythmic and she scraped her hands down his powerful shoulders, across his back, and pressed her mouth against the base of his throat.

The pale sun glowed in the sky beyond the shuttered

windows as they made fierce, greedy love in the radiance of the new day.

And then, as the sun began to burn with more strength and power and the rest of the world began to waken, they held each other and made love again, as gently and slowly as the blossoming of dawn.

Chapter 24

BILLY CORNERED DAFFODIL IN THE FRONT OF THE diner as she was wiping down table three.

"You want to tell me what happened to your face?"

It was midafternoon and rain clouds were moving in, muddying the diamond blue sky, turning it a murky greenish-gray. The lunch crowd had cleared out and only old Sam Garrett, who worked part-time at Merck's hardware store, was still lingering over his fourth cup of coffee near the window. In the kitchen, Katy was basting pork ribs with her special honey barbecue sauce, but neither Billy nor Daffodil paid the least bit of attention to her or anyone else. They simply glared at each other.

"What's wrong with my face?" Daffodil snapped. She'd done a pretty good job of covering the bruise with two kinds of concealer and makeup, and no one else had mentioned a word to her about it, not even Ms. Templeton. Leave it to Billy to give her grief.

"You run into a Mack truck?"

"Very funny. Just get out of my way." She lifted the cleanup bucket filled with empty glasses, plates, and Fantastik cleaning spray, and started toward the kitchen, but Billy nimbly blocked her path. He took the bucket from her and set it down on the floor.

"Not so fast, Daff. Not until you answer my question."

"I fell out of bed, okay?"

"Bullshit."

He seized her arm, then as she winced, he glanced down and saw that there was a black-and-blue bruise beneath his fingers. Rage choked him. And he felt sick to his stomach at the same time. He dropped her arm, wishing he would have seen that bruise before he touched her. "Did that asshole do this to you?" It was hard to keep from shouting. "Tell me!"

"What do you care?" Daffodil gave him her haughtiest look. "You're not my boyfriend anymore."

"Yeah, now you've got a real prince. A guy who beats you up."

"He didn't—I told you, I fell out of bed."

"Daff, why the hell are you covering for him? Don't you see what a loser he is? The girl I knew wouldn't have wasted a second of her time on a creep like Corey Dillard."

For a moment Daffodil couldn't remember a thing about why she had started dating Corey in the first place. His being handsome had something to do with it. And he was cool. A lot cooler than Billy, whose only sport at school was science lab. That had been her sport too, before she'd decided to stop being a geek.

"The girl you knew was as big a loser as you are, Billy. She had mousy brown hair and dorky clothes and no life— all she ever did was work all day. Everyone thought she was a boring nerd. Now everyone knows different. Corey thinks I'm hot. And I . . . I love him," she blurted, and in the next breath was appalled at what she'd said. After what had happened the other day, she didn't even think she wanted to see Corey ever again. She was scared of him. Scared of what he'd done, of what he was capable of doing.

But maybe it was her fault. Maybe she'd just overreacted, gone about trying to reason with him in the wrong way, and he'd lost his temper. Maybe nothing like that would ever happen again...

She almost started to cry just thinking about it. But she wouldn't cry in front of Billy. He was staring at her like she'd just crawled out from under a rock.

"A boring nerd?" His lip curled. "Yeah, you have to be a hair spray model to be interesting, right? Can't be too smart or the cool guys won't like you."

She flushed, then brushed past him and grabbed the bucket. "Get lost. I have work to—"

At that moment, the door swung open and Corey strolled in. He was wearing khaki pants and a white T-shirt and his sunglasses hid his eyes.

"Hey, baby, what's up?" He breezed toward Daffodil, ignoring Billy.

"I'm working." Her voice came out all wooden. Just the sight of him made her want to back up and it was all she could do to stand there calmly and act like he wasn't some kind of monster or something.

"Take a break. Let's go for a walk. Your boss won't mind."

"Yeah, she will. She was really mad about... about the other day."

"Screw her." He gave Daffodil a lazy smile, took off the sunglasses, and dangled them from the collar of his T-shirt. "Just tell her you're taking a ten-minute break. I think it's a law that employees are supposed to get a ten-minute break every—"

"Knock it off, Dillard. Maybe she doesn't want to take a walk with you. Maybe she doesn't ever want to see you again."

Corey threw Billy a scornful glance. "Stay out of this, wimp. This is between me and my girlfriend. Got that?"

"I got news for you, Dillard. You ever lay a hand on her again and I'll kick your ass back to where you came from."

Corey stiffened and his eyes turned cold. The glance he shot at Daffodil made her heart skip a beat.

"What did you tell him?"

"Nothing! I swear! Billy, you don't know what you're talking about. Just because I fell out of bed you're making up all kinds of stories that can only get you in trouble."

"You're the one who's headed for trouble, Daff." Billy spoke quietly. "Unless you quit hanging around with this jerk. I mean it, just tell him to get lost. Quit letting him use you for a punching bag—"

"Shut up! Just shut the hell up!" Corey lunged toward Billy and hit him before the other boy could block the punch. Billy went down, sprawling backward on the floor with a crash that brought Katy running from the kitchen.

"What's going on here?" When she saw Billy on the floor, her eyes widened. She rushed toward him, but he was already scrambling to his feet and he shook off her hand as she tried to help him stand. He was starting to launch himself at Corey, when Daffodil jumped in front of him.

"No, Billy, stop it!" Daffodil was shaking all over. Corey was taller and heavier than Billy . . . and he'd taken tae kwon do. He'd love an excuse to beat up Billy, and if he got started, even Ms. Templeton might not be able to stop him. "I'm going for a walk with Corey," she announced quickly. "Corey, you still want to go for a walk with me, right?"

"Yeah. Right." He licked his lips, glancing contemptuously at Billy, then into Daffodil's pleading eyes. He had to set her straight and keep her straight. Make sure she didn't open her mouth. "Ms. Templeton, I'll bring her right back, I promise. Come on, Daff."

Katy watched, her gaze troubled, as the screen door slammed behind them.

"Billy, are you all right?"

"Yeah. He surprised me, that's all." Billy was rubbing his

jaw, staring out the window at Corey and Daffodil as they headed toward the bench across the street, outside the real estate office.

Katy decided it was time to cut to the chase. "You still care about Daffodil, don't you?"

He shook his head. "Nope. She can do whatever she wants. She's already done a damn good job of flushing her life down the toilet."

"What do you mean? By dating Corey?"

"That's only the last straw," he muttered. He picked up the bucket Daffodil had left on the floor and trudged back to the kitchen, with Katy following him.

"I told you she used to be a straight-A student. She wanted to go to a Big Ten university, wanted to become a scientist."

"A scientist? Daffodil?" It was hard to imagine the spacey blonde bombshell who spilled a Coke on herself almost every day handling Bunsen burners and test tubes.

Billy sighed. "She may be klutzy and act like a ditz, but Daff has a brain. She won two science fairs in a row during grade school. And she did this physics thing with a gyroscope in eighth grade that all the teachers went crazy over. When we were together, she told me all about how she was going to need to win scholarships for college because her mom couldn't afford to help her. All because every cent Mrs. Moline makes goes toward helping Rose become a movie star." He rolled his eyes. "Her mom always told Daff that she was the smart one, and Rose was the pretty one. And that the smart one could take care of herself."

"It sounds to me like Mrs. Moline is the one who needs some education," Katy said. She felt a twinge of anger. She hadn't spent all that much time getting to know Daffodil, but she knew that if her own daughter had lived, she'd never have tried to pigeonhole her, or brush off her dreams. She'd have helped her become the best she could be and would have given her all the support she could.

"What does this have to do with her screwing up her life?" she asked Billy slowly. "Besides dating Corey, that is."

"Daff *could* have gotten scholarships, if she'd kept her grades up. But everything changed when we hit high school." He started loading dirty plates and cups from the bucket into the dishwasher, not looking at Katy.

"We were friends from the time we were little kids—we used to play together all the time. In eighth grade, we both realized how we felt...well, you know...she became my girlfriend. Then we hit high school. Bam. Suddenly Daff just went crazy. I don't think she cracked a book all freshman year. She was too busy chugging beer at a bunch of parties."

Katy saw the scowl on his face deepen.

"She dragged me along at first. But I wasn't cool enough for her new friends," he added in a sarcastic tone.

"Billy, that must have been a pretty rough time for you."

"Yeah, well, it got worse." His shoulders slumped. "She dyed her hair blonde on Thanksgiving Day our freshman year, and then she broke up with me that night when I came to her house for dessert. Right after Thanksgiving dinner." Anger throbbed through his voice.

"And just like that..." He snapped his fingers. "She started dating Tommy Tucker, and then she moved on to some other jerk on the football team. She's barely given me the time of day since then. As if I wanted her to," he added swiftly.

Katy eyed him sympathetically, but before she could speak, he rushed on. "You should have seen her when Corey Dillard moved to town. She hooked up with him faster than a dog can lick a dish. And now, you know what? She's going into her senior year, and her grade point average is the pits. And it's her own fault."

Katy had been listening in growing dismay. "So she's blown any hope of a scholarship?"

"You got it. And what's she left with? That loser who beats her—" Billy broke off, slumping over the work counter. "Someone's got to talk some sense into her," he muttered.

I already tried, Katy thought in dismay. *And got nowhere.*

"What about her mother? I think I'm going to pay Mrs. Moline a visit."

"She's in L.A. with Rose."

"Still?" Katy stared at him. "You mean Daffodil's staying there all alone? She told me her mom was coming home yesterday or today."

"She probably just wanted to get you off her back."

If it was true that Corey had been the one to inflict those bruises, Katy knew it wasn't safe for Daffodil to be staying alone. She glanced out the front window and saw Daffodil and Corey still sitting on the bench.

"When she gets back, I'm going to talk to her."

Billy stashed the bucket in the storage closet and closed the door. "Hope you like talking to a brick wall."

When Daffodil returned, Katy did her best to convince her to stay with a friend or relative until her mother got home, and at last the girl shrugged and agreed to spend a few nights with her friend Marcy. It seemed to Katy that she was trying hard to appear nonchalant and far more indifferent than she felt.

When Mrs. Moline comes home, I have no choice but to warn her, Katy decided, as she finally returned to basting the ribs. *Daffodil needs help fast. She needs to know that she can get out of this relationship with Corey, and that there are people around who will help her.*

It was no surprise that Luke Dillard's nephew appeared to be as much a macho bully as his uncle had been. If Corey had really struck Daffodil, he deserved to be prosecuted for assault. Maybe Daffodil would at some point even consider pressing charges.

I never even thought of pressing charges against Luke the night he almost raped me, she thought. *I just wanted to forget all about it.*

Regret twisted inside her. Who knew how many other women Luke had hurt in the following years? She remembered how he'd laughed when the straps of her dress had ripped when he'd grabbed her. How he'd tried to hike up her skirt as he pinned her against the passenger seat of his truck . . .

She'd never fully been able to forget that if not for Jackson, Luke would have done a lot worse to her. And if Daffodil didn't dump Corey and get some support and protection, Corey might do worse to her the next time . . .

Jackson.

Thinking of him soothed her. As she closed the oven door and left the ribs to bake in the rich sauce, her thoughts shifted back to last night, to the beautiful ways he'd made love to her. The gentle touch of those big callused hands grazing her body, the warmth of his lips on her throat, on her breasts. And the triumphant gleam in those astonishing blue eyes when they'd clutched each other and held on for dear life, writhing and rushing toward the most explosive and exquisite climax Katy had ever known.

It was too soon. Too soon to be having such intense feelings for anyone. But there it was. If she wasn't careful she'd be getting in way too deep with Jackson Brent, a man who'd broken more hearts than Russell Crowe.

It wasn't smart and none of this should be happening. But thinking of last night, and of the way Jackson had been there for her every time she needed him ever since she came home, she couldn't deny that she was starting to have feelings for him. All the wrong feelings.

The knowledge scared her. It scared her almost as much

as the idea of someone having killed Matt, of that person being on the loose, perhaps closing in on her.

It would seem that her life was in danger. But almost as unnerving, Katy thought as she sliced vegetables in the warm quiet of the diner, so was her heart.

Chapter 25

Mojo wandered into Katy's bedroom as she leaned toward the mirror and applied silky taupe lipstick, his tail wagging as he watched her.

"You miss everybody, don't you, boy?"

Ambling forward, the dog regarded her hopefully.

"In a few more days everyone'll be home. Just hang in there."

She glanced at her watch as the lab settled down on the rug, resting his dark head on his paws. Jackson would be here any minute to pick her up for dinner, and butterflies tumbled in her stomach at the knowledge that within moments she'd be seeing him again.

What are you, sixteen years old? she asked herself, but she couldn't help the way she felt. The past two nights she'd spent at his cabin had reawakened her to life and all its vibrancy in a way nothing else had since the day she'd lost the baby.

The hurt of that was still there, and the pain of her divorce, but for the first time, life felt good. Almost good. Even if it wasn't safe to stay alone at night in her own house, even if there was a murderous creep out there waiting for another chance, she knew at least that she wanted to live and she wanted to be happy—and she could be.

She didn't know exactly how Jackson felt about her and not long ago, the uncertainty of that would have scared her out of her wits. She'd have run like hell from any kind of involvement with him, rather than risk being hurt again. But now, she wasn't sure exactly how it had happened, but being with Jackson was a risk she was willing to take. A risk she *wanted* to take.

Katy Templeton. Taking a risk again. Will wonders never cease? She closed her eyes. And prayed she wasn't headed for disaster.

Dabbing on perfume, she heard the tires of Jackson's truck crunching outside. Her heartbeat quickened. Mojo bounded from the bedroom barking, and she heard his paws thumping down the stairs. Hastily she added a whisper of blush to her cheekbones and stood back from the mirror to survey the results.

Not bad. Black capris and sandals, a silky topaz tank top just short enough to show a hint of her belly button, and slim silver hoops in her ears. Her hair was caught back from her face in a high ponytail, wrapped in a black leather band.

She was probably overdressed for dinner at Margie and Lee's—black jeans and a cotton shirt would have been fine—but she'd wanted to dress up for Jackson.

"You're crazy," she told herself and grabbed her purse, but just as she started out of the room, the phone rang and she whirled back to snatch up the cordless handset from the nightstand.

"Katy, it's Stan Harvey."

"Sheriff Harvey." Her hand tightened on the phone. "Is there some news?"

"Sure is. Good news and bad news."

Her stomach quivered. What did that mean?

"I've been checking things out," the sheriff continued in his deep, rusty voice. "And I had a conversation with Donna Kirk—Crystal's mother—a short while ago. It seems she didn't exactly tell you the truth the other day. Looks like Crystal did make it out of Thunder Creek after all."

"What?"

"Her mother says she saw Crystal about a week after she left here, and spoke to her again some months later. Twice more since then, the final time a year ago last April."

"Oh, my God. But why did she tell me she hadn't seen her or spoken to her?" Stunned, Katy could scarcely believe her ears. "Why did she say that Crystal never showed up?"

"Well, it seems Crystal left home under real bad circumstances. She fought with her father when she was sixteen and ran away in the middle of the night. Ed Kirk never forgave her for that. He disowned her, said his daughter was as good as dead. When you called, Ed was standing right there. The mother didn't want him to know she'd seen Crystal. According to her, he blew a gasket when he heard she was coming back—threatened to throw Donna out if she let Crystal step inside his house. So Donna and Crystal actually met in secret, someplace away from the house, and the husband never even knew about it. Donna never even told him she'd talked to the girl again. I guess Crystal was a real sore spot between them."

"He was hostile when I spoke to him on the phone," Katy said. "He called Crystal a little bitch."

"Yeah, well, I guess that's why the mother didn't tell you the truth with him standing right there. She knew it'd set him off but good." Katy heard him sigh. "Sounds like she's terrified of the guy."

"So . . . she lied to me." Relief seeped through her. "Crystal really did make it out of Thunder Creek that day."

" 'Pears so. And that would mean that the sketch Matt drew wasn't based on his seeing her dead body. Now, I don't know why he drew her that way—maybe he was just using his imagination. Or maybe she was only sleeping or . . . who knows? To tell you the truth, and without having seen the sketch, I just can't figure it out. Not without more information, anyway."

"So . . . what happens now?" she asked dazedly, struggling to take it all in.

"Now I try to find Crystal and officially verify she's alive. I don't have much of a lead, but I'll give it my best shot."

"Did she tell you where Crystal was the last time they talked?"

Jackson was knocking at the door, and Mojo was barking frantically downstairs. She headed into the hall.

"Yep—San Bernardino, California. But that was over a year ago. Could be a cold trail by now. But I'll start there and see what I can find. At least we know this isn't a murder investigation, Katy. That's the good news."

The sheriff cleared his throat.

"Okay. So tell me the bad news," Katy said quietly. But she was already starting to fill in the pieces.

"The bad news is that we're now back at square one as far as that attack on you is concerned. I've got two theories: one is that for some reason your asking questions about Crystal and about that supposed pact of Matt's might have shaken somebody up—enough to drive that person to break into the Triple T and attack you. We'll know a lot more about the likelihood of that if we can find and question Crystal. Until then, I'm not ruling it out."

She reached the bottom of the steps and opened the door to find Jackson standing there looking more handsome than any man had a right to be. He wore dark jeans that sublimely fit his long, lean torso, and an open-necked white shirt that emphasized his deep tan. His thick hair gleamed like dark silk in the fading gold-tinged sunlight, framing that lean, hard-jawed face. Her eyes sought out his and she reached for his hand, drawing him into the house as Mojo leaped madly about, and Sheriff Harvey continued in his steady tone.

"There's another possibility, Katy, and we have to take a

look at it as well. A serious look. Maybe whoever came after you the other night didn't do it because you were digging into the past. Maybe right now in the present there's someone who has a grudge against you. Can you think of anyone?"

"No, no one," she replied, startled. She tried to wrap her mind around this new theory.

"You sure? No one who'd want to harm you or scare you out of town?"

"I'll . . . I'll have to think about it, Sheriff, and get back to you. Nothing springs to mind right now."

"Well, give it some thought. In the meantime, you go on being careful, honey. Keep all the doors and windows locked, and keep your guard up."

"I will."

When she set the phone down, Jackson wrapped his arms around her waist. "You look like someone just stole your saddle right out from under you. What's up?"

"That was Sheriff Harvey," she said slowly. "Crystal Kirk is alive."

"What? He's sure?"

"Yes. Her mother admitted she lied to me because her husband was in the room—she *has* spoken to Crystal since she left Thunder Creek. Jackson." She drew an unsteady breath. "Do you realize what this means? Matt's fall *was* an accident, after all. He didn't see Crystal lying dead somewhere. There was no murder. We were wrong."

"I guess that's good, right?" Jackson's arms tightened around her even as his mind rapidly processed this new information. He hated the strain and confusion he saw in her face. He spoke against her hair as she rested her head on his shoulder. "We'll get to the bottom of this, Katy. We'll take our time and get it all figured out—"

Suddenly, he tensed, and eased her back so he could look into her eyes. "Hold on. If Crystal's alive, then why did someone come after you the other night? Why did your questions hit such a nerve?"

"Sheriff Harvey has two theories. He thinks someone might have still been shaken up by the questions and come after me, or that someone has a grudge against me and is trying to scare me out of town. But if that was the case, why would whoever did it steal Matt's sketch? And warn me to stop asking questions. Unless that was only a cover..." She took a deep breath. "Do you think that's possible?"

"Damned if I know." A muscle clenched in his jaw. He didn't like this, didn't like any of it. Stealing the sketch made no sense. But then, neither did someone attacking Katy.

He remembered the way she'd looked when he'd found her on the kitchen floor. The next time he might not be there, the next time the bastard might have a chance to finish what he'd started. Fear pumped through him, and with it, anger. He subdued both with an effort.

"Okay, let's focus on the theory of someone wanting to scare you out of town. Any idea who that might be?"

"Someone who didn't like the food at the diner?"

"Not funny."

"Well, Tammi and Wood really want me to sell them the diner. But I can't believe they'd stoop to threats and violence to chase me out of town, thinking I'd sell the diner to them before I headed for the hills."

"You never know," Jackson said. "Wood Morgan didn't get where he is today by playing by the rules. From what I've heard, he's broken a few along the way, twisted a few arms to get what he wants. So has another one of our local big-shot ranchers."

Her eyes met his. "You're talking about Luke."

"You've made it pretty clear you want nothing to do with him. And Luke doesn't take rejection well. There were rumors he roughed up Dixie when she asked him for a divorce. And when Corinne dropped him for Roy Hewett he started stalking her. Nothing major or too obvious, nothing that she could prove—but she said it was creepy."

"Yes, but... I don't know. It sounds crazy," Katy muttered. Not that she would ever defend Luke. But the thought of him sneaking into the house, cutting the lights, choking her, and hitting her over the head...

Trying to maul her in his truck was one thing, but breaking and entering and assault—all these years later?

Maybe he'd carried a grudge against her since that night. Maybe against Jackson too, which would explain Ajax getting shot.

"You still think he shot Ajax, don't you?"

Jackson's lip curled. "Let's just say I think his alibi isn't worth a bucket of spit. And just maybe there's a connection between all of this."

"Do you really think he carries that much of a grudge from all those years ago? That's sick." But an icy tremble ran through her. Shooting that dog was sick. Grabbing her in the dark and choking her was sick. Still...

"I'm leaning toward Wood." The words spilled from her suddenly. "He could have two possible motives. Not only does he want Bessie's Diner, he also had a big problem with my asking questions about Matt and Crystal—and the pact. Something must have happened back then that he doesn't want anyone to know about."

"You could be right." Jackson frowned. "In that case, let's call Harvey tomorrow and steer him in that direction."

"In the meantime, we'd better hurry," Katy suddenly realized. "We're already late for dinner."

"Margie will forgive us." Jackson tipped her chin up and studied her. "Are you all right? You look kind of shaky. Gorgeously beautiful," he added with his slow grin. "But shaky."

"Thanks. It's just a lot to take in. I'll be fine."

"Yes. You will." Jackson's eyes held hers. She looked so

elegant, so fragile, all he wanted to do was hold her and protect her. It was difficult seeing the doubt and worry in those
striking eyes. Even the rich sensuousness of her silky tank
top couldn't disguise the tension in her body. "No one's going to lay a hand on you again—except me," he assured her
with a flash of a grin. Her answering smile hit him like a jolt
of bottled lightning.

"Promise?" she teased.

He answered lightly but there was a tightness in his chest.
"Word of honor."

By the time they returned to the Triple T it was nearly eleven.
Katy had barely been able to taste her food, but had forced
herself to eat two helpings of Margie's famous lasagna—
a wonderful recipe she'd stolen and reinvented at the Rattlesnake—and to push a slice of Better Than Sex chocolate
cake around her plate until it looked like she'd eaten more
than a handful of crumbs.

Despite her lack of appetite, the glass of wine she'd sipped
at dinner had helped take the edge off her nerves, and so had
Jackson. He and Lee and Margie had an easy friendship that
pleased her. And when the baby had woken up and Margie
had brought him out and dumped him into Jackson's arms, a
thrilling rush had shot through her. Jackson held the baby
easily, and his face had relaxed with pleasure as he'd surveyed the squirming bundle. Some men looked awkward
holding infants—Seth had always avoided it when they were
visiting friends with babies, joking that he'd wait for his
own—but Jackson looked comfortable, and he'd laughed,
his eyes lighting when Cooper grasped his thumb for dear
life in his tiny pink fingers.

And only once, when they were doing the dishes together
in the kitchen, had Margie even tried to pry information out
of her.

"Okay, spill." Margie had handed her a dripping platter to dry as they stood side by side at the aluminum sink. "I want to hear everything about what's up with you two. Wood Morgan told Smoke that you and Jackson were at the Tumbleweed together."

"It wasn't like that. It wasn't a date," Katy began, her cheeks going pink, but Margie interrupted with a grin.

"Oh, honey, you don't have to tell me if you don't want to. But geez, I saw how he looked at you when I brought out the Better Than Sex cake. Like he couldn't imagine anything better than sex with you. I nearly dropped my fork. For a man who's pretty cool about his emotions, Jackson's practically wearing his heart on his sleeve. But," she continued, as Katy's blush deepened, "you don't have to tell me a thing. I'm just nosy. And . . ." She paused in the act of rinsing soapy water out of the lasagna pan, and spoke more softly, a thread of emotion running through her voice.

"I want you to be happy. I want to believe that Jackson is helping to heal that stomped-on heart of yours. Is he?"

"Yes." Katy took a deep breath. The word seemed so inadequate to describe what was between her and Jackson, what she knew she felt for him. Despite all caution, all common sense, she couldn't stop the hot tumble of feelings that possessed her whenever she was near him—or even thought about him.

"This is so cool." Margie's grin widened. "My best friend and the heartthrob of Thunder Creek High. I *never* would have seen this coming."

She wasn't the only one, Katy reflected later, when she'd returned home shortly before midnight, let Mojo outside into the yard, and then proceeded to pack a few things for her overnight stay at the cabin.

If anyone had told her a month ago that she'd be in danger of falling in love with her brother's best friend, she'd have thought they belonged in an insane asylum. But then, if anyone had told her that Matt had been hiding some big dark secret all those years ago, she wouldn't have believed that either.

But he wasn't murdered, she reminded herself as she tossed a black satin bra and thong into an overnight tote, along with a matching camisole. *Neither was Crystal.*

She still couldn't quite accept that the sketch Matt had drawn meant nothing, even though it had been stolen—and that someone attacking her in her own house was unrelated to the questions she'd been asking about the past.

During the drive home tonight, Jackson had told her he'd learned from Elam that Crystal had lived at the Pine Hills Apartments south of town. Only yesterday that kind of information had seemed so important—now it no longer mattered.

Yet she fervently hoped that Sheriff Harvey would manage to locate Crystal. Having a chance to talk to her personally might be the only way to clear up the last nagging questions about Matt and the sketch—as well as whatever secret pact he'd made and kept, and taken to his grave.

Mojo was scratching at the front door and she ran downstairs with her tote. But as she opened the door and the dog trotted inside, she suddenly saw Jackson sprinting from the barn. He halted when he saw her come out onto the porch.

"Looks like it's game time," he called. "Cleo's water just broke."

"My God." Her pulse started to race. She grabbed the porch rail. She and Jackson had been keeping careful track—this was only the 337th day of Cleo's gestation, and her prior gestation date had been day 342. This was probably the very earliest date Cleo could deliver and still have a good chance of the foal's lung function being strong enough for it to survive.

Thank God they'd come back tonight—Jackson was here, just in case something went wrong...

"I just remembered—her appetite was off today," she gasped. "Riley noticed it too." *I should have noticed that sign. I wasn't paying enough attention. Because I was too immersed in everything else,* she thought with a rush of guilt. "Jackson, does she . . . does she look all right?"

"Far as I can tell, she looks perfect," he called over his shoulder, already sprinting back toward the barn. "Come see for yourself."

Darting upstairs, she kicked off her high-heeled black sandals and stripped out of her clothes, tossing them on the bed. She yanked on gray sweats and stuffed her feet into sneakers, then rushed downstairs and out of the house.

Her heart was thudding by the time she reached the barn and saw Cleo in her stall. Cleo was past the initial pacing stage and was already lying down on her side, quiet, only her ears twitching back and forth as she endured her contractions. She groaned once and her body strained mightily as Katy entered the back of the stall. The white bubble that was the amniotic membrane had already appeared, and within it, Katy suddenly saw that the first of the foal's feet was visible. The sight of that foot filled her with a rush of hope, and the fervent wish that her father could have been here to see this.

There was another contraction, and Cleo groaned again, her body straining.

"Don't worry, girl," Katy whispered, anxiety knotting her stomach. "Your baby's going to be perfect."

Jackson dragged his gaze from the laboring mare to glance at her. Hope and worry mingled on her beautiful face as she stared intently at the mare, as if willing her with every ounce of her being to come through the pregnancy alive, with a healthy foal. He could only imagine the emotions running through her—hope for Cleo's pregnancy to be successful, along with memories of her own failed one, and of the baby she'd wanted so badly to bring into the world, and had ultimately lost.

"She's doing great," he told her softly. "There's the other foot now, sole down, exactly in the right position. Atta girl, Cleo."

When the foal's nose appeared two minutes later, Katy squeezed Jackson's hand with excitement.

"Looking good," he said in a low tone. They both knew the whole process shouldn't take more than twenty minutes, and that most of the problems that usually occurred during delivery would have appeared by this stage. Katy realized she'd been holding her breath, and released it, for the first time actually starting to believe that Cleo would give birth to a healthy foal.

The next few minutes flew by, and suddenly, the rest of the foal's neck, front legs, and shoulders emerged, then its torso and hips. It was over so quickly that all Katy could do was stare in wonder at the miracle before her—the chestnut mare breathing heavily on her side, and the wet, trembling, utterly beautiful colt she'd just presented to the world.

"She did it! Oh, my God, Jackson, she *did* it!" she breathed, grabbing his arm. Tears burned at her eyes. Hot, happy tears, and it was all she could do to keep her voice low, so as not to scare Cleo or the colt. Her whole being wanted to shout and dance with joy.

"Damn straight she did." Jackson grinned from ear to ear. "I bet that colt will be up on his sternum in under ten minutes—and standing in twenty." He pulled Katy to him and kissed her, a quick triumphant kiss that made her heart sing even more wildly.

And he was right, in less than the usual thirty minutes, the colt was standing on shaky legs, the cord broken. When he nickered, Cleo rose too. She nuzzled and licked him affectionately as he began his instinctive search for her teats. Spellbound, Katy watched them, joy rising in her with each passing moment. She wasn't going anywhere until she saw the colt start to nurse, and she knew Jackson wasn't either—especially not until the placenta passed.

Cleo had her foal. A healthy foal. A huge burden slipped from her shoulders as before her eyes, the dusky colt gave a lusty sigh and began to nurse.

Happiness shook her at the sight of mother and newborn. *Good for you, Cleo. Take care of him, love him.*

Beside her, Jackson noted the passing of the placenta. Just like clockwork. He couldn't seem to stop grinning.

But when he turned to Katy, and saw the wonder and joy in her face, the shimmer of tears on her eyelashes, his own throat thickened with emotion. A powerful mingling of tenderness and lust surged through him in a way he'd never experienced before.

"Why don't we clear out and give these two a chance to get to know each other." He slipped an arm around her waist and drew her from the stall.

The moment they were out of the barn, Katy and Jackson looked at each other in the cool moonlit darkness, then started to grin. Katy felt like she could lift her arms and fly. She grabbed Jackson's hand and began to run, pulling him along with her toward the ranch house. Laughing, exhilarated, they raced through the shadows, whooping like children. By the time they'd pounded up the stairs and stripped off their clothes and tumbled into the glass-enclosed shower stall in the upstairs bath, they were more than ready for each other.

"That was the most incredible thing I've ever seen!" Katy gasped as the hot spray of water drenched her hair and skin, washing away the grime and sweat and straw of the barn. She grinned as Jackson ducked completely under the water, his hair streaming across his brow and into his eyes.

He was magnificent, and desire spilled violently through

her at the sight of his dripping, naked body. Water glistened across his chest, and down his powerfully muscled arms and legs. And he was ready for her, more than ready, she realized with an indrawn breath. Her breasts tingled, their peaks hardening as she nestled closer, curving herself against him. With one arm snaked around his neck, she seized a cake of soap, and with a saucy smile began lathering every bronzed delicious inch of him.

Jackson couldn't decide whether to groan or grin as she washed him. Her hands tormented him with their soft, soapy strokes, while her wet, rosy-tipped breasts pressed against his chest.

"God, you're beautiful." His lips caught hers, his teeth nipping at the soft bottom lip, and then he grabbed her bottle of body wash and poured it into his rough palms. It was tangerine-scented, fresh and delicate—like her, he thought, as he worked the fragrant liquid into a lather and began stroking it over her shoulders, and in soapy circles around those firm, lovely breasts. She moved sensuously in his arms, murmuring, locking her body against his, even as her hands slid downward to touch and stroke him, arousing him to an even more intense and pounding need than before. Their lips met and clung beneath the steam and hot water. The kiss was endless and powerful, as deep and cleansing as the steam and the soap.

Steam swirled thick as a forest mist through the bathroom as the hot water pummeled them, as their bodies responded to one another. Katy's murmurs of pleasure changed to breathless moans as Jackson's hand stroked downward to the wet silky hair between her thighs.

"Jackson, I need you," she gasped. "I need you right now."

"Yep, sweetheart, I know just what you mean." He chuckled devilishly but his voice was hoarse. "But you're going to have to hold on a little longer."

His eyes gleamed into hers as one arm slid around her,

and his other hand slipped inside her. Katy drew a deep shuddering breath. His kisses became darker, more furious and demanding.

Oh, Lord. Katy gulped in those kisses, unable to breathe without them. He had such strong hands. Yet such an arousingly gentle touch. The hunger in his eyes denied the leisure of those touches, as he stoked the eager circles of flame inside her until she was ready to explode.

The world became a blur of their two bodies enveloped by mist, thrumming water, and the hot dance of kisses under silver rain. By the time he shifted her against the wall of the stall and lifted her up, by the time she wrapped her legs around him and he slid inside her, the need and the fire were bursting through them both like lava and Katy's head fell back as Jackson's mouth pressed greedily at her throat.

They made love wildly, ecstatically, and after their bodies reached a shuddering climax that left them spent and shaken, they held each other still. Katy's face burrowed into his neck, her hands clutched tightly at his shoulders. And every part of her felt clean and new and alive, as if he'd awakened all that had been numb and hidden inside her.

Eventually they tumbled into bed—her bed—too relaxed and tired to drive back to the cabin. Besides, they wanted to check on Cleo and the foal first thing in the morning.

"What are you going to name him?" Jackson asked as he lightly stroked her hair. They were both naked, curled like spoons in the narrow bed, as moonlight glistened across the yellow coverlet that protected them from the cool night breeze.

"Midnight," she murmured, thinking of the dusky colt born so close to the stroke of twelve. "Unless my father has his heart set on something else."

"I think he has his heart set on your sticking around. And that's about it. Your mom told me he's missed you all these years more than he'd ever admit."

"That's Big John for you." She twisted around, facing him, reaching up a hand to draw her fingers through his still-damp hair. "I wonder how he'd feel if I decided to stay."

Jackson's eyes searched her face. "I can tell you how I'd feel."

She couldn't breathe for a moment. "Don't let me stop you." She tried for a light tone, but Jackson immediately pulled her toward him and shifted so that she was on top of him, her mouth no more than a breath away from his.

"On second thought, I'm not much of a talker." He ran his tongue slowly, deliberately around the edges of her lips. Then he gently bit the lobe of her ear. "Why don't I just show you instead?"

And that was all the talking either of them did for a very long time.

Wood Morgan scowled at the moon as Elam opened the door of the Land Rover and swung nimbly into the gray leather seat. The car was parked on a back road half a mile from the Tumbleweed, the windows rolled up, the air conditioning running. It was three in the morning and Wood guessed that aside from the two of them, only the bats and owls and coyotes were awake.

"What are you waiting for? Tell me," Wood ordered, not even turning his head. "Tell me everything Brent said today."

"He wanted to know where Crystal lived. There was no harm in it, so I told him. That was it. I figured he'd hit me with another bunch of questions, but he didn't. Still," the bartender added, studying Wood's scowling profile, "it shows that he and Katy Templeton haven't dropped it—they're still asking questions. So there goes your big theory that they'd give it up and quit poking into Matt Templeton's ashes."

Wood's stomach roiled. "Those idiots. Those fucking idiots. I can't afford this."

"Ain't that the truth," Elam drawled. He leaned back in the seat.

"If Tammie ever found out, she'd divorce you before you could spit." He nonchalantly stretched his long legs out as far as he could, and chewed a little more on the wad of tobacco that had been rolling around his mouth for the past hour. "She'd take you for everything you've got. If she didn't kill you first," he chuckled.

"Shut up. You think this is funny? I'll give you funny. I haven't paid you hush money all these years just to get screwed now by Matt Templeton's little sister sticking her stuck-up nose in something that's none of her business. If I go down, Elam, I guaran-damn-tee you, you're going down too. If Paxton ever finds out what happened in the bar that night you're out on your ass. And if the Templeton girl and Brent ever find out—"

"They won't," Elam said softly. "I'll take care of it."

There was a pause during which Wood could almost hear the drops of sweat trickling down his own forehead. For a horrible moment he thought he was going to have to lean out the window and barf.

Damn it, he'd made one lousy drunken mistake that night and he'd been paying for it ever since. Paying in sweat, in nightmares, in guilt—and in bucks. Big bucks. But he damn well wasn't going to let one stupid error in judgment get in the way of everything he'd built in this town. No way.

No one could find out. No matter what it took.

"I still don't like you telling them she hailed from Tucson," he growled. "What if they followed up on that?"

"No one in Tucson can help them find what they want to know. But if I'd lied about it, and they found out, that would've brought them straight back to me. And that would have been bad news for you."

"Don't threaten me, Elam. Don't ever threaten me."

Wood Morgan turned his head then to stare at the man in the passenger seat beside him. Sweat dribbled down the rancher's temples, but his light brown eyes were as cold and flat as stone in the beams of moonlight, the eyes of a man to whom ruthlessness had become second nature.

Even Elam felt a quick chill at their expression. "Hey, Wood, you know I'm on your side," he backtracked quickly. "Haven't I kept your secret all these years?"

"Our secret, Elam. Don't forget it's *our* secret."

"Sure, but you've had the most to lose. And I've kept my mouth shut the entire time."

"For a price. You've been well paid for your silence and for your help," Wood snapped.

"So now I'm ready to help you some more. Katy Templeton and Jackson Brent haven't quit asking questions as of today. So what's our next move?"

There was silence for a moment, except for the whir of the air-conditioner in the dark, silent night. Wood Morgan spoke at last, grimly, biting out the words. He really had no choice.

"*Your* next step is to do exactly what I say. Nothing more, nothing less. Wait for my call. And then, if you succeed in shutting Katy Templeton down once and for all, I'll pay you ten thousand dollars."

Ten thousand dollars. Hot damn, Elam thought.

Over the years, Wood's fear of discovery had helped Elam build a nice little nest egg. But the well had run dry for a while—until Katy Templeton came to town and started asking questions. Now things were looking up again, looking up big time.

Another ten thousand dollars, he reflected with satisfaction, *just for getting Katy Templeton out of Wood's hair. Sweet.*

"Don't worry about a thing," Elam assured Wood as he opened the car door. Stepping out, he grinned cheerfully back at the somber-faced rancher whose face had taken on a sickly green sheen in the moonlight, as if he'd eaten something that violently disagreed with him.

"Like I always tell you, Wood, you can count on me. Just say the word and Katy Templeton won't be a problem for long."

Chapter 26

"HEY, BILLY, COME HAVE LUNCH WITH US!"

Marcy Hubner, eating a bacon, lettuce, and tomato sandwich across from Daffodil in the diner as Daffodil took her lunch break, winced as a sandaled foot kicked her under the table.

"Ow!" Marcy complained, loudly enough for Billy to hear.

Billy saw that kick, and saw Daffodil's wary expression as she glanced over toward him, then quickly away. His eyes narrowed, but he shook his head at Marcy.

Carrying his own burger and fries to a table at the rear of the diner he proceeded to eat his lunch, determined to keep his distance from Daffodil. If she was stupid enough to want to continue seeing that asshole Corey Dillard, that was her problem, he told himself. Not being able to get over Daffodil, still remembering how much fun they'd had dating in eighth grade—four whole years ago—that was his problem.

Why don't you concentrate on Marcy? he told himself, shifting his gaze to the buxom, brown-haired girl wearing cut offs and a V-necked red T-shirt. He'd dated a few girls in high school, no one seriously, but he knew when someone was interested in him, and Marcy was definitely interested.

The trouble was, he really wasn't—at least not in her.

He scowled at his pile of fries as he chewed his burger. He'd heard Katy ask Daffodil this morning if her mom had returned from Los Angeles yet.

She hadn't.

But he knew she'd been staying at Marcy's house in the meantime. That made him feel a little better.

Daffodil Moline is all screwed up, he told himself. *But you're not. You've got plans, and you're going to college and you're going to make something of your life. And if she wants to throw herself away on some asshole who beats up on her, it's none of your business.*

Yeah, right, he thought glumly, and wished that Corey Dillard would walk in right at that moment, wished he could get just one more shot at punching a hole in his smug little face.

But the doors to the diner remained closed, and the soft whir of the ceiling fan was the only sound other than the chatter of the girls in the booth toward the front. The lunch crowd had gone, the afternoon lull had set in, and as soon as he was done he needed to give Katy a hand in the kitchen.

By the time he carried his plate back to the sink, Katy was seasoning the ground beef for tonight's Marvelous Meat Loaf special, shaking in garlic salt, pepper, oregano, and onion powder, then adding two cups each of grated onions and mushrooms. The meat loaf, garlic mashed potatoes, and a green bean soufflé were on the menu tonight, as well as the usual fare.

"Just in time, Billy. I need you to start peeling those potatoes." She covered the huge stainless steel bowl of ground beef with plastic wrap and set it on the top shelf of the refrigerator.

"Okay, sure," he mumbled.

She threw him a sharp look. "What's wrong?" Walking to the sink to scrub her hands, she studied him. Billy looked even more serious than usual, and his voice was curt and low, the way it sounded when he was angry. "Is it Daffodil again? What did she do now?"

"She's taking a long lunch, for one thing."

Katy glanced into the dining room and saw Daffodil and Marcy lingering over their sandwiches.

"It's all right. There's not much for her to do until later anyway. I noticed you two still don't seem to be speaking much these days."

"Why should we be?"

Because you still care about her. And from the way she jumped in front of Corey the other day when he was coming after you, I think she cares more about you than she'd ever admit. But aloud she only said, "It's a bit awkward working together and not speaking, isn't it?"

"Doesn't bother me," he said, trying his best to sound in-different. "I've got nothing to say to her that she wants to hear. But..." He paused, potato peeler in hand. "You're still going to speak to Mrs. Moline when she gets back, right? If she ever does get back," he muttered.

"Definitely. Billy, I'm as concerned about Daffodil—and Corey—as you are."

"I just don't like to see any girl used as a punching bag, that's all. Even one who's gotten to be too stupid even to stand up for herself."

Too stupid, Katy thought, *or too down on her own sense of worth to realize she deserves better? Or*—she remembered the frightened way Daffodil had looked at Corey when he'd gone after Billy—*too afraid.*

Like Crystal Kirk's mother was afraid to tell the truth in front of her husband.

You need to stop thinking about Crystal, she told herself. *You need to think about who in the world would want to scare you into leaving town—or worse.*

It was chilling to think she had an enemy here in Thunder Creek, an enemy who would lock Mojo in the barn, cut the lights, and choke her from behind. An enemy who had struck her over the head, who might have killed her if Jackson hadn't shown up when he did.

"Wood Morgan's out front." Daffodil sailed into the kitchen, dumping the dishes she and Marcy had used in the sink. "He wants a slice of apple pie and coffee on the double."

"The coffeepot's out there." Billy jerked a thumb toward the dining room.

"I know that." Daffodil glared at him. "I came in for the pie."

"I'll take it to him," Katy said suddenly. Even as she directed the girl to empty and reload the dishwasher, fill the ketchup bottles, and assemble napkin and flatware setups for all the tables before the early dinner crowd arrived, she began slicing the still-warm apple pie, then centered it on a plate.

After she brought Wood the pie, a fork and napkin, and filled his coffee cup, she slid into the booth opposite him.

"Mind if I join you?"

His brown eyes flicked coolly over her, showing nothing of what was going on behind the bland, good-ol'-boy smile that slid onto his face. "My pleasure, Katy. I hope this means you're considering selling the diner after all. That would make my day. Tammie could use some good news."

"Oh? What's wrong?"

"Our two boys came down with chicken pox. Both of 'em. She's going out of her mind. They're quite a handful. And if that's not enough, she doesn't like the architect's plans for the dude ranch. Wants me to get some more bids." He took a sip of coffee. "That woman's a perfectionist. She wants everything done just so—but I have to say, she knows what she's talking about. We have a half dozen potential investors lined up already, wanting in on the dude ranch. Not that we need a one of 'em, mind you." He gave her a sly grin. "If the numbers come out the way I want, I'm ready to go it alone. Too many cooks spoil the broth, isn't that what they say?"

He chuckled, vastly amused by his own joke, and Katy managed a smile.

"I haven't changed my mind about the diner," she said. "But you can tell Tammie that at some point I might be willing to supply pies and baked goods to the dude ranch, if she's interested."

In truth, she'd never considered such a thing until this very moment. But she wanted to see how Wood reacted.

"That's real nice of you, Katy, but actually, we're hiring Elmo Panterri as chef. I reckon he'll be able to handle just about anything we need."

Elmo Panterri, chef to the stars. Despite herself, Katy was impressed. Elmo Panterri had owned his own restaurant in Los Angeles until he sold it for millions a few years ago, had an avid following for his cable cooking show, had catered countless celebrity weddings, and was considered one of the foremost of the new breed of American chefs.

"He might run a little cafe for us in town as well—the Cowpoke Cafe," he added. "For when our guests are shopping and sightseeing, you know. Tammie came up with the name. Hope you won't mind the competition," he said, those light-brown eyes turning shrewd. He was watching her reaction to this news, as closely as she'd been watching him.

Katy kept her expression neutral, but she almost felt relief. She suddenly began to doubt that Wood was behind the attack on her at the Triple T. This was a man who was too cunning, too clever to have to rely on physically mugging people—he just coldcocked them in business instead. He was the ultimate businessman, and if he wanted to please his wife by snaring Bessie's Diner for her to turn into a gift shop, he went about it not by hiring a hit man but by hiring a world-class chef to try to draw away all of Katy's customers and bankrupt the diner.

Of course, that didn't mean he wouldn't hire a hit man to stop me from asking questions about Matt and Crystal, she reminded herself.

But not without trying some business bludgeoning first, her instincts told her.

"Cowpoke Cafe—cute. Sort of like . . . Rattlesnake Cafe?"

"Hell, Katy." Wood paused with his forkful of pie halfway to his mouth. "You know, I'll bet Tammie never thought of that." His broad clever smile belied his words.

Never thought of it, my ass. You're a liar and a ruthless bastard. And maybe a killer.

"Well, Elmo or no Elmo, I think there's always going to be a place for Bessie's Diner in Thunder Creek." She managed a shrug. "I bet the dude ranch is going to create a lot of new jobs, bring new people to town. They all have to eat, so there should be plenty of business to go around."

"You never give an inch, do you?" Wood shook his head and set his fork down on the plate. "I've got a feeling Tammie's going to lose this one."

"Think so?" Katy smiled.

"I told her that the Templetons don't give up easy, not one of them. You may have moved away to the city, but you're still a tough Wyoming gal at heart, aren't you? And not so different from Big John—or from Matt," he added, "when he got something into his head."

"I wasn't aware you knew Matt that well."

"We didn't hang around together in high school, but everyone knew Matt Templeton. He was Thunder Creek's golden boy."

Was it her imagination or was there a slight edge to his voice?

Her pulse quickening, Katy kept her gaze steadily on his face. "Even a golden boy could get into trouble now and then."

"Like you said, Matt and I weren't close enough for me to know anything about that."

"Are you sure? Because I think you do know something. I think you might know what was troubling my brother before he died. Something having to do with Crystal Kirk."

She leaned forward, suddenly imploring him. "If you know, Wood, just tell me. Matt was hiding some kind of secret before he died. I can't rest until I know the truth—but it doesn't have to go any further than the two of us. Tammie never needs to know—"

"I told you. I don't know what you're talking about." His voice was colder than the bottom of the Atlantic. He glanced at his watch and slid from the booth.

"Afraid I have to make tracks."

His expression and his voice had both hardened, and Katy had the distinct impression that he'd just found out what he'd actually come to the diner to discover: if she was going to drop the matter—or not.

He set me up, she realized with a start. *He deliberately led the conversation to Matt, trying to see what I would do. And I told him what he most wanted to know—that as far as I'm concerned, the subject isn't closed.*

"Got a three o'clock meeting with a contractor," Wood said curtly. "Need my bill."

"No problem."

She had the feeling he was no longer even seeing her, that his mind had moved ahead to a place she couldn't begin to follow—a place she wouldn't *want* to follow, she thought uneasily.

Katy handed him his change, then slammed the register shut as Wood strolled out of the diner and let the screen door bang behind him.

"Excuse me. Katy?"

She turned and for the first time noticed the woman

seated at the corner table near the window. It was Corinne, the waitress from the Tumbleweed.

Katy hurried over. "Sorry to keep you waiting. What can I get you?"

But Corinne smiled and shook her head. "I'm fine— Daffodil brought me a lemonade. That's all I want. I really came in . . . to talk to you."

When Katy gazed at her in surprise, Corinne went on quickly, "I overheard you talking to Elam in the Tumbleweed the other night—you and Jackson were asking him a bunch of questions. About Crystal," she added softly. "And I think he . . . he lied to you about something. I know it's none of my business, but I haven't run into Jackson in the past few days to tell him, and . . ." She moistened her lips. "It looked to me that what you were talking about seemed real important to you, so I figured you'd want to know—"

"Yes." Katy sat down on the chair next to Corinne. "Yes, please, I do want to know. Everything you can tell me."

Corinne nodded. "Okay, but . . . you won't let Elam know I was here, will you?" She was keeping her voice low, Katy noticed. Her lips twisted ruefully. "I don't want to get fired."

"You won't. I promise you, this is between us. What did Elam lie about?"

"Maybe it's not important, but . . ."

She glanced over her shoulder, as if to assure herself that Wood had really gone, and that no one else had come into the diner. "He told you that Wood Morgan never dated Crystal when she worked in the bar. I heard different."

Katy went still. "From who?"

"Tina, this girl who worked there with me when I first started a few years back. Crystal was long gone by then, but Tina had been there forever and used to work with her. And she talked about Crystal sometimes."

Katy waited, her heart thrumming.

"I don't know much about her, or why she left or anything, but I do know she and Wood Morgan had a little flirtation thing going. And they had a few dates, according to what Tina told me. And most everyone who worked in the bar knew about it. Elam did, for sure," Corinne added. "When I heard him tell you that she never dated Wood Morgan, I thought you might want to know the truth."

So Wood dated Crystal. And he and Elam both lied to me about it, Katy thought. She wondered what else they were hiding. Aloud, she said to Corinne, "Wood Morgan was already going steady with Tammie back then, wasn't he?"

"That's what I heard." Corinne pushed a strand of blonde hair behind her ear. "I guess his seeing Crystal raised a few eyebrows in the place. But no one really talked about it outside of the bar because Wood's father and Ted Paxton, the Tumbleweed's owner, were good friends. And Ted would have probably fired anyone who got on the wrong side of the Morgan family. Everyone's always known the Morgans have more money in their back pocket than almost everyone else in Thunder Creek put together. So Tina said she and Elam managed to keep it pretty quiet—but Tina did tell me about it after a few drinks one night when I'd been working there a few months."

"Did she tell you anything else? Any guesses as to why Crystal left? Did she ever hear from her after she did leave?"

"Not that I heard of," Corinne replied. "Apparently Crystal had stopped dating in general, but Tina and Elam were sure she had a regular boyfriend, someone who was buying her nice stuff, some new clothes, pretty earrings—I guess Crystal loved earrings—things like that. And when she left town..." Corinne stirred her lemonade with the straw... "she told Tina she'd be back, and she and this boyfriend were going to get married, and everyone at the Tumbleweed would be invited to the wedding. But..." she shrugged, "she never did come back."

Katy felt a chill. Once again, Matt's sketch filled her mind's eye.

"Look, Katy," Corinne said quietly. "I'm no gossip, even though I'm sure I sound like one. But it looked to me like you had something pretty serious on your mind the other night, and I knew Elam was lying to you—about Wood Morgan, at least. So I wanted to let you know. I hope this helps."

"It does. It helps a lot, Corinne." Still feeling a little dazed, she managed to smile with real gratitude at the other woman. "No, no, it's on the house," she said, shaking her head as the woman started to dig in her purse. "I can't tell you how much I appreciate you filling me in."

"No problem. Just don't let Elam find out I ratted on him," Corinne added with a rueful smile. "Now I have to head to work, but... good luck."

I'll need it, Katy thought, staring after Corinne, and trying to digest this new wrinkle.

Somehow, no matter how much she wanted to forget about Crystal and about the sketch, there were now two things making it almost impossible.

One was that she'd been lied to. And the other was the sketch itself. Why had it been drawn, and why had it been stolen? Why would whoever had broken into the house the other night have bothered with it if it didn't matter? Why would he have even noticed it in the dark, when Jackson had been pulling up in the truck and had nearly caught the intruder in the act?

She could find only one answer. Sitting at the table staring into a near empty glass of lemonade, Katy felt goose bumps rise on the nape of her neck. Because she suddenly knew that the sketch *did* matter. It had to—just as she had thought all along.

It was a threat to someone. A clue to the truth. Even, perhaps, it was proof.

Proof that Crystal had been murdered. Proof that, despite what her mother had told Sheriff Harvey, she'd never made it home at all. Proof that there was a reason for all these lies, and that someone was covering up at least one murder—and, she thought, fury and grief stabbing her heart, possibly two.

Chapter 27

KATY MADE THE CALL AS SOON AS THE DINER CLOSED, and Billy and Daffodil both left. She still had the phone number back at the Triple T, but she couldn't wait until she got home—she dialed directory assistance for Tucson and was given Edward Kirk's phone number for the second time.

She had to persuade Donna Kirk to tell her the truth. For whatever reason, Crystal's mother had lied. Not to her, but to Sheriff Harvey.

If I have to go to Tucson and speak to her in person, I will, Katy decided as the line began to ring.

You've reached the Kirks. Me and Eddy aren't here right now, but we'll call you back when we get home. Just leave a message and your number...

She left her number, but no message—only her name and a request that Donna call back as soon as possible. She wasn't convinced the woman would be so quick to return the call, but if not, Katy would simply call her again later from Jackson's cabin. And she'd keep trying until she reached her and got some answers.

Katy's cell phone rang twice while she was driving home to change her clothes before meeting Jackson at the cabin, but neither caller was Donna Kirk. Only her attorney, updating her on the latest go-around with Seth's lawyers, and then happily, Bessie, calling from the lobby of Caesar's Palace to say she'd just won $240 playing blackjack.

"The dealer was hot, but not as hot as I was," her grandmother chortled gleefully. In the background, Katy could hear the roar of the casino, the ring and jingle of slot machines, the clamor of countless voices.

"Good for you, Gram. You're not tiring yourself out, are you? Big John will have my head on a platter if you come home and have a relapse," Katy warned.

"No chance of that. How are things at home, and at the diner?"

Just great, Katy thought. *Someone tried to kill me at home and the diner's going to have competition from Elmo Panterri. Plus, Matt was mixed up in something terrible, and someone might have killed him.* "Everything's fine, Gram. Cleo had her foal—a healthy colt. I'll fill you in on the rest when you get home."

"Any word from those parents of yours?"

"A postcard. Mom wrote it, of course."

Her grandmother snorted. "Of course. I have to go, Katykins. Ada just ran out of nickels, so we're going to grab lunch and then hit the quarter slots again. I'm feeling lucky!"

Lucky. I'm feeling lucky, too, Katy reflected as she turned Gram's Blazer into the long drive leading up to the Triple T. *Like I'm finally going to get some answers and nail down the truth.*

Whatever it took, and no matter what she had to do, she wasn't going to give up until she'd unearthed what had really happened to her brother all those years ago, and what secret had linked him with Crystal Kirk.

She'd planned to bring Mojo to the cabin with her tonight, but she found him trotting after Riley at the ranch, and in the end, Riley offered to take him home for the night. Katy agreed, and by the time they caught up on ranch business and looked in on Cleo and her foal, it was getting late, and the early evening sky hinted of rain.

Rain. She could smell it in the air as she climbed into the Blazer and slammed the door. She hoped it would hold off until she was at least closer to the cabin, or it would slow her down even more—and she was anxious to get dinner started. She'd planned to surprise Jackson tonight with a candlelit meal, one of her favorites: tenderloin tips in brandy sauce, rice, and salad, but now food was the last thing on her mind. Still, they could discuss everything she'd learned from Corinne over dinner—if she could focus long enough not to burn everything to a crisp.

Driving toward the cabin she reviewed everything Corinne had told her, and compared it against her own impressions of Elam and Wood that night in the Tumbleweed, marveling at how easily Elam had lied to her face, how Wood Morgan had coldly stonewalled. Somehow or other, her mind became preoccupied turning over the bits and pieces of information she'd uncovered and she suddenly noticed she was not on the road she'd intended to take at all.

She was on Coyote Lane. She'd completely missed the turnoff for the more direct route to Jackson's cabin, Big Tree Road.

"Damn," Katy muttered, frowning ahead of her. She knew Coyote Lane would eventually intersect with Big Tree up ahead, but first it would lead her two miles out of her way.

Still, it would take longer to turn back, so she thumped down on the accelerator. She hadn't taken Coyote Lane for years. She'd avoided it every time she came home, and for good reason.

Coyote Lane branched off—just ahead—to a rutted, narrow trail that led to the Jenssens' place. The place where Matt had died.

There was little other traffic, only a lone car far behind

her. She slowed as she approached the trail. The turnoff point was nearly obscured by old tree stumps and brush. Her hands trembled on the steering wheel as she stared through the gathering gloom, peering down that dismal-looking offshoot of Coyote Lane.

A few raindrops sprinkled the windshield, and flannel-gray clouds were moving in slowly, almost stealthily.

But Katy didn't see them—she saw only the old trail, the trail that led to a place she'd dreaded and avoided for half of her life.

She hit the accelerator suddenly and swerved to her right, taking the turn a little faster than she'd intended. Drawing a deep breath, she clenched the steering wheel as the Blazer jolted forward toward the Jenssen place.

The ranch was abandoned now. She'd heard the Jenssens had sold the land to a development company that had never done anything with it, and the family had moved away.

Weeds grew higher than the wheels of the Blazer. The windowpanes in front were cracked, the porch steps all crumbling. The house and barn were both in disrepair—faded, dilapidated, as gray and colorless as the leaden sky.

Katy pulled up before the barn and got out. She walked through the dirt and the weeds until she was no more than ten feet from the barn, then stared up at the roof—that high, sloping roof from which her brother had fallen.

She didn't know what had made her turn onto Coyote Lane—perhaps it was her subconscious. Perhaps after all these years, this is what she had to do before she could ever put the past to rest.

Face this place. Find the truth.

I will, Matt. She whispered the words into the air. *I promise.*

Words whispered in the air.

I promise, Katy, I'll teach you to be the best softball

pitcher in the girls' league. Easy, now. Put some muscle be-
hind it. Right here. Throw it right here . . .

Tears filled her eyes.

Katy, this is your lucky day. I'm going to do you a favor. I
won't tell Mom and Dad this time, but if you ever sneak out
of the house again and I catch you, I will tell them. And I'll
tell them that it wasn't the first time. And remember how I
was grounded during football tryouts? Well, you'll be
grounded forever if they find out. And take off all that eye
gunk, you don't need it. You're pretty enough as it is.

Rain pattered down, light as the kisses of ghosts. She
stared at the broken windows and saw her brother's face—an
eighteen-year-old face, handsome and golden as only youth
could be, the face of a young man with things on his mind
and places to go. He'd been solemn and in a rush that last
night, wearing his oldest jeans and a paint-spattered plaid
work shirt as he bolted out the door to his truck. Rushing,
rushing.

And now she knew why. He had to paint the Jenssens'
barn, and study for his chemistry quiz, and help Allison with
the homecoming decorations and . . . go to see Sheriff Harvey
about a dead girl . . .

If not that night, the next day.

And then, he was going to tell Dad.

The sound of a car door slamming jolted her from the
world of memories and ghosts. She spun around, staring
through the rain and gloom, but there was no car on the trail
behind her.

But she'd heard it. She was almost positive.

Maybe it had come from the brush flanking the trail, she
thought, her heart jumping into her throat. Maybe someone
had followed her, pulled off the road, hidden their car.

You're imagining things. No one followed you. But she
suddenly remembered that car trailing far behind her on
Coyote Lane.

Fear swept her as she stood in the drizzle, scanning the overgrown trail and the trees and the brush as thunder clapped in the distance, and rain streamed down the roof of the abandoned barn like God's tears. *You're overreacting.*

No, I'm getting the hell out of here, she thought, and ran toward the Blazer.

A shot rang out from the trees, every bit as loud as thunder. Then another, the bullet skidding into the dirt only yards from her feet.

She screamed and lunged toward the shelter of the Blazer, ducking behind it. For a moment she thought of jumping in, locking the doors, making a run for it—but he could shoot her right through the window. Panic swept through her as she realized she was trapped.

Calm down. Think. Get Big John's gun.

She eased open the Blazer's door, reached for her purse, open on the seat. As she dragged it toward her, her cell phone tumbled out onto the floor, but even as she cursed, another shot blasted, keeping her pinned down. She thrust her hand into her bag and came up with the gun.

"What do you want?" she yelled, as she checked the chamber and clicked the safety. "I've already called for help."

There was silence, a frightening eerie silence. Only the sound of her own ragged breathing and the patter of rain greeted her straining ears.

Where the hell was he? She edged her way to the front end of the Blazer and peered around it at the dismal landscape, the jutting trail and wet trees. She saw nothing, no one.

No more shots.

Suddenly just as she was gearing up to jump in the Blazer and make a run for it, she heard a twig crack behind her and spun around.

A man in a gray rain slicker, heavy black boots, and a ski mask stood less than fifteen feet away, pointing a rifle at her.

"Drop that gun—" he shouted, to her surprise recoiling as he spotted the revolver, but he was too late. Katy reacted instantly, firing as Big John had taught her. One shot, two, three, and then she dove to the ground.

Chapter 28

"WHAT THE *HELL*!" THE MAN STAGGERED, DROPPING heavily to one knee. As Katy stared at him, noting the blood spurting from the hole in his slicker just below the shoulder, she saw the rifle slip from his grasp and hit the ground with a thud.

"Don't move," she gasped. Her heart in her throat, she scrambled to her feet and aimed the revolver at him again as rain pelted her face and soaked her hair.

"You damn near killed me," he shouted, shoving a hand against the spurting wound.

"You were *trying* to kill *me*." But an awful queasy feeling trickled through her as she stared at the blood flowing from the wound, streaming down his slicker into the weeds. She tried to keep her gaze on his face, struggling to discern his identity beneath that ski mask. "And I want to know why," she added, her fingers tightening on the revolver.

"I wasn't...trying to kill you," he rasped as the rain pounded all around them. "I was just trying to scare you. If I'd wanted to hit you, I would've. *Damn* it."

"Wh-who are you?" she demanded.

He groaned, clutching harder at his shoulder as a crack of thunder shook the sky. "To...hell with you!"

She thought she recognized his voice. "Take off that ski mask, Elam."

Silence. He stared at her, then lost his balance and sank down onto both knees. "What'd you call me?"

"Elam. You're Elam Lowell. Now take off that mask."

He lifted his head and stared at her, and the combination of the resolution he saw in her face and the bullet she'd put in his shoulder crumpled the last of his defiance. He'd already screwed up big time. No way out now except possibly through negotiation. Unfortunately, he wasn't in the best bargaining position, being on the wrong side of the gun. And the wrong side of the woman holding the gun. *Shit.*

He took his bloodied hand from the wound and tore off the mask with a grunt. He'd been beat up before, hit over the head with a bottle in a bar fight, stabbed in a Tijuana brothel, but never shot. It hurt like hell. "Satisfied?" he rasped.

Katy's heart pounded in her ears, almost as loud as the boom of thunder that crashed while she stared into Elam's pain-twisted face.

"I'm going to call an ambulance," she said, still feeling queasy. "And then I'm calling Sheriff Harvey."

"No! No ambulance, no sheriff. You can't do that."

"Can't I? You need medical help and I need Sheriff Harvey to arrest you and get the truth out of you."

"Damn, it...no." He winced in pain and then said, more pleadingly, "Please. Don't...call anyone. Give me a chance...just hear me out."

The pain in his eyes and the blood running down his slicker sickened her, but Katy tried to steel herself against them even as his pleading rang in her ears. She'd never shot a man before, only targets. From the time she was eleven until she was fourteen Big John made her target practice with tin cups on a fence post at least two hours every single week. But he'd never prepared her for what it felt like to actually shoot a man, to see the aftermath, the pain, the blood. She hoped to God she wasn't going to faint, because she still wasn't sure Elam wouldn't kill her if he had a chance.

But he did have a chance, she reminded herself. *The gun was pointed at you when you turned around. He could have shot you in the back, unless . . .*

Unless he really only wanted to scare her.

"Talk then, and make it fast. Tell me what this is all about. And the first thing I want to know is if Wood Morgan sent you here to shoot me."

He said nothing a moment, then grimaced, his head bowed in the rain. "Let's go . . . inside the old barn to talk."

"No. Here and now. Start talking."

"I'm not mentioning names," he muttered. "But I came here to scare you, to try to get you to stop asking all those damned questions about what happened fourteen years ago. The past is dead and gone, and it's going to do nobody any good to bring it up now."

"Least of all Wood Morgan, right?" Katy blinked the rain from her eyes. "Tell me about Wood and Crystal—and how my brother got mixed up in whatever was going on between them."

"It wasn't like that. You won't . . . like what I have to say. I was told to fill you in if I couldn't get you to back off . . . and I will . . . but no names."

"I already have your name, don't I?"

"Do you want to hear this or not?" Elam shouted, and for a moment Katy thought he was going to lunge for his rifle. But he sagged down on the ground once more, and she could see he was growing weaker. She'd have to call the ambulance soon.

"Make it fast. You're probably going into shock," she told him.

"There was one night," he continued, as if she hadn't spoken. "One night when things just got out of hand. It wasn't anyone's fault, and it definitely wasn't your brother's fault.

But everyone did things they regretted later—probably Matt most of all. I know for a fact he didn't want anyone finding out. He was having trouble living with it himself."

Cold struck her, and it wasn't from the chill of the rain. "Go on," she managed, but her voice sounded ragged even to her own ears.

"From what I heard, your brother had one of those nights kids have sometimes when they start questioning everything in their lives. You know? He showed up at the Tumbleweed same time as . . . someone else—another kid, someone Crystal had dated a few times before she quit seeing everyone. She'd taken up with a man—no one knew who—and she'd just up and quit going out with any of the guys who used to hang around her. Anyway, both these boys sneaked into the place that night, looking for a good time, and to blow off some steam, and I let 'em stay. And, yeah," he said, his breath coming in hard rasps, "I served 'em some beers. They got a little drunk and spent the rest of the night flirting with her. Just flirting," he added defensively, "you know, harmless stuff."

"Get to the point," Katy said, but her heart was already beginning to pound uncomfortably in her chest.

"Crystal was in a strange mood. I guess maybe she'd had a lover's quarrel with this mystery guy she was seeing. I knew for a fact she wanted him to marry her, wanted it bad, and I figured maybe he was giving her a hard time about it, because she was a little reckless that night, a little wild. Like she was mad underneath it all. By the time I closed the place, she was still flirting pretty heavily with Matt and . . . the other boy."

The other boy. *Wood Morgan, or I'll eat my calculator,* Katy told herself.

"By that time everyone else was gone. The three of them put on some music, danced a little more, and—"

"Did you dance with her too?"

"Seemed no reason not to." Elam was pressing hard against his wound as the rain continued to beat down. "All three of us danced with her—we took turns," he muttered. "It got a little rowdy. And we played pool. And...drank some more. I gave the boys and Crystal some of the hard stuff, maybe I shouldn't have, but..."

Katy felt sick. Am image of Matt drinking, dancing, playing pool in the closed bar with Crystal swam through her mind. But Elam wasn't done.

"That wasn't even so bad," he said thickly as the rain beat down steadily, "not compared to what happened next..." He broke off and pressed his lips together, whether from pain or chill or remorse she couldn't say.

"Go on," Katy ordered, her heart racing. "Wasn't so bad compared to what? Tell me!"

Elam hunched over, his head bent. "The other boy, not your brother, pulled out a joint. And something else—a Baggie with some coke in it. I didn't touch any of the drugs and neither did Matt but...this other boy, he talked Crystal into trying it."

God, no. *No.* Her stomach cramped. "Crystal was... *drugged*?" she asked in horror. She couldn't even visualize her brother being a part of that. How could he...

"Not drugged, no...well, not exactly...she took it of her own free will. But she wasn't herself that night, and she'd been drinking..."

"What else?" Katy's throat was tight. "Tell me the rest, damn you."

"I don't remember whose idea it was. Maybe it was mine," Elam muttered. "But we got out a deck of cards and we...we played poker. Strip poker."

Katy stared at him. "Strip...poker?"

"She wasn't too good at cards. Crystal...she kinda... lost her shirt, I guess you'd say. She was laughing though, she didn't seem to mind at all. And I can tell you, no one else did either."

"Did you . . . did they . . ." She couldn't get the words out. "Did someone . . . rape her?" she asked in a voice that sounded completely unlike her own.

"*No.* No, it wasn't like that. They . . . we . . . had sex with her, all right? Your brother, he passed out right around the time she took her panties off. Just passed out under one of the pool tables. Me and the other kid, we took turns. It was her idea—"

"I don't believe you!"

"I swear on a stack of Bibles," Elam croaked, and something in his expression penetrated the fog of sick fury in Katy's mind. It occurred to her suddenly, dully, that he just might be telling the truth. Not that it meant anything. Crystal had been drinking, she'd been given drugs. She was mad and wild and high and they'd taken advantage of her, taken advantage of whatever freaked out, drugged out state she'd ended up in . . .

"She was willing, I swear to you, she was willing! She went from one to the other of us. Laughing. Then she cozied up to Matt, but the kid was out cold. So she came back to . . . to the other kid. And then, sometime later, I was half passed out myself, but I saw Matt wake up. He looked around, dazed like, and he looked real sick. He barfed on the floor, and then he tried to stand up, and he saw them . . . Crystal and this other guy, on top of the bar, going at it like monkeys. He ran over there, I think he thought at first that Crystal was in trouble, but she just laughed her head off—she was high as a kite by then—and she told him to wait his turn."

Elam shook his head, his voice thinner now, weaker. "It was a wild night, that's all. A crazy, wild, night. It never shoulda happened." With an effort, he lifted his head and met Katy's stunned gaze.

"Matt never did screw her though. He staggered out of

there, never even unzipped his pants. But he still felt sick about the whole thing later. Felt like he never should have been there in the first place, never should have watched Crystal take off her clothes, or let that other kid give her those drugs. He had some dumb idea about telling his girlfriend, fessing up, even though he didn't actually cheat on her, but we talked him out of it. We told him if anyone found out, it would only make Crystal feel worse, and she didn't deserve that. We got him to make this pact with us. A pact of silence, we called it. All three of us swore to it, swore to protect Crystal and each other. Because if word got out, we all knew that wouldn't go over real well for any one of us—not in this town. And Crystal was the last one who wanted anyone to know—so we figured, if no one talked, no one'd get hurt." He was breathing heavily now, struggling through the pain.

"We all agreed. And we all kept the pact. And that's it," he said through clenched teeth. "You know the whole thing, I swear it."

"Just how bad did my brother feel about this?" Katy managed in a low tone, her hand that clutched the gun beginning to shake.

Elam stared at her blankly. "Well, like I said, real bad," he began, and then broke off. "Hey—are you thinking he jumped off that roof on purpose? Now . . . that's something I couldn't tell you."

No. No, Matt would never do that. He'd have come to one of us before then, he'd have confessed, broken down. He'd never have taken his life because of one stupid, horrible night.

She closed her eyes for a moment, as if blocking out the whole ugly story and all the images in blinding color it carried with it. The next thing she knew, she heard a grunt, a scrabble in the wet grass and even as her eyes flew open,

Elam bore down on her and snatched the revolver from her grasp.

"I'm leaving," he said hoarsely, and she saw his face was a sick pale gray. He wasn't pointing the revolver at her. He threw it toward the barn, as far as he could and stooped for his rifle.

"I'm going home and tending to this wound, and if you know what's good for you, you won't tell anyone about this. You don't want this whole story coming out, fourteen years later, do you? You don't want your brother's squeaky-clean reputation spoiled in this town. Can't imagine Big John, or your mom, or Bessie would be too pleased with that."

"Neither would Wood Morgan," Katy said, her throat tight with anger and a rising bile.

"I never mentioned no names." Elam started walking, slowly, wearily, toward the trail. But he paused at her next question, called out to his back.

"What happened to Crystal? Did you kill her to keep her quiet? Did Wood Morgan pay you to kill her, just like he paid you to come after me today?"

Elam turned around, swaying a little on his feet. He shook his head. "She was leaving town. It had nothing to do with that, it had to do with her boyfriend, I swear it. She told me so the night she left. She didn't want her boyfriend to know what she'd done, all she wanted was for him to marry her. She was having a hard enough time with him—without him knowing about what she did that night."

"What you all did," Katy corrected sharply.

Elam grimaced again. "The night before she left, I gave her a little gift. One thousand dollars—just to ensure she kept her mouth shut. She was happy to get it. Believe me, she had no intention of letting that story come out. All she wanted was to see her mama, and maybe pick up some advice about getting this guy to marry her. She planned to come back and have a big splashy wedding, and she was going to invite all of us at the Tumbleweed. Crystal probably had more to lose by that story coming out than anyone."

He turned and headed away from the barn, toward where his car was presumably parked in the trees. "Don't call no one," she heard him say wearily. "Don't tell no one. Now that you know, just let it be."

Katy watched him walk away, her stomach churning and her mind struggling to put all the pieces together. Matt... something terrible, a pact... the sketch.

None of this explained the sketch.

Elam had slipped into the cover of the trees.

If he'd wanted to kill me, he could have just now. He'd walked away, she realized in shock.

Thunder boomed overhead and she stumbled forward toward the barn to find her father's gun. She scooped it up, clicked the safety, and headed back to her Blazer.

Elam's words still hung in the air. His blood soaked the ground. And the rain mingled with the tears she hadn't even known were streaming down her cheeks.

Somehow she found the strength to hoist herself back into the Blazer. She pushed the gun deep in her purse. And realized her cell phone was ringing.

She fumbled for it on the floor.

"Is this Katy Templeton? This is Donna. Donna Kirk."

"Mrs. Kirk." Katy slammed the door of the Blazer, stared blankly ahead of her. It seemed like months ago, not hours, that she had called the number in Tucson.

"What is it now?" Donna Kirk's thready voice scratched plaintively in her ear. "If you have more questions about Crystal, you're wasting your time. I really don't know what else I can—"

"This won't take long, Mrs. Kirk," Katy said. "Please. I... appreciate your returning my call. Is your husband at home right now?"

"My husband? No. Eddy's at the plant. What does that have to do with anything?"

"You told Sheriff Harvey that you weren't free to talk openly in front of your husband—and I wanted to make certain that we have an honest conversation today, Mrs. Kirk. I need to know the truth, all of it. It's very important."

"What are you talking about?" Donna Kirk's voice rose half a dozen octaves. "I already told you the truth. And who's this Sheriff Harvey?"

Seated behind the steering wheel, Katy froze. Her eyes were fixed rigidly and unseeingly on the raindrops sliding down her windshield.

"Sheriff Harvey," she said in a faint, clear voice, as if speaking to a small confused child. "Our sheriff here in Thunder Creek. Remember, he called you and asked about Crystal. I imagine he asked many of the same questions I did, but you told him you'd seen her, and had spoken to her— the last time was a little over a year ago."

There was silence on the other end. Then Donna Kirk's voice crackled, taut and furious. "Is this some kind of joke? I never told anyone any such thing. I never heard of this Sheriff Harvey. I told you, Crystal's gone."

On the last word, her voice broke, and for one horrible moment, Katy listened to racking, helpless sobs. Then Donna Kirk got ahold of herself, managing to speak in a harsh whisper.

"She never showed up, never called me. Not once in all this time. I really don't like talking about it, but ... if *you* know anything, if you think *you* know where she's gone, then tell me. Please. I'd ... I'd just like to talk to her, I wouldn't tell her how I found out."

Confusion, shock, and a jarring sense of unreality tumbled through Katy. She spoke through dry lips. "I don't know where she is, Mrs. Kirk, truly, I don't. But if I find out ..." She swallowed past an acrid taste in her mouth. "You're sure...there's no mistake? You never spoke with Sheriff Harvey, never told him—"

"For Pete's sake, how many times do I have to tell you?" The woman nearly shrieked. There was a world of grief and loss beneath the rage. "The only person who's even mentioned Crystal's name to me for years is *you*. Lord knows, Eddy and me never talk about her. You can believe me or not, I don't care. But if you don't know where my daughter is, don't call back!"

And she hung up. Numbly, Katy held the disconnected phone in her hand, staring at it with dazed eyes. Thunder boomed again over the mountains and the rain crashed down.

Chapter 29

"OH, *DAMN*." DAFFODIL MOLINE STARED IN DISMAY AT the gas indicator of her Jeep as it sputtered to a stop. *Empty. Great. I'm out of gas, just what I need.*

She was a good two miles outside of town—and probably the same distance from Marcy's house.

Her feet already hurt. And it was starting to rain.

Just another sucky day in the life of Daffodil Moline, girl idiot, she muttered to herself as she jumped out and scowled at the world in general.

A few drops of rain fell on her cheeks and upturned nose. A little water won't kill you, her mother always said. *Yeah, but it ruins your hair,* she thought as she turned back toward Thunder Creek and began to trudge along the road.

She had gone about twenty feet and had convinced herself that at least her life couldn't get much worse when a car rumbled toward her from the direction of town. She gritted her teeth when she saw it was Billy's dented old pickup.

Don't stop, don't talk to me, don't ask any questions, she implored him silently. *Just keep on going.*

"You've got to be kidding. You ran out of gas?" Braking alongside her, Billy stuck his head out the window.

"What I did or didn't do is none of your business, Billy Stone."

"Want a ride back to town?"

"No." She kept walking, only more briskly, heading away from him as a sprinkling of raindrops peppered her bare arms and the fabric of her blue T-shirt. She heard him turning the car around on the narrow road and cruising back toward her.

"Don't be a jerk, Daffodil. Get in."

He was keeping pace with her as she walked, but she refused to even glance at him.

"You're getting soaked," he pointed out.

"What do you care?"

"I don't." His jaw tightened, and he was about to stop, wait for her to pass, and then turn the car around and go on his way, when a clap of thunder sounded and he saw her jump. Daffodil had always hated thunder.

"Tell you what, Daff. I'll drive you to the gas station, bring you back with the gas can, and I won't say a word. You don't have to talk to me, not a single word. Just get in the car."

She hesitated, her footsteps slowing. Another rumble of thunder brought her to a halt and she stood there, hugging her arms around herself. "You promise? Not a word?"

"I'm only going to make this offer once."

If she wasn't getting soaked and her feet didn't hurt, she wouldn't have considered it, Daffodil told herself as she dashed around the hood of the pickup and yanked open the door.

They hadn't driven more than a hundred yards when Billy said, "Any word from your mom? Like, when she's coming back?"

"You said I didn't have to talk to you, remember?"

"So sue me." He shot her a grin. She'd forgotten how cute Billy looked when he grinned. That slightly crooked smile. The dimples peeping out. Something twisted inside her. He hadn't done anything but scowl at her since the Thanksgiving night she'd broken up with him.

"Come on, Daff, this is me. I know how much you hate staying alone."

"I'm not alone. I'm staying at Marcy's."

"For how long?"

She sighed. "Till sometime next week, I think. Mom called last night and said Rose has some callbacks in the next few days. One is for a shampoo commercial—Mom wants to stay and see how it goes. But she promised she'd come home as soon as they find out if Rose got the part."

"You haven't told her yet, have you? About Corey roughing you up?"

"He didn't!" But her cheeks turned red, and she had to fight the urge to rub the bruises on her arm. "You have no idea what you're talking about. You don't have any idea what happened between me and Corey, so just . . . shut up about it."

"Why don't you tell me then?"

"Corey is the best thing that ever happened to me. He's wonderful! He thinks I'm the hottest girl in school, and he . . . he says he loves me—"

"So that's why he hit you?"

"He only did that because—" She broke off and bit her lip. *Me and my big mouth.* Humiliation surged through her. "I have nothing more to say to you," she told him between clenched teeth.

Billy slammed on the brakes so suddenly that if she hadn't been wearing her seat belt she'd have flown forward.

"So he did hit you!"

His face was pale with fury. "Damn it, Daff, why'd you let him get away with that? You're never going to see him again are you? Tell me you aren't!"

"Billy, I—" Staring into his eyes, seeing the depth of anger there, startled her. "I . . . I don't think so. I don't want to." To her frustration, her voice began to quaver. "It's not that easy. You don't understand. Nobody understands."

"Try me." Billy grabbed her arm, then remembering the bruises, slid his fingers down to her palm. He clutched her hand, his grip gentle. So gentle it made her feel like crying.

"Tell me, Daff. Come on, I have to know."

Chapter 30

THE WORLD HAD TURNED UPSIDE DOWN AND KATY didn't know how to right it.

She gripped the steering wheel as if it alone would keep her grounded, keep her focused on the shocking words Donna Kirk had just spoken.

I never heard of this Sheriff Harvey... the only person who's even mentioned Crystal's name to me for years is you.

Cold fear settled in her chest. She heard again Stan Harvey's deep, rusty voice. *I had a conversation with Donna Kirk—Crystal's mother—a short while ago. It seems she didn't exactly tell you the truth the other day. Looks like Crystal did make it out of Thunder Creek after all—her mother says she saw Crystal about a week after she left here...*

Lies. All of it. *Lies.*

She was shaking so hard it was difficult to turn the key in the ignition, but finally she managed it and swung the car around, tearing back toward Coyote Lane.

Dazedly, she switched on the windshield wipers as the rain tumbled faster and more thunder growled from the mountains like a monstrous grizzly.

Keep quiet, act like nothing happened, Sheriff Harvey had said. He must have been buying time—but for what?

To silence her? Just as he'd silenced Matt? And Crystal? Had he told Matt not to tell anyone too, when Matt had come to him after seeing Crystal's dead body?

Her stomach churned. *Don't jump to conclusions. There could be other explanations.*

Yet as she swerved back onto Coyote Lane, she found herself scanning both her rearview mirror and the empty road ahead, half expecting the sheriff's car to appear out of the gloom, as if somehow he knew what she'd discovered.

What she *might* have discovered, she corrected herself desperately.

He wanted her to think that the sketch didn't matter, that whoever had attacked her had nothing to do with Crystal, or Matt, or with events that happened fourteen years ago. That she had an enemy here in Thunder Creek, an enemy unrelated to Matt's sketch or the questions she'd been asking about the past.

But the sketch had been stolen. It *had* to matter. And if it did . . . if Crystal was dead, and had never gone back home, had never been seen or heard from since the day she supposedly left Thunder Creek . . . then Sheriff Harvey was the one who had lied.

Panic skittered through her and she bore down on the accelerator, gravel spewing from beneath the tires as she sped toward Jackson's cabin.

The idea that Stan Harvey, her father's old friend, the respected sheriff of Thunder Creek for nearly forty years, had killed her brother seemed ludicrous. Her hands were clammy on the wheel as she saw his rough, kindly face in her mind's eye, heard the calm authority of his voice.

Maybe right now in the present there's someone who has a grudge against you . . . Keep all the doors and windows locked, and keep your guard up.

Oh, God. Confusion and terror swept through her. *Who do you call, she thought, her heart pounding, when you can't*

call 911, when you can't trust the law? When nothing makes
sense?

The trees began to wave violently in the wet tearing breeze
as she grabbed her cell phone and punched in Jackson's number, as she drove like a madwoman for the cabin.

Pick up, she thought frantically, as the line began to ring.
Please, Jackson, pick up.

Smoke MacIntyre and Lee Davis couldn't help a little good-
natured ribbing as they cornered Jackson Brent in the check-
out line at Merck's hardware store.

"So, Big John'll be coming back real soon. You and he
goin' to have a little talk?" Lee asked casually.

Jackson took his change from Ned Merck and stuffed the
bills into his wallet. "What about?"

Distractedly, he picked up the can of paint, the new
brushes, and the nails he'd just bought for refinishing another
section of the clinic. His mind was on Katy, on trying to figure out who in hell had come after her at the Triple T. Due to
the dearth of suspects—or motives—Luke Dillard was still
at the top of his very short list. He'd exchanged greetings
with Smoke and Lee but was too intent on trying to figure
out if Dillard was just a stalker-bully or truly psychotic to see
the winks they'd exchanged.

"You know, Jackson—about the question."

"What question?"

"Oh, c'mon." Smoke fought to keep a straight face.
"You're going to ask Big John's permission first, aren't you?"

That finally got his attention. "Permission for what?" His
tone was suspicious, his eyes wary beneath the low brim of
his hat.

Both men broke into grins. "To pop the question, of
course." Lee clapped him on the shoulder. "Asking Big John

first would be a nice touch. Old-fashioned, respectful. I'd go that route, if it was me."

"On the other hand," Smoke pushed his lower lip out, speculating, "our Katy's a downright independent woman if I ever saw one. She might get pissed off if you were to ask Big John before posing the question to her—"

"You two think you're funny, don't you? Well, you can take your comedy routine to *Saturday Night Live*. They could use you guys." Jackson hefted the paint can in one hand and the bag of nails and brushes in the other and headed for the door.

"Margie's already planning a bridal shower," Lee called after him.

Jackson spun around. "You're kidding, right?"

He flushed when they burst out laughing. Damn it, were they kidding—or not? There was a cold, sick sensation dive-bombing the pit of his stomach. It free-fell when Lee shook his head.

"Hell, no."

Even Ned Merck, behind the counter, gave a snort of laughter.

"Can't a man even go to a friend's house for dinner with a woman before people start writing their wedding invitations for them?" It came out like a growl, which only increased their amusement.

"Not in Thunder Creek." Smoke slapped a package of batteries down on the counter. "You should know that by—" He broke off as he spotted the commotion outside the window, heating up at Slade's gas station across the street. Smoke whistled under his breath. "Well, now, take a look at that."

Jackson turned, frowning at what he saw. Over at the gas station, Billy Stone and Corey Dillard were fighting, slugging it out beside the gas pump as Luke Dillard watched. Daffodil Moline was there, shrieking at the top of her lungs as Luke Dillard held her back. It looked to Jackson like she wanted to dodge into the fray and somehow try to separate the boys.

Billy was getting the worst of it. As Jackson, Lee, and Smoke watched, Corey did some martial arts moves, a bit more jerkily than Jackson had seen in the movies, but they worked, and Billy was on his knees, bent over, and appeared to be wheezing. Grinning, Corey advanced and kicked the other boy, catching Billy in the head with his boot.

Even as the kick connected, Jackson was already sprinting for the door, with Lee and Smoke on his heels.

"Hold it right there, you two! That's enough," Jackson called out and ran across the street.

But he didn't have time just yet to see if the boys heeded his order, there was something else he had to see to, something that wouldn't wait. He confronted Luke Dillard.

"Let Daffodil go, Dillard. *Now.*"

The other man flicked him a glance of contempt. "I'm just trying to keep it a fair fight, Brent. Stay out of it." He held tight to Daffodil's arms as the girl twisted and fought, her rain-soaked blonde hair streaming over her eyes. "This little hellcat has no business mixing in—neither do you."

"Take your hands off her."

"Go to hell. I'm damned if I'll take orders from—"

Jackson moved fast, wrenching the other man's arms from Daffodil, pulling her free.

"You all right?" he asked her, but she never had a chance to reply because Luke Dillard jumped toward him, shoving Daffodil aside and slugging Jackson in the stomach. He doubled over as Daffodil gasped, and Smoke and Lee leaped between the two men.

"All right, this is getting out of hand," Smoke said sharply, glaring at Luke. "I think those boys have tussled enough, it's time to rein this in, not make it worse."

Jackson straightened, breathing hard. Much as he wanted to go after Dillard, he resisted the urge. Billy was more important. The boy was clearly no match for the Dillard kid. But even as he turned toward the two boys, still trading punches, a sobbing Daffodil flew into the fray.

"Don't, please, Corey," she screamed, the tears streaming down her face, mingling with the rain as she tried to push Corey back. "Don't hit him anymore!"

"Daffodil, get out of the way!" Billy lunged forward desperately but wasn't in time to prevent Corey from shoving her hard into the gas pump.

As Lee swore and hurried toward Daffodil, Billy launched himself at the other boy in a furious blur. Corey went down, yelping and groaning as Billy pummeled him in a rush of adrenaline that clearly stunned his opponent.

"All right now—that's enough." Jackson hauled Billy off the other boy, inwardly pleased that Billy had managed to get a few good licks in. He reached down a hand to help Corey to his feet.

"This is over," he began, but at that moment, before Lee and Smoke could even yell a warning, Luke tackled him in a flying dive that sent him barreling down onto the concrete.

Luke landed on top of him and slammed a fist into Jackson's face. Eager to press his advantage and get in as many blows as he could before anyone interfered, he started to draw his arm back for another punch, but Jackson moved faster. He grabbed Luke's arm—Dillard was strong, but Jackson was stronger—and heaved Dillard off. Then, with swift brute strength and the adroitness for which he'd been famous in his football days, he reversed their positions.

He pinned Dillard beneath him, and his fist thwacked straight into the other man's nose. Ignoring Dillard's grunt of pain, and the spurt of blood, he hit him again.

Behind him, Daffodil had run sobbing to Billy's side. Corey watched open-mouthed and disbelieving as his uncle lay helpless beneath the bigger man, unable to defend himself. Smoke and Lee folded their arms across their chests and observed in grim silence, both of them thinking the same thing: Dillard had asked for it.

"Get up, Uncle Luke!" The cut above Corey's left eye was oozing blood. "Come on, don't let him win, get up!"

But though he struggled mightily, Luke Dillard couldn't topple the man holding him down, or stem the rain of punishing blows.

"This one's for Katy," Jackson said between clenched teeth. He hit Luke in the jaw, feeling cold satisfaction as the man slumped beneath him, too beaten even to struggle.

"Hey, Jackson, that's enough." Smoke stepped forward at last and pulled on Jackson's arm.

Lee spoke from only a foot away. "Let him up now, buddy."

"Not yet." Breathing hard, Jackson stared down at Luke, remembering how he'd nearly raped Katy back in high school, wondering if he'd also been the one to attack her at the Triple T. "You like picking on women, don't you? And dogs. I told you what would happen if you shot Ajax."

"I . . . didn't . . . shoot . . . your . . . damned . . . dog . . . asshole," Luke gasped. Blood ran from his mouth and his nose, and there were already bruises puffing above his eye and across his jaw.

"Like hell you didn't." Jackson eyed him in disgust. "Admit it, you bastard. Admit you shot him."

"I . . . didn't . . ."

Jackson raised his fist as if about to hit him again. "Admit it!"

"No! Doc Brent, let him go!" It was Daffodil's voice, high-pitched, frantic. In surprise, Jackson glanced over at her.

She was kneeling beside Billy, who sat in the dust beside the gas pumps, looking dizzy and winded. Her arms were around him, supporting him, but her face was pale as a December sun, and her eyes bored frantically into Jackson's.

"He didn't shoot your dog—I swear to you. He wasn't even there. I was, so I know—"

"Shut up, you goddamned little bitch!" Corey spun toward her. He took one step in her direction, but with a burst of strength Billy scrambled to his feet and planted himself in front of her.

"You're never touching her again," he warned, his fists clenched, his breath coming in ragged pants.

Jackson glanced down once more at the man bleeding beneath him, then he drew a deep breath and climbed off. He walked toward the three teenagers. Billy still stood protectively in front of Daffodil as she clutched at his arm.

"It's okay, Billy. I'm not afraid of him. I'm sick to death of being afraid. I'm ready to talk, and Mr. Corey Dillard can just go to hell!"

Corey stood frozen, aware of Smoke, Lee, and Jackson all seeming to close in around him. His uncle was still groaning on the ground, not even trying to stand yet.

He felt trapped. They were all staring at him, surrounding him. Damn that stupid little bitch for her big mouth.

"I've had it with you, Daff." He spoke sneeringly. "No one wants to hear what you have to say, least of all, me."

"Yeah? I bet Doc Brent wants to hear," Billy shot back.

"You'd win that bet." Jackson regarded Daffodil through the thrum of rain. "You were there when Ajax was shot?"

She nodded.

"Want to tell me who did it?"

"Keep your mouth shut, you slut—"

Billy sprang forward and his fist shot straight at Corey's mouth. The boy was sent spinning and fell to his knees.

"Stop, Billy. That's enough. Please." More tears filled Daffodil's eyes as Billy turned back toward her. Looking at Jackson, she spoke through trembling lips.

"It was Corey. Corey shot your dog. I was with him, I left work to go with him. He said we were going to have some fun. At first we drove to the Dairy Queen in Winston Falls, and then we headed back. Corey had a six-pack in the car and we parked for a while and drank some beer and then he . . . he drove to your clinic, Doc Brent. He went on past it, clear out to your cabin and we saw Ajax outside, on his lead. N-no one was around."

"Shut up, Daff!"

She spoke louder. "Corey cut your dog's lead and Ajax . . . he took off. He started running toward some trees, and I . . . I thought that was all Corey was going to do, but he jumped back in the car and we . . . we sort of followed him as best we could. We caught up with him somewhere near Bear Road, and all of a sudden, Corey took a rifle out of the backseat and . . . and . . ." She broke off, her eyes wet and fierce. "I tried to stop him, Doc Brent, I swear I did! I grabbed his arm, and begged him not to do it, but he pushed me away, and then he got out of the car and before I could get there he . . . he shot Ajax."

Daffodil was sobbing violently now, and Billy had his arm around her. Corey Dillard slumped to the ground, his head down, not even looking at her.

"What happened then?" Jackson asked grimly.

"Corey was mad that he'd only wounded the dog. He said he was going to try again, but I tried to get the rifle away and I told him no, we had to get out of there. He pushed me away. So I told him if he fired again I'd tell, and he'd be in big trouble and then he—"

"Go on, Daffodil, honey. What'd he do next?" Smoke prodded. His eyes were narrowed and grave beneath the dripping brim of his hat.

"He hit me." She stepped away from Billy and toward Corey, who still didn't look at her. "He hit me across the face. And then he grabbed my arms. I still have what's left of the bruises to show for it." She held out her arms as Billy stood by in tight-lipped silence.

The men looked at the bruises, then both turned to regard the boy slumped on the ground.

Daffodil lowered her arms. "He told me that his uncle had warned you, Doc Brent, that he'd shoot the dog if he came on Dillard land again. He said he was only protecting his uncle's cattle, because the dog would have gotten free of his lead one day anyway, and might have come after the calves."

Standing in the rain, she started to shiver. "He said he was just trying to help his uncle and have some fun at the same time. That's what he said—he thought it was *fun*." She swallowed hard and finished in a rush. "I wanted to call for help or . . . tell you . . . but he told me if I did that he'd . . . that he'd . . ."

"He told her he'd beat her up if she talked." Billy spoke up. "And then he hit her again, just to make sure she understood."

Jackson didn't have to ask Daffodil if this was true. The answer was in her eyes—he'd never seen such a mixture of anger, shame, and contempt.

"I'm sorry, Doc Brent," she said after a moment, her voice breaking. "I should have told you right away."

"It's not your fault, Daffodil. You just need to pick your friends better. Next time you will."

He turned to Corey, still sitting on the ground. He didn't dare touch the boy, for fear he'd lose control. Instead he let Lee step forward.

"Is that what happened, son?"

"Don't answer him." It was Luke Dillard. He'd finally staggered to his feet. "Not a word, Corey. Not one goddamned word. You hear me?"

"Tell the truth, Corey." At the sound of Jackson's level tone, the boy's head came up a few inches and he cast Jackson a sullen look. But there was fear too, behind the defiance in his eyes.

"It'll go easier for you if you tell the truth now," Jackson said.

"He's right." Smoke nodded. "There's no backing out of this trouble, but you can at least face up to it like a man."

Corey's mouth seemed stuck together but he forced the words out somehow. "Yeah, all right. I did it. You going to throw me in jail?"

"That's for Sheriff Harvey to say." Rigid control only just managed to keep a lid on Jackson's fury. "But you'd better believe I'm going to press charges against you. And I hope Daffodil will too. What you did to her is called assault."

Jackson turned his head to study Billy and Daffodil. Billy was banged up pretty bad, wet and bleeding and bruised, and Daffodil was shivering in the rain. They looked like a couple of soaked, battered pups. "Why don't you kids get inside, get warm somewhere."

Billy nodded and drew Daffodil closer. "Let me take you home so you can put on some dry clothes. Then we'll come back for your car."

"Okay." She leaned in against him, drawn to the warmth of his body. Despite being soaked and miserable, she felt better—better than she had in a long time. A weight had been lifted from her, and the funny thing was, she didn't feel afraid anymore. She felt . . . fine. Comfortable. Safe. Just like she'd always felt when she was with Billy. He didn't expect her to always look "hot" and he'd always listened when she'd felt like talking about hydrogen fuel cells or the anatomical differences between Cro-Magnon and Neanderthal skulls. He was just Billy. And she was just herself.

"Let's go," she whispered. And then she did something she hadn't done in a long time—at least that's how it seemed. She smiled at Billy. And tucked her icy, wet hand in his.

Jackson's cell phone rang as he watched Billy and Daffodil trudge back to the pickup—two slight bedraggled figures in the slanting gray rain.

"Jackson Brent." He spoke curtly, still thinking about Luke and Corey, and what a scummy pair they made. And about how big a mistake Luke's sister-in-law had made sending her son here to try to straighten him out. The kid was more screwed up than ever.

"Jackson, thank God! Thank God you're there!" Katy's voice, tense and breathless. Tension whipped through him at the raw panic jolting through the phone.

"What's wrong?" Everything else was forgotten. "Where are you?"

"I'm on my way to your cabin. I'm all right." He heard her struggling to keep her voice steady, and his gut tightened.

"I'm on Coyote Lane. Can you meet me at the cabin right now?"

For the first time, lightning sizzled across the sky and there was a sudden burst of static from the phone. When it died out, he spoke tersely. "Are you still there?"

"Yes. I'm here. I'm fine. At least I will be when the shock wears off."

"I'm on my way. Talk to me."

He was already at his truck, having spared only a cursory nod to Smoke and Lee, and not even a glance at Luke or Corey. His paint and other purchases were still sitting on the ground—he'd forgotten all about them listening to Katy's taut, rapid words.

"I just found out something important, Jackson—I think Sheriff Harvey lied to me—to us." Her words poured out, thrumming with shock and fear. "Mrs. Kirk said he never called her. She said she never did hear from Crystal again since the time she planned to leave Thunder Creek. If that's true, Jackson, it means Sheriff Harvey lied. And that he's involved—he's covering up something. All this time he knew the truth, he knew that something bad happened to Crystal. And maybe Matt's accident wasn't really . . ."

She broke off, and Jackson's chest tightened. He felt cold all over.

"Okay, Katy, listen to me. Get to the cabin." He vaulted into the truck and slammed the door. "Don't stop for anything—or *anyone*." He fired up the engine even as thunder roared like cannon fire and the rain pelted harder. "When you get there, lock the doors. I've got a rifle and ammo inside my bedroom closet. If it'll make you feel better, take it out and load it up until I can get there—"

"I have Big John's revolver in my purse," she said quickly, refraining from telling him she'd already had to use it once today.

"Good. So just wait and hang tight, and when I get there we'll figure it out together."

"Yes, yes, I'll be fine. I'm just—in shock."

"I can see why." What she'd told him was sinking in, not fully, but a good part of it, and he didn't like the feeling in his gut. "Don't open the door for anyone but me. Got that? No one."

"Don't worry, I won't." She gave a short, ragged laugh, then he heard her quick intake of breath. "Jackson, come soon, will you?"

"Count on it, sweetheart. Just hang on."

The solid strength of his voice soothed some of her nerve endings that seemed to be dancing on barbed wire. Her hand holding the phone was shaking. She could barely hold it as she fought with the steering wheel on the increasingly rough road. Rain slashed furiously across the windshield, and the sky was growing so dark she switched on her headlights. "I'm okay. See you soon."

She dropped the phone on the seat and concentrated on driving. *Calm down,* she told herself, for the hundredth time. *All you have to do is get to the cabin.*

By the time she passed the clinic, the wind had picked up and the sky had turned a sickly greenish-gray. Tumbleweed blew across the road as the windshield wipers rushed to beat back the rain. Relief flooded her when she reached the cabin. It stood solid and safe and welcoming against the storm, its isolation comforting under the circumstances. There was no danger here, only the cabin where she'd had coffee and bagels with Jackson yesterday morning, only the bed where they'd made love all night while the stars burned in the sky. As she grabbed her purse and made a run for it through the slash of the rain, she thought of hot tea and a fire. And Jackson. Jackson was coming. He'd be here soon.

She used the spare key he'd given her and burst in just as thunder boomed and lightning flashed again across the mountain, so close together she gasped. She slammed the door against the wind and rain, and twisted the dead bolt, then leaned against the door and for the first time since she'd hung up the phone with Donna Kirk, her heartbeat slowed. She let herself take a long, deep breath.

Then it struck her. How quiet the cabin was. Where were Regis and Cammi and Ajax?

Fear sliced through her, but even as it did so, she saw Cammi dart into the living room, glance at her, swish her tail. "There you are."

She sighed at her own jumpiness and followed Cammi as she spun around, gave another nervous swish of her tail, and leapt back toward the bedroom. "Where's your pals? Curled up all comfy on the bed, I'll bet."

In spite of the situation she couldn't help a small, relieved smile. "Too lazy even to come out and say hello—"

She broke off at the sight that greeted her as she reached Jackson's bedroom. Regis and Ajax were sprawled on the floor in front of the bed. They were asleep . . . deeply asleep.

Something turned over in the pit of her stomach. Why hadn't they barked, or come to greet her, why hadn't they so much as lifted their heads now that she was standing only a few feet away?

"Ajax . . . Regis . . ." Her heart skittered as they remained motionless. Oh God . . .

Cammi had leaped onto the nightstand and was watching Katy nervously. She swallowed hard, fear clutching at her as she knelt beside the dogs. They were breathing—she could see their chests going up and down, but . . . She touched them and they never stirred. They might have been dead . . .

She sensed someone behind her even before he spoke. The chill chased down her spine like the blade of an ice skate.

"They're not dead, Katy." Stan Harvey spoke calmly, matter-of-factly, even as she shot to her feet and spun around to face him. He was holding his revolver as casually as if it were one of his cigars, not even pointing it at her, but his eyes were keen, watchful.

"Though they will be soon," he went on as he watched her face drain of color. "And so, I'm real sorry to say, will you."

Chapter 31

"YOU DON'T SEEM SURPRISED TO SEE ME."

Stan Harvey eased his gun up just a bit so that it was pointed directly at Katy's chest. He noted the expression of determination entering her eyes, overtaking that initial flash of fear, and he prayed she wouldn't act on it. If he had to shoot her, it would ruin everything.

Because everything depended on following the plan.

"You couldn't have figured it out already, could you?" he asked.

Her throat was almost too dry to speak, but she managed to get the words out without her voice shaking. "If you mean, do I know that you lied about talking to Donna Kirk, and that Crystal never showed up at home after she left Thunder Creek, yes, I figured it out. And I also figured out that you killed her." Her voice broke then. "Just as you killed Matt."

"Think you're pretty smart, don't you?"

"What have you done to these dogs?"

"Nothing serious. It's only chloroform. They won't ever know what hit them. And neither will you. Or Jackson." Sweat sheened his face, but he held the gun steady, like the pro that he was.

"It's going to be a clean easy death, Katy. Painless. I owe you that much. And Big John too."

Regret glistened in his eyes. "I hate having to do this." Desperation threaded his voice. "But you've given me no choice."

"Of course you have a choice. You can stop this right now."

"It's way too late for that. Fourteen years too late."

He waved with the gun toward the living room, his tone becoming crisp, businesslike.

"So, get on out there, Katy. I'm sure Jackson will be along soon and I want to be ready. We wouldn't want him surprising us, now would we?"

A new terror swept through her. Jackson was coming— because she'd called him. He'd burst in here, unsuspecting, to find her, help her. And he'd be caught too.

There'd been no sign of a car or of anyone else at the cabin, so Jackson would have no warning. He'd be as unprepared as she'd been. And every bit as vulnerable.

"Actually, Jackson has nothing to do with this," she said quickly. "This is between you and me."

"Not since you blabbed to him about that sketch your brother drew. Not since the two of you started asking questions, trying to dig into something you had no business interfering in. Sort of like disturbing the dead. The dead are better left alone, Katy. Too bad you didn't realize that before. Now let's go."

Trembling, she stared at him. He wanted her to walk? Right now her legs felt so weak she could barely stand. Even now, even with a gun pointed at her, what she was facing was hard to believe. This man whom she'd known all her life, who had sipped coffee in her mother's kitchen, who'd played poker with her father every other week for years, who'd kept the peace in Thunder Creek for as long as she could remember—this man had killed her brother. He'd come to the funeral, he'd watched her family grieve, he'd witnessed firsthand the agony he'd caused.

And now he wanted to kill again.

"It was because Matt saw what you did to Crystal, wasn't it?" Her gaze held his, dazed and fascinated and repelled. Part of her wanted to delay going into the living room, delay whatever he had planned next for as long as possible, and part of her just wanted to know, at last, the truth. All of it.

"Matt saw her body," she said. Her voice was low, quiet compared to the harsh drum of the rain beating at the roof. "But he didn't see you. He had no idea you were the one who killed her. Or else he wouldn't have come to you. He did come to you, didn't he? You lied to me about that as well."

"Right you are." Stan Harvey nodded. "No one else except Matt ever knew she was dead, or ever would have known. As far as the world was concerned, Crystal Kirk left town. End of story."

He licked his lips. "I need folks to keep on believing that, Katy. That's why I'm here right now."

"Why did you kill her? Why did you even have an affair with her—she was half your age."

"She was a grown woman, very much so," he corrected her sharply. "And what goes on between a man and a woman in the dark is no one's business. But she was going to tell Ardelle everything, unless I got a divorce and married *her*. She was out of control, and I knew she meant what she said. I couldn't let her destroy Ardelle. I couldn't let that happen."

"Then maybe you shouldn't have had an affair."

"Don't judge me." For the first time, temper flared in his face, that solid, rough-hewn face she knew so well. "Don't you dare judge me. I never wanted to hurt my wife. But she was sick for a long time—she was weak and delicate. And we couldn't...well, let's just say a man has his needs. Crystal Kirk took care of those needs. But she was jealous, crazy-jealous—a lot more than I realized at first. She wanted marriage, babies, all that crap. She wanted everyone to know she was good enough to be Sheriff Harvey's wife."

His hand tightened on the gun. "But she wasn't," he said with contempt. "And she got out of hand."

His eyes seemed to flatten. "When I heard her crying on the phone to her mama, feeling all sorry for herself because I wouldn't ask Ardelle for a divorce, I thought at first *Good. Let her go home. Let her cry on her mama's shoulder so her mama could explain the facts of life to her—that white-trash tramps-on-the-side don't get wedding rings from men who were only looking for fun.*" His mouth twisted. "But she never made it that far. Things happened that morning, the morning she was supposed to leave. Things...got out of control."

"How?" She kept her gaze glued to his face, but all the while Katy was listening, listening desperately for Jackson's truck over the rain.

Harvey shifted his weight from one foot to the other. He seemed relieved to be telling her his side of the story, relieved to have the chance to prove to her that none of this was his fault.

"I went to her place early, while she was still packing, and I told her it was over. Told her not to come back to Thunder Creek, that we were finished. Just as I figured, she started crying, carrying on. So I pulled out this envelope—it had five thousand dollars in it. I thought it was a nice good-bye present, that it would make the breakup easier to swallow." He grimaced. "But instead she went nuts. Threw the cash in my face, then came at me with her claws. I pushed her away and she started screaming, screaming that she was going to tell Ardelle. Screaming that I'd pay."

His eyes grew darker, seeming to shrink into the furrows of his face. "She kept shrieking about what I'd done to her, how bad I'd treated her, yammering and yammering—getting more hysterical by the minute. Then she screamed that I'd upset her so much she'd done something awful and horrible things happened to her, and it was all my fault. I didn't have a clue what she was talking about, but then she let loose—about all of it—about that night in the Tumbleweed, about your brother and Elam Lowell and Wood Morgan. She claimed she'd been drugged, claimed she didn't know what was happening, claimed it was my fault for the way I'd upset her. But anything Crystal got was her own damned fault," he said heavily, and now Katy could see a muscle jerking rapidly in his cheek.

Her stomach clenched. "Is that why you killed her?" she asked. "Because of that night in the Tumbleweed?"

"She was threatening to tell Ardelle," he exploded. "She was nothing but a dirty little tramp and she was going to destroy my wife! She wouldn't shut up, she just kept screeching, throwing things, coming at me..."

Sweat glistened on his face as if he'd stuck his head out the door into the pummeling rain. She saw his hand shaking on the gun, ever so slightly, and suddenly she was afraid he'd lose control and squeeze the trigger.

"I hit her—once, only once—but she just kept screaming. I started choking her to shut her up, and before I even realized it..." His eyes had a faraway look. "It wasn't supposed to happen," he finished hoarsely. "But...she wouldn't shut up..."

Suddenly he jerked free from the reverie. The stare he gave Katy was stone-cold. "I'm damned if I'm going to spend the rest of my life in prison because I protected my wife."

"Your wife is dead now." Her eyes locked on his. "And you're still trying to kill people to protect yourself."

"Damn straight. I have a good life here, a reputation to think of. I've got respect. Not to mention a tidy little four million dollar fortune my wife entrusted to me. I'm just doing what I have to do to keep what's mine, to keep my life."

"And my brother?" Katy didn't even realize her voice had risen. She was shouting. "What about his life? He found

Crystal's body somewhere, didn't he? And he went to your office to report it. You told him not to tell anyone. You told him to wait, while you looked into it, just as you told me."

"You're a smart girl, Katy. Too smart." There was an edge to his voice. He didn't like the way she was talking to him. She wasn't showing him respect.

"I didn't want it to come to that, Katy. I didn't have anything against Matt. But he made a big mistake: he went to see Crystal the morning she was leaving town, got there soon after I'd dragged her outside. She was way back behind the trash bins in the weeds that run all the way up to the railroad tracks. Her nose had been bleeding when I hit her, and I guess he saw a spot or two of blood on the carpet outside her door. And more on the stairs. I hadn't had a chance to come back yet and clean up the scene; I'd just dumped her body in that field of weeds and went home for a shovel and gloves. While I was gone, it was Matt's bad luck to find that little bit of a blood trail—and follow it."

Katy's stomach lurched. The sheriff paused as Cammi darted out of the bedroom past him. Then his gaze returned to Katy's face, his expression sour. "Yep, he found Crystal all right—hidden in all those weeds, just short of the tracks. But by the time I got back to bury her, he was gone."

"He went to your office later," Katy said shakenly. "He told you about seeing Crystal."

Harvey nodded. "He was waiting outside my door, quakin' like there was no tomorrow. It was a lucky thing I was the one he came to first. I was able to get him to hold off on telling anyone—convinced him to wait until I'd seen the body myself and started my investigation. He'd really wanted to tell Big John, I guess because he was so shook up and all, but I impressed on him the importance of waiting. And then, you see, I had no choice but to make sure he couldn't tell anyone. Ever."

"You bastard." She couldn't help it, the rage burst out of her. "He came to you for help, he trusted you!"

"You don't think I wanted to have to kill him, do you?" Stan Harvey said. "Your father's been my friend for a long time. And Dorsey's one of the sweetest women I've ever known, next to my Ardelle. The last thing I wanted was to hurt Matt. Or you, for that matter," he added. He sounded sincere, she realized in shock. But his face was grim, set. Katy could read the resignation, and the resolve, in his eyes.

"In my line of work, a man has to do a lot of unpleasant things. You get used to it. Sometimes it's the only way."

"The only way to protect yourself, you mean? After you kill an innocent girl?"

"Crystal was a far cry from innocent. She turned out to be a slut—and a loose cannon. But right now, I'm concerned with you, Katy. You brought this on yourself, after all, even more than Matt. I gave you a warning at the Triple T that night. I felt it was my duty as a lawman to at least warn you first."

"Your little warning nearly killed me," she bit out.

"I could have killed you then—easily. But I gave you a chance to back off, even though I didn't really expect you'd take it. And sure enough, you and Jackson wouldn't let it go. I heard he was still asking questions about where Crystal lived, and I'll bet you called Donna Kirk again too, now didn't you?"

He gave a thin smile at her startled expression. "I know everything that goes on in this town. Too bad you didn't realize that sooner."

Stan Harvey motioned once again with the gun. "Come on, Katy. For the last time, get in that other room. We're done talking."

She walked in front of him, her steps dragging, her brain racing. The rain was still pounding against the windows, and the wind had begun to scream like a wild thing, trapped, desperate. She strained for any sounds of Jackson's truck pulling up, but she couldn't hear anything over the rain and wind and thunder.

"Close those shutters," he ordered her. "We don't want Jackson getting a sneak peek of what's in store for him, do we?"

"What is in store for him?" She tried to sound calm as she touched shaking fingers to the brass knob on the shutters. For a moment she had a brief glimpse of the world outside. The road was empty, but for blowing rain and twigs and tumbleweed. He'd be here soon. She had to do something—stall, fight, somehow change the balance of power, so Jackson wouldn't be walking unawares into this trap.

Turning from the shutters, her glance shifted to her purse. She'd dropped it onto the small table beside the sofa, next to the bronze sculpture. She edged toward it as Sheriff Harvey slipped the gun into his holster and then reached into the pocket of his black rain slicker, drawing out a length of rope.

"What I've got planned is nothing too terrible," he said. "I don't want either of you to suffer. It'll be quick, and it's going to look like an accident, of course. I'll have to tie you up first so you won't be in the way when Jackson comes in. I'll have to coldcock him, but don't worry, I won't hit him too hard— just enough to stun him while I tie him up. We don't want any broken skulls or visible lacerations on the corpse."

Katy's legs trembled. *Corpse.* She reached the table. "And then what?"

"A little chloroform, then when you're both unconscious, I'll remove the ropes. We can't have any hint of foul play getting in the way of an accidental death ruling from the coroner, now can we? Then I'll light some nice romantic candles and set the fire. It's a shame how a little romance can get out of control." He was breathing hard now, looking a little sick. A little wild.

"You'll never feel it though, Katy, not the heat, not the flames. It'll be a peaceful death."

"You can't do this." She was as pale as Bessie's bone china, but her voice was quick and forceful. "It'll never work. Someone will realize—two members of the Templeton family dying accidentally? Sort of a weird coincidence," she pointed out desperately. "Someone will put two and two together—"

"No way," he cut her off. "It's been fourteen years since I knocked over that ladder while Matt was climbing down. That's a long time, Katy. No one's going to connect this fire with that. And as far as the world can see, neither of them has anything to do with me. And if you think Wood Morgan or Elam Lowell will say one word about anything, or question what happened to you, you don't have a clue how desperate Wood is to keep Tammie from ever finding out about that sleazy little night fourteen years ago. He and Elam will be silent as Christmas Eve."

He was right. He'd thought this through too well, worked his plan like a professional. What was she thinking? He *was* a professional. A professional liar. And killer.

"I won't tie your bonds too tight, Katy. Don't want you to be uncomfortable." He started toward her, dangling the rope, his eyes intent, chillingly purposeful.

Katy pounced forward and snatched up her purse. She plunged her hand in, digging for the revolver, but even as she yanked it out he lunged at her. Seizing her wrist, he easily twisted the gun away, then shoved her backward, purse and all.

"Damn you, that was stupid."

"So is expecting me to submit quietly to being tied up and killed!" she gasped.

"I expect you to be smart enough to realize that fighting won't do any good." He dropped Big John's gun into his slicker pocket and, scowling, started toward her once again.

"Now then—"

Katy grabbed for the bronze sculpture and hurled it at his head. He tried to duck but he wasn't fast enough and it glanced off his temple with a solid thud. She was already bolting for the door, clutching her purse, reaching for the dead bolt.

Her fingers shook as she twisted it hard. She heard him coming at her, and yanked the door open. Panic tore through her as she plunged outside into the storm, into a shrieking wind that sucked at her hair and bombarded her with sleek gray torrents of rain.

Still clutching her purse she ran, veering from her car as she saw him dodge that way, expecting her to try to reach it. Instead she raced around the cabin, running hard, her feet slipping on the wet grass as she fled toward the rocks and the trees and the jumble of rising switchbacks that crisscrossed the trail up Cougar Mountain.

He was coming after her, his boots pounding through the night, and she imagined those strong arms closing in on her, grabbing her, yanking her back...

Fear drove her, drove her blood, body, and soul. She ran for her life, plunging between the trees like a wild creature, trying to lose him in the soggy, windswept darkness.

Had Crystal had a chance to run?

Matt hadn't.

For a moment in her mind, she thought she heard her brother's voice, urging her on. "You can do it, Katy. You can do it."

The rocky trail wound and climbed and she scaled it breathlessly, scrambling, scraping her arms and her face on rocks and branches. It was impossible to hear him now, over the rush of the rain and the wind tearing through leaves and branches, but she knew he was there... he was coming.

Her breath rasped through her lungs as the trail opened up and became steeper still. Bound by rocks on one side and a steep granite drop on the other, Katy fled up Cougar Mountain. Once, she glanced back, and saw what looked like headlights below, near where the cabin was shrouded in a blur of rain and darkness.

Jackson!

She wanted to scream his name, but she couldn't. Stan Harvey might hear her. Her only hope was to keep going, to get as far away as she could...to hide and if need be, to fight—with the only weapon she had left. If she could find it in time...

She tripped over a rock and went sprawling down onto a jutting boulder. Its roughness tore at her hands and arms, and with the wind knocked out of her, she lay frozen a moment, trying to catch her breath, then realized she had reached a ledge. The trail wound away to her left, twisting and uneven, leading higher still up the mountain. Ten feet to her right was only roaring empty space where a narrow precipice dangled above a dizzyingly steep chasm that dropped straight down to a rocky gorge below.

Hurry. He's coming.

Precious seconds ticked past and there was no time to pause any longer, to catch her breath and gather strength. She was ice cold and soaked, her arms and legs ached, and her teeth were chattering, but she had to go on. She had to run and she had to fight.

Her purse had slipped from her hands when she fell. She grabbed it, her fingers stiff and icy, and scrambled up, shoving her wild hair from her face. With her head bent against the slashing rain, she thrust her hand inside her bag, fumbling frantically.

Suddenly over the wind she heard a sound. Her head flew up just in time to see Stan Harvey launching himself onto the ledge, his face every bit as thunderous and full of fury as the night sky.

She screamed, and even as she did so, her hand closed

over the canister of pepper spray. As he hurtled straight at her she brought the canister up and sprayed it directly into his face.

His tortured yell of pain drowned out the wind.

Stan Harvey clutched at his eyes, screaming. The scream turned to an agonized rasp as his mouth opened and closed, opened and closed, as if pumping for air. He staggered back, then sideways. Then forward, blind and gasping.

"Bitch!" he gasped out. "I'll make you pay—"

Katy moved fast as he tottered toward her, sidestepping him, reaching into the pocket of his slicker and seizing her father's gun. She darted back out of reach even as Harvey's arms thrust out, groping blindly for her. He missed and nearly lost his balance.

"Keep back, damn you, or I'll shoot," she shouted over the rain. Then she heard as if from far away a faint sound. A truck's engine? Or merely the wind? Turning she peered through the driving rain and the darkness and again saw lights far below. This time they definitely looked like headlights.

Hope spiked through her. She veered past the sheriff as he groaned again. All she had to do was start down the mountain. Harvey couldn't follow her, not yet, and she'd run down to Jackson, to light and safety, and later they'd come back for this murderer. But even as the thoughts rolled through her mind, even as she set a foot on the path, Harvey skidded, lost his balance, and stumbled into her. His hands grabbed wildly, latching onto her shoulders and holding fast. In horror, she stared up into his blind, fire-red eyes.

"Let go, damn you!" She struck him in the face with the barrel of the gun, but still he held on, and dragged her with him as he ducked sideways, only to lose his balance yet again. They fell together on the hard, slippery ground, rolling, rolling straight toward the precipice. She felt the gun spin from her hand as they tumbled across the slick treacherous trail. Then they were at the edge—over it—with only dark rushing air beneath them.

Her scream soared up toward the heavens as she grasped wildly for the ledge, even as Stan Harvey, screeching, hurtled past her.

She didn't see him fall, but his final yell roared through her ears. It echoed, lost and furious in the wrath of the night, and into the depths of her soul, even as she clung like an ant to the wall of Cougar Mountain, hanging on with every bone and muscle and pore of her body.

"Jackson," she called feebly, sobbing, her nails digging into rock and brush, her feet scrabbling to keep their toehold on a slick narrow perch just beneath the lip of the ledge.

"Jackson, I'm up here," she gasped into the wind, knowing he couldn't possibly hear her.

The rain drove at her, twigs blew against her cheeks, caught in her hair. She burrowed her face against the jagged rock, and tried to anchor her feet. Thunder grumbled, seeming to shake the mountain. Lightning slashed. Her cheeks were streaked with tears and dirt and rain.

Katy closed her eyes against the ferocity of the night. She pressed her body to the wall of rock, and held on.

"Katy! Do you hear me? Katy, give me your hand! Just reach up—and give me your hand."

She thought she was dreaming, but she wasn't. It took all of her courage, but she moved her head away from the wall several inches, and tilted it up, just enough to see Jackson flat on his stomach atop the ledge, reaching his hand down to her.

"Come on, baby. You can do it. Give me your hand."

She blinked but he didn't disappear. A tiny flicker of hope broke through the dazed terror that had overtaken her.

"Jackson," she croaked over the wind. "You . . . came."

"Damn right I came. I promised, didn't I?" Sweat and rain poured down his face. She looked like death warmed over, like a puff of air would send her careening down the gorge. Terror flailed him. "Now I'm going to get you home and safe, Katy. Give me your hand, and we'll get out of here."

"I . . . can't."

"Yes, you can. I'm taking you to the cabin."

The cabin. Jackson's big warm bed, the thick down comforter. A fire blazing . . . *Fire* . . .

"Jackson, I have to tell you," she shouted, gasping as the wind tore at her. "In case I fall, you have to know. It was Sheriff Harvey." The words came out in a jumbling rush. "He admitted it. He killed Matt . . . and Crystal."

"Okay, baby. We'll talk about it later. Give me your hand."

"He . . . chloroformed Ajax . . . and Regis . . ."

"Later, Katy. You can tell me later. Right now, you just have to reach up and take my hand."

She closed her eyes at the thought of what he was asking her to do. "I c-can't. I'm afraid to move . . . afraid to let go."

"Nothing to be afraid of. I'm right here, I can almost reach you. Look, see my hand, Katy?"

He held it down to her, the tips of those long, strong fingers only inches above where she huddled. "Just reach for me. I won't let you fall. Trust me, baby."

I want to. I want to trust you. "I . . . can't let go," she cried, tears mingling with the rain on her cheeks.

"Then I'm coming down."

"No! It's too dangerous! We'll both fall—"

"The hell we will."

"Wait, I'll do it—I'll reach up . . ."

He held his breath as she released her viselike grip on the jagged rock she clung to. Her hand inched upward. Suddenly lightning speared the sky and the wind surged, and Katy grabbed the rock again, sobbing.

Her entire body trembled. Panic spliced Jackson's insides

as he stared down at the soaked and shivering woman clinging to the face of the mountain. She looked as fragile and
precarious as a feather in a hurricane. Her face was white
and she was probably in shock. He'd called Smoke from his
cell phone the moment he'd reached the cabin and seen the
door flung open, and found the rope and toppled bronze
sculpture inside—only seconds before he found the dogs.
Help should be coming soon, but he couldn't afford to wait.
She could slip or faint or even sway at any moment, and the
damned storm just wouldn't let up.

"You're okay, Katy. You're fine. Take it easy. I'm right
here."

"Don't l-leave me."

"I'm never leaving you, sweetheart. Never."

She glanced up in time to see him edging out over the lip
of the ledge, the upper half of his lean, hard body hanging
down as he stretched his hand toward her. The wind whipped
at his dark hair, rain battered his face, but Jackson didn't
even blink. His fingertips brushed the rock wall less than a
foot above her head. He edged lower still.

"Jackson, don't, you'll fall!"

"No, I won't. And neither will you. Reach up now, only a
little. You can do it."

Could she? Clammy sweat sheened on her skin. Waves of
cold seeped through her. It seemed to her that at any moment
the fury of the wind would simply blow her off the mountain,
straight down into the gorge...

She held on tight, gasping, her fingers digging into the
rock.

"Katy, look at me." His voice was firm and calm despite
the raging storm. She focused on that, on how steady and
sure Jackson was, how certain he was he could pull her up.

Trust me.

She looked up and saw his face, that dark, determined

face. Water streamed past his eyes, his jaw was set. Stubborn man. Wonderful, beautiful, stubborn man.

She squeezed her breath in, let go of the rock, and slowly, ever so slowly, lifted her hand.

The wind howled, and she bit her lip. Then lifted her hand higher...

"I've got you," he said swiftly as his fingers locked around hers, strong as iron. "Easy does it."

The human touch, the warmth of his hand even through the storm, revived her spirit, her will to fight, and as if awakening from a dream, she scrabbled to help him as he pulled her up and over. She landed at last on the ledge with a thud. Immediately, Jackson dragged her from the rim, back toward the trail, and then he gathered her in his arms and cradled her icy body against him as the night screamed around them.

"My God, what did that bastard do to you?" Searching her face, he cupped her cheeks between his hands. "If he's not dead, I swear I'll kill him. I'll *kill* him."

Then he was kissing her face, her hair, her hands, kissing her over and over and Katy kissed him back, her lips clinging to his the way her hands had clung to the mountain.

"He's down there... somewhere..." she gasped between kisses, and Jackson's brows drew together in a frown.

"Then he's dead. But even if by some chance he survived the fall, he's got to be hurt bad enough so he's not going anywhere. Smoke can check it out when he gets here. I don't give a damn. I'm getting you down to the cabin before you freeze to death. I thought I'd lost you, Katy, but now that I haven't, I'm damned if I'm going to stand by and watch you get pneumonia."

"You could get pneumonia too," she whispered, her teeth chattering. To warm them she kissed him again, holding tight to his shoulders, to the strength and solidity of him.

"Then let's get the hell out of here." He buried his hands in her streaming hair and kissed her again, as once more lightning illuminated the sky, a flash of vivid hot gold in the wild black night.

Neither of them saw it. They saw only each other, and the love pulsing between them, stronger and more permanent than any quick flicker of light. They saw a reflection in each other's eyes of promises to be made and kept, of life to be lived, of possibilities opening, theirs for the taking.

With their arms wrapped around each other, their heads bent against the wind, they walked together down the mountain.

Chapter 32

"I THOUGHT I'D FIND YOU OUT HERE."

Katy reached the corral post where her father stood watching Cleo and Midnight frisking beneath the summer sun. It was only midmorning, yet the air blazed with heat and Big John looked uncomfortable in his crisp white shirt and black string tie. He didn't say a word to her, but kept his gaze trained on the horses.

"It's time to leave for the memorial service." She touched his arm, then dropped her hand when he jumped as if she'd pinched him. "Daddy, are you all right?"

"I'm fine. Just don't know if I'm going."

She suppressed a sigh. Ever since her parents had returned from Paris and found out the truth about Matt's death—and about Sheriff Harvey—her father had been more closed off than ever. He barely spoke, rode the range on horseback or Jeep most of the day, and locked himself in his den as soon as dinner was over. There was an even grayer cast to his skin beneath his tan these days, and a tightness around his mouth that never seemed to ease.

"All right. If it's too much for you, there's no need to go. Mom will understand." She always did. "I'll stay home with you if you'd like," she ventured after a moment.

"Do I look like I need mollycoddling?" he snapped.

Katy's slim brows rose. "You look like you need to let off some steam." She slanted a glance up at him, resisting the temptation to plop her hands on her hips. "Go ahead, Dad, say whatever you want. You're mad at me because I forced you to go to Paris, because you missed the birth of Cleo's foal. Because I found out what really happened and stirred up all these memories and emotions about Matt's death. You'd have been content never to have to mention it or think about it again, much less go to a memorial service and stand at his grave. I'm the one you're mad at, so why don't you just admit it and say what you have to say? Get it off your chest for once in your life and—"

"You almost died." The words broke from him, ragged and hoarse. As he spun toward her, arms hanging taut at his sides, she saw grief and naked fear shining in his eyes. And something else, something akin to panic.

"You almost died, Katy," he repeated, as if he could scarcely take in the words. "While I was gone."

"But . . . I didn't." She stared into his eyes, stunned by the emotion she saw raging there. "I'm fine, Dad," she said faintly. "Fine."

He shook his head, his eyes still glazed with fear and grief that echoed from deep within his soul. "That son of a gun almost killed you. A man I called my friend almost took you away from me."

"Oh, Dad . . ." She edged closer, her throat tight. "We all thought he was our friend. No one knew," she said quietly.

"I should have known."

"There was no way you could have. Stan Harvey was a pro at deception. There was a side to him no one ever saw." And a side to her father she was glimpsing now for the first time ever.

"It wasn't your fault, Daddy." She touched his arm again, and this time she felt the tension vibrating through him, but to her surprise, he didn't pull away. "And neither was your being gone when everything started to unravel. You don't control the world, you know, none of us do."

"I should have been here, Katy. I should have protected you better." Fierce pain radiated from his eyes, and a swell of emotion made her chest ache.

"I think I did a pretty fair job of protecting myself." She spoke lightly, and tried to smile. But something of her father's emotion touched her too, giving rise to a rush of tenderness and protectiveness toward this big, fierce bear of a man. "And of course, there was Jackson."

"Thank God for that," Big John muttered.

"He's a pretty good man to have around in a crisis. If it wasn't for him, I don't think I'd have made it off the mountain."

"Jackson's a good man to have around anytime. I guess you've figured that out."

"Yes." Her smile was soft, lighting her eyes. "I guess I have."

Suddenly, Big John turned and leaned against the corral post, his head bent forward. There was a silence in which she heard the whickering of the horses in the corral, Mojo barking in the distance, the bang of the screen door. Then she heard the horrible low sound of her father's sobs, and saw his broad shoulders heaving with emotion.

"Daddy." In dismay, Katy's arms flew around him, straining to reach across those broad, powerful shoulders. "Please, what is it?" she whispered, suddenly remembering the old adage *Be careful what you wish for.* For years she'd wanted her father to open up, loosen up, stop holding everything in so tightly. Now he seemed to be bursting at the seams with pent-up emotions and her heart broke at the sight of his pain.

"I never told you." He struggled to speak coherently through the sobs coursing through him. "I'm sorry about . . . your baby. Everything. I never knew . . . what to say . . ."

"I know, Dad, I always knew. You don't have to—"

"Don't you see, Katy?" He wheeled toward her, those gray eyes moist with the tears that streamed down the rugged planes of his face. He seized her shoulders in a desperate grip. "I almost lost you on that mountain, and I never told you...how much I love you. How proud I am of you. You could have died, and I'd never have said those words...never have had the chance to say how glad I am you're back and..."

He broke off, the sobs consuming him, and Katy went to him as he enfolded her in his arms. She stroked his back, and hugged him tight, tears welling in her own eyes at the cascade of emotions tumbling from this man who guarded his emotions as if they were entombed in Fort Knox.

"Is this a private party, or can anyone join in?" Dorsey Templeton's quiet voice broke through the mingled sobs of father and daughter. Katy lifted her head from her father's shoulder and offered a watery smile.

"Group hug," she gasped, and then Big John opened his arms to his wife, and the three of them embraced, their tears mingling beside the corral as a fresh summer breeze swept down from the mountains.

And as she stood with them both, letting the grief and the love flow between them, Katy was infinitely glad that she'd made the decision she had—the decision to protect Matt's secret. What good would it do to expose the stupid mistake Matt had made that autumn night, when he'd become involved in a situation that went way too far and landed him in way over his head?

He'd been a teenaged boy, a boy who was all too human, and not some kind of saint, however much she might have worshipped him. He'd acted wildly and irresponsibly that night, running on angst and impulse and hormones—not to mention alcohol—as teenaged boys were wont to do. And from everything she'd discovered, no one had regretted what had gone on inside the Tumbleweed after the bar had closed more than he had.

Oh, Wood Morgan had regretted it because he feared Tammie would find out, and that fear had chased him through all the years of their marriage. Elam probably hadn't regretted it at all—especially since Katy had discovered that Wood paid him well to keep his mouth shut over the years. And Crystal?

She'd died filled with shame, anger, and regret.

But Katy knew one thing down to her soul—Matt had worried about Crystal after that night. No doubt trying to assuage his guilt over the entire sleazy episode, he'd sought her out, driving to her apartment before school that last morning before she left town, trying to make sure she was all right, trying to find some measure of forgiveness. But his efforts at kindness, at repentance had gone horribly wrong—instead of bringing him peace, they'd resulted in his death.

Wood Morgan, of all people, had filled Katy in, privately, after hours in the diner, when no one was there except the two of them. After Elam had been shot and had told Wood everything that had happened at the Jenssens' barn, Wood had come to her, knowing the gig was up. He'd explained that he'd only sent Elam there to try to scare her, and if that hadn't worked, to fill her in on what she wanted to know. Elam had been given the okay to tell her everything about that night and about the pact—leaving out only Wood's name.

"You know Tammie," he'd muttered to Katy, having the grace for once in his life to look uncomfortable, if not ashamed. "She'd never forgive me for cheating on her, even though it was long before we were married, and she'd have my hide for keeping it from her all these years. And then," he'd drawn a deep breath, "there was the drugs..."

His voice trailed off, and he ducked his head. "If I had it to do over, I'd never have fooled around with them and sure as hell never have given 'em to Crystal. If Tammie knew about the drugs, hell, if this town knew..." He drew in a deep breath.

"It'd ruin my business and my standing in the community. But the worst part, Katy, is that it'd ruin Tammie's life—our life together. That woman hates being humiliated. I think she'd divorce me, she's that damned proud and stubborn. Do you want to be responsible for breaking up my marriage—for her moving out and taking our kids with her? I'm telling you, Katy, I can't afford to have it come out—not now, not ever. I have a place in this community, and so do my wife and kids. I'm asking you, Katy—*begging* you—don't tell anyone. No one needs to know. Even Matt agreed to keep it quiet," he'd added desperately. "Matt hated what happened that night, but he did agree to the pact. Don't you think you should honor it for him?"

"Don't you dare talk to me about what I should do for my brother." She'd stood beneath the circling ceiling fan in the diner and glared at him. "You only care about yourself. You didn't care about Matt, or Crystal. Only about protecting your precious reputation."

"It wasn't so bad, that night," Wood had tried to argue. "Yeah, it was kinda sleazy, I admit, but...we were drunk. And a little high—some of us, at least. But only Elam and me actually...did the deed with Crystal. Matt passed out, and when he woke up and saw what was going on, man, he looked sick. You think your parents want to know about that? Come on, what good would it do, after all these years? It's bad enough they find out he was murdered—but do they need to know the stupid stuff he got mixed up in one damned night, right before he died? Do you really want them to be as disillusioned about their precious perfect golden boy as you are?"

Katy had clenched her fists to keep from hitting Wood Morgan across the face. "I'm not disillusioned—not with Matt," she'd shot back.

"He regretted what he did, and would have owned up to it. Elam said Matt wanted to go to Allison and be straight with her about it. You were the one who talked him out of it, who wanted to keep it secret. You convinced Matt to enter into that pact, and you paid Elam for his silence. You lied to me, and you sent Elam to fire shots at me to scare me off." She'd taken one furious step closer to Wood Morgan.

"You never cared about the effects of your actions on anyone else, and you never will—you just don't want to get caught."

"Katy—" Wood's tanned skin had gone ashen at the fury in her face. "Does this mean you're going to tell your folks? I'll do anything, pay anything . . . you can keep the diner, I'll get Tammie to back off—"

"Great, you do that, Wood," she interrupted. "Keep Tammie away from me—and you stay away too. I'm keeping the diner, all right, but not because of you."

"I didn't mean it that way. I just want to negotiate something here so that we both get what we want—"

"I've got what I want. The truth. That's all I wanted from the beginning."

She'd walked to the front of the diner and held the door open for him. Dusk was painting the summer sky with faint strokes of charcoal. She felt the anger draining from her as quickly as it had come, leaving only distaste for the man who followed her to the door and stepped past her onto the porch in uneasy silence.

"I'll let you keep your dirty little secret, Wood, but not for your sake. Only because no possible good can come from revealing it now. Only pain. And there's been enough pain stemming from that night. I won't add to it."

"I'm grateful, Katy. More than I can say. If there's anything I can do—ever—just say the word. Whatever you want—"

She let the screen door slam between them. "Good night, Wood."

. . .

The memorial service was to be a small affair. It had been Dorsey's idea—a desire to hold a moment of silence at her son's grave after all these years, a time to contemplate and acknowledge his death in light of what Katy had uncovered. Matt Templeton had not died an accidental death: he'd been murdered. He'd tried to befriend an unfortunate girl and ended up in the wrong place at the wrong time, falling victim to her murderer. They would gather and reflect and say good-bye once more in light of these new circumstances, paying silent homage to the son, grandson, and brother who had discovered a murder and sought to bring it to light, only to have his own life extinguished.

And so they stood quietly together beneath a burnished blue sky as hawks swooped overhead and the rustle of squirrels in the brush brought the rustle of life to this lonely place. In the distance, beyond the sea of headstones and the rows of aspens, were the cottonwood-dotted banks of Thunder Creek.

Katy stood between Jackson and Bessie, her head bent, gazing at the glistening white headstone carved with her brother's name.

Today was different from that other day, Matt's funeral, when she'd been fourteen, crazed with grief and anger, when she'd hated and blamed Jackson Brent every bit as much as she mourned her brother. Now she slipped her hand into Jackson's, squeezed it tight, and knew that he belonged here, that Matt would want him here, that she wanted him here.

His fingers closed around hers, those long, strong fingers, and she wondered what had become of the cold emptiness in her heart. Now it was full. Where there had been loneliness, bitterness, there was peace. And as she thought of Matt and his zest for life, his kindness and patience, his short "golden" life, she felt through her sorrow a renewed sense of hope. It seemed to Katy that the trees looked larger, their leaves greener, that the scent of the wildflowers she'd gathered and laid upon her brother's grave wafted through the air with a sweet pungent fragrance more intense than any store-bought bouquet, that the blood and pulse and energy of the close friends and family gathered around her soothed and stimulated her soul. And she glanced at the quiet, handsome man beside her and smiled up into his eyes, seeing there a reflection of her own grief, her own loss, and her own peace as she finally, fully, let the pain of Matt's death go.

It was a very private gathering. Margie and Lee were there, as were Smoke and Ellen, his parents, Ada and Billy, Pat and Riley, and some of her parents' other friends. And to Katy's surprise, Allison Leggett was there too.

She and her husband hovered well behind those assembled around the grave during the moment of silence. When everyone headed back to their cars, Allison approached the Templetons alone. After paying her respects to Dorsey and Big John and Bessie, she drew Katy aside.

"I had to say good-bye to him," Allison said simply. "This time, it's for good."

Katy searched her face. Allison had never asked her if she'd discovered what terrible secret Matt had been hiding. She obviously still didn't want to know. And that was her choice, Katy reflected. And maybe after all these years, it was for the best.

But there was something different today about her brother's former girlfriend. She looked less tense and somehow less sad than she had when Katy and Jackson had visited her. She almost looked . . . happy.

"I'm glad, Allison. Glad you're saying good-bye. It's time."

"More than time. I guess I should have realized that before. You were right. I wasn't being fair to myself, or to my family." She glanced over her shoulder at the man standing with his hands shoved in his pockets, his face sober. "Rusty's a good man." She shrugged. "No one's ever going to be like Matt—he was my first love, my special love—but Rusty loves me, too and . . . you know what? I love him. I love my boys." Her small gold earrings glittered in the sun as she lifted her chin. "And I've decided to make the most of what I have. And that's a lot." She smiled into Katy's eyes. "Rusty and I talked it over, and we're both going to work harder, try harder. We both want things to be better. I wasn't doing my share, and it wasn't fair, not to any of us, but I'm going to now. Matt would want me to be happy . . . and you know what, Katy? I want to be happy too."

Katy's heart lifted. "From what I can see, there's every reason you will be. Rusty didn't mind coming here today?"

"No. We've been talking a lot, especially about the past, about letting go—and about the future. We're leaving in a few days for a vacation. Our first vacation without the kids since Neddy was born. We're going to Aruba—and," she laughed, sounding almost like the carefree young girl Katy remembered, "Rusty told me this morning he booked the honeymoon suite at the hotel. For the first time in years it's only going to be the two of us, a king-sized bed, a Jacuzzi, and the beach. A vacation isn't a cure-all, we both know that, but . . . it's going to mark a new beginning."

"It sounds wonderful." Katy hugged her. "Will you come back to the house for lunch? We'd love to have you and Rusty join us."

"No, we need to get home to the boys. But thank you." Allison touched her arm. "I'm sorry for the way it turned out Matt died, and for what you had to go through, but I want you to know, that day you came to see me, and got me thinking about things—that day changed my life."

It changed mine too, Katy reflected later in the dining room as she and her mother and grandmother served the simple luncheon they'd prepared for those who came back to the Triple T from the cemetery—cold chicken salad, a green bean casserole, and strawberry shortcake. It was Allison's identification of Crystal in the sketch that had set off the chain reaction of events that still reverberated up to this very day.

The revelations about Sheriff Harvey hadn't ended when he'd fallen to his death on Cougar Mountain.

The state police who'd taken over the investigation had found Matt's sketch inside a false-bottom compartment of Harvey's desk at the Last Trail ranch, along with some pictures of Crystal posing for him in the nude, and an address book containing the names and phone numbers of half a dozen women in Montana, Utah, and Oregon. Following up, the police had learned that on many of the occasions when Thunder Creek's sheriff had claimed to be at some law enforcement conference or seminar, he'd actually been taking trips with young women, trips to places like Palm Springs, Atlantic City, and Hilton Head. Most of these trips took place after Ardelle's death, when he'd already inherited the money it would take for the first-class air tickets and hotel rooms he'd always booked. But still he'd kept this part of his life secret, apparently wanting to preserve the image of endless faithfulness to his wife and dedicated service to his community, an image he'd nurtured and protected for so long.

Stan Harvey, never taking a vacation except to fish or to hunt. Stan Harvey, devoted husband, still mourning his wife after an illness that lasted so many years.

He'd murdered Crystal in a moment of rage and Matt in an act of premeditated desperation. He'd snuffed out the lives of two vibrant young people and had managed to keep both crimes, and his true nature, hidden for fourteen years.

"That poor girl." Her mother might have been reading her mind. She paused, dish in hand, and pursed her lips. "Lying in an unmarked grave all those years. No one even knowing what had become of her. No one even having a chance to murmur a prayer over her grave. If not for Matt and his sketch, and for you, honey," she gave Katy a soft smile, "...her parents might never have known what happened to her."

"At least now they can give her a proper burial—and say good-bye," Katy said soberly. Crystal's body had been found and exhumed from its anonymous grave behind the Pine Hills apartments. Her parents had been notified, and after investigators determined that she'd died of a broken neck, her remains had been shipped home to her family in Tucson.

Somehow or other, the national news media had picked up on the story of the small-town sheriff who had killed two people fourteen years earlier, and had fallen off a mountain to his death while trying to commit yet another murder to cover up his crimes. CNN and FOX News had been calling nonstop trying to interview Katy, her parents, the state police, and everyone who'd ever known Stan Harvey, which was pretty much the entire town. Seth had called too, wanting to know if she was all right, and for once not even bringing up company business in their brief, surprisingly cordial conversation.

Seth. How far away he seemed. Physically and emotionally. It no longer cut her to the quick to think of him, of their failed marriage. Of the way he'd abandoned both her and their dead baby.

Her heart still ached, would always ache, for the child she'd lost, but she was able to look forward now, to see a future for herself, to feel something again, something whole and positive and wonderful.

She didn't feel lost anymore. She'd found what she was seeking—she'd found herself again. Here in Wyoming. Somehow she'd found again what mattered most, deep down to her soul: her family, their land, her grandmother's diner, her old dear friends—and Jackson.

A delicious shiver curled down her spine as she pictured his cool blue eyes, the way they glinted at her when they made love. She remembered the clean pine scent of his skin, the thickness of his hair, the way his mouth slid into that easy, blinding grin that made her giddy. She could remember the feel of his arms holding her close in his bed, and best of all, she could look forward to many more of those delicious nights and mornings—and maybe even a few afternoons.

"There's a mighty handsome young man waiting for another glimpse of you, Katykins." Bessie burst into the kitchen with an armful of dessert plates and coffee cups, with Ada ambling right on her heels. "Scoot on out there and rescue him," she ordered. "Most everyone's left, but Big John and Riley are talking his ear off about shipping fever in those newly arrived feeder steers. You go on out there, I'll take over here."

"We're almost done." Katy slid the last of the dishes into the dishwasher even as Ada wagged a finger at her.

"If I were thirty years younger I wouldn't keep a man like Jackson Brent waiting," she announced.

"You run along, honey." Dorsey dried her hands on the dish towel. "We can finish up here."

"If I didn't know better, I'd think it was a conspiracy." Katy grinned at the three women and relinquished her spot by the sink, not at all unhappy to join Jackson in the living room.

He stood up when he saw her, excused himself from the conversation with Big John and Riley, and came toward her.

"How about going for a ride? You, me, Shadow Point."

"Tempting." She tilted back her head, eyed him. They hadn't had much time alone together since her parents and Gram had returned, what with all the police interviews and reports, and the general uproar in Thunder Creek about Stan Harvey's death and secret life. Katy was stunned by how much she missed him.

"Horses or wheels?" she asked.

"Horses. Go change out of those fancy duds, city girl, and I'll get us saddled up."

Ten minutes later she had changed from her black Armani slacks and cream silk blazer into jeans and a T-shirt, and had pulled on riding boots and smoothed her hair into a ponytail. Jackson helped her to mount Charleyhorse and then swung up on Myst, a gray gelding with white spots on his forelegs.

They rode for the better part of an hour, following a secluded trail that wound past the creek, and up into the hills where Shadow Point jutted out over a deep wooded valley.

But when they reached it, they found they weren't alone after all. A girl and a boy lay snuggled together in the long grass, arms and legs entwined, lips joined in a kiss.

The young couple heard their arrival at exactly the same time Katy and Jackson noticed them. Billy shot upright, his eyes wide, and Daffodil gave a startled shriek as she recognized the two figures on horseback.

"Hey, there, sorry to scare you two." Jackson was working hard to keep from laughing out loud at the sight of the two flush-faced teenagers who looked like they'd been caught stealing instead of just French kissing up at Shadow Point.

"We were uh, driving around and we got out to take a walk and . . . we ended up here . . . uh, resting. We gotta go . . ." Billy stammered.

"Don't let us chase you off. We'll find another spot to, um, have our picnic," Katy offered helpfully, already starting to turn her mount.

It was Daffodil who scrambled up, pulling down her T-shirt with one smooth motion, and adjusting her cut-off shorts on her hips with a quick tug. "Picnic? But I don't see any picnic basket, Ms. Templeton. Or even a blanket to sit on."

Jackson gave a chuckle deep in his throat.

"Wait a minute—you two were coming to Shadow Point to hook up!" Astonishment flashed across Billy's face. "I didn't know grown-ups even knew about this place."

"Hey, careful who you call a grown-up." Jackson laughed again. "This place has been around for a long time."

"And Doc Brent has probably been here more times than most of the town put together," Katy added.

He threw her an amused glance.

"Well, don't let us stop you or anything." Daffodil grinned, shoving her messy blonde hair from her eyes. "I really have to get home. Really," she insisted, as Billy looked crestfallen. "I've started studying again for the ACTs. I did so bad last year when I took them, and if I can bring my scores up, I might still have a chance at a scholarship. Come on, Billy, let's go."

Stretching down a hand, she tugged him to his feet. He slid an arm around her waist and Katy couldn't help but notice the completely relaxed way she leaned into him.

"Yeah, well, I guess we should go back," he said reluctantly, gazing down into Daffodil's eyes.

From the way he was staring at her, and the way she looked at him, it was clear that all they really wanted to do was get back to necking in the grass.

"Ada was still at the Templetons' when we left." Jackson spoke casually. "Looked to me like she and Bessie were going to sit around jawing about Las Vegas all afternoon."

"Yeah?" Billy's face lit up. Obviously the prospect of his grandmother being away, and an empty house appealed to him almost as much as Shadow Point. "Well, then, uh, we'd better get going. It'll be nice and quiet at my house and Daff can get a lot of studying done."

"Um-hmm, yes." But the girl spoiled it with one small giggle.

"If you're sure." Jackson was already dismounting, and

taking hold of Charleyhorse's bridle. When he grinned up at Katy, she wanted to burst out laughing. He obviously didn't care a bit that they'd interrupted the two teenagers. All he wanted was to get Katy alone in this spot.

Even as he helped her down from the horse, his hands lingering at her waist, she felt the thrum of electricity crackling between them.

She was about to slide her arms around his neck when Daffodil's voice interrupted her.

"I just wanted to say thank you, Ms. Templeton." The girl left Billy's side and turned back, approaching Katy with slow steps. "You were right—what you told me about Corey. About what he did...to me..." She cast a quick glance at Billy, who sobered at the mention of Corey's name. "I was stupid to cover for him. Stupid to let him get away with treating me like that...with hurting me. And hurting Doc Brent's dog. For a while there, I was pretty mixed up. And pretty dumb."

"You were scared, Daffodil. Even the smartest person can make mistakes when they're scared." Katy remembered Jackson's description of the fight outside the gas station. "But in the end, you stood up to him," she pointed out. "And you dumped him. You should be proud of that."

"I guess. I should have done it sooner, though. I just felt trapped—and alone. My mom's back now. I told her what happened and she forbade me ever to see Corey again. Like I would," she added with a snort. "Even if his mom hadn't come and taken him back to Sioux Falls with her, I'd never have gone out with him again in a million years. I am so over him." She rolled her eyes, then threw a saucy smile over at Billy. She started to turn away, then suddenly looked at Jackson.

"Doc Brent, what's going to happen to Corey now? Are you going to press charges against him for shooting Ajax?"

"Not if his mom does what she promised and gets him

into a counseling program. If he sticks with it, and doesn't get into trouble for six months, I'll let it go."

"That's better than he deserves," Billy muttered darkly.

"What about you, Daffodil?" Katy asked. "You could press charges as well. What he did to you was assault."

The girl shook her head. "He's gone, and with any luck he won't be coming back. And maybe that counseling will teach him a thing or two. I don't think living with that uncle of his was a very good influence. If you ask me, Luke Dillard could use some counseling too."

"I doubt there's a counselor in the world who can change Luke Dillard into a decent man," Jackson growled. "But maybe his nephew stands a chance."

Katy bit her lip. She understood too well Daffodil's reluctance to press charges. She hadn't wanted to even tell anyone what had happened between her and Luke back in high school, much less bring charges against him. True, things were different now, and date rape and date violence were both recognized as common dangers for women, but maybe if she'd filed charges then, if Luke had had to face some consequences he'd have grown up to be a better man, and set a better example for his nephew. Or maybe not.

She knew she wasn't responsible for Luke's behavior. He was a slime, had always been a slime. And he probably always would be. But she guessed he wasn't going to bother her anymore. Yesterday she'd confronted him in the diner—sliding into the back booth across from him during the postlunch lull, and telling him in no uncertain terms that if he ever harassed her again, if she ever heard even a whisper about him stalking or harassing any other woman, she'd let everyone in Thunder Creek know exactly what he'd tried to do to her back in high school. There was a name for it now and it was prosecutable. And Jackson was her witness. If he didn't want every single person in town to know what kind of a lowlife he was, he'd better keep his distance. And clean up his act.

For good measure, she'd warned him that she planned to file a report with the new sheriff—once there *was* a new sheriff—about what had happened all those years ago. It might be too late to press charges now, but if any woman ever accused Luke of hurting or frightening her, there would at least be a record of accusation from the past.

For one moment she'd thought Luke was going to lean across the table and punch her, but then he'd merely shoved his plate away and stomped out of the diner without saying a word, and without paying for his burger. She had a feeling he'd be steering clear of her from now on.

That was something—maybe not enough—but it still felt good to have put him on notice finally and let him know she'd be holding him accountable.

Corey though was another matter. She could only hope that the boy wouldn't continue to follow in his uncle's footsteps, that he'd never hurt another girl. She thought of the conversation she and Jackson had had with Luke's sister-in-law before she took Corey back. They'd told her not only what he'd done to Ajax, but to Daffodil as well. Rhonda Dillard had been stunned and heartsick, and when she'd promised to get help for him, Katy had believed her.

Daffodil was regarding Jackson uncertainly. "Doc Brent, how's Ajax now?"

"Pretty good for a dog that's been shot and chloroformed in the space of a week. He's bouncing back. And Regis and Cammi are none the worse for wear. Why don't you and Billy stop by and visit him? Ajax doesn't hold a grudge." Jackson spoke offhandedly, but the message was clear: neither did he.

"Visit him? I'd really like that." Daffodil looked eager. "Thanks."

Katy watched Daffodil and Billy start down the hill, heading down the back trail she and Jackson had avoided, the one that led to the road where Billy's car was no doubt parked. She turned back to Jackson.

"You're a very nice man, Jackson Brent."

"Yeah? How do you figure?"

His arms came around her as a bird began to sing somewhere in the trees. His nearness, the warm, sunlit afternoon, the horses grazing nearby in the shadow of the hills lifted her heart.

"I've seen you in action. You could have nailed Corey's hide to the wall. But you're giving him a chance."

"I felt sorry for Rhonda."

"You take in stray animals. You put up with Gram's and Ada's blatant matchmaking. And you let my father talk your ear off about shipping fever and feeder steers. Shoptalk, on a Sunday. Need I say more?"

"What you need is to understand that I'm just angling for a reward."

"Oh, a reward." Her arms slipped around his neck. She pulled him toward her, breathing in the scent of Lever 2000 and horses and Wyoming sagebrush. "What sort of reward?"

He bent his head and kissed her, a long, slow, provocative kiss that left her lips burning. Her heart racing. "That's not it," he whispered against her mouth.

"It...isn't?"

"It's a bigger reward than that."

"Does it involve taking our clothes off out here and hoping no one else comes by to neck?"

"Eventually. That would be part two."

"What's part one?"

Jackson's hands moved up from her waist to cradle her face. He took a deep breath. "Say you'll marry me, Katy."

"M-marry you?"

"It's not supposed to be a question. It's supposed to be an answer. *I will marry you.* Like that."

"You've never even said 'I love you.'"

"Do you think I'd ask you to marry me if I didn't?" He grinned and his finger traced her delicate jaw, then her lips, with a slow, sensuous tenderness that made her knees melt.

Beneath the casual lighthearted tone she saw the intensity in his eyes, and felt the tension in his body. The next moment she heard it in his voice.

"Katy." He smoothed a hand ever so gently through her hair. "I love you."

She closed her eyes, trying to breathe. Trying to stay calm and simply breathe.

"I need you," he went on. "I want you. I never thought I'd say this, because I never wanted to need anyone this much, to love anyone again, but I love you and I want you in my life, by my side... always. I want the whole deal, Katy. I want to have a family with you, to go to bed every night with you, to cook a big Sunday breakfast with you. I want to make a home for you, for us—and we'll just keep adding more and more bedrooms the more kids we have—"

"How many do you want?"

"Three... four. If that's okay with you."

"What happened to Mister Noncommitment? Mister I'm-Not-in the-Market-for-a-Lifetime-Partner—"

"He fell off that mountain the moment I hauled you up from that ledge and safely into my arms."

"Jackson." She pulled his head down, kissed him, her lips clinging to his.

When she broke the kiss, Jackson's voice was hoarse. "I never wanted to need like this, to love like this, Katy. It was too scary knowing I could lose it if I got it. But now, the hell of it is, I'm more scared of never having it at all. And the only woman I'd ever want those things with is you. Baby—"

"Yes. Jackson, *yes*."

He stared at her. "You mean—" He broke off, looking ridiculously, wonderfully, sexily hopeful. And stunned.

"You heard me, cowboy," she murmured against his lips. "Yes, I'll marry you. You're not backing out on me, are you?"

"Not on your life," he vowed and suddenly scooped her up into his arms. Spinning her around, he gave a whoop that Katy was sure could be heard throughout Natrona County.

"Jackson!" Breathless laughter bubbled in her throat. "Put me down, you crazy cowboy!"

He set her on her feet, then immediately backed her against a tree and kissed her until they were both breathless. The hillside air was cool, but their skin was hot. And so was the hunger in their eyes as they retreated into the shadow of the trees and proceeded to undress one another and make slow, delicious love.

The world retreated and there was only the two of them, alone in Shadow Point, with only the mountains to witness the vows they made to one another, and only the birds to hear the sweet words they exchanged, or to sense the thunder and the joy when they made love beneath the Wyoming sky. They both knew that life could be cruel, that fate could be harsh, but they also knew that there was beauty and love and happiness at their fingertips. And they would find it, build upon it, wrap themselves in it, here in Thunder Creek—together.

Epilogue

TWO YEARS LATER ON A CRISP CLEAR NOVEMBER DAY, with fat snowflakes whirling down from the peaks of the Laramie mountains and a sharp wind dancing across the grazing lands, valleys and treetops of Thunder Creek, Jackson drove his wife and baby daughter home from the hospital.

Smoke plumed from the chimney of their cabin, which had been enlarged with two additional bedrooms and a screened-in porch out back, facing Cougar Mountain.

The moment he opened the door, they were greeted by two hurtling dogs, the curious stare of Cammi the cat, and the enticing aroma of chicken and dumplings wafting from the kitchen. A fire popped and crackled in the fireplace, a welcome antidote to the bluster of the winter wind.

"Well, it's about time. I've been watching the clock this past half hour." Bessie rushed out of the kitchen, wiping damp hands on her apron. "Everything's all set in the nursery," she added, her eyes bright and focused on her beaming granddaughter and the tiny bundle in Katy's arms. "You don't have to lift a finger."

"Thanks, Gram. It smells heavenly in here. Did Mom and Daddy call?"

"You bet they did. Their flight from Shanghai was delayed

five hours—they just landed in L.A. They're boarding a plane for Denver in another hour. Your mother's ready to commandeer the plane and leave right this minute and your father, well . . . I'm warning you, he's fit to be tied. He said he should've known you'd give birth three weeks early—that you're just as unreliable and thoughtless as Cleo."

"Now he's comparing me to a horse. Nice," Katy muttered, but she couldn't help grinning back at Jackson as he let out a bark of laughter and closed the door.

"I think I can guarantee that your mother won't be dragging Big John away on any trips ever again, at least not while any female in his herd is pregnant," her husband remarked.

"Forget Big John." Bessie waved a dismissive hand. "The great-grandma is the only one who really matters. Now let me see this little muffin."

As Jackson shrugged out of his coat, and the dogs clamored for attention, Katy obediently peeled back the blanket that had shielded her daughter's tiny face from the wind and cold. She gazed down in wonder at the baby staring up at her, and her heart was so full of happiness she thought it would burst.

"Gram, this is Mattie," she murmured, as Bessie's eyes lit like Christmas lights. "Mattie, meet your great Gram."

Matilda Brent's wide blue eyes flitted over the beaming old woman who reached out a finger to stroke her little cheek. She blinked and her lips puffed out, then they twitched. And Katy knew that no baby in the world had ever been as beautiful, as alert, or as clearly intelligent as the priceless child she held in her arms.

"She smiled!" Gram exclaimed. "Did you see that? This is one smart little girl—she smiled at me!"

Jackson couldn't seem to stop grinning, until he glanced at Katy's face. Despite the glow in her eyes, she looked pale and tired. It had been a difficult birth, nearly eighteen hours of labor. She'd been worn out by it all, but in the end, everything had gone off without a hitch.

And Mattie, at six pounds, ten ounces, was tiny, healthy, and perfect.

During Katy's long and arduous labor, he hadn't been able to do anything but encourage and coach her through it. Now, though, he could take charge.

"You need to rest."

"I'm fine."

"Yeah, and I want to keep it that way. Down, mutts," he ordered the dogs, and lifted the baby gently from Katy's arms.

"To bed," he ordered Katy, and her slim brows rose.

"Just because you're a father now, you don't get to act as bossy as Big John," she told him, but she had to admit that the idea of their big bed sounded good. It would sound even better if he would lie there with her, hold her, and enjoy their baby with her.

Gram gave a cackle of laughter. "Oh, don't argue with him, Katykins. Let him spoil you. You deserve it, after bringing this little beauty into the world."

"She's a wise woman. Listen to her," Jackson said.

"Go ahead, both of you, gang up on me. I'm going to bed. But only if you bring Mattie to me—once you've changed her diaper."

"I suppose I can manage that." Jackson's eyes met hers and they were filled with a depth of love and tenderness that took her breath away. For a moment their gazes clung, lingering, reluctant to part. Then, slowly, Katy smiled.

"Don't be long," she murmured.

Bessie Templeton's sharp eyes missed nothing of the silent, intimate exchange. Satisfaction curved her thin lips into an even bigger smile.

"I'll just keep supper simmering for you two and be on my way. I'd best look in on the diner and see if Ada needs a

hand at the cash register. You were right about that new waitress, Katy. She's good. And not a bit clumsy or ditzy like
Daffodil Moline."

"Daffodil simply had other things on her mind." Katy
moved toward the bedroom. "And now she's able to give
them her full attention."

Daffodil was in college now, as was Billy, both of them on
scholarship at the University of Wyoming, both of them still
helping out at the diner over summer and winter breaks.
While Billy was studying physics, with an eye toward teaching, Daffodil had chosen to major in molecular biology.
Maybe in a few years, Katy thought as she slipped into a
thick terry robe and sank into bed, Mattie will be calling
them for help with her science homework.

It wasn't long before she heard the front door slam, and
Gram drove off through the lightly falling snow, handling her
new black Explorer like a general charging forward in a tank.
Katy watched the Explorer disappear over a ridge, her gaze
taking in the snowflakes tumbling like sparkling crystals
over the mountains.

Then Jackson came in with Mattie in his arms, snug
against the flannel shirt that covered his chest, and her heart
turned over.

"Got something for you," he said.

"Come over here, both of you." Katy held out her arms.

When he set Mattie in her arms, Katy couldn't do anything but stare down into that sweet, tiny face. In her yellow
cotton sleeper with the bunny embroidered on the front,
Mattie looked like a miniature angel. With her tufts of light
brown hair and those amazingly alert eyes, she looked as if
she were pondering where best to perform some good and
wondrous deed.

You've already done it, she thought, kissing the baby's
cheek. Warmth and contentment stole over her. *You came
into our lives.*

"Jackson, do you think Matt knows that his niece is named for him? And how beautiful she is?"

Jackson stretched out beside her, and his breath ruffled her hair.

"Sure he does. And if I know Matt, he's going to keep a good eye on her. Our Mattie has her own special guardian angel."

"I feel like I do too." Her gaze met his. Love flooded her, rich and warm and flowing like the sweet waters of a river through land that had been barren and parched.

"I know exactly what you mean." Jackson leaned over and kissed her, his lips tender, tasting, as if sealing their love, and this moment, forever.

"I think I figured out what I'm going to get Mattie for her first birthday," he said, drawing Katy and the baby closer. "Or maybe her second."

"What's that?"

"Cleo's foal. Midnight."

"You want to buy Midnight for Mattie? Isn't it a little early to be thinking about riding lessons?"

"It's never too early. When did you start?"

"Age three."

"Me, too. Well, okay, she can just get to know him for a while before she starts actually riding him." He grinned. "In the meantime, I have a present right now for Mattie's mother."

Delight swept over her as he reached into the drawer of the bedside table and pulled out a small box wrapped in gold paper embossed with silver hearts.

"Oh, Jackson . . ." She stared at the gift nestled inside the box. It was a bracelet—a slim dazzling gold bracelet with a diamond and ruby heart dangling elegantly from one stunning platinum link.

"It's gorgeous," she gasped. "It's the most gorgeous thing I've ever seen."

"No—you are." He spoke quietly. "You and Mattie. You're my treasures. My life—and my future. Always."

Her eyes lifted to his, shining with happiness. With love.

Tenderness was reflected in the depths of his, right back at her.

"Jackson, you're spoiling me," she laughed. "But don't stop. I love it so much. I love you so much."

He shifted closer, touched her hair, her cheek, as gently as he'd touched Mattie's. His voice was husky. "I love you more."

She'd never realized how full her heart could be. Inside this cabin, where a fire blazed cozily in the living room and her grandmother's chicken and dumplings warmed on the stove, she had everything she'd ever wanted.

Family, home, happiness.

And love.

More love than she'd ever thought possible.

Jackson bent to kiss her again as Mattie yawned in her arms. And outside the window the snow fell faster, thick and swirling as it tumbled wildly—the way it had for centuries—over Thunder Creek.

About the Author

Jill Gregory is the *New York Times* bestselling author of over twenty-five novels. Her novels have been translated and published in Japan, Russia, Norway, Taiwan, Sweden, and Italy. Jill grew up in Chicago and received her bachelor of arts degree in English from the University of Illinois. She currently resides in Michigan with her husband.

Jill invites her readers to visit her website at http://members.aol.com/jillygreg.

Return to

THUNDER CREEK!

Join Jill Gregory in her next riveting novel . . .

Look for it in July 2004

Read on for a preview . . .

on sale July 2004

JOSY GLANCED WEARILY AT HER WATCH WHEN the phone rang in the design studio Friday night— Lord, it was a quarter past nine. She hadn't even heard everyone else leave.

"Josy Warner," she mumbled into the phone, weakly remembering that she hadn't had a bite to eat since the bagel with cream cheese and cucumber slices she'd wolfed down at lunch.

"Josy, it's me." Ricky Sabatini's voice on the other end of the phone was raw, tight and urgent. "I need you to get me the package back—*now*."

"Now? You mean...right now?" She shook her head, trying to cast off her fatigue and to digest what he was saying. Suddenly, the driving urgency of his tone registered and she clutched the phone tighter.

"Ricky, what's wrong?"

"Don't ask me questions, there's no time to explain. I'm not in town, so you'll have to bring the package to Archie. He's a friend, maybe the only one besides you I can trust. Write down this address. Fast."

Her heart was pumping. Frantically she grabbed for notepaper and scribbled down the street number he gave her. "It's in Brooklyn—Windsor Terrace—right off Prospect Park. Tell the cab driver to wait," Ricky ordered, "and as soon as you give the package to Archie, get the hell out of there. You hear me?"

"Yes, but—"

"Go now. Right now."

He hung up.

Josy stared at the phone, her throat dry. Ricky didn't sound good. It couldn't be the trial—it hadn't started yet. There'd been a postponement. But... why did he need the package now?

What the hell difference does it make? she thought, dropping the phone into its base and springing out of her chair, sending her colored pencils clattering to the floor. He needed the package right away. And she was more than glad to be rid of it.

She left the studio in a run, hailed a cab at the corner, and gave the driver her address as she jumped into the back seat. When she reached her building she spared only a quick nod to the doorman as she rushed past him and punched the elevator button. She'd never heard that note of frantic urgency in Ricky's voice before. Even when they were kids on Jefferson Street, there'd been a cool firmness about him that had made it appear he had no problem keeping every emotion in check. Tonight he'd sounded almost unraveled.

What the hell is in that box? she wondered as she jammed the key in her lock.

She half expected the package to have disappeared when she opened the bottom drawer of her dresser, but it was right where she'd left it, under her sweaters.

She stuffed it into her black leather work tote and in less than a minute she was hailing another cab.

It took nearly an hour to get to Brooklyn zooming straight across the Manhattan Bridge, down Flatbush and cutting through Grand Army Plaza, and by the time the cab turned onto Vanderbilt Street and braked before the small brick house on the left side of the street, her nerves were shot. She felt queasy, her hands were shaking, and she didn't know if it was from having skipped dinner or from anxiety over the contents of the package in her tote, but she heard herself ask the driver to wait in a breathless voice that sounded completely unlike her own.

Clearing her throat, she climbed out of the cab and hurried up the cement steps, feeling the package swaying inside her bag. It was nearly ten o'clock, and the windows of many houses on the street were open to the hot, sticky night. She heard a radio blaring rap and smelled the aroma of pizza drifting from one of the windows. Down the block, a dog yapped, rapid and staccato. She saw kids skateboarding around a corner—a few people sat on porches in aluminum chairs.

She rang the doorbell and waited.

Thirty seconds dragged by. There was no answer. She rang the bell again and rapped sharply on the door.

Still no answer. This wasn't right. And it wasn't good, not at all.

She checked the slip of paper again, confirming the address, then turned to the cab driver.

He was hunched over the steering wheel, watching her, looking irritated as hell. "One minute," she called frantically, her heart beating in time to the rap music. She pounded on the door again.

Damn it, Ricky, she thought. Maybe Archie was late. Maybe she should leave the package on the front porch for him.

Or . . . inside.

She gave the doorknob a little jostle, praying it wouldn't turn. But it did. The door gave, and she pushed it open an inch just to see if she could.

Damn. She didn't want to go in there. The entire situation was freaking her out. But if she went in, she could leave the package on a table or something and when Archie got here, it'd be safe.

The cab driver leaned out the window. "Lady, I'm not supposed to just sit. You want me to take you someplace or what?"

"Yes, yes, I do. Wait one more minute."

She shoved the door open and stepped inside. There were lights on, and a window air conditioner whirred somewhere.

"Archie?"

No answer.

The house was warm, though, and cluttered, with a tiny hall and a brown-carpeted living room filled with a mismatched jumble of older furniture that contrasted with the gleaming, sleek wide-screen TV dominating one wall. There was a wood coffee table in front of a cracked black leather sofa and she hurried toward it, planning to leave the package right there, next to three empty beer bottles and a pile of laundry. But then she heard a noise coming from a back room.

Not just any noise—one that made the skin on the back of her neck prickle. It was a moan.

For a moment, Josy froze, then she started toward the sound. She heard another moan—it seemed to be coming from the kitchen up ahead.

She saw him as soon as she reached the doorway. He was lying facedown on the linoleum floor. There was blood everywhere—beneath him, on the counter, the refrigerator, the floor. The queasiness rushed to her head and she sucked in a deep breath to steady herself.

"Oh, God." Shock ripped through her. She ran to him and knelt down. His face was turned toward her and she saw that his eyes were open. They looked glazed, sad . . . dim. She also saw the bullet hole that had torn through his shoulder blades and gouged out a hole in his faded green cotton shirt.

"Archie?" she gasped. "Archie, hold on, I'll get help."

She groped in her tote for her cell phone, but before she could find it, he wheezed, "No . . . get outta here. Take the package . . . get out. . . ."

She ignored him and punched in 911, still on her knees beside him.

"A man's been hurt. He's bleeding. We need an ambulance." Her voice was high-pitched, rapid. "The address?" She gave it in a rush. "Yes, he's conscious, but there's blood all over the—"

Somehow, the wounded man managed to reach out and grab the phone. With his thumb he pressed the END button, and then, groaning, he threw the phone as far as he could. It slid to a rest only five feet away, against the base of an electric stove.

"No . . . cops," he told her, but his voice sounded even weaker than it had before. "Get out—take the package—go . . ."

Her cell phone rang and she scrambled across the floor to grab it, half expecting the emergency operator to have traced the call and called back for more information.

But Ricky's voice yelled in her ear. "Josy, change in plans. Don't go to the address I gave you—"

"I'm already here. Ricky, a man's been shot. I think it's Archie! You're Archie, aren't you?" she asked the man on the floor, whose eyes were now closed, scaring her half to death.

"Yeah. Lemme...talk to...Ricky—tell him... hammer..."

"Ricky, what's going on?" she shrieked.

"How bad is he hurt?" Ricky asked, ignoring her question. "Did you call an ambulance?"

"Yes, they're on their way—"

"Then get out of there, Josy. Now!"

"Oh, no. Ricky...Ricky, I think..."

The man's eyes were closed again. He wasn't even moaning now. *Please,* she prayed silently, forgetting about Ricky, forgetting about everything except the man lying in his own blood on the floor.

"Archie," she cried. She set the phone down, reached for his wrist, felt for a pulse. She hadn't done this since they'd learned it in health class in high school. She hadn't been good at it. She couldn't feel one now. Shouldn't she be doing something else? Mouth to mouth? Putting pressure on the wound?

She couldn't feel a pulse. He looked so still, so...

"Ricky, I think...he's dead!"

She heard the scream of an ambulance in the distance.

"Josy, you still got the package? Take it with you

right this minute and get the hell out of there!" Ricky roared into the phone.

"But I can't leave—"

"Yes, you can. For me, Josy. I can't let the cops get that package, you see? Get outta there. If he's going to make it, the paramedics will save him. All you can do is get the hell out!"

She was still frozen, still staring at Archie, who hadn't moved a muscle, when she heard something else.

The front door, squeaking open. Low voices.

Pure instinct had her surging to her feet, trembling, edging out of sight of the front part of the house. She held her breath, clutching the cell phone, trying not to panic.

"Josy, do you hear—" She hit the END button to blot out Ricky's shout and turned off the phone. Whoever was out there, it sure wasn't the paramedics. Maybe whoever had shot Ricky had come back to finish him off. Though from the looks of it, there was no need, she thought, her gaze shifting to him and then quickly away.

She'd never seen a dead man before tonight but she was pretty sure she'd seen one now.

She wanted to scream, but she clenched all her muscles, took a deep breath and leaned forward ever so slightly so that she could peek around the doorway and down the hall. She just caught a glimpse of a man with dark blonde hair dressed all in black— black blazer, black slacks, and a black gun in his hand. *Now there's a fashion accessory I can do without,* she thought on a sob, jerking back out of sight.

Ricky was right. She had to get out of here.

There was a side door off the kitchen. She edged

toward it, praying the floor wouldn't creak. She took one last look back at Archie, who hadn't moved or spoken a word, and opened the door.

It led outside into a small unfenced yard. Carefully, she stepped out and closed the door after her.

It took a moment for her eyes to adjust to the hot darkness, but the moon riding high overhead helped and she saw a maze of yards on either side of her.

She ran to her left and glanced at the street, praying the cab was still there, knowing it was her best chance.

It was gone.

Choking down panic, she veered away from the street, clutching her tote close, running faster than she'd ever thought she could in sandals with two-inch heels.

She dashed through yards, past swing sets and fig trees and marigold gardens, running, running. She nearly ran over a couple of teenagers drinking beer on a beach towel spread across the grass and slowed down long enough to ask them where the nearest subway station was.

They pointed her toward the Fort Hamilton stop, and she stumbled on. She had no idea how long she ran before she reached it. Every so often, she twisted her head around, trying to see if she was being followed. She wasn't—yet. But even when she reached the F train and sank into a seat in the back, she couldn't believe she'd gotten away.

"Faster," she urged the train silently, as she slumped back, clutching her sides. Her head was pounding with the vision of a dead man on a linoleum floor, and another man with a gun, searching the house, looking for . . . what?

The answer was obvious. For her. Or the package. Possibly both.

I know I owe you, Ricky, she thought miserably, *and I'll always be grateful—but what have you gotten me into?* A shudder racked her shoulders, and serious nausea clogged her throat.

She pulled the tote closer and peered inside at the dark shape of the package. She needed to know what was inside it. And more importantly, she thought, fear eating through the inner lining of her stomach, how was she going to get rid of it?

By the time she reached the door of her apartment and had to try three times to fit her key in the lock because her hand was shaking so badly, she'd decided that things couldn't get any worse.

But then they did. She opened the door at last and gasped.

Her lovely, tidy, chic, and comfortable studio apartment, the one place that felt more like home to her than her childhood bedroom before her parents had died, looked like a hurricane had blown through and left a wake of destruction.

The sofa cushions had been slashed and dumped on the floor, lamps were knocked over, the coffee table kicked aside. Her lovely rose silk bedding was in a heap on the floor and the drawers of the antique Regency dresser she'd so painstakingly refinished had been overturned, her clothes strewn everywhere imaginable.

Even her trash can in the kitchen had been upended. Garbage lay everywhere on the previously shining white-tile floor, alongside pots and pans, cracked dishes, and boxes of Cheerios and macaroni and cheese and broken chocolate chip cookies.

Shock and anger raged through her, along with the slick rush of fear.

What is so damned important about this package? she thought furiously, and reached into her tote to pull it out. She glared at it a moment, then started to rip the brown paper off, but she stopped dead when her apartment phone rang.

"Josy! Josy, are you there? Damn it, Josy, why'd you turn off your cell? Answer me!" Rough fear throbbed through Ricky's voice. Somehow, she found her own.

"They were here, Ricky. In my apartment. They've ruined . . . everything."

"They tossed your apartment? Jesus. Josy, I'm sorry." She heard him suck in his breath. "You don't know how sorry I am. Things weren't supposed to go down this way. I never thought . . . listen, you need to get out of town. *Now.*"

"Out of town? No, Ricky, that's crazy. I need to call the police!" She sank down on her stripped-down bed, still holding the parcel.

"Josy, listen to me. That's the worst thing you can do. They want what's inside the package and they'll kill you to get it."

"That's why I have to get rid of it—fast." She heard her voice rising, on the brink of hysteria. "The police can take it off my hands and—"

"Josy, I'm not sure who we can trust at the police department. I was set up . . . and until I know who did that to me . . . if it's one guy or half the damned department. . . . I can't go to them and neither can you. Pack a bag and—"

"Are you crazy? I have a job. My boss is expecting me to turn in sketches for the fall collection in two weeks. Running away is *not* an option—"

"Neither is dying," Ricky yelled at the other end of the phone.

That stunned her into silence. Ricky continued more quietly, but with that same urgency she'd heard the first time he called about the package.

"I never should have got you mixed up in this. I swear I didn't mean for this to happen. I thought... never mind. You have to get out, Josy, tonight, right now. I'm nowhere near the city, or I'd get you out myself, but I can't come back. I can't be found, not yet... and you can't be found either. So pack a bag, take the package, and go somewhere no one would expect. Not to any friend, anyone they could find out about or locate. Go someplace where you can get lost for awhile, until I can get to you and take the package back."

"Ricky..." She could barely speak. Her voice was a hoarse, sick rasp. "Do you know what you're asking?"

"Yeah. I'm asking you to save your life. And mine. You know I wouldn't unless this was really important, Josy. These guys don't fool around. They can't get that package, and they can't catch up to you. They're not the type to ask questions and leave quietly, you know what I mean?"

Her heart was pounding like the roar of the subway. She felt as if she was in a movie, the loud, violent, gritty kind of movie she didn't especially care for... only it wasn't a movie, it was her *life*.

"How're you going to find me? Shouldn't I tell you where I'm going?"

"Not now—not on this line. Just go... and I mean

now. Grab the package and get out—don't use your cell phone once you disappear; buy a disposable and don't use it until I tell you. Send me an email when you're settled and safe, and I'll get you instructions. Not my regular screenname. Middle name, Josy. You know the one. *Middle name.* I'll contact you when I can and take the package off your hands. Oh, hell, I gotta go—"

And then there was nothing. Ricky had vanished.

Just like she had to do.

She fought down a sob, dragged her suitcase from the closet and grabbed an armload of clothes.

Two hours later she was at LaGuardia, boarding a plane for Salt Lake City. She had her tote, her suitcase, and her sketchpad, and she made it on the plane in one piece.

That was something, Josy thought, as the jet taxied the runway before take-off.

There was only one place she'd thought to go. A place far from New York, where she could lose herself, lay low, have time to think, to work, and maybe put some pieces of her life together while she was trying to save that same life.

A town where a woman named Ada Stone lived. A town as different from New York as crystal was from cowhide. A town where she could try to recharge what was left of her creative batteries, and meet the one living relative she had left in this world.

A town called Thunder Creek.